DROP DEAD RED

Mercy Watts Mysteries Book Four

A.W. HARTOIN

ALSO BY A.W. HARTOIN

Historical

The Paris Package (Stella Bled Book One)

Strangers in Venice (Stella Bled Book Two)

One Child in Berlin (Stella Bled Book Three)

Young Adult fantasy

Flare-up (An Away From Whipplethorn Short)

A Fairy's Guide To Disaster (Away From Whipplethorn Book One)

Fierce Creatures (Away From Whipplethorn Book Two)

A Monster's Paradise (Away From Whipplethorn Book Three)

A Wicked Chill (Away From Whipplethorn Book Four)

To the Eternal (Away From Whipplethorn Book Five)

Away From Whipplethorn Box Set (Books 1-3, plus bonus short)

Mercy Watts Mysteries

<u>Novels</u>

A Good Man Gone (Mercy Watts Mysteries Book One)

Diver Down (Mercy Watts Mysteries Book Two)

Double Black Diamond (Mercy Watts Mysteries Book Three)

Drop Dead Red (Mercy Watts Mysteries Book Four)

In the Worst Way (Mercy Watts Mysteries Book Five)

The Wife of Riley (Mercy Watts Mysteries Book Six)

My Bad Grandad (Mercy Watts Mysteries Book Seven)

Brain Trust (Mercy Watts Mysteries Book Eight)

Down and Dirty (Mercy Watts Mysteries Book Nine)

Small Time Crime (Mercy Watts Mysteries Book Ten)

Bottle Blonde (Mercy Watts Mysteries Book Eleven)

Mercy Watts Mysteries Book Set (Books 1-3, plus bonus short)

<u>Short stories</u>

Coke with a Twist

Touch and Go

Nowhere Fast

Dry Spell

A Sin and a Shame

Paranormal

It Started with a Whisper (Sons of Witches

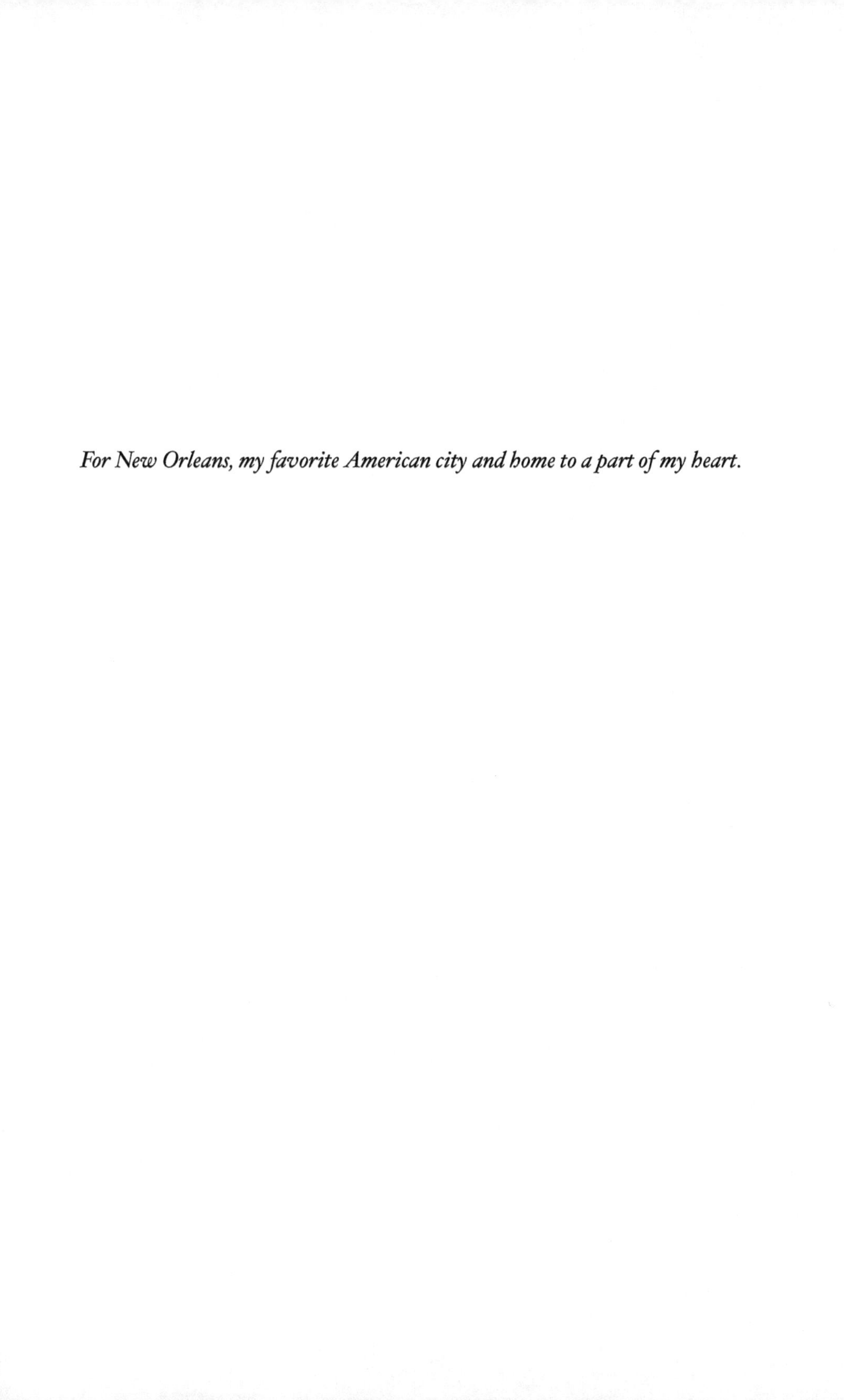
For New Orleans, my favorite American city and home to a part of my heart.

CHAPTER ONE

My penance was about to begin. Or rather, it would begin if I ever got out of my truck. The convent sat on a hill under low clouds, fat with snow. With its high stone walls and arched windows, it could've been transported from Provence. The convent was beautiful, a place of hope and tranquility, but it contained the terror that was my Aunt Miriam.

My family had kept the truth from her for as long as they could. But news of my modeling contract with the bad boys of rock, Double Black Diamond, had finally slipped out at my Aunt Tenne's birthday party last week, thanks to my so-called partner, Aaron. He'd been bragging about being hired to cater the shoot, and Aunt Miriam's sharp ears picked it up. Honestly, it was almost a relief. It'd been a month since I'd signed, and I kept waiting for the sound of a cane hitting my door with everything an elderly nun could muster. She might actually hit me with that big stick. It wouldn't be the first time. She was much fonder of it than she was of me. Like with a spanking, the waiting was the worst part.

Now the waiting was over. I'd been summoned to the convent for lunch. I didn't know what to expect. This had never happened before. There could be a bunch of nuns with canes waiting for me. Canes are big with my aunt's friends. I could just hear their hushed accusations. "You've disgraced the name of Watts." "Your poor parents. How could you?" "Mercy Watts, you are now a brazen hussy." People considered me a hussy no matter what I did, but I still didn't want to hear it again. Especially not from a nun. That's why I was sitting in my truck, wasting gas and praying that something would happen to stop me from going in the convent.

Nothing did, of course. But I could just leave. Nobody would stop me. My best friend, Ellen, needed me to...to take her to someplace that was imperative. Not good. I had the flu. No, no. I was at risk for Ebola. I was a nurse. That was perfect. I could avoid Aunt Miriam and her dreaded disapproval and lengthy lectures on decorum for weeks. Finally, irrational fears were working out for me. I grabbed the gearshift and smiled.

Crack!

I screeched like someone put an ice cube down my back and looked out the window, then I screeched again. Aunt Miriam stood at my window with her cane raised up, ready to strike my window a second time.

I gave her a rather limp finger wave and she rapped my window in response. I kind of wished I had a communicable disease. An isolation ward was sounding pretty good. I cranked down my window slowly. One of those times when having a vintage truck paid off.

"What are you doing out here?" asked Aunt Miriam with frozen breath streaming out in a rush.

"Um...nothing."

"You've been out here for fifteen minutes. I don't have time for this. We have a situation to discuss." Steam jetted out of her nose, making her look dragon-like in appearance as well as character.

"I'm sorry. I know I've disappointed you," I said in my best repentant tone.

"I'm not best pleased with your recent shenanigans, but that's not the situation I want to talk about. Get out of this truck."

"Really?" I asked.

"Get out of the truck."

I shut off the engine and climbed out like I was older than Aunt Miriam. "So what's the situation?"

She hit me. Her spindly arms hauled back, she assumed the stance of a major league baseball player, and she whacked me good on the shoulder.

"Ow! You said it wasn't about the modeling," I protested.

"It isn't. It's about your godmothers." Aunt Miriam planted her cane on the icy blacktop and glared at me.

"What happened to Myrtle and Millicent?"

Her cane went back to hitting position again.

I held up my hands. "Whatever it is, I'll take care of it."

Aunt Miriam dropped the cane and gave me a piercing look. "I know you will."

"Then why'd you hit me?" I asked, trying not to whine. She hated whining worse than bikini shots and that was saying something.

"How else will you ever learn? Nothing else has worked." She turned around and marched up the stairs to the convent.

I wanted to protest, but I would definitely remember that pain the next time I was tempted to do something the family wouldn't approve of. I would probably still do it, but I'd remember.

"Are you coming?" she yelled over her shoulder.

"Are you going to hit me again?"

"Does it matter?"

It didn't. I had to go, or my mother would demand a reason why. Saying that a ninety-pound nun might hit me wasn't going to cut it. So I followed, keeping myself out of cane range. Mom would say that you can't pick your family. Obviously. Nobody would pick this.

It took a good twenty minutes to get to Aunt Miriam's studio apartment in the elder wing. We were slowed down by several novitiates, wanting to say hello to Aunt Miriam and asking advice about prayer and whatnot. They smiled, their earnest faces glowing with goodness that I could never hope to aspire to. Even more disconcerting was Aunt Miriam. She smiled. She took their young hands in her wrinkled age-spotted ones and counseled them warmly. What the heck? The woman just whacked me with a cane.

One sister, with a pink round face surrounded by her snug veil, took my hand as we passed by and said, "You are so blessed to be Sister Miriam's niece."

"I wonder why I'm so blessed all the time," I said in all seriousness.

"It is His will and I will endeavor not to envy you in your blessing."

"You should never envy me," I said, thinking of my aching shoulder.

The sister hugged me and hurried after the other novitiates. I watched them go and, for the first time, wondered if a religious life wasn't the sanest choice for someone like me. No. It would never fly. Nobody would buy me as a nun. They barely bought me as a nurse, even when I was wearing scrubs and a hospital badge. Vows were out.

I caught up with Aunt Miriam at her door as she was turning the big brass key. She eyed me. "What did you say to Sister Clarence? I hope you didn't crush her spirit. She has a warm, generous heart."

"I don't crush people's spirits. Why would you say that?"

"You wreak havoc wherever you go." Aunt Miriam tossed her cane onto her love seat, she only carried it for intimidation purposes, and went into the little galley kitchen.

"I do not." I watched her dig around and, to my dismay, pull out pimento loaf. I didn't actually hate pimento loaf. It was more the idea of meat in a loaf that I hated.

"People die when you show up."

"Not true. Nobody died in Honduras."

"Luck."

"Nobody died in Colorado."

"Close enough. That boy will never be the same." She gave me the stink eye as if I was the one who did the deed. "I've been praying for him, and you should, too. It's all your own fault that you'll have to handle this situation. Your father's too busy, thanks to you."

"I'll take care of whatever it is." And I would, too. Dad was a retired police detective gone private. Business was always good due to my dad's media presence and reputation, but, since my latest havoc-wreaking in Colorado, it'd gone through the roof. The name Tommy Watts was everywhere and somehow the media made it sound like Dad had sent me to Copper Mountain to save Mickey Stix's wife, Nina, and solve an attempted murder. Dad had nothing to do with it, but it was paying off in new clients.

Aunt Miriam slapped together a couple of sandwiches and gave us each ten baby gherkin pickles. She put the plates on the tiny breakfast bar and ordered me to get the mustard and mayo out.

I put the mayo on the counter and found an empty mustard jar tucked away in the back of the fridge.

"Aren't you going to ask me about your godmothers?" Aunt Miriam asked.

I already did, you crazy old bat.

"What happened with Myrtle and Millicent?" I asked, dutifully.

"What's wrong with that mustard?"

"It's empty."

"It's not empty. I can get six or seven more sandwiches out of that jar. Microwave it." Aunt Miriam hadn't grown up during the depression, but you'd never know it. She never threw anything out. It was amazing that she hadn't poisoned herself with her five-year-old salad dressings.

I popped the nearly empty jar in the microwave and pondered how long to choose. Asking would only get me a lecture.

"I had a visit yesterday," said Aunt Miriam.

"Oh, yeah?" I picked fifteen seconds. A good wholesome number.

"From a member of the Klinefeld Group."

I stopped breathing and the microwave beeped. The Klinefeld Group was the nonprofit trying to get control of my godmothers' fabulous art collection, using any means necessary. There were even accusations that The Bled Collection included art stolen from Jewish prisoners during the Holocaust, which it didn't.

"Mercy. Mustard."

"Of course." I got the mustard and, the second it cleared the microwave, the top exploded off and shot the remaining six sandwiches of mustard straight up onto the ceiling in a spectacular starburst pattern. I think I screamed, but I'm going to pretend I didn't.

I did look at Aunt Miriam. She sighed and said, "You were saying something about not wreaking havoc."

"It was an accident."

"It always is with you," she said. "There's a sponge and cleaning spray under the sink. I assume you'd like mayo on your sandwich now."

"Yes, please." I went to get her step ladder. She kept one in her bathroom because she couldn't reach the top shelf of her medicine cabinet.

Aunt Miriam force fed me my pimento loaf sandwich and a glass of Tang before I climbed the ladder.

"Are you going to tell me what the Klinefeld Group wants with you?" I asked after chugging the Tang.

"When you're done cleaning my ceiling."

Groan.

I sprayed one spray before my phone belted out the Darth Vader theme song. Aunt Miriam took my phone out of my purse and glared at me. "You gave your father the Darth Vader ring tone?"

"I thought it was funny," I said.

She pursed her lips so hard they went white. At least it wasn't my mother. Her ring tone was the Wicked Witch of the West. That would've gotten me another caning.

Aunt Miriam started poking random buttons on my phone without success. Couldn't she just let it go to voice mail? Seriously? I was cleaning mustard off a ceiling. That counts as busy.

She finally hit the right button. "Hello, Tommy. It's Auntie." She paused and then said, "Your father wants to talk to you."

"I'm cleaning here. You don't want this mustard to set."

She held out the phone. "I'll risk it."

I took the phone, while balancing on the rickety ladder. "Hi, Dad."

"Aunt Miriam doesn't sound happy. What did you do?"

"Nothing."

Silence.

"Well, there may be mustard on the ceiling," I said.

"Sounds about right. Clean it up and get over here."

"Where are you?"

"Gioia's," he said and my mouth began to water. House-made salami. Not a loaf in sight.

"I'm having lunch with Aunt Miriam."

"How is it?" he asked with plenty of amusement in his voice.

"Delicious," I said with a winning smile at Aunt Miriam. She narrowed her faded blue eyes at me. How did she always know when I was lying? I was a decent liar. Some would say an excellent one. No one related to me seemed to think so though.

"Bullshit. Get over here. We've got a situation to discuss."

"No more situations. I just came back from Colorado. That whole thing was a nightmare." I didn't mention the Klinefeld Group thing in case he didn't know.

"Look here, girl. One of your people needs you. You'll get over here and you'll smile while you're doing it."

"I don't have people. I have patients."

Dad snorted. "Patients. Whatever. I'm waiting."

"Dad, I can't. I have a thing. Aunt Miriam needs me to—"

Click. He hung up on me. Unbelievable, but not wholly unexpected. Dad wasn't fond of the word 'no'. And what did he mean by 'Patients' with a snort? I was a nurse. A darn good one, in my unbiased opinion. Dad usually described me as a 'sort of nurse', which was, I supposed, a dig at my PRN status. I worked through an agency and filled in when someone was short a nurse. My parents considered it one shift short of a real job. But they didn't complain when I was available to do all the scut work at my dad's agency. Then they liked it just fine.

Aunt Miriam tapped my ankle. "What thing do you have?"

"This, right now, is a thing."

"Use proper sentences."

"Do you want me to clean this or not?"

"Tommy wants you to go to Gioia's, so you go. The ceiling can wait."

Forever, I hope.

"What about the Klinefeld Group?" I asked.

"Come back promptly at six and I'll tell you."

Groan.

"Fine." I climbed down and dropped the sponge in the sink. "But give me a hint."

Aunt Miriam narrowed her eyes at me. "I'll tell you at six."

"I'm not going until you tell me," I said, crossing my arms. I was stubborn, too. Where did she think I got it from?

"Don't make any other plans. Tonight's movie night."

The blood drained right out of my face. "What?"

"You heard me. We will have dinner, discuss the Klinefeld Group, and watch a movie."

I pointed at her. "I can't believe it. You planned this."

Watching movies with Aunt Miriam could not happen. She loved horror. It was super creepy, a nun loving horror. *The Exorcist* was her favorite, followed closely by *Saw*.

"Don't be ridiculous. I couldn't plan that you would spurt mustard all over my ceiling." She smiled and I doubted every word.

"If anyone could, it would be you. Where's Sister Francis? She's your movie person."

Aunt Miriam whipped out a DVD case from behind a stack of cookbooks. She had it there the whole time, waiting for her chance to pounce. "Francis is out of town visiting family. You'll have to do. I've been saving this one just for you."

"*Annabelle*? That's still in theaters," I said, backing away. If I watch that, I'll never sleep again.

"Tommy found me a bootleg copy. Such a sweet boy." She followed me, waving the DVD. "Tonight. Six."

"What about Sister Clarence? She loves you. I'm sure she'd be happy to watch it."

"*Annabelle* would scare Clarence."

"It'll scare me. I can't handle horror. You know that."

She backed me up into the door. "Don't be ridiculous. You were nearly murdered in a funeral home."

"That's right. I probably have PTSD."

"There was that girl in that disgusting bar, the scuba diving incident, and who knows what all? You can handle it. You're tough."

"No, I'm not. Ask Dad. He called me a pansy yesterday."

"Tonight at six."

"I'll clean your mustard," I said, crossing my arms.

"I need a movie-watching partner. It's no fun without someone to scream with."

"It's no fun at all."

"Do you want to know about the Klinefeld Group?"

"Yes."

"Then you'll be here," said Aunt Miriam.

"I'll find some other way to get the info."

"No, you won't. Don't make me get out The Exorcist."

"Please don't make me do this," I begged.

Aunt Miriam's pocket started to ring. It had to be Dad. He never gave up and Aunt Miriam wouldn't have any problem with caning me to get me to obey.

Aunt Miriam managed to answer it after she tried fifteen different buttons. Cellphones weren't her thing.

"Hello, Tommy," she said in a sweeter tone than she ever used for me. Probably because Dad taught self-defense classes to the Sisters of Mercy. That was an idea I wished he'd forget.

Aunt Miriam held up the phone and Dad's voice exploded out of it. "What are you waiting for? Don't make me come over there!"

I think there was even a breeze coming out of it.

Aunt Miriam crossed her arms.

"How did he know I wasn't leaving?" I asked.

"He's your father. Will you be leaving or shall I make another sandwich for Tommy?"

I stomped out without answering. No good could come of it.

CHAPTER TWO

Traffic brought me to a dead stop under a streetlight banner proclaiming in green, white, and red that I had arrived on The Hill. I didn't need a banner to know where I was. The Hill was unique in the St. Louis landscape. The turn-of-the-century brick buildings were filled with family restaurants and shops that had been in business for decades. The Italian flag's colors were everywhere, just so you would know exactly what The Hill was all about. Food and family. I loved it. The Hill was cozy and warm on the coldest days and there was a sense of history that could only be matched in the Central West End, where I grew up and still lived. If I ever moved, it would be to The Hill.

I leaned to the left to try and see around a ginormous sport utility vehicle. I got a glimpse of a detour sign and groaned. A cop stepped in front of the sign and waved for the line of vehicles to start moving. I thought I'd make it through, but I got the hand and the cop waved the cross traffic through instead. Macklind Avenue was blocked off and that was where Gioia's was. Great. I couldn't see what was going on, but it had been happening for a while. There were cop cars and white tents cordoning off the area.

The cop was replaced by another broad-shouldered man in blue and the first cop headed in my direction. I quickly cranked down the window. "Excuse me!"

He turned, his face drawn and his young eyes accented with heavy bags. It said O'Connor on his name tag. "Yes, ma'am."

"What's up with blocking off Macklind? I gotta get to Gioia's."

"The detour will get you..." He trailed off as he leaned in to get a better look at me. "Holy crap! You're Mercy Watts. You really are a dead ringer for Marilyn Monroe. I can't believe I'm talking to you. I met your father once. He rocks. I mean, he's a great cop. A great detective, he was, I mean he is. He *is* a great detective. He was a cop. You know that. Everybody knows that."

"Breathe," I said, suppressing a smile. Dad's fans got so flustered.

"Sorry. I just didn't think you'd be here. I mean, you have to be somewhere, but not here. You could be here. I can't believe I'm meeting Tommy Watts's daughter. You're the DBD cover girl. Holy crap. Can I have your autograph?" asked O'Connor.

What started out as fun had rapidly turned depressing. I was famous, but not for anything good. I was Tommy Watts's daughter. DBD's cover girl. I had Marilyn's face. None of that was about me, the real me. It was all window dressing. I was famous for belonging to someone else. That stunk. I was supposed to belong to me.

"Sure," I said with a sigh. "Got paper and a pen?"

He gave me his ticket pad and I signed the cardboard backing. That was a new one.

"So...are you going to tell me what's going on down there or what?"

"You're joshing me, aren't you? You and your dad are probably on the case. Is there a case? They have the guy. Maybe they don't. Do you know something?" asked O'Connor.

I slapped my forehead. "I don't even know why I'm sitting here. What happened?"

"Seriously?"

"O'Connor, your partner's about to wave me through. Tell me or I'll run you over."

"Tulio's down there."

I blinked.

"The shooting. Mass murder."

"I…I forgot. I've been working a lot," I said, my stomach growing queasy with the pimento loaf and the thought of all those people.

"What's the case?" whispered O'Connor. "I won't tell anyone."

"I'm a nurse. There's no case."

He held his finger to his lips. "Mum's the word. You are not on this case. Got it."

Oh dear Lord.

The other cop waved to me and I drove away from O'Connor, who would undoubtedly inform everyone he met that I was working the Tulio mass murder case, which I wasn't. Like he said, they got the guy. Kent Blankenship had confessed to walking into Tulio, one of The Hill's best restaurants, and opening fire with a TEC-9. He killed or wounded twenty-six people in the small elegant dining room in the space of 22 seconds before a waitress named Monique Robertson, who bore an uncanny resemblance to the actress Mo'Nique, tackled him. After Blankenship was arrested and charged, his idiot lawyers tried to claim police brutality, only to discover that Monique had brutalized him in every way an unarmed woman possibly could. She kicked him, bit him, punched him, clawed him, and stabbed him with a fork multiple times. Blankenship's mug shot made him look like the victim, instead of a thirty-year-old busboy that got fired from Tulio's for incompetence. Monique was lauded as a hero and every news program known to mankind featured her for days. The Tulio case didn't need me, it had the epically badass Monique.

I had been working a double shift in St. John's ER the night it happened and I'd done my best to forget about it ever since. The victims didn't come to our ER, too far away, but it was all over the news. It was a miserable, heartbreaking night made worse by my history. Again, I was famous for all the wrong reasons. People felt compelled to ask my opinion about it because I'd nearly been murdered and was obviously an expert on murderers. Surviving didn't make me an expert on anything, except for crappy hospital food, but nobody believed that. Nobody except Dad and my cousin by marriage, Chuck. They got that you can solve a crime, see the motive, and not truly see the person behind it. Murderers were all unique and they kept escaping their pigeonholes, no matter how often we stuffed them in there.

Why in the world did Dad decide to have lunch at Gioia's on that day of all days? Blankenship had done his deed three days before. I loved The Hill, but it was the place to avoid on that afternoon. If I hadn't been so good at blocking out Tulio, I would've insisted on having lunch somewhere else. I didn't care if Gioia's had the best salami in the world, thinking about Tulio was too high a price to pay.

I followed the detour signs in a roundabout way through the back-streets of The Hill. I wasn't sure why twenty turns were needed to get me to the other side of Macklind, but the cops seemed to think it was necessary. My truck barely fit into a parking space down the street from Gioia's. The street wasn't that crowded on a Saturday night. Gawkers and news people had taken up all the spaces, and I hoped they were spending money at the places that didn't have the misfortune to hire homicidal busboys.

Gioia's was packed, but it always was. I squeezed in the door and spotted Dad at one of the few rickety metal tables. The line wrapped around him, crowding his tall, spare form, but he ignored them. Dad was hunched over a tablet, typing in notes with amazing speed.

I pushed past a couple guys discussing the merits of Italian-style beef and headed for Dad. Before I made it, I was cut off by Joe Funaro, a local baker.

"Hey, Mercy. Thought I might be seeing you, since the old man is here."

"It's under duress, I assure you."

"Yeah, I get it. Your dad is something. So what do you make of that whole deal down at Tulio? That's some shit, ain't it? I can't get nothing out of Tommy," said Joe.

"To tell you the truth, I'd forgotten all about it," I said, trying to maneuver past him.

"You forgot? It's all over *Headline News*." He leaned to the side and looked out the plate glass window. "There's a rumor that Robin Meade might come out to cover the trial." He gave me a rakish look. "What do you think? Do I have a shot?"

I rolled my eyes. "Not even a little bit."

"Hey! Give a guy some hope."

"First of all, Robin Meade doesn't cover trials. She sits in the studio. Second, she's married."

"She's a Hollywood type. They don't mate for life," said Joe.

"Or for a decade, usually," I said.

"Exactly my point. Do you think I should get my chest waxed?"

"Please don't," I said, shuddering. Joe's hairless chest didn't bear thinking about.

"But girls like it," he said

"Not all girls. I still have a huge crush on Magnum P.I." I slipped away, leaving Joe to ponder Tom Selleck.

I sat in a chair next to Dad and said, "Why here? Seriously, why?"

Dad glanced up, but not at me. Our table was being eyed by customers desperate for a table. There was a conspicuous bulge under his right arm. Being armed helps when you're not vacating quickly. Tables were at a premium and we were going to be there for a while. Dad had two unwrapped sandwiches in front of him, some bags of my beloved Billy Goat chips, and a couple of iced teas. Dad's would have a pound of sugar in his. Mom was from the South, but it was Dad who loved the sweet tea.

"It's the right place. You needed to be down here today," he said, still eyeing the customers until they backed off.

"Why would I need to be *here* today? Traffic is a nightmare," I said.

I got you a Sydwich," he said with the lazy smile he was said to use on suspects quite effectively. It lured them in. I refused to be lured.

I crossed my arms. "Dad, I don't like Sydwiches. That's you."

"Damn. Honest mistake." He rubbed his hands together. "I guess I'll have to eat them both."

Honest mistake, my foot.

"What's Mom going to say?" I asked.

He grinned, stretching his freckles and popping out his ever-so-charming dimples. "Nothing. My ulcer has resolved."

"Really?"

"Really. What sandwich do you want?"

"Nothing. Aunt Miriam fed me pimento loaf and Tang," I said.

He sneered. "You need real food."

"Just a salami," I said.

Dad raised a long arm. "Shrimpy, a salami on garlic cheese."

"On it!" hollered Shrimpy, one of the expert sandwich makers, from the back.

The rest of the patrons stared at us, mouths open. The service at Gioia's was iffy. They were busy, having the best freaking salami in the world will do that, so they didn't have time for the niceties.

Fifteen seconds later, Shrimp yelled, "Incoming!" He launched my sandwich in the shape of a white papered torpedo across the dining area, Dad's long arm shot up and snatched it out of the air. "Thanks!"

"You want some tortellini salad with that, Tommy?"

I held up my hand. "No, no. I'm good." Nobody needed a container of tortellini flying around.

"It's a pass, Shrimpy!" yelled Dad.

"Sure thing!"

I unwrapped perfection and breathed deep the smell of a century-old recipe. The garlic cheese bread didn't hurt either. But before I took a bite, I asked, "So Dad, why are we here?"

"Ameche. What'd you think?"

"Ameche?" I took a bite. Oh my god. Why'd I eat that pimento loaf? I'd wasted valuable stomach space.

"He's your people. You gotta be on this."

"Ameche isn't my anything. What are you talking about?"

"He's your people. You got to take care of your people."

I sipped my tea, unsweet and therefore palatable. "He helped me with a case one time. That hardly makes us attached at the hip."

Dad inhaled a Sydwich and gulped his tea to cool down the spicy giardiniera. "Where's your loyalty? I raised you better than that."

Dad didn't do much raising to be honest. He was an up-and-coming homicide detective when I was young and worked as much as possible. Sometimes more. Most of my raising was left to Mom and my godmothers, Myrtle and Millicent Bled. Dad filled the role of pain in the butt. He still did, eyeing me while he unwrapped his second Sydwich, having lost all the charm he used on suspects.

I chewed slowly, just to bother him, and then said, "Fine. What's wrong with Ameche?"

"Haven't you been watching the news at all?"

"No. I've been avoiding it like herpes."

Dad started on his second Sydwich and then pondered me. "The incident at Tulio really bothered you?"

"Of course. I'm not a fangirl for murder. And I wouldn't call it an incident. It was horrific."

He reached over and pulled me close. His forehead touched mine and a lock of his red hair brushed my forehead. It was tender and comforting, not like Dad at all.

"Just tell me. I can't take the suspense," I said.

"I'm sorry you have to be involved."

I jerked back. "I don't."

"You do, I'm afraid. You met Ameche's sister, Donatella?"

"No. Why?"

"Her husband and his entire immediate family were killed at Tulio." Dad's voice was soft and steady, no ups or downs. They were just words that couldn't hurt me but somehow still did.

My sandwich stopped halfway to my mouth and Dad pushed it back down to the paper. "Mercy?"

"There were kids in there," I said.

"Two nephews and a niece."

"Oh my god. Have you talked to Ameche?"

"He called me this morning. There's an issue with Donatella and he needs our help, your help specifically."

"My help? What for?" I asked, my throat dry and scratchy.

Dad pushed my sandwich closer. "I'll tell you. Eat up."

"I'm not hungry anymore."

He nodded and told me about Donatella Ameche Berry and Tulio. Donatella was Ameche's older sister. She was married and lived in New Orleans. Friday, the night of the murders, was her in-laws 40th wedding anniversary. The family was celebrating at Tulio. Donatella's husband, Rob, flew in on Thursday to spend some extra time with his family and Donatella was supposed to fly in after the kids got out of school on Friday. Their flight was at five. Donatella pulled the kids out early and managed to get on an earlier flight so they wouldn't have to go straight to Tulio from the airport. That change in plans saved her kids' lives.

They became violently ill on the plane and an ambulance met them on the tarmac. They made it to the hospital in time and were diagnosed with a form of bacterial meningitis that would've killed them in flight, had Donatella stuck to the original schedule. As it was, she and the kids were at the hospital when the shooting at Tulio took place. Once the kids were out of immediate danger, Rob went to the restaurant to tell the family what had happened. He was there in time for dessert and for Kent Blankenship to open fire.

Dad wrapped my hands around my iced tea and insisted I take a drink. It was hard to get a sip down; my throat was so dry.

"They're all dead?" I choked out.

"Yes. All of the Berrys that were there. They had the misfortune to be seated in the center of the restaurant because of the size of the table. Line of fire."

"That might be the worst thing I've ever heard."

"I'm not done," said Dad.

I looked up into his blue eyes. They were so much like Aunt Miriam's, but without the critical appraisal for once. "Donatella's kids?"

"Still alive. Still in the ICU."

"So…"

"There are surviving Berrys, the ones not invited to the anniversary dinner, and they think Donatella hired Blankenship to kill her husband and his family."

"Are you freaking kidding me?" My cheeks flushed and the top popped off my cup.

"Nope. That crew is on fire and they blame Donatella for the massacre."

"I thought Blankenship confessed."

"He did, but they're pushing for an investigation into Donatella." Dad sucked the last ounce of sweet tea out of his giant cup.

"Her kids almost died. Are they crazy?"

"Ameche says they're dirtbags and the dirtbags think the meningitis was pretty convenient for Donatella, since it saved her life and the kids' lives."

"What do they think, that she gave them meningitis?" I asked.

"That's exactly what they think and they're pushing hard."

"Who has the case?"

Please don't say Chuck.

"Sidney Wick. Good guy and he's taking it seriously."

"Ameche must be totally losing it."

"That's putting it mildly."

I wrapped up my sandwich for later. One does not throw away a Gioia's salami, even when one thinks they might throw up. "I'm so afraid to ask, but what do you want me to do? I assume Blankenship didn't implicate Donatella, so this isn't going anywhere."

Dad shook his head. "You've been around, Mercy. That isn't close to the end of it. People have been sent to death row on nothing more than circumstantial evidence."

"And I'm supposed to…"

"You're a nurse. I want you to nip this in the bud. Talk to the doctor and find out if it's remotely possible that Donatella could've orchestrated this illness thing. Off the top of your head, what do you think?"

"With what you've told me, I'd have to say yes."

Dad sat bolt upright. "Are you serious?"

"I'm not saying it would be easy, but it could be done. Donatella would have to be willing to risk her own children's lives to do it. You'd have to study the disease course and time everything perfectly, but you could do it, if you infected the children directly."

"Shit."

"You didn't expect that?"

"Hell, no. Change in plans. When do you work again?"

"Tonight at eleven. I can't do anything else. I have to sleep. I'm working to seven."

"Sleep's for wussies." Dad wasn't joking. He really thought that sleep was for the undisciplined. "I need you out at Hunt in an hour. Yeah…I can swing it in an hour."

Hunt? What the heck is Hunt?

"I'll have to pull a few strings, but I'll get you in," he said.

I sipped my tea and watched my father think. You could see everything on his face. Of course he could hide absolutely every emotion when necessary, but that day he didn't bother. His eyes darted around. His mouth moved. He looked like a total nutter.

"That's what we'll do. First, Hunt. And then, the hospital. I'll handle Morty. Agreed?" he asked.

"What's Hunt?" I asked.

"Hunt Hospital for the Criminally Insane. Think, Mercy."

"Holy crap! Why would I ever, in a million years, go there?"

"Because you're going to interview Blankenship."

"What's he doing out there? Why isn't he in the regular lockup?" I started looking for an escape route through the lunch crowd.

Dad snorted and shook the remaining ice in his cup. "He had a psychotic break in lockup. Duty officer now has eight facial fractures. They should've shot Blankenship."

"Wasn't he cuffed?" I asked. A visit to Hunt was sounding less appealing all the time.

"Did it with his head. The powers that be decided they couldn't handle him and sent him out to Hunt for the experts to deal with. Best to get that bastard out of the city anyway. Best, if you think a lynch mob isn't a good option."

"Sidney must've interviewed him about Donatella. There's no point in me going," I said, sliding back my chair. It made a hideous screech on the linoleum and everyone looked at us again.

"Sidney is a fifty-year-old bald guy with gout and rosacea. You're beautiful."

I think my mouth dropped open. Beautiful? My dad had never said that to me before. I'd heard other dads say it about their daughters. 'Look at my daughter. Isn't she a beauty?' 'This is my beautiful daughter.' They'd say it even if their daughter looked a whole lot like Ben Stiller, but not my dad. He avoided the B-word completely. I heard 'pretty' once when I modeled my prom dress and Mom made him say it.

"What?" Dad asked.

"You called me beautiful."

"Like that's news. Don't get a big head." He slapped a manila folder on the table. "Here."

Since the complimenting was over, I opened the folder. It

contained a slim amount of data on Kent Blankenship. "That's it? He's got no history."

"That's right. Blankenship is about the most boring murderer I've ever heard of. I take that back. He is the most boring. He was perfectly normal until three days ago."

I flipped through the pages again. "Well, I wouldn't say that."

A flicker of a smile passed over Dad's lips. "Oh, really."

"Blankenship has an IQ of 143, but he barely graduated from high school. I wouldn't call that normal. No romantic relationships. No life, as far as I can tell."

"And that's why you're going to talk to him. He's a smart loser. You ought to be his wet dream."

"Dad, that's gross."

"I agree. But if he's going to accuse Donatella to deflect blame for a plea deal, we need to know it."

"I do not want to go to Hunt." I closed the file.

Dad gathered up our trash and tossed it. The second I stood up, a couple of guys pounced on our table. I tucked my sandwich in my purse and waited while Dad paid. That's how I knew that he was really serious about me going to Hunt. Dad never took me to lunch. He never paid, not once, since I became an adult.

Dad ushered me outside and down the street to my truck. I got in and said, "I really don't want to go to Hunt. There has to be a hot female cop who can do it."

Dad put Blankenship's file in my lap. "You saw the IQ. He might just be smart enough to smell a cop. You can be his friend."

My lip curled at the thought and I pictured Jodie Foster standing in front of Hannibal Lector's cell.

Dad laughed. "It's not *The Silence of the Lambs* out at Hunt."

"And you know that for sure?" I asked.

"Pretty sure." He slammed my door and walked down the street with his cellphone pressed against his ear.

Pretty sure? That was just great.

CHAPTER THREE

Hunt Hospital for the Criminally Insane had had a change of heart or at least a change of name. The sign said, "Hunt State Hospital for the Mentally Ill." Maybe a PR firm told them that Criminally Insane wasn't so comforting for the people who lived in the town of Hunt. I doubt that anyone was fooled. The razor wire and guard towers were a dead giveaway that the hospital wasn't for the mildly unwell.

Hunt did surprise me, though. It was built in 1840 and looked a lot like a college campus from the front, if you were able to ignore that pesky razor wire. The entrance was another surprise. I turned in and stopped at a guard shack. I had to get out of my truck while they searched it. The guard ran a hand-held metal detector over me before I was allowed back in. Then I got to drive through the first gate, which closed after me and I was then sandwiched between two gates. I went through the whole thing a second time with the addition of a hand swab for explosive material. Then the second gate made a loud clank and rolled back, allowing me through. By the time I drove into a parking spot, my hands were clammy and the hair on the nape of my neck was sweaty despite the frigid wind blowing across the parking lot. I got out and a portly man rushed out of the visitors' entrance, waving to me. He had a thick head of iron-grey hair and the jolliest expression this side of St. Nick.

"Glad to see you got here alright," he said, extending a mittened hand. "Wilson Cleves, director of Hunt."

I shook his hand. "Mercy Watts. I believe you're expecting me."

"We are indeed. I thought it would be your father visiting us today, but it's wise that he sent you instead."

"My father's been here before?"

"Oh, yes. We see him almost on a regular basis," said Mr. Cleves.

Unbelievable. Dad acted like he'd never seen the place. What a pain in my neck.

"Parole hearings?" I asked.

"On the rare occasion. Mostly visiting. Tommy's uncommonly compassionate, especially for a cop, if you don't mind me saying so."

"He is," I said, because I was supposed to. My dad visited the criminally insane. The thought was uncomfortable for some reason. I couldn't put my finger on why. I knew he visited other prisoners, those who had committed crimes under a particular set of circumstances. There was a severely-abused woman who'd created a detailed plot to kill her husband, carried it out to the letter, and was given a life sentence. Dad liked her. He brought her books. What do you bring to the insane?

Mr. Cleves swiped a keycard and punched in a code. "Come right in."

I hesitated at the open door. "Who does he visit?"

"I can't release that information. Visitor logs are private. You understand."

I nodded, but I still wanted to know. I was as nosy as my mother.

We went in a large arched door and entered a waiting area with some grubby sofas and a glass-enclosed reception desk. There was an armed guard behind the desk and an older couple sat on one of the sofas. They were squeezed together, holding hands. They didn't look at me but stared off at a spot on the opposite wall.

"Harve, can you give Shelley a buzz for me?" asked Mr. Cleves. "And have him brought into the fishbowl."

"Sure thing, Wilson." Harve picked up the phone and asked for

Shelley to come up to the front, then punched in another number. "Julius, Wilson wants Blankenship in the fishbowl ASAP. Full rig." He paused and glanced at Mr. Cleves, who nodded. "Yeah, fire it up."

I must've been sporting a freak-out expression, because Mr. Cleves patted my shoulder. "It's fine. You'll have absolutely no trouble at all. This is what we do."

That did not make me feel better in the least, but I nodded.

"You'll wait here for Shelley. She'll take care of you. You'll be searched, full body scan, and then you'll be all set." He said like it I was about to win a prize.

"Great." Why did I say that? I should've said, "Holy crap. I'm leaving."

Mr. Cleves patted me again and Harve buzzed him through a thick metal door, the kind of door you never want to go through.

I turned to find a sofa to perch on and found the older couple standing and staring at me. I jumped and stepped back.

"I'm sorry," said the woman in a quavering voice. "We didn't mean to startle you."

"It's okay," I said. "I'm just a bit jumpy."

"You're going in to see Kent Blankenship. He's our son, but they won't let us in."

"Um..." I looked at Harve behind the glass.

He grimaced slightly, like this was the worst part of his job. "Inmates have the right to refuse visitors."

The woman nodded. "But...but he isn't refusing you. Who are you?"

"She's not really a visitor, ma'am," said Harve.

"I'm here about another matter," I said.

Mrs. Blankenship began to shake and her husband pulled her tight to his side. "Is there something else? The police didn't say that. Did he do something worse?"

I held up my hands. "No, no. I don't know that he did anything...else."

They let out tensely-held breaths. "Thank God."

Mr. Blankenship dropped onto the sofa and buried his face in his hands. His wife stepped toward me and extended her hand. I didn't take it. I didn't know what to do.

"Will you tell him something for us?" she asked.

I looked at Harve and he shrugged.

"Okay. What do you want me to say?"

"Tell him that we still..." Her shoulders spasmed. "Just tell him we're here."

"Okay. Sure," I said.

She collapsed next to her husband and sobbed into his shoulder. I stood there, watching. I didn't move. I couldn't. I'd seen their names in Blankenship's file. But here, in front of me, were the real people that raised him. Nothing in his file suggested that it was their fault, but something went wrong and they had a front row seat.

"Mercy Watts?"

I turned and saw a woman with thin brown hair and a corrections officer uniform standing in the doorway that Mr. Cleves had gone through. "Yes."

"Come through."

I walked away from the Blankenships and their howling grief. I felt stiff, like it had enveloped me, and I couldn't move properly anymore.

"I'm Shelley. I'll be with you the entire time you're here."

"Hi."

"Are you okay?" she asked.

"How come nobody's with them?" I asked.

"Who should be with them?"

"I don't know. It just seems weird. I mean, they're out there by themselves."

Shelley frowned. "You get used to it."

"Really?"

She shrugged. "Yeah."

Shelley led me into a room with two stern male corrections officers. Shelley patted me down, ran me through the body scanner, and had me sign a stack of paperwork that basically said I wouldn't sue anyone, if I got my face eaten off. Proceed at your own risk, baby.

We left the screening room and the tension left Shelley's face. She walked me down a series of corridors with office doors that had locks but weren't too serious about it. It could've been any drab office building until we reached a barred door. Shelley identified herself and me to the camera. It made a loud clank and opened. We walked down a cinder block hall that definitely was not an office building.

"So," she said with a smile, "you're the new Clarice."

"Huh?"

"Pretty girl sent in to talk to a maniac for information."

"That's me, I guess."

"Who sent you?" she asked.

"My father," I said, smiling for the first time.

She gave me a sideways glance with furrowed brows. "Who's your father?"

"Tommy Watts."

She brightened up considerably. "Oh, Tommy. He's a great guy. He wouldn't send you, if he didn't think it was fine."

Well...

Shelley gave me a run-down of the rules. They were pretty obvious. No touching, stuff like that.

"Here we are," she said, stopping in front of yet another grey metal door. "This is the fishbowl. We call it that because you'll be visible on all sides. We use it for lawyer visits. Visitors that need privacy."

"Do I need privacy?"

"Someone thinks so."

"Can I pass on the privacy?" I asked, feeling like a complete wuss. This woman worked here, daily.

"He's already in there. Don't worry. There will be four guards watching you at all times. He's shackled, hands and feet, to a chair that's bolted to the floor. As an added precaution, we've wired him up. If he steps out of line, I'll give him a jolt that'll stop him in his tracks. You okay?"

"How many problems have you had in the fishbowl?"

"None with visitors. If there's a problem, it's while we're getting the inmate in or out. You're not involved in that. Let me give you some advice."

"Don't get near the glass," I said.

"There's no glass." She took a walkie-talkie off her belt and said into it, "She's coming in."

I heard the locks click as they were unlocked in the door, sending my blood pressure soaring. "So what's your advice?

"I've worked here for eight years. I've seen it all. Stuff you wouldn't believe. Blankenship isn't special. His problem is that he thinks he is. When you go in there, his perception is your reality. Don't let him suck you in too far."

Too far?

The door opened and an unsmiling guard nodded and waved me in. I took a deep breath and walked in. There wasn't any glass. It was a square room, white walls and a grey tile floor. On one side sat Blankenship, shackled and bolted to the floor as advertised, sitting in a metal chair behind a wide rectangular table. He wore a grey jumpsuit with no ID number on it, presumably everyone knew who he was. His head was bowed so that I couldn't see his face, but there was a red mark on his neck that could've been a handprint.

Shelley led me to another metal chair across from Blankenship behind a second metal table. I looked at Shelley.

"People feel better with their own table." She pointed up at a camera in the corner. "We have views of every inch of this room. If anything happens, we'll be in in under three seconds."

"You've timed it?" I asked.

"We have. You get ten minutes. Longer is out of the question. Things will start to occur." Shelley nodded to me and I sat. She left the room through another of the four doors, but there wasn't any sound of locking. Thank goodness for that.

Blankenship didn't look up. I expected him to be curious, to want to know who this visitor was that was being forced on him, but there was nothing. I would have to initiate the conversation and I hadn't a clue how to do it.

"Mr. Blankenship?" I asked.

Nothing. He wasn't currently drugged. They'd had him on anti-psychotics when he was first brought in but found it unnecessary. Shelley said he was docile, but she said it in a way that made it clear that she didn't expect it to last.

"Mr. Blankenship, I need to ask you a few questions," I said.

Blankenship's head nodded and a chill went through me. I hadn't expected him to move, I guess.

"Why?" he asked in a soft, rather high voice.

"Because I've been ordered to do so."

He tilted his head up. His face was blank, not disinterested, not anything. I paused and took note of his injuries. One eye had multiple popped blood vessels, his lip was split in two places, and he had what looked like rug burn on his nose and right cheek. Monique had worked him over pretty good or maybe the cops helped out. I didn't care which.

"Do you know Donatella Berry?"

"No."

"Had you ever heard of Donatella Berry before the police mentioned her to you?"

"No."

It was pretty straightforward. Dad thought, for some reason, I'd be able to tell if he was lying. I couldn't. There was nothing to see.

"Did you know any of the people in Tulio the night you opened fire in the restaurant."

"Yes."

"Who did you know?"

"Jackson, Curt, Sierra." Blankenship went on to name every member of the staff working that night at Tulio, but he didn't name a single customer. I'd memorized the list.

"Why did you open fire at Tulio?" I asked.

"I wanted to kill them."

"The staff?"

"Everyone."

"Including the customers?"

"Yes."

I wanted to shift in my chair, but his brown eyes were on me and squirming equaled weakness. What would he think if he saw that? Was this what Shelley meant by his perception would be my reality?

"Are you uncomfortable?" he asked.

I hesitated but decided to be honest. "Yes. Are you?"

"You're the first person who's asked me that."

"I'm not surprised. So, are you uncomfortable?" I asked.

The first expression flickered in his eyes. "Yes."

Then I got it and I managed to contain a smile. "You didn't expect to be uncomfortable."

"I expected to be dead," he said flatly.

"You must be disappointed."

He nodded and I went on to ask him all the things I was supposed to ask, exactly way Dad told me to ask them. Blankenship admitted nothing about Donatella. The only thing I was sure of, was that being alive was a grave disappointment to him. In a weird way, I started to warm up to the psycho. I'd expected him to lie, blame the victims, and scream obscenities. But there was none of that. I asked questions. He answered. Short and to the point. He had no interest in me. His eyes didn't roam over my chest, and he didn't throw out the Marilyn comparison. It was like talking to a dead person, whose body just doesn't know it yet.

"Is that it?" he asked.

"Not quite," I said. "Your parents are here and they asked me to tell you that."

His face froze and his head dropped back to his chest. We stayed like that, me watching and his head down, for at least a minute. I couldn't tell if he was having an emotional reaction to his parents or what. He looked dead. Maybe it was a good time to start again if he was emotional.

"Who was your partner?" I asked.

"I didn't *need* a partner." Blankenship didn't look up.

Need. Need was interesting. And it was important to him. So what did he have that he didn't need?

"Not to do what you did, obviously. But there was someone."

The door opened and Shelley came in. "Time's up."

Under any other circumstances, I would've begged for more time. Maybe I could get him to look up, maybe I could see the answer in his eyes. But that was not happening. Shelley took me by the arm and marched me to the door I'd come in earlier. Another guard opened it and Shelley ushered me through. At the last second, I looked back at Blankenship and caught him gazing at me with a glint in his eye. A tiny smile curved the edge of his lips. When our eyes met, both vanished instantly. Then I was out the door and it bolted automatically behind me.

"Okay?" asked Shelley.

I nodded.

"So not okay."

"I don't know what I am right now."

"He got to you."

"No, he didn't," I said, walking back down the hall beside her.

She shook her head. "Don't come back. Not even if Tommy wants you to. Don't do it."

The leaving process was much faster than the entering. I got my stuff back and was taken out through a different set of doors, so I didn't see Blankenship's parents again. That was a relief. I don't know what I would've said to them.

Mr. Cleves put me in my truck and I drove through the two gates and turned onto the narrow road that led to the prison. When I was out of sight of the guards' shack, I pulled over and dialed Dad.

"There was a partner, but he's never going to tell us who."

"How do you know?" asked Dad.

"I just know."

"That's my girl."

CHAPTER FOUR

The door whipped open before my knuckles touched the wood. Aunt Miriam glared at me and she had her cane in hand, ready to strike.

"You're late," she said.

"I'm not late. It's five till," I said a little more sharply than I intended.

"Did you bring wine?"

I suppressed a smile. "Was I supposed to bring wine?"

"You are a guest. You are supposed to bring wine or a hostess gift," Aunt Miriam's freckled cheeks flamed pink.

"Do people still do that? Wasn't that over in 1963?" I held up my purse. "I have orange Tic Tacs and a used tissue."

She slammed the door the way a silver screen diva would. Think Lauren Bacall, only meaner. I laughed a little, and it was tempting to walk away, but what would I tell Mom? In my family, leaving after Aunt Miriam slams the door in your face means that you didn't try hard enough. I did not want to try harder. I wanted to go home and sleep before my shift, but that definitely wasn't happening. Aunt Miriam would call Mom. Mom would call me. Dad would call me. Aunt Tenne would call me. There would be a whole lot of calling and no sleeping.

I sighed and picked up the wine bottle I'd hidden beside the door. I was a bad niece, but sometimes I couldn't resist bothering the old crab. She sure bothered me. I held up the bottle in front of the peephole and knocked.

"Who is it?" hollered Aunt Miriam. I'm pretty sure hostesses aren't supposed to holler.

"Who do you think?" I hollered back.

"Someone who ignores the lessons I've taught her."

That was pretty accurate.

"I was born in a barn." I continued the hollering thing. It was fun.

The door whipped open again and Aunt Miriam was mid-rant when she saw the bottle. She swiped it out of my hand and eyed the label. "Bordeaux?"

"It goes with meatloaf," I said, dipping down my chin to look properly chastened.

"How did you know we were having meatloaf?"

Because we already had pimento loaf.

"It's snowing. Seemed like a meatloaf night," I said.

She stepped back and let me in like it was a real honor. "Sit down. I'm ready to serve."

I sat, as ordered, and watched as she popped the cork out of the bottle with a slim little screw better than a man with bulging biceps. I had to have one of those special cork removing gizmos that take no arm strength whatsoever. Aunt Miriam poured me exactly one ounce of wine, because I was working later, and then plated the famous Watts meatloaf. It was famous because it was Aunt Miriam's mother's recipe from the depression. Meat was scarce, so Great Grandma Cecile filled her meatloaf with boiled eggs. At some point, whole olives got added to the mix. Nobody knows who did that.

Eating Aunt Miriam's meatloaf was an art, one that depended on being visually impaired. Just eat it. Don't look at it. I was lucky she didn't make liver and onions. Gag. I really wanted the info on the Klinefeld Group, but I wasn't sure I wanted it that bad.

After we finished and I washed the dishes, Aunt Miriam handed me the stepladder and pointed at the mustard on the ceiling. I was hoping she'd forget. Who was I kidding? She never forgot anything.

"Are you going to tell me about the Klinefeld Group?" I asked, while spraying the mustard and getting the mist in my eyes.

"Yes," she said.

"Well?"

"Scrub."

"I am." Boy, did I scrub. The mustard had set. It did more than set. It stained the ceiling. I scrubbed so hard the paint came off, but the stain didn't even budge. How was that even possible? "I can't get it."

Aunt Miriam sent the ceiling a scorching look. I'm surprised the mustard didn't peel off in fear. "Alright. I was afraid of this. You will have to paint it. Touch up paint is in the storage cupboard. Sister Margaret Anne has the key."

I nearly fell off the ladder. "Are you kidding me? I have to work tonight."

She patted my calf and laughed. "I'm funny. Come down."

Hilarious.

I climbed down and we settled in for movie terror night. Before she pressed play, I put my warm hand on her cold one. "Tell me about the Klinefeld Group."

"After the movie," she said, her eyes not straying from the small screen.

"I promise I'll watch and be scarred for life. Just tell me."

"Fine. His name was Jens Waldemar Hoff and he was extremely polite."

It was the only time I'd ever heard Aunt Miriam call someone polite with disdain in her voice. She didn't warm to Hoff, despite his good attitude. He'd come about The Girls, my godmothers Myrtle and Millicent Bled, and the Bled Collection. Jens Waldemar Hoff came with a promise and a threat. He wanted me to get The Girls to give the Klinefeld Group all the WWII artifacts in the Bled Collection, or they would expose the family as thieving racists that stole from the Jews even as they were forced into the gas chamber. They would expose Stella Bled Lawrence as a collaborator with the Nazis. They would ruin the Bled family, my family by association, and get the artifacts anyway.

"He made it sound like he was doing us a favor by sparing The Girls the humiliation," spat Aunt Miriam.

"That's all ridiculous. They can't prove any of it. Stella smuggled those things out of Nazi-occupied territory at the request of the families. She was a spy for Britain, for crying out loud."

"The Klinefeld Group will say that she was a double agent and everyone was fooled by her pretty face."

"They can say whatever they want. It's stupid."

Aunt Miriam frowned and put a hand on my leg.

"What?" I asked. "Stella was a hero, even if the world doesn't know it."

"The world *doesn't* know it. Her records have never been declassified." Aunt Miriam's eyes got all misty. "She had to do a lot of things that could be construed in a negative light. She got close. She knew them."

"Who?"

"Top Nazi officials. Stella played many roles and they never knew who she really was. She did things that she regretted. They can use those things against the family now."

"She was a hero."

"I believe that, but what will the public believe?" Aunt Miriam asked. "The Girls are old. Do you want them put through this?"

"They won't give up those pieces. They swore to protect them. You know that."

"I do know. I wanted to find out what you think about it. They are your godmothers and you know them better than anyone."

"I don't know about that," I said.

She scoffed, "Don't be silly. Everyone knows that you are their child and you know them best. Hoff wants to speak to you."

"I have nothing to say to him."

Aunt Miriam gazed at me, searching my face, and I waited. Asking what she was looking for wouldn't help at all. There might be yelling or a pinched cheek. Aunt Miriam was the boss and I always knew it. Just when I was about to get nervous, she said, "I can see that. Good. I told him nothing and I'm glad you won't either."

"Of course, I won't."

She took my hand between hers and pressed it firmly. I could feel the bones under the thin blanket of translucent skin. "It's not the collection that he wants."

"Huh?"

"There's something in particular he's after. They're only using Stella and the pieces she smuggled out to get it."

"How do you know?" I asked.

"He was asking questions about the size of the pieces."

I frowned and planted my elbows on my knees, rubbing a bit of mustard into my skirt. "Like...how big are the paintings?"

"He wasn't interested in the paintings at all or the sculptures. He asked about boxes and furniture."

"What kind of boxes?"

"The kind that The Girls might not have opened. Do you know about anything like that?"

"No. Why would they have a box and not open it?"

"I have no idea, but he wants something, and he thinks it's hidden within the collection. He thought he was too smart for an old nun like me. A fool to the marrow, he was."

"Are you sure?" I asked.

"I know people, Mercy. I'm a nun."

That didn't sound like the greatest recommendation for knowing people. Knowing God, sure. People, not so much.

"Okay. I'll look into it."

"What's your plan?" she asked.

"I guess I'll figure out what he wants and keep him from getting it."

She gave me a peck on the jaw. It was the highest point she could reach. "Good girl. Now to the movie.

We watched *Annabelle* and, for once, being totally exhausted worked out for me. I kept falling asleep, so I missed most of the horror. The horror in the movie anyway. I dreamt of Blankenship in the fishbowl with his smile. It wasn't a nightmare exactly, but it certainly wasn't pleasant.

When the movie was over, Aunt Miriam stood up and rummaged

around, coming up with *The Exorcist*. "I'll start it and make some popcorn."

She was almost gleeful. Talk about creepy.

"I can't. Work," I said, stretching.

"That movie didn't count. You went to sleep."

"Well, I had a long day, and I'm about to have a long night."

Aunt Miriam got pensive and then smiled. "*American Horror Story: Asylum*. I've been saving the season."

"For when you really hate me?" I asked.

"Don't be silly. We're family."

I didn't know what that meant, but it was best not to inquire. I watched Jessica Lange chew up her dialog from behind a throw pillow. Aunt Miriam sat on the edge of her seat with her hands clasped in joy. When the first episode was over, she was genuinely sad that I had to go. I was, too. I had to go out in a frigid black-as-pitch night and walk through the grounds of an old convent. If that wasn't a good opening for a horror movie, I didn't know what was.

Once it was time to go, Aunt Miriam practically shoved me out the door with a meatloaf sandwich and a promise/threat that we'd do it again soon. Great. More movie nights with Aunt Miriam.

I walked alone through the silent half-lit halls of the convent, but it wasn't the shadows that bothered me. It was my own thoughts. Blankenship wasn't barred from sending or getting mail. He could have visitors. I might be right about him. What was to stop Blankenship from telling his partner about our little visit? He'd smiled, and I'd seen it. People knew me and now he did to. The feeling I had, while walking through those long corridors, was that I wasn't alone. I was known and Blankenship was with me.

The visitor's parking lot was empty, except for my truck and a Mercedes coupe. I stopped at the top of the staircase. Snowflakes whizzed by me and I squinted at the image of luxury below me. I didn't know anyone who drove that car, and from what Blankenship's bio said, he didn't either. I got out my handy dandy pepper spray anyway and slowly walked down the stairs.

I found the Mercedes empty and let out a tense breath. Empty. Of course, it was empty. No one who drove that car was lying in wait for me in a convent parking lot. That was just stupid. It was some high-class donor meeting with the Mother Superior.

I relaxed and went around it to my truck. When I made it to the headlights, I saw a head, slightly bowed next to my driver's side door.

"Mercy Watts. It's about time."

I knew that voice and I didn't want to hear it.

Oz Urbani straightened up and grinned at me over my side mirror. I hadn't seen him since August after I'd gotten back from Honduras. He was just as handsome with a light tan and soft dark curls waving back from his angular face. He rocked a scarf like no man I'd ever seen. Outside of *GQ Magazine,* that is. Oz was better than anyone that Blankenship might send my way, but I wasn't thrilled. I'd done Oz a favor and he'd done me one in return. It had been a fruitful relationship, but I had hoped to never ever lay eyes on the nephew of Calpurnia Fibonacci again. Connections to organized crime wasn't something I wanted on my résumé. But the Fibonaccis didn't ask permission last time and they wouldn't this time either.

"What are you doing here?" I asked.

"Waiting for you. What took so long? Sister Miriam's meatloaf can't be that good," he said.

"I don't even want to know how you know about Aunt Miriam's meatloaf."

"Everybody knows."

"Are you stalking me?"

"My cousin is Sister Mary Carlotta," he said, grinning wider.

I tried to push him aside to put my key in the lock. "So you're here to see her. Great. See ya."

"I'm here to see you. Do you think I'd stand outside in this weather for a cousin?"

"I don't know what you'd do, which is kind of the problem." I used my shoulder to try and knock him off balance. No luck. Oz was slight, but strong. "Get out of the way. I have to go to work."

"I'm glad to see I don't scare you," he said, crossing his arms.

"Why would I be scared? Our so-called relationship is over."

"Well…"

I hip-checked him. "No way. Hit the road. This is not happening again. Forget you know me."

The grin vanished. "I just want to know what Blankenship told you today."

I stopped pushing him. "Oh my god. No. Don't tell me you're interested in him, because I'm not doing a damn thing for that psychopath."

"It's not Blankenship that I want to help," he said.

"Who then?"

"Donatella Ameche. Look. I know you went out to Hunt today. I want to know what he said about her." The snow picked up and he squinted at the blast.

"How do you know I was at Hunt? Do you have a cousin there, too? Which ward?"

"I have a friend. Several, actually. So what about it?"

"Who's Donatella to you?" I asked, brushing the hair out of my eyes and pulling my stocking cap down farther over my ears.

"Old friend. I know the Berry family is trying to implicate her in the Tulio murders, and I don't want that to go anywhere. Donatella is a good person. Truly kind and warmhearted. She would never arrange anyone's death. You're on the case anyway. You may as well share what you have with me."

"I'm not *on* the case. It's police business. Please get out of my way. I have to go. I'm going to be late," I said.

"I can't," he said, his dark eyes pleading. "I have to know how much trouble Donatella's in."

I bit my lip. Dad would kill me if I said anything. On the other hand, what could it hurt? "Is this just between you and me?"

"I swear. My family doesn't know I'm here and I won't tell them." Oz took my hands and pressed them between his buttery soft leather gloves. "Please."

"Blankenship didn't implicate her. He claims he doesn't know her and appears to have no interest in screwing her over. But keep in mind that he's a mass murderer, so pretty much all bets are off."

"What else? There's something else," said Oz.

"I don't think it's Donatella, but there's somebody in the mix. He wasn't completely alone in the shooting. Someone was involved somehow."

"Are you having one of your father's famous feelings?"

"I guess so."

"Good. Someone else being involved is good for Donatella. I'll put some feelers out and see what I can come up with."

I yanked my hands away. "You said you wouldn't involve your family. They're going to know about me."

"Not necessarily. Tulio is my aunt's favorite restaurant. We've known the owners for fifty years. My family will want to help. They don't need to hear your name," said Oz.

"You'll tell me what you find out?"

"And you can filter the information through your father. Everybody wins."

Usually when someone says that, I'm the one who loses. But I nodded anyway. "Can I go now?"

Oz stepped aside and then looked up. "Check it out."

I peered through the window of my truck and there, at the top of the stairs, was Aunt Miriam. No coat. No expression. The increasing snow half obscured her. If it weren't for the wind whipping her veil around, I would've thought she was an illusion.

"Oh, no."

"That woman is scary," said Oz. "She reminds me of Sister Constance at school. She hit me. A lot."

"You have no idea. Quick. Go before she writes down your plate number," I said.

"Do you think she will?"

I jumped in my truck. "Count on it. Go."

Oz walked to his car like he didn't care that the world's scariest nun was giving him the stink eye. His car turned over on the first try and he drove away before my ancient truck even thought about starting. The engine finally revved and I looked back up, praying she wasn't coming down for 'a talk.' The top stair was empty. Aunt Miriam had vanished into the swirling snow. If only her memories of Oz would vanish as well. But they wouldn't and, when I least expected it, Aunt Miriam would happen to remember a handsome member of the Fibonacci family in a wintry parking lot. Eventually, this meeting would come back to bite me in the butt.

CHAPTER FIVE

My night in the ER was as nutty as a Watts family reunion, but without the drunk uncles and lectures on the importance of being Irish. A guy zipped his penis up in his jeans. Another guy got amorous with a lightbulb. Radiology will keep those films forever. A fight broke out at a Furry convention. You haven't lived until you've treated cuts and bruises on six guys in fox costumes. On the normal side, there were a few accidents involving people who didn't understand the concept of black ice. I managed to stay awake with the help of burnt coffee and stacks of charts that needed to be updated.

I finally walked out into the icy morning air at 7:30am. My truck was more enthused about starting, and I was about to pull out when Dad's ringtone started in my purse.

"No. I'm not answering." I put my truck in reverse.

Dad hung up and then my phone started again. This time with the Wicked Witch of the West ringtone. Come on. Who was next? Uncle Morty?

I sighed and dug out my phone. "Hello."

"Hi, honey," said Mom. "Here's Dad."

Damnit.

"Mercy, what are you doing?"

"Is this a trick question? I just got off work," I said, rubbing my eyes and smearing the remains of my mascara on my fingers.

"Excellent. Head over to Children's. Donatella is expecting you. The kids are in the PICU," said Dad.

"It's the crack of dawn. It can wait."

"Remember Ameche."

"Like you'd let me forget," I said. "I'll go over after I sleep. Seriously. It was a busy night."

"It was not. I have a scanner, girl. You caught five MVAs. None of them over thirty-five miles an hour. You were bored senseless. Get over to Children's."

"What's the rush?"

"I'll let the doc explain that." Dad hung up like there was no chance I wouldn't disobey. The odds were actually in favor of disobeying, but somehow, I turned right when I should've turned left. Damn my curiosity. Dad always knew how to get to me.

St. Louis Children's Hospital was surprisingly busy, especially for a weekday morning before eight o'clock. Children got sick, too. Sometimes I forgot that. I wanted to forget that very much. Not that Children's was an unpleasant hospital. It was the only hospital that didn't make me somber. There were colors, real colors. Not just soothing earth tones, but primary colors. I trotted past a red sculpture of an elephant and dashed in under a pretty portico that an artist designed to be welcoming, not an apology for having to be there.

I rode the elevator to the kangaroo floor and was just starting to feel chipper when the door opened. There was Chuck, hunched over like someone recently kicked him in the groin. Sidney Wick stood beside him, looking the way Dad described him, not beautiful.

We all stayed put until the elevator doors started to close. Chuck's long arm shot out and stopped it. "Fancy meeting you here."

"You should be totally shocked. I know I am," I said, stepping out onto the animal print carpeting.

Sidney shook his head. "You're not going to cause me any problems, are you, Miss Watts?"

"Who me?" I asked. "I wouldn't dream of it."

"Why are you here then?"

Chuck stayed silent. He clearly already knew.

"Ameche's my friend and I'm a nurse. I can deal with the medical stuff. Explain things. It helps to have an expert when the family's under so much stress," I said.

Sidney's heavy rounded shoulders relaxed. "Ameche didn't mention that you were helping out."

"Why would he? Medical explanations have nothing to do with what happened at Tulio."

"Let's hope not." Sidney went onto the elevator. "You coming, Watts?"

Chuck let go of the elevator door. "Be down in a minute."

Sidney raised an eyebrow at us, but the door cut him off before he could insinuate something I'd rather not have insinuated.

I spun around and headed for the PICU doors, but Chuck grabbed my arm. "Hold it right there, Missy."

"Missy? Are you high?" I asked, shaking him off.

"I don't know where that came from. I'm so damn tired, I'm not sure what your real name is."

"Carolina."

"Oh, yeah," he said with a wan smile, and then he sniffed me. I hate when men sniff me and it happens more than you'd think. "Is that Aunt Miriam's meatloaf?"

"You don't know my name, but you can recognize the meatloaf smell."

"It's distinctive," he said.

"I'll give you that." I shoved him toward the elevator. "Go to bed."

Chuck grinned and the sleaze came roaring through the exhaustion. "I will, if you come with me."

"Gross."

"No, it's not. Everyone says so."

I wrinkled my nose. "That's why it's gross."

"That didn't come out right," said Chuck.

And yet it's true. Slut.

"See ya. Gotta go."

Chuck snagged my arm and steered me to a cushy bench done in orange. "So you caught this case?"

"I didn't catch it. It hit me in the head at Dad's insistence."

"Maybe you can calm the Berrys down. They want someone to blame for Tulio."

"Do you think it was random?" I asked.

"Blankenship says it was and Sidney believes him. He wanted to ruin the restaurant after they fired him. He didn't know the Berrys."

"That sounds so stupid when you say it out loud. All those people. Children. Over getting fired."

"Agreed. What did *he* say?" asked Chuck.

I grimaced and crossed my arms.

"Come on. Tommy told me that he was sending you out to Hunt." There was a sharpness in his voice that surprised me. Chuck was Dad's protégé and I'd never heard an ounce of criticism come out of his mouth before.

"You got a problem with me going out there?" I asked.

Chuck's lean form bent over me and he whispered, "You bet I do. I told Tommy not to send you. It wasn't right to ask that of you."

I was so surprised. I couldn't say anything. Chuck was more protective of me than my own father. Come to think of it, it wasn't so surprising. Dad had sent me to places nobody should go. It was a no-brainer to think I shouldn't go to Hunt.

"How bad was it?" asked Chuck.

I shrugged. I didn't really know what to say.

"That bad?"

"Not really. Blankenship was..."

Chuck's face went hard. "Did he threaten you?"

"No. Nothing like that. It was just weird, being in that place and looking at him, knowing what he did."

"You're sure you're okay?" he asked.

"Of course. You must think I'm a serious wimp."

"Not at all. Did you get anything from Blankenship?"

"Not really." I didn't want to say anything about Blankenship having a partner, in case Dad wanted that information close hold.

"Good. Promise me you won't go out there again," said Chuck.

I had absolutely no intention of even driving by Hunt's gate, but I didn't say that because I could do whatever the hell I wanted, "I will not. I'll do whatever I have to do to help out Ameche and Donatella. You should know that."

"I do. I wish I didn't." He grinned and was still charming, despite the dark circles under his eyes. "Missed a spot." He kissed my cheek and I caught the scent of good whiskey underneath coffee and a mint.

"A spot of what?" I wiped his nonexistent spit off my cheek.

"Whatever." Another winning grin.

But I was not won over. "Save it for Philippa."

"We broke up. Didn't she tell you?"

My hands went to my hips. "I hope you didn't break her heart."

"That's not what I do. She knew it would never get serious anyway."

I didn't ask why. Philippa was great and Chuck was obviously an idiot.

He let go of my arm and I headed for the PICU doors. I could feel him watching me walk away. Maybe Philippa was lucky after all.

I pressed the button next to the PICU doors, identified myself, and was buzzed in. The PICU was just as cheerful as the rest of Children's, but it was very quiet. I walked down to the desk and saw Clementine Collier going through a stack of charts with her back to me. Her waist-length steel-grey dreadlocks were held back by a purple bandana and she wore a pair of black cat ears and a tail. That was so Clementine. I met her when I was fourteen when my friend, Ashton, fell off the top of our cheerleading pyramid, shattering her pelvis and puncturing her lung. Clementine made a huge impression on me and was the reason I started thinking about a career in nursing. Dad blamed her for keeping me from my true vocation which was, of course, law enforcement. But I was never going to be a cop, even if Ashton had better balance. The smell of Dad when he came home from the morgue, when Mom didn't catch him before he got into the house, cinched it for me. I didn't want to shower in the basement or smell like that on a regular basis.

"Hey Clem," I said.

She spun around, and her hair beat a drum solo on the cabinetry. "Ah, shit. Are you on the schedule? I can't remember a damn thing."

"I'm here about the Berry kids. It's a friend thing."

Clem leaned on the desk and cocked an ear at me. "You can tell me. I won't tell any complete strangers. The entire staff will have to know, my husband, Channel 5, CNN, just my regulars. Why are you really here? Big investigation, huh? Case of the decade. Your hotty cousin was just here. He was up to no good, but that's normal for Chuck. You know, he's dated half my staff. Looking for love in all the wrong places, if you know what I mean."

"How much coffee have you had?" I asked.

"The shift's barely begun. One pot...maybe two."

I was grinning like an idiot. "You're going to give yourself an ulcer."

"Got it covered. It's been a rough month." Clem came around the desk and hugged me so hard she realigned my spine, then hooked her arm through mine. "Let me introduce you to my crew."

Our first stop was Payton Stills, a thirteen-year-old burn victim. I was touted as a nurse/detective and forced to tell the story about how I once captured a bigamist with the help of a giant black poodle. I must've told it well, because I made Payton laugh. Next was leukemia patient James Laird. Clem told him how I was once clobbered at a funeral home and stuffed in a red casket. I was never stuffed in a casket, but James declared that it was awesome. There were three more patients in the PICU and I was trotted out for all of them, me and my various mishaps. By the time we got to the Berry kids' rooms, I wasn't tired anymore. Not a bit. You forget how easy your life is until you meet Clem's crew.

Clem stopped in front of Abrielle Berry's room. The curtain was drawn across the glass panel, so I couldn't see who was in there. She reached for the door handle, but I touched her shoulder. "Wait."

"I knew it," said Clem. "This isn't a social call."

"I know Joey Ameche, the uncle, but you're right as always. My dad wants me to look into the medical stuff as a favor to Ameche to help his sister."

"I figured it was something like that."

"What exactly do they have?" I asked.

"Exactly? We don't know. It's a form of bacterial meningitis, listeriosis. Unbelievably bad. Colton coded in the ER. They got him back, but it was tight. Keep in mind that this was one hour and forty-two minutes after the first signs that the kids were ill. Freaking crazy. They were both in a coma for over a day."

"Will they recover fully?" I asked.

"They're coming around. Abrielle's healing faster, but she wasn't as bad. Colton's out of the woods, but he's going to have some problems. Speech, motor control. It'll be a long haul. You want to go in?"

"Not necessary. It's a terrible time for them. I don't want to disturb the family. Who's the doc?" I asked.

"Elise Lydia. You know her?"

"I might. Young, pretty?"

"That's her. Damn good, too," said Clem. "She's in with Colton. You go to the family waiting area and I'll get her."

It took a while and I was nearly crashed out when Dr. Lydia came in and I could see why Clem liked her. Lydia looked about twenty. She wore enormous fuzzy boots with claws on the toes, plenty of sparkly jewelry, and her fingernails were painted with orchids. Lydia wasn't your typical doctor. I liked her instantly.

"So you're the famous Mercy Watts." She shook my hand and plopped down on a green beanbag. "What can I do for you? You're involved with the Berry case."

"As a friend of Joey Ameche, I'm looking into the medical stuff," I said. "Any idea where they picked up the listeriosis?"

"That's the big mystery," said Dr. Lydia. "There are no reported cases in New Orleans or even the state of Louisiana. The CDC is looking into it. But until we have the strain pegged, there's not much to do except treat the kids and get them well."

"Any idea what food was tainted?"

"None. But they ate something that no one else ate."

I didn't like the sound of that. Coincidences happened, but, seriously, that was some pretty bad luck to come down with a mysterious form of meningitis on the day, the very day, half your family is massacred.

"What did the kids say?" I asked. "Have they given you anything to go on?"

Dr. Lydia shook her head and her dangly earrings made a tinkling sound. "I wish. Colton isn't completely aware of his surroundings yet and Abrielle doesn't remember anything but eating cereal for breakfast. Their school verified that they ate lunch at the cafeteria with a hundred other kids. None of them are sick. None of the school employees have so much as a cold. This is isolated."

"A little too isolated." I rubbed my eyes and shifted in my bean bag.

"What are you getting at?" asked Dr. Lydia.

I was too tired to dance around the subject. "I'm supposed to make sure that Donatella didn't poison the children in order to save them from the shooting that killed their father and the rest of the Berrys."

She stared at me and I could see she wasn't getting it.

I yawned and said, "The remaining Berrys think she arranged the murders at Tulio to get rid of her husband's family and him, of course."

Dr. Lydia's mouth fell open and she closed it with a snap. "I hadn't heard that. I admit it was pure luck that the children lived. Did you hear about how Donatella got standby slots?"

"I did."

She shook her head hard and her earrings went crazy, banging into her cheeks. "Donatella loves those kids. I don't think any decent parent would take the chance, even if she desperately hated the husband, which I doubt."

"Why do you doubt that?" I asked. Parents weren't always rational and sometimes their kids got dead because of it. The thought was abhorrent, but it happened.

"Because I was in the room when Donatella got the news that her husband was dead. I've given a lot of horrible news, but none so bad as that. She wasn't faking. I'd stake my license on it."

"What did she do?"

"She didn't believe it. She thought it was a mistake. Kept calling her husband's phone. Wanted to go to Tulio. She wouldn't answer any questions, because she just didn't believe it. She was hysterical. Finally, Clem turned on the TV in the break room and took her in there. Then she went into absolute shock. Her pressure dropped into the basement and her lips turned blue. She couldn't fake that. It's not possible. I'm telling you. Donatella had nothing to do with Tulio or with the listeriosis."

That was good enough for me. Job well done.

CHAPTER SIX

Two days later Spidermonkey was waiting for me in his usual spot. He did like a good blaze and Café Déjeuner had a big fireplace with lots of crackling logs and a set of brass fireplace tools. My cyber spy spotted me over his *Wall Street Journal*, nodded, and went back to reading as I headed for the barista. She was blond, twenty-something with the unlikely name of Sally on her tag. I ordered a cinnamon roll and a latte and leaned on the counter, careful not to look at Spidermonkey. It wasn't easy, but he liked to, for whatever reason, pretend we didn't know each other and decided to sit together on a whim in a tiny café in Laclede's Landing, because *that* would happen. Spidermonkey did have his oddities, but he was worth it. He was a high-level snoop and he'd been working for me since The Girls' nasty nephew sued them in an effort to get control of the Bled Collection and their money. Oz Urbani was the one who had gotten Brooks off The Girls' back, but the case hadn't ended there. Brooks' lawyers had implied that my dad had done something illegal in order for The Girls to give him our house. So far Spidermonkey had discovered that Dad had taken a mysterious flight to Europe that coincided with the disappearance of Josiah Bled, The Girls' uncle and a multimillionaire. That had led us to The Klinefeld Group, a not-for-profit trying to get control of the Bled Collection through the St. Louis Art Museum.

Sally gave me my latte and cinnamon roll and I pretended to be unable to find another place to sit in the empty café. Spidermonkey offered me a seat at his table, like the white-haired old gentleman he was.

"So..." I said.

"So the name is fake. Jens Waldemar Hoff doesn't exist. Sloppy. He never thought we'd look as far as Germany. The name was unusual enough for me to trace easily. There have been two real, or shall I say possibly real, Jens Waldemar Hoffs residing in Berlin. One died in 1963 and the other is four."

"How do you know this Hoff isn't real? Maybe he moved and they didn't update the website."

"Because he told your Aunt Miriam that he just flew into St. Louis and there's no one by that name on any flight manifest for the last six months. Plus, I found a woman in Vancouver who made a complaint to the German embassy in Canada about a Jens Waldemar Hoff of The Klinefeld Group because he was harassing her."

"So what?"

"Her description doesn't match Aunt Miriam's. Different ages, hair color, build. It's two different guys using the same name."

Why do I feel so nervous?

"What was that Hoff bothering her about?" I asked.

Spidermonkey smiled. "Guess."

"Artwork, circa WWII?"

"Bingo."

"Who is she?"

"A pharmacist with absolutely no artwork from the war or any other era. Her name is Amber Patterson. Ring a bell?"

"Not even a little bit. Why would he bother her if she doesn't have any artwork? She has to be something more than a pharmacist."

"You'd think so, but no. Amber is who she says she is. But according to her statement Hoff was threatening and insistent. He left the country and the embassy dropped it."

"I don't get it. What the heck does this have to do with our house, my parents, and the Bled Collection?"

"I don't know yet, but I will."

"So we're nowhere," I said, wanting to put my head down on the table.

"Except…" said Spidermonkey.

I raised an eyebrow. "Except?"

"The one that died in '63 had a wife with the maiden name of Klinefeld. What are the chances of that?"

"What did you find out about him?"

"Nothing yet. His records are inconveniently missing."

"Define missing," I said.

"As in, he doesn't exist before 1950." Spidermonkey smiled and I could see that all his juices were flowing. This was a tasty bit of mystery.

"So what are you thinking?"

"It will take serious digging. Other than the death record, I have nothing. I may have to resort to hand sifting in Berlin. A picture would be helpful. If I can get that, we'll be on our way."

"But you don't know if this has anything to do with the Klinefeld Group. How much is this going to cost?" I was getting even more nervous now. There were only so many double shifts I could pull and my modeling job for Double Black Diamond hadn't started yet. I'd already spent my advance by paying off my debts.

"What do you say we split the cost?" he asked.

"Why would you do that?"

"I have a special interest."

"In a guy that died in 1963?" I asked.

"Yes." Spidermonkey took a drink and became thoughtful. "I have a connection in the Mossad. He's retired, you understand, but still in the know."

"*The* Mossad? What can an Israeli do for us?"

"Think about it, Mercy. What does the Mossad do so well?"

"They're spies, aren't they?"

"And…"

Then I remembered Myrtle and Millicent discussing Simon

Wiesenthal, a friend of Stella Bled Lawrence and a recently revealed Mossad agent. "Nazi hunters. Do you think Hoff was a Nazi?"

"That's exactly what I think."

I drank my latte and stayed silent.

"Aren't you intrigued?" he asked, frowning.

"I am," I said.

"But?"

"I don't want to get sidetracked. This is ultimately about The Girls and my parents for me."

"I understand and I can do both, if it comes down to it. Are we agreed?"

We shook hands over the table and, all of the sudden, I was involved in tracking down a possible Nazi.

Spidermonkey leaned in. "I need you to see what you can find out about Stella Bled Lawrence and her activities in Europe throughout the war. Do The Girls have letters, diaries, anything like that?"

I thought about the scrapbook Florence Bled made of Stella's covert activities but didn't mention it. Nobody was supposed to know about that. "I'll see what I can do. You want to know if Stella knew this Hoff during the war, I assume?"

"I do. Anything about Berlin could be helpful, too. Make a list of any German names you come across."

I agreed to do that, but I hadn't a clue how I was going to accomplish it. Myrtle and Millicent weren't keen to let any info about Stella's activities go. We got up to leave. I put on the warm camelhair coat Mom gave me for Christmas and I felt safe in its folds. It even smelled like Mom, although she'd never worn it. For some reason, the thought of Mom led me to think of Dad. Long term investigations were his favorite thing. Now the Klinefeld Group was leading me into the distant past, his past, and I had to go. There were questions to be asked and answered.

"Wait," I said as Spidermonkey opened the café door and a blast of January air came in. "How did Jens Waldemar Hoff die in '63?"

"I was wondering when you'd ask that. The death certificate says, roughly translated, death by misadventure."

"What does that mean?" I asked.

"We'll find out." And he left me wearing a warm coat and holding a cold latte.

CHAPTER SEVEN

It was my last shift in the St. John's ER, so it had to suck. That was the rule. Last shift must be miserable. I'm sure it's written out somewhere with my name in bold. To make my shift worse, I'd pulled the short straw and got assigned the nursing student. Brittany was smart, earnest, and sweet, which sounds great, but she also had the steely nerves of a stressed Chihuahua. Her hands shook every time she attempted to put in an IV line. I say 'attempted,' because she never actually succeeded. Word got around and patients started their consultations with, "Not Brittany." That included a guy who came in with head trauma from a golfing accident. You know it's bad when a guy is more concerned about who's going to do his IV than who's going to stitch his face.

It'd been very long night. I was thrilled that it was almost over. We had a half hour left when Brittany and I left the room of a fourteen-year-old boy who was experiencing severe leg swelling. And I do mean severe, as in I was surprised his skin hadn't split open.

Allison, the phlebotomist, started to go in when Brittany stopped her. "He's so scared and it's my fault."

Allison shot me a glare and then settled a patient look on her experienced face. "Brittany, did you do the IV?"

Brittany teared up. "I tried. I hope I didn't wreck his veins."

I patted her quaking back. "You only did one stick. He's fine."

"I'm a disaster. Why did I think I could be a nurse?"

Allison rolled her eyes and headed in with her blood draw tray. At least the boy got her. With Allison, he'd barely feel the needle.

I steered Brittany away from the door. The last thing the patient and his distraught parents needed to hear was her snuffling. "He'll be fine."

She wiped her eyes, removing the last bit of electric blue eyeliner she had on. "What do you think he has? It looks serious and he's so young."

"It's probably post-infectious glomerulonephritis. He'll be fine," I said in the voice I usually saved for patients. Brittany couldn't take the voice she deserved.

"How do you know?" she asked.

"He had strep two weeks ago and his heart's solid. Come on," I said. "I need some coffee."

And a shot of Dad's good whiskey. Maybe two.

Brittany brightened up. "You've been so great. I wish I could be with you on all my clinicals."

God wouldn't do that to me.

Before we made it to the break room, Christine, the charge nurse, cut us off and held up two charts. "Take your pick. We've got two infections, ear and toe. Which one do you want?"

There was no way Brittany could handle prying off a toenail. There was a little spatula involved. Messy business. She'd already dry-heaved over a pus-shooting boil that I lanced. Okay. The pus did hit the ceiling, but that was nothing compared with the toe spatula.

"We'll take the ear," I said.

Christine grinned and handed Brittany the chart. "Wise choice. You're out after the ear."

"Thank god." I grimaced with guilt. "I mean, it's been wonderful working with you, Christine."

"Yeah. It's been a barrel of laughs around here tonight. Let me know when you leave." Christine booked it down to the toe and Brittany and I went into Room 3, where there was an elderly woman tugging on her ear lobe.

"I just couldn't take it anymore," she said, apologetically.

I had Brittany scrub and glove up. She could handle an ear infection. Lancing ear drums had been out for decades. "It must be pretty bad to get you here so early."

"I haven't slept in days."

"We'll get this taken care of and you can go back to bed. How's the pain on a scale of one to ten?"

"Sometimes a ten, but other times, it just bugs me."

I introduced Brittany and explained my student would be taking a look in her ear to assess the infection before the doctor came in. Brittany got the otoscope ready and her hands were even steady. We were going to rock this infection. Mrs. Silverstein laid back and folded her hands over her stomach and waited peacefully.

Brittany smiled, said something professional, put the scope in Mrs. Silverstein's ear, and let out an eardrum piercing scream, "Oh my god!"

"Brittany!" I yelled.

She dropped the scope and ran out of the room at her top speed. Mrs. Silverstein had her hands clamped over her poor ears and my own ears were ringing.

Christine ran in with a suture kit, poised to stitch. "Where is it?"

"What?" I asked.

"Whatever happened."

"Nothing happened. Go get Brittany before she runs out into traffic."

"Right. I'll get her and then I'll kill her." Christine spun around and marched out.

"Mrs. Silverstein, are you okay?" I asked my wide-eyed patient.

"What?" she yelled.

I peeled her hands off her ears. "Are you okay?"

"I'm fine. What's wrong with that girl? She seems to have a nervous condition."

"That's one way to put it. Brittany's just a little high strung."

"Then, honey, you better tell her that nursing's not for her. This is just a little ear infection. What'll happen when somebody chops their foot off?"

"Heaven knows." I got out a fresh scope and took a peek in Mrs. Silverstein's ear, expecting to see the equivalent of a pus shooting boil. What I did see took me aback. There was a little scream. Maybe a grimace and repulsed body language, but I kept it all on the inside like nurses do. No matter what crazy crap people have or do, we keep it on the inside. I looked in that ear and saw eight eyes looking back.

"So how bad is the infection?" asked Mrs. Silverstein.

I straightened up, gave an involuntary shiver, and said, "Great news. It's not an infection."

"Really? How come it hurts so much?"

"You have...something lodged in there. I'll take care of it and you'll be out of here in a jiff."

I did a warm lavage on Mrs. Silverstein's ear and washed out a tiny little spider into a pink emesis basin. Then, and only then, did I tell Mrs. Silverstein what was in her ear. She took it very well and insisted that we release the spider into the wild, which I did after we were done.

"I'm going to write you a good review," said Mrs. Silverstein.

"I don't know if they have reviews for nurses," I said.

"They should. That girl was unprofessional and she wears too much perfume."

"I'll talk to her about it." I finished the chart and handed off Mrs. Silverstein to my replacement. When I found Christine to tell her I was out, she was at the desk, trying to talk sense to a sobbing Brittany. No sense was getting in that dripping mess.

"I told her to leave, but she won't go," said Christine.

"I'm going to fail. They'll fail me. My parents will be so upset," wailed Brittany.

I looked at the ceiling and said, "I'll take her with me."

"Would you? Thank goodness." Christine ran away before I could change my mind. I gathered up the still sobbing Brittany, got our stuff, and half-carried her to the parking lot. The sun was coming up and the interior lights had shut off so it was dim in the garage. We walked five steps toward Brittany's Prius when I jerked her back.

"What's wrong?" she said.

"I don't know. Quiet."

For once, Brittany was quiet. I clutched her to my side and looked around. I had to scan twice before I saw him. A slim figure, dressed in jeans and a dark grey hoodie with a baseball cap, stood in the shadows directly under a surveillance camera, but he wasn't worried. Nothing conceals a face like a cap and a hood. He stood completely still, but something in his stance said he was both confident and dangerous. He didn't react to my look.

"I see him, too," whispered Brittany.

"We're going back inside."

"Uh, huh."

We took a step back and he ducked behind a pillar the second he realized I'd made him. We ran inside, bursting through the door just as Raymond, the night security supervisor, was coming out of the stairwell.

"Hold on, girls. What's up?" he asked.

"There was a man in the garage," cried Brittany.

Raymond went from friendly to pissed in an instant. He yanked his walkie-talkie off his belt and told Jack to get the hell up there. "You girls don't move. I'm going to check this. I told them we need to patrol this garage. Pretty nurses coming and going. It's like chum for sharks. I'm gonna—"

The closing of the door cut him off and a second later Jack arrived, breathless and holding a donut. "What happened? You okay?"

"We're fine." I told him what happened and mentioned that the security footage might help, but I doubted it. That guy knew what he was doing.

"He was waiting for us, wasn't he?" Brittany was chewing her blunt fingernails.

"I suspect he was waiting for me."

Jack gave me the once over. "Yeah, probably. I got to call your dad."

"You know him?"

"I retired two years after he made detective. Hell of a cop. He is going to be pissed."

"You could call Chuck Watts. He's less likely to lose it."

"That's not what I hear, but I'll call him."

Raymond came in, huffing and puffing. "He's long gone, but that bastard was definitely waiting for a victim. There are six cigarette butts next to the pillar. One's still burning. He didn't want to miss you."

Not a comforting thought for me or for Brittany, who'd begun to shake. I needed to get her out of there.

"What do you need from us?" I asked. "It's been a long night. We're worn out."

"We need statements. The cops will want to talk to you," said Raymond.

Jack turned around and held out his phone. "Chuck, for you."

Ah crap.

"Hi," I said.

"Do not leave. I'm on my way," said Chuck, breathless.

"Are you running?"

"Damn straight I'm running."

"We're fine. Nothing happened."

A car door slammed. "It could've."

"But it didn't. I need to sleep."

"Do not leave."

My phone yelled Dad's ring tone and everybody stared at my purse for a second and then started to laugh.

"Did you call my dad?" I asked Chuck.

"No. Stay there." He hung up on me and I groaned.

Raymond and Jack were still laughing.

"Tommy Watts is your Vader," said Jack.

"He is an omnipresent force." I reluctantly pulled out the yelling phone.

"I can see that," said Raymond.

I leaned on the cold concrete wall and said, "Hi, Dad."

"Good. You're off work. Get over to Children's ASAP."

"What is it this time?"

"Ameche called me. There's a situation. Handle it and check in later."

"Where are you going?"

"Quincy. I got a lead on the Abbott kid."

I had no idea who the Abbott kid was, but at least Dad wouldn't be showing up and throwing a hissy fit. "Okay. You nab the kid and I'll go to Children's."

"On it." Dad hung up and I heaved a sigh of relief. I couldn't deal with Dad after the shift I'd had. I was full up on screaming.

"I have to go to Children's," I told Raymond and Jack.

"Chuck wants you here," said Jack.

"Tell him it's for Ameche. He'll understand."

"I doubt that."

Brittany shook more violently. "Can I go with you? I don't want to stay here alone."

"You're not alone. Raymond and Jack are here. The cops will be here in like, two minutes. You have to give them a statement."

"I'm a terrible nurse," she wailed.

That was out of nowhere, not that I could exactly argue with it. "You just need some seasoning."

"Did you need seasoning?" she asked hopefully.

"My dad is Tommy Watts. I was sneaking peeks at crime scene photos when I was six. I came to nursing preseasoned."

"I know who you are."

"You do?" I was genuinely surprised. Brittany had shown no sign that she recognized me at all.

"You grew up on Hawthorne. I live on Longfellow. My parents are live-ins for the Strahans. I've always known about you."

"You hid it well. Most people can't. There's hope for you yet."

"Huh?"

"The key to nursing is a strong stomach and the ability to hide what you really think. You can do that."

"I screamed in Mrs. Silverstein's face," she said with a sniff.

"Well, you need to work on that."

"How?" Brittany looked at Raymond and Jack who shrugged in unison.

"I'll tell you what. If you stay here and deal with the cops and the statement, I'll help you out."

Brittany threw her arms around my neck, thanking me profusely. Just like that, Brittany the dry-heaver became one of my people.

CHAPTER EIGHT

Clem met me at the door of the PICU, wearing bunny ears and a cotton tail. "Glad you're here. You'll have to wait a minute. There are too many visitors right now."

"Who's here?" I asked.

"The Ameches and some little weird guy they brought in with them," she said.

Little weird guy.

"Did he have food with him?"

"How'd you know?"

"Lucky guess."

We walked by the desk and it had Aaron written all over it. There were no less than five large containers of muffins, house-made sausages, pancakes, and mouth-watering hash browns. Three nurses sat behind the desk eating in a stupor I recognized as Kronos induced. Kronos was my investigating partner's restaurant. It was Star Trek-inspired and weird to the max, but seriously good. No one cooked like Aaron. I carried around the proof in my generous rump.

"I've died and gone to heaven," said Kayla. "Hi, Mercy."

I waved and grinned. I knew Kayla from nursing school, back in the days when she was always on a diet. Those days were over.

Before we got to the Berry kids' rooms, Dr. Lydia came out of Payton Stills' room. "Mercy. That was quick. Joey called your father only about forty minutes ago."

"It sounded important, so here I am," I said.

Dr. Lydia frowned. "I'm not sure if I'd call it an emergency, but the Ameches will be happy to see you."

"Why?" I asked, swallowing hard. The smell of Aaron's food was making me drool.

"You have a way about you."

I frowned.

"It's not the Marilyn thing. It's you."

That would be nice if I believed it. People had feelings about Marilyn Monroe. If they were good feelings, they felt good about me. It wasn't the same thing as liking me, not the same thing at all.

"So what's up?" I asked.

"The lab results are back. Both Abrielle and Colton were infected with a strain of listeriosis meningitis that was previously unknown before this case," said Dr. Lydia.

"New strains develop," I said.

"Not out of the blue in a completely isolated incident," said Clem.

"You're suspicious?"

"We are," said Dr. Lydia.

"How are the kids?" I asked.

"Improving daily. They're both having migraines. Abrielle can barely function. Clem and I made statements and the cops have cleared Donatella of any involvement."

"That's excellent news. What's the problem?" I asked.

"How'd they get it?" asked Dr. Lydia.

I looked down the hall at Abrielle's door. How indeed?

"What did the CDC say?"

"Not much. It doesn't look like an outbreak, so I don't think they're all that interested. They called it a singular aberration or something like that. They're going to follow-up, but let's face it, between the West Nile virus, all the measles and mumps outbreaks, and Ebola, they have their hands full."

"What do you want me to do? I'm no infectious disease expert," I said.

"You are a nurse and an expert in figuring things out."

Abrielle's door opened and an older couple came out. They looked to be in their late sixties or early seventies. Like Blankenship's parents at Hunt they held each other's hands as they came down the hall and silently passed us.

"You can go in now," said Dr. Lydia.

I didn't want to go in that room, like so many others I would rather have avoided. But Ameche was my people and you take care of your people. I opened the door and walked into the fabulous smell of Bananas Foster.

Abrielle lay in the bed under dim lighting with her eyes closed. She was older than I'd imagined, about fourteen. A thin headband held back her straight brown hair and accentuated her heart-shaped face. Next to her stood Aaron with a bowl and a spoon. Abrielle gave a slight nod and Aaron gave her a little bite of Bananas Foster.

On the other side of the bed sat Ameche with his arm around a woman who I assumed was Donatella. She looked up at our approach and my mouth formed an "O." Donatella was stunning. She had pale flawless skin and masses of dark red curls that went down past her elbows. When she looked at me, I saw no recognition or expectation in her eyes. They were dull and lifeless. No spark and she should've had a spark with that hair. I would never have expected her to be Ameche's sister. It's not that he or their parents were unattractive. They were a normal amount of attractive. Donatella was something else and I suddenly knew why Oz was so interested in her.

Ameche saw me a second after his sister and jumped to his feet. "Mercy." He dashed past Abrielle's bed and flung his arms around me.

I hugged him as little as possible. There's a small truth about me. I don't like people touching me, not even my people. It could be because I get touched plenty and it was rarely welcome.

"I'm here. Of course, I'm here," I said.

Ameche gave me one more fierce hug and backed up. "Sorry. I don't know why I did that."

"It's okay."

Donatella edged out of her seat like she was in severe physical pain and Ameche took her arm. "This is Mercy. She's going to help."

Donatella held out her hand but looked like she had no real interest in whether I took it or not. I did because I couldn't leave the pale limp thing hanging out there. Her hand was freezing. I mean seriously cold.

"Has anyone taken your temperature lately?"

She blinked. "Temperature?"

Abrielle opened her eyes to slits and watched us.

Dr. Lydia took Donatella's hand and then her pulse. "Let's go out to the family area, so you and Mercy can chat."

"But Abrielle..."

"I'm sure Joey and..."

"Aaron," I filled in.

"Would be happy to stay."

Ameche assured Donatella that he wouldn't leave her side. That he'd pee in a pitcher, if he had to. That got the tiniest smile out of her and we went out into the hall.

"Clem, can you get some blankets out of the warmer?" asked Dr. Lydia.

"I'll do it," I said. Better for Clem to stay. She was an expert in parental support in a crisis. I dashed off to the staff room and grabbed three toasty blankets out of the warmer, and then went to the desk. The nurses were still there, gorging.

"Did he happen to bring any thermoses?" I asked.

They didn't speak, only chewed and pointed to a trio of thermoses next to a pile of charts. The first one had a fruity coffee blend and the second had hot chocolate. I snagged it and headed for the family room. Dr. Lydia had Donatella curled up on an over-stuffed blue couch. I tucked the blankets in around her and poured her a cup of Aaron's best French hot chocolate. I could tell it was French by the whiff of bittersweet chocolate when I poured it. I was getting better at Name That Chocolate.

"Drink this," I said.

"I'm not hungry."

"I know, but this will help."

We all three waited until she agreed and took few sips. Drinking hot chocolate almost looked like it was too much for her. Clem had to help her bring the cup to her lips. The full light of the family room showed what shape Donatella was really in and I had to agree with Dr. Lydia's opinion. This was not a woman who risked her children to kill her husband. She looked worse than terrible. I'd looked after my mom's best friend Dixie after her husband, Gavin, was murdered and Donatella made Dixie look put together. Her glorious mass of red hair was matted and greasy. She probably hadn't bathed since it happened and she'd chewed her lower lip bloody. Her fingernails had traces of a top end manicure, but she bit them past the quick and the tips were red and swollen. It would take a pretty high level of commitment to do that to yourself. I couldn't. Fingertips have a lot of nerves in them. Even if it weren't for Ameche, I would help her. I'd never seen such a picture of need. I was in it for the long haul, so I pulled up a beanbag. Besides, how often do you get the chance to sit in a beanbag?

"I'm happy to help in any way I can. Since the police dropped the investigation, I'm not sure what you're looking for." I squished down and got instantly sleepy.

Clem took Donatella's temperature with a temporal scanner rolled across her pale forehead. She didn't seem to notice the touch of the metal ball or Clem's frown after.

"I'm going to buzz Dr. Bergamo," said Clem and she left.

Donatella spoke, her voice was whisper soft. "They're suing me."

"Your husband's family?" I asked.

She scoffed. "Family. Those people aren't family. They're vultures. They're the ones that recommended Tulio to Rob's mom in the first place and they want to blame me for what happened. Rob hadn't talked to any of them in years. Now they're acting like they knew him, like they were close. Rob was my best friend in the world. He was my world. It's disgusting."

"They're suing you for what? Wrongful death?" I asked.

"That and custody of my children. None of them have even seen Abrielle or Colton in their whole lives. They're saying that I'm unfit. Me. Their mother. They don't believe the police. They have the man that did it. I don't know him." Donatella began hyperventilating and tears streamed down her cheeks. Dr. Lydia produced a paper bag and she had Donatella breath into it. The bag puffed out and collapsed with each breath and I took the time to absorb the information. This must be what Dad was worked up about. He wouldn't care about strains of listeriosis.

Ameche came in, looking nearly as bad as his sister. He wasn't a big guy, but he'd lost ten pounds at least. "Mom came back," he told Donatella and then turned to me. "So I take it she told you."

"She did, but you shouldn't get too upset about it. The courts will see this for what it is, a money grab. The cops have cleared Donatella. This'll barely get off the ground."

Donatella rammed the bag into her lap. "But it will get off the ground. You know how people are. They'll talk. There will be stain on my character. My kids will hear the rumors. Their father is dead and then they get to hear whispers about how maybe their mom did it. Do you know how much that will hurt them?"

I couldn't imagine growing up the way Abrielle and Colton would. Murdered father. Accused mother. Even if the accusation was crap, it was still out there. A question that hadn't been answered.

"I have some small idea," I said. "So I assume you have a plan or I wouldn't be here."

"We want to hire you," said Ameche. "We want to prove where the listeriosis came from, so we can show that my sister didn't have a damn thing to do with it."

"I thought so. What about my dad? He's the professional."

Donatella twisted the bag into a tight rope. "I'd rather have you, if you don't mind."

"Why's that?"

"Nothing against your dad. He was great to get involved at all, but you're a young woman. I'm sure you need the money more than your dad. He was on 20/20 last week." She held out her hand to Ameche. "I've followed your career. It's impressive, even if you're not technically a professional."

"I've been lucky a lot."

"I'd like you to get lucky for me. Plus, you helped out, Joey. He's moving up, thanks to you. My family owes you."

I shook my head. "That was my dad's doing. I just passed along his name."

"The nursing thing will help," said Ameche. "You know your way around diseases and stuff."

"I do, but I can't say I'm any expert on meningitis."

Donatella dropped her brother's hand and took mine. It was cold and sticky with fresh tears. "What you don't know, Dr. Lydia will tell you. Will you do it? I need a medical professional. Your dad gave me his price. I'll gladly pay it to you."

Dad's price. Yes!

"You have to understand that I don't have a license," I said.

"That doesn't matter to me. I just want this settled before the children realize something's happened. They still don't know about their father and the rest of the family. I want this to go away before they're told.

"I'll see what I can do." I got out my phone and opened my note-taking app. "Okay. Tell me everything that happened that day."

Donatella straightened up and blew her nose. "Right. Everything. I'm afraid it's not very exciting."

She was right about that. It was a pretty typical day for a regular family. Rob left the day before Donatella and the kids to hang out with his brothers, so they were alone on Friday. They all got up at six. Donatella took Abrielle and Colton to school and she went to work at the French Quarter elementary school my mom attended. Donatella picked the kids up early from school and drove to Tulane, where her oldest son was a freshman. They picked up his gift for his grandparents, a drawing of them on their wedding day. Christopher couldn't come, because he had a huge test in calculus and his grade wasn't great.

"You have an eighteen-year-old kid?"

Donatella looked like death on a bad day, but still not old enough to have a kid that old.

She gave me a wan smile. "I got pregnant my freshman year of college."

"Was Rob Christopher's father?" I asked.

"No. We met later." She flushed and then said, "Why are you frowning? Christopher was an accident, but he's a great kid."

"I don't doubt it. I'm thinking that the Berrys can use it against you."

"What?" asked Dr. Lydia. "So what if she had an out-of-wedlock child?"

"The one child who wasn't poisoned isn't Rob's kid. Their lawyers can twist it. Donatella didn't care about Rob's kids. She wanted to get rid of all the Berrys. That kind of thing."

"But Christopher really had a test," said Donatella.

"Please tell me he's here," I said.

"Christopher? Of course. He flew in on Saturday."

"Good. It would've looked bad if he didn't. What happened after you saw Christopher?"

Donatella continued her story, sounding stronger by the moment. They flew out of New Orleans after getting on standby for an earlier flight. The kids weren't feeling good when they boarded, but Donatella just thought it was carsickness. That wasn't unusual. Colton was the first to feel ill. It started with a terrible headache and quickly progressed to projectile vomiting. Then Abrielle started with the headache. They landed at St. Louis in the nick of time. The pilot called ahead and there was an ambulance on the tarmac. Rob met them at the hospital. The anniversary dinner was at eight. Once they were stabilized, Rob couldn't do anything and decided to go tell the family what had happened in person. Rob was killed at restaurant, but Donatella didn't know anything about it. She didn't want to know. The play-by-play was too much for her.

"This sounds like an incredibly short incubation period," I said to Dr. Lydia.

"It came on very fast."

"A large amount of the bacteria would have to have been ingested then."

She nodded. "Definitely direct contact, but this is a new strain and we don't know how they got it."

"Has to be food," I said.

"I believe so." Dr. Lydia became pensive and avoided my eyes while Donatella ran down all the food they ate. Cereal for breakfast, school lunch, and pretzels at the airport. She ate the cereal herself.

Clem came in. "Donatella, Dr. Bergamo is coming up and Colton is asking for you."

I gave her all my numbers and promised to update her daily. She gave me her house key and security code and left with Clem supporting her.

"So what are you not saying?" I asked Dr. Lydia.

She leaned her elbows on her leopard print pants and said. "I can't say anything for sure."

"Then say what isn't for sure."

"This hit them hard and fast. That combined with the lack of other cases in the kid's vicinity…"

"You think they were infected on purpose," I said.

Ameche put his face in his hands

"It's just a feeling," she said.

"I have a deep respect for feelings, so let's go with it," I said. "If you were going to infect someone with meningitis, how would you do it?"

"Well, I'd have to have access to the bacteria first of all."

"Let's say you do."

"I'd inject it. That'd give me a fast infection."

"Did you find any suspicious injection sites?"

Dr. Lydia shook her head. "By the time we started questioning where they got it, the injection site could've healed enough so as not to be detectable."

"But you found nothing on either child? No bruising?"

"No. Both children were in excellent health at the time they got sick. Colton had bruising consistent with playing soccer, mainly on his legs. Abrielle had no bruising whatsoever."

"What's your second choice?"

"I'd have to get bacteria on their mucus membranes, nose or mouth."

"So, like using a sick person's fork."

"Except there are no other sick people."

"So it's food."

"Donatella didn't get it at home. And like I said, there were no other cases at their school or the airport."

"If their lunches were the only ones contaminated, Abrielle and Colton were specific targets," I said.

"I remember lunch lines at school. It would be pretty hard to make sure Abrielle and Colton got the contaminated trays. You never know where a kid is going to be in a line. It'd have to be lunch personnel and they'd have to do it right in front of the kids and the other adults."

"That's true, but they got it somehow. Maybe it wasn't the food. Maybe it was the forks. It'd be easy to pull a fork out of a pocket and put it on a specific tray," I said.

"It could be done but keeping the bacteria live on a dry surface isn't easy. I think it would have to be a good-sized amount, too. We'll know more when we know the strain."

"When will that be?"

"Four or five more days."

"I take it you haven't told Donatella you think someone did this on purpose," I said.

Ameche's head popped up. "No way. She couldn't deal with it. She's already lost Rob and rest of his family."

"We're not sure," said Dr. Lydia. "There's no reason she has to know."

"I agree, so I think I'll start at the other end."

"What does that mean?" asked Ameche.

"Instead of worrying about how, I'm going to figure out who. If this wasn't an accident, someone hates that family enough to kill the children. I just have to find out who."

"I'd begin with the family that's suing Donatella days after her husband was murdered," said Dr. Lydia.

I rolled out of my comfy beanbag. "My thoughts exactly."

CHAPTER NINE

The security guard acted like I was a loon for wanting an escort out to my truck mid-morning. I didn't care what Julio thought. Parking garages were gloomy at the best of times with plenty of places to hide. Plus, Dad and Chuck would ask if I got someone to walk me out and neither of them were above calling security to confirm my story.

Julio put me in my truck and I locked the door immediately. I saw him roll his eyes and mutter something as he walked away. Probably how I was a lunatic. Maybe so, but I wasn't a kidnapped lunatic and that was all that mattered.

I pulled out of the garage, looking for the guy in the hoodie and dialing Uncle Morty.

"Shit! It's you," he snarled into the phone.

"I love you, too," I said.

"Yeah. Yeah. What do you want?"

"It's the Ameche case."

"What of it?"

"I need the address of the Berrys that are suing Donatella," I said.

"*You're* gonna pay them a visit?" He chuckled like I was some kind of candy ass girl. I'd done stuff, survived stuff.

"Yes. Why is that funny?"

"'Cause the last time you interviewed a family of suspects you missed the murderer."

It was true, but how was I supposed to know. It was my first murder investigation, which also happened to be Dixie's husband's murder. I was upset. It was personal. The interview was short and it's not like they were wearing 'I ♡ murder' hats.

"Can't we forget about that?"

"Loser."

"Are you going to tell me where they are or what?" I asked.

"You paying?" he asked, suddenly all business.

"The client will be paying."

"Holy shit. You got a paying client. Tommy'll throw a parade."

I pulled onto the highway and longed to throw my Bluetooth out the window. "Whatever. How long will this take?"

"Got it now. Well, well, well. Somebody thinks they done hit the lottery," he said.

"Why?"

"They're staying at the downtown Westin at 350 a night. Two rooms."

"So? Donatella didn't blink at Dad's rates. The Berrys must have money," I said.

"Some Berrys have money. The ones that are dead."

I yawned and asked, "How much money are we talking about?"

"It's not Bled money, but they were comfortable." Uncle Morty explained to me that there were two lines of Berrys. One brother, Rob Berry's grandfather, invested in McDonalds in the mid-sixties. The other brother, grandfather of the surviving Berrys, headed a pyramid scheme that landed him in prison in 1972. That line never recovered and, for some reason, blamed the other side for their problems. Rob Berry, Donatella's late husband, was a partner in a high-class real estate firm in New Orleans and she was a school administrator. Their children, Abrielle and Colton, would inherit several million dollars, since they were the surviving heirs to the successful Berrys. The other side would get nothing.

"Unless Donatella were sent to prison and they got custody of the kids and control," I said.

"Yep," said Uncle Morty.

"I don't suppose—"

"Already checked. The other Berrys have never been to New Orleans and have had no contact with anyone in the city."

"They still could've had the kids poisoned but if the whole family was supposed to be dead anyway, why bother?"

"Good question." Uncle Morty hawked up a phlegm wad and made me involuntarily hork.

"Don't do that. It's too disgusting." I shuddered. "Any connection between Blankenship and the other Berrys?"

"Not yet, but they all live out in Belleville. It could've been arranged face to face. You think Blankenship had someone in the mix, right?"

I pulled onto my street and got lucky with a space in front of my building. "I got that feeling. So the other Berrys aren't *connected*, are they?"

Uncle Morty snorted. "They wish. The mafia wouldn't have any use for them." He gave rundown of their jobs, arrests, etc. They had some drug dealer connections, so we couldn't cross them off. In the world of the internet, poison could be a website away. But did they have the brains for it?

I wasn't hearing a lot of evidence of planning ability and poisoning the kids was a strategic plan to kill them in flight. I still had to interview the other Berrys. People can be a lot different on paper than in person. Google me and you'd see that I'm everything from a nurse to a drug-addled moron slut. Face to face is the only way to go when it comes to capabilities. Hopefully, when I talked to them, I'd be able to tell if they had two brain cells to rub together.

"I guess I'll be paying a visit to the other Berrys."

"Damn straight. The lazy bastards just got up, so you can catch them," said Uncle Morty.

I scanned the sidewalk and my building's entrance. No lurking men in hoodies. Good. I got out and dashed through the icy air to unlock the door and slip inside.

"Hello?" bellowed Uncle Morty.

"I'm afraid to ask, but how do you know they just got up?" I asked.

"Ordered room service. You wanna know how the bastards like their eggs?"

"How do you—never mind. I'll shower and get over there. Call my dad, will you?"

"Already texted him. He knows about the guy in the hospital garage, too."

"Great." I did an internal groan. "I've got to go."

"Mercy, you gotta be careful with this crew. They're trash, but they're not stupid. Hit 'em with what you got."

"What do you suggest?" I asked.

"Full Marilyn."

I sighed and hung up. It'd been a long night and an even longer morning. I wasn't sure if I had a full Marilyn in me. I clomped up the stairs, went into my apartment, and my morning got longer.

"Skanky!"

My cat, Skanky, named as such because he was Skanky and never more so than that morning. He lay twisted up on my sofa, covered in vomit and surrounded by shredded paper.

"Yow."

"What the hell did you do?" I needn't have asked. It was obvious. Pete had been foiled again. My boyfriend, Pete, had taken to leaving me little gifts of chocolate when he stayed in my apartment. He was a surgical resident and I hardly ever saw him. He slept at my place some-times because it was so close to the hospital, and I've been known to have food. I appreciated the specialty chocolates from around the world, but Skanky usually found them before I did with gross conse-quences. This time he must've tried my Tigger cookie jar, because it was lying smashed into a million bits next to my breakfast bar.

Skanky gave out a pathetic yow and attempted to clean. He failed miserably. Tongue didn't even make it to fur.

"Don't give me that," I said. "Nana gave me that jar. It was a collec-table." I didn't really care that it was a collectable as much as I cared that my grandmother had given it to me, and I had to clean up the mess.

"Yow."

I snapped on a pair of examination gloves and carried the limp yowing Skanky into the bathroom and washed him in the sink. He hated it and there was a certain satisfaction in that.

"It's your own fault," I said.

"Yow."

"I'm not even calling the vet this time."

"Yow. Yow."

"I should. Maybe there's a shot she can give you."

Hiss.

"Yeah, whatever. I'm so scared of the terribly sick four-pound cat." I toweled Skanky off and put him on my bed. He tried to clean again but fell over in a little fuzzy heap. "Yow."

I rolled my eyes and got into the shower. Idiot cat. There was a tiny bit of guilt for not calling the vet, but, honestly, she didn't want to hear from me anymore. After Skanky ate an entire pound of Belgian dark chocolate and survived, she declared him indestructible and quite possibly the stupidest cat she'd ever worked on. The vet claimed that cats learned what not to eat, but not my Skanky. Oh, no. He never learned anything. I was lucky he used the cat pan.

After my shower, I felt mostly human and rifled through my closet to find my best Bled funeral suit. It was a Valentino, purchased by Myrtle and Millicent, so I had something stunning to wear to their Cousin Dorothy's funeral. They hated Dorothy and they wanted me in full Marilyn. I hardly ever had the chance to wear it. The suit was the height of funeral fashion, coal black in the style of the forties with shoulder pads and a nipped-in waist. The stand-up mink collar framed my face, making me paler and somehow more refined.

I curled my hair the way Marilyn Monroe did, waves off the face to emphasize my widow's peak and I applied heavy makeup. I hardly ever did, unless I was pulling out all the stops with plenty of sooty mascara and a thick coat of Harlot Scarlet on my lips. I didn't like to do it, but I had to admit the effect was startling. If I wanted them to be thrown off balance, full Marilyn was the way to go.

The suit slipped on like it should never have been taken off. A pair of seamed stockings and five-inch stilettos finished the look.

I twirled for Skanky. "How do I look?"

He barfed on my pillow. I guess I asked for that. I stripped off the pillowcase and stuffed it in the washer on my way out. Pete had to stop giving me chocolate. It was sweet, but so not worth it.

I sat in the Westin St. Louis lobby for twenty minutes before the manager decided to move me to a small conference room. Apparently, I was distracting to the guests and staff and must be shut up in a wood-paneled room before I could cause any trouble. I had no intention of causing trouble, but it was nice to know I could.

The other Berrys finally came down to meet me ten minutes later. I decided to make them come to me, instead of the other way around, because it said something if they obeyed. They didn't give orders. They took them.

The manager opened the conference room door with an appropriately solemn face. After all, half the Berry family had just been murdered, but I don't know why he bothered. The other Berrys were anything but morose. They ambled into the room with pleasant, curious expressions. I'd chosen a seat behind the door so they'd have to look around for their visitor, giving me a few seconds to look them over. Mourning wasn't the word for the other Berrys. They, all four of them, wore brand new athletic wear. The Rams were pretty big with them. They had the jerseys, sweat pants, hats, and wristbands. They were logoed up and that stuff wasn't cheap, especially if your biggest earner was an assistant manager at a Walgreens.

It took them a good two minutes to spot me and the Westin manager raised an eyebrow at me before he closed the door. That eyebrow said a lot. I was, despite the whole Marilyn thing, his kind of people. The other Berrys weren't.

"Oh, shit," said the oldest, a man in his seventies with a narrow face and a large nose. "There you are."

"Oh, shit is right. Holy fuck," said the woman beside him, presumably his wife. "You look exactly like Marilyn Monroe."

I uncrossed my legs and stood up slowly. They stared at me and I smiled. "I'm here about Abrielle and Colton."

"Who?" asked a guy who was a forty-year-old version of his father.

"Abrielle and Colton Berry."

"Oh, yeah. The kids," said the woman on younger guy's arm. She obviously wasn't a Berry. Her face was round where the Berrys had a narrow pinched look about them.

"Yes," I said. "The kids."

"What about them?" she asked.

I walked over with plenty of swing in my hips and extended my hand. "I'm Mercy Watts and you are…"

"I'm Ken," said the older man. "This is my wife Stacy and my son, Willy, and his wife, Gina. What exactly are you here about?"

I flashed them Dad's card and said I was there on Abrielle and Colton's behalf. It took them another second to remember once again who the kids were. I implied that the court had sent me to make sure they were fit to care for the kids and the Berrys were all over that. They had a nice house for the kids to live in, a good school district, and a dog named Trigger. Ken showed me pictures and the house was a nice split-level with a well-kept lawn. Trigger wasn't mangy or gross, which was more than I could say for my cat.

"It's a lucky thing, but why weren't you all at the anniversary party at Tulio?" I asked.

"Weren't invited," spat out Gina. "They said we could come to the house after, if we wanted to. As if."

I put on my sympathetic face. It wasn't a good fit at that moment. "Didn't you recommend Tulio?"

"Yeah," said Willy. "I heard it was good, but I never been. It's lucky they're rude, or we'd be dead, too."

"So you weren't close?" I asked.

Stacy snorted and leaned back in her chair. Her arms were crossed. "Why do you care?"

"I need to know how well you know Abrielle and Colton, if you're going to be raising them."

"Oh, well…we don't know them. They live in New Orleans and they never invited us down to stay."

"That's a shame. New Orleans is a great town. I love it."

Gina eyed me. "Who made that suit? It's hot. Mink collar?"

Definitely not stupid.

"Yes, it is," I said.

"You've got great taste. I need a suit like that," said Gina.

Gee. I wonder how you plan on paying for it.

"It's a great suit. Very comfortable. Do any of you have medical training?"

Ken shifted in his seat. He didn't like that question. "I could've gone to medical school, but there wasn't enough money."

"It's very expensive. Medical school. So do any of you have medical training?"

"Why?" asked Stacy.

"Because Abrielle and Colton may need special care."

"Their mother, that Donatella, poisoned them," said Willy. "I don't care what the police say. She did it."

I widened my eyes. "How do you know?"

"She's the type. Have you met her? She's one of those hot-tempered redheads. She wanted to get rid of our family so she could get all the money."

"I met her this morning at the hospital. I don't think she's left their side," I said.

"Well, she has to make it look good," said Gina.

"If she's going to get all the money for herself," said Willy.

Ken broke in. "Not that we care about the money. We'll keep it all for the kids for when they get older."

Sure you will.

"I saw them this morning, too," I said.

"Who?" asked Stacy.

"Abrielle and Colton."

"Good. You got to keep an eye on that Donatella. She's a slippery witch for sure. Did you know she got herself pregnant at eighteen, but the guy wouldn't marry her? Just goes to show."

I had no clue what that was supposed to show me.

"Andrew's going to fix her wagon," said Ken. "We aren't dropping this by a long shot."

That much was clear. The other Berrys had a plan for the future and they wouldn't give up their two little lottery tickets easily. I asked a few more questions. Uncle Morty was right, as usual. The other Berrys weren't stupid by a long shot, but I didn't see them as criminal masterminds, either, just typical greedy relatives. I brought up Abrielle and Colton a couple more times and none of the Berrys ever asked me how they were. They had no interest in the kids whatsoever. Ken was curious about whether or not his late relatives had wills and how long it would take for the kids (he didn't use Abrielle or Colton's names) to inherit. I had no idea and told them so. Willy was mostly interested in my body. Gina and Stacy wanted to know the price tag on my suit and what brand of makeup I wore. They answered every question without hesitation, they were so transfixed by the idea that I hadn't had any work done to achieve the Marilyn look. The full Marilyn served its purpose. It pays to be distracting.

I had sixteen messages by the time I got back to my apartment. Two were from Uncle Morty. Chuck called once and the rest were from Dad. He found the Abbott kid, but he wasn't happy about it. The kid got picked up for public lewdness ten minutes before Dad got there. Now he was waiting through arraignment and bail, which meant he wasn't able to yell at me in person. He much preferred yelling in person. I didn't so much. The phone wasn't great either.

"Do you know what happens next?" he yelled.

"I'm going to New Orleans."

"Well, thank god she figured that out."

"*She* is right here, Dad. You don't have to yell," I said.

"You went into a parking garage alone. That guy could've nabbed you, knifed you, shot you."

"I know!" I yelled back. "And I wasn't alone!"

"You do something for that Brittany girl. She might've saved your life."

"I will!"

"Why are you yelling? I'm the one that's pissed," said Dad.

"Not anymore."

"Call Claire and have her book you a flight tonight. I want you out of town with a quickness. We're dealing with a mass murderer whose partner's in the wind. You can stay at the grandparents in the Quarter. Come over and pick up the key before you leave."

"I'm not staying with Nana and Pop Pop. I'll never get anything done. They'll be all over me."

"They're in New York with your Aunt Tenne and Bruno for his big show," said Dad.

"Fine!"

"Damn straight it's fine. It's about time you stop arguing with me."

I screeched and hung up. My gorgeous suit went back onto its deluxe padded hanger and I collapsed next to Skanky. He'd given himself a good cleaning and was snoring on my pillow. New Orleans wouldn't be so bad. I loved Nana and Pop Pop, but I was their only grandchild and did they love me. My grandparents made my parents seem uninvolved and distant. I'd have to thank Bruno for being a brilliant artist and luring them away. My Aunt Tenne had met Bruno on our trip to Honduras. They've fallen inexplicably in love and she'd brought him back to the States. Nobody expected it to last. Bruno was fifteen years younger than my aunt, but, if anything, they were more devoted to each other. Tenne was managing Bruno's career and had proved to be good at it. Bruno did nothing but paint and sculpt, while she handled the business. It worked out for everyone and the family had embraced Bruno as only we could. His studio was on the third floor of my parent's house and Mom kept him in food and supplies. Bruno remained his shy self, but I think he liked our family.

At that moment he was the only one. My phone was ringing again. It was Uncle Morty. He wasn't a real uncle. He was my dad's best friend and an honorary uncle, but he was more annoying than my blood uncles. I had to go through the meeting with the other Berrys step by step and then listen to Uncle Morty grumble about how I should've gotten more out of them. But I wasn't the dirty laundry person that he was. He could dig through their financials, looking for a connection to New Orleans or Blankenship. I had things to do.

"All I know is that they are not giving up," I said. "So I'll just have to find out where the listeriosis came from to clear Donatella beyond any reasonable doubt."

"You'll have to lock it up tight. Stewie can smell a big payday a mile away," said Uncle Morty.

"Who's Stewie?"

"Stewie Suydam, biggest ambulance chaser west of the Mississippi. Real dirtbag, but good unfortunately. He called those Berry bastards, not the other way around."

"So the Berrys didn't think of this on their own," I said.

"Naw. They had plenty of help. Call me when you get something."

I hung up and I called Claire about New Orleans. Claire was my old high school rival, who was now my dad's transcriptionist and secretary. She said she'd take care of it and would email me the reservation. I rolled over and petted Skanky until he woke up and started to clean his rear. Why did he always start at the bottom? I'm sure his ears were just as dirty. Something about the rhythm of his licking made my eyes close. Maybe it was the grossness, but I went right to sleep without eating or putting on a tee shirt.

It felt like only a second later when my eyes popped open. "Stewie!"

"Yow."

"Where's my phone?"

I found it under Skanky all warm and hairy. He'd chewed on a corner until he'd gotten through the case. I briefly wondered if he could get shocked from biting a phone and then decided I didn't care. Electric shock therapy might be just what he needed.

I dialed and received my usual greeting, "What do you want?"

"Uncle Morty. It's me. Who did you say was the other Berrys lawyer, the ambulance chaser?"

"You take a blow to the head? It's Stewie Suydam." He paused. "Why?"

"Because they didn't mention any Stewie. I think their lawyer is named Andrew."

"Andrew. Who the hell is Andrew?"

"I don't know, but Ken said Andrew was going to fix Donatella's wagon. I assumed it was their lawyer."

"I'm on it." He hung up on me and I checked my email. Claire got me a six o'clock flight and it was almost four. I grabbed my suitcase and started throwing in an assortment of warm weather clothing and shoes, lots of shoes. Then I texted Oz. It was a simple message designed to not get a response. Of course, it failed.

"Why are you going to New Orleans?" asked Oz after I finally broke down and answered the phone.

"I have to track the listeriosis."

"To clear Donatella."

"That's the idea. Do you have anything for me?" I wasn't sure what answer I was looking for. No matter what Oz said, I was getting dangerously close to the Fibonacci radar again.

"The word is out. Aunt Calpurnia was already working our connections. She's pretty torn up about Tulio."

"Nothing yet?"

"Nothing yet, but believe me, she's serious. They're kicking over all the rocks."

"And my name is out of it?" I asked.

"You have my word."

I took my favorite red wrap dress, the causer of many a problem, rolled it up and tucked it in my suitcase. "Oz, have you by chance heard the name Andrew associated with Blankenship or Tulio?"

"Andrew what?"

"Just Andrew." I told him about the other Berrys and what Uncle Morty said. Oz said he'd ask around and see what he could find out. I promised to text with any developments and then turned my attention to the task at hand, the trip, but instead the guy in the hospital parking garage appeared in my mind. It was quite unexpected. I wasn't afraid often, but there was something about the way he stood there, waiting. I'd had a few situations, but I usually went to the perpetrator like I did in the funeral home incident or swam to them as in Honduras. Never before had anyone come for me, unless you counted the occasional stalker. But that guy in the hoodie was no weirdo, looking to smell me. I could just tell.

I went to my sweater drawer and felt between my Christmas sweaters, pulling out the Mauser, a World War Two relic brought back from Europe by my great grandfather. I never carried it, but I had all the paperwork. There was a full clip in my handy box o'clips and I found the carrying case Dad got me under a pile of shoe boxes. I packed up Grandpa's Mauser and made sure I had all my permits and then, and only then, did I get the cat carrier.

"Skanky. Sweet boy. Come here and get some treats." I had no treats, but Skanky had proven how dumb he was.

"Bacon. I've got bacon."

No luck. Skanky had jumped off the bed during my frantic packing and disappeared. It was the suitcase. I should've nabbed him first and then packed. I didn't have time for this. I ran out to my neighbor, Mr. Cervantes. His door creaked open and his wrinkled brown eyes peered out at me over the chain.

"Hi, Mr. Cervantes. I'm in a real bind. Could you possibly watch Skanky for me? I can't find him and I have a plane to catch in under two hours," I said, all in a rush.

Mr. Cervantes smiled and undid the chain. "I'd be honored to help. Big case?"

"Not sure yet. I have to go to New Orleans. You don't mind?"

Mr. Cervantes didn't mind. He was thrilled, especially when I gave him my key and Aunt Miriam's cellphone number, in case he had a problem. Mr. Cervantes liked Aunt Miriam. He'd known her forever, even before she was a nun. I never got the story there. Half the time he appeared terrified of her, like everyone else. The rest of the time, he probably would've asked her on a date if that were allowed. I thought he was lucky she was married to God. She'd eat him for lunch.

I gave him the vet's number, just in case Skanky ate a tennis ball and then I ran out to drive to my parents' house on Hawthorne.

The winter light was fading and I screeched to a halt in the alley behind the house. Dad's car was parked next to Mom's, so he must've gotten the Abbott kid out of jail. Time 4:15. Not bad. I went up the walk, past the sad barren flower beds, to the back porch. Dad had finally replaced the dry-rotted roof after Mom threatened him with a divorce and a contractor. It was the combo. Divorce alone wasn't enough to do it.

I let myself in and took a second to breathe the cool air of the butler's pantry. It was my favorite place in the house and it didn't bother me at all that the builder, Josiah Bled, The Girls' uncle, might've buried his lover, Bernice Collins, under the floor. Nobody knew what happened to Bernice and I was more interested in what happened to Josiah seventy years later. I hadn't heard anything from Spidermonkey. He was the one person who hadn't called me, but, then again, Spidermonkey only called with updates, not to bother me.

I went to the key cabinet at the far end of the pantry and looked at the rows of keys on the little brass hooks. None were tagged, of course.

"Mom, Dad, I'm here. Where's the key?" I called out through the pantry door.

No answer, so I went into the toasty kitchen filled with the smell of cheesy noodles, our family's version of comfort food. Cheddar cheese, grilled chicken, pasta, and curry. It was heaven. There was also, to my mother's deep shame, a can of cream of chicken soup in our family casserole, but I wasn't to tell anyone about that on pain of disinheritance. Mom was serious about that. She went so far as to hide the empty soup cans in our neighbor's recycling bin. She was so crazy.

"Mom!"

Still nothing. I came around the table to find Mom's evil Siamese, Swish and Swat, sitting in the doorway to the rest of the house. They stared at me with their pale blue eyes. I was pretty sure they were thinking about how they would eat me when I was dead.

"I don't have him," I said to them. "You'll just have to torment somebody else's cat for a change."

Swish hissed and Swat extended his claws. They loved it when I dropped off Skanky. He was their favorite chew toy. When I went camping last summer, they licked off all his hair and he had to wear a sweater for a month out of sheer embarrassment. His, not mine.

"Okay. Get out of the way," I said.

Hiss.

"I will kick you. Don't think I won't." The last time I tried to get past the evil Siamese, they shredded my ankles. I had scars to prove it, but Mom blamed me for startling her babies. Please. Nothing startled those two. They were like wolverines in cat clothing. It was either kick or risk the ankles. Neither was a good option. I grabbed the broom out of the pantry and brandished it at them. "Prepare to eat bristles."

Swish and Swat yawned, pointedly showing me their needle-sharp teeth as if I needed to be reminded. Then they stalked off down the hall and went up the servant staircase. I trotted past the stairs and heard the murmur of voices down in what Mom insisted on calling the parlor. It was the living room. I heard my name and hesitated at the door. If Mom found out that I told my best friend Ellen about the cream of chicken soup, I wanted to know before she disinherited me.

"You don't know that he'll be there," said Dad. "She's never seen him before."

"Mercy's never been there alone before," said Mom. "He will be there."

"It'll be fine. Mercy's no shrinking violet. She can handle herself."

That sounded suspiciously like a compliment. I was shocked.

"I don't know," said Mom.

"It's less expensive to stay at your parent's. It's no big deal."

"It's unnerving. I never told her."

"No reason to tell her. What would you say anyway?"

I walked in. "Never told me what?"

My parents were standing in front of the blazing fireplace with whiskey sours in hand. Mom was in full Marilyn, but she always was. Mom couldn't help it. She loved lipstick and lashes, pencil skirts and stilettos. Her look always matched her face.

"When did you get here?" Mom blurted out.

"A couple of minutes ago. Who were you talking about?" I asked.

"You shouldn't eavesdrop. It isn't polite."

"I wasn't eavesdropping." Not much anyway.

Mom sipped her drink and eyed me coldly over the rim of her vintage glass. "Why do you have a broom?"

I looked down, surprised to see the broom still in my hand. "I was...sweeping."

"Did you smack my cats?" asked Mom with a strange glint in her eye. When it came to the evil Siamese, she forgot who her flesh and blood was and who was purchased from a breeder in Chicago.

"Mom, I would never smack Swish and Swat."

Mom put her glass on the mantel and crossed her arms. Dad sipped his whiskey sour and smiled so that his dimples danced on his cheeks. He towered over Mom at six four and was seriously lanky with red hair and a special charm that was somehow evident even when silent.

"Okay, so I need the key," I said, anxious the leave the cats behind.

"That's all you have to say for yourself," said Mom.

"Um...yeah."

"You didn't even call me."

"About what?"

"The stalker in the parking garage. I had to hear it from Morty," she said.

"I thought Dad would tell you."

Mom turned her glare on Dad and he quickly said, "You need keys."

Dad tossed me the keys and ushered me out of the parlor while Mom chased us, yakking about the darn cats. The devils watched as we went by the servant stair. I swear, they were smiling.

"Carolina, she doesn't have time. Six o'clock flight." Dad took the broom out of my hand and tucked it away around a corner. "Hide the weaponry next time."

Before I knew it, I was through the pantry and at the back door.

"Hey Dad, I want to know who you were talking about. What's unnerving?"

Dad opened the door and pushed me through. "I want to know why your mother keeps making me salads when she knows I don't like the color green. Life's full of mysteries. Have a good flight."

"But—"

He closed the door and locked it. My father locked me out. I had a key. But still it was weird. I was about to go back for another try, but I checked my phone first. "Oh crap!"

There wasn't enough time for a fight. New Orleans and something unnerving awaited.

CHAPTER TEN

Claire booked me on a non-stop flight to New Orleans and I was alone on it. I expected to see Aaron standing at check-in, eating a Twinkie and looking confused. But there was no Aaron at check-in or anywhere else. It was good to be on a flight alone with a magazine, but it felt a little weird. I kept expecting him to pop out of the bathroom, holding a giant salami or something. My row was empty, except for me, and the flight half-full. Once I got used to the idea of flying without constant chatter and the smell of hotdogs, I wadded up my coat and prepared to snooze for the two-hour flight. But it was not to be.

There was a mother and her two darling little red-headed girls in front of me. And when I say darling, I mean it. They were the most adorable children I'd ever seen, even the three-year-old who continually sang *Let It Go*. Not the whole song, just the one line. Their mother apologized and gave me M&M's. I'll put up with a lot for an endless supply of M&M's. Plus, the small girls were the only children in two weeks that I'd seen that weren't throwing up, concussed, or otherwise injured. It was refreshing.

My flight arrived on time and I was out in the humid air, grabbing a cab within twenty minutes of landing. My cab driver didn't share my attitude and was visibly pissed that I wasn't going to a hotel in the French Quarter. My grandparents were on a street he'd never heard of and didn't believe existed. I told him to put the address into his GPS and silently calculated a lower tip for telling me that I didn't know where my own grandparents lived.

We zoomed toward downtown, past a sign that made me smile. "Eat local. Breastfeed." My cab driver didn't find it, or me, amusing. He grumbled all the way to the Quarter and made sixteen turns before he found the street. I didn't care. I was smiling. New Orleans always felt like another version of home. A grubbier version, but home none the less. I love the faded, but colorful, houses with their wrought iron balconies overloaded with fat ferns and flowers.

The cab jerked to a halt. It didn't make the driver any happier that he was wrong about my grandparents' address. He tossed my suitcase onto the sidewalk and his tip evaporated. When he realized it, he gave me a look like he knew I was a jerk all along. Not staying in a hotel. What kind of tourist was I anyway? He squealed his tires down the short street and ran up on a sidewalk, narrowly missing a couple of obviously drunken businessmen who were probably looking for Bourbon Street. They were going the wrong way and would end up at St. Louis Cemetery No.1.

I righted my suitcase and dug out the keys. There were two. One for the wrought iron gate, between two pink buildings butted right up to the sidewalk, and one for the door. I wrestled the old gate open and carried my suitcase into the narrow alley. It was unpainted brick with tiny ferns growing on the walls out of the mortar. Ferns don't need dirt, I guess. I locked the gate and walked back to the courtyard. My grandparents' place had been in the family forever and had an old-style courtyard between the main building and what used to be the servants' quarters out back. The fountain was bubbling away, surrounded by potted palms and ferns, because you can never have enough ferns. The far wall had a little stream of water that spurted out of a plump cupid's mouth into a pool in the raised flower bed below filled with twisting red bougainvillea. Nothing changed at Nana's house. Mom said it was the same when she came to visit her grandparents when she was a kid.

I turned to the main house and unlocked the rather rickety door in the wall of windows that overlooked the courtyard. Nana and Pop Pop never closed the shades, even though their property was no longer private. When Pop Pop retired, my grandparents decided the place was too big for them alone and they started a vacation rental business. The servants' quarters now had four vacation rentals in them and they did a brisk business. So the shades remained open to make them accessible.

That back room was Pop Pop's TV room and it was filled with over-stuffed leather furniture, local artwork, and an enormous brick fireplace next to the equally enormous TV that usually had some sport on it. I carried my suitcase into Pop Pop's room and stopped at the sofa to look at the framed family tree that hung behind it. There was something about seeing my name there among all those other names and generations that made me feel small and sort of precious. I was the last leaf on a very big tree. If I didn't continue the family line, it was over and that tree would stay as it was forever. I said hello to the tree and went up the stairs to my room. It overlooked the courtyard, had toile wallpaper, and a flowery bedspread on the cushy bed. Never has a bed looked so inviting, but I needed some food. Lucky for me, Matassa Market was a block away. If I hurried, I could get to the deli before they shut it down. I unpacked the Mauser and, after thinking it over, I put it in the side table drawer. Dad wouldn't be happy, but it didn't feel right to go to neighborly Matassa with a gun, so I pocketed a key ring-sized pepper spray and headed out.

Matassa was located on a convenient corner but didn't see a load of tourists. It was the sort of place you'd never find in the Central West End. A full grocery store was stuffed into the space normally allotted to a barbershop. Matassa didn't feel clean. It felt like family, messy friendly family. I said hello to a mildly interested clerk at the front and headed straight for the deli. The French Quarter was the one place were Marilyn Monroe look-alikes weren't unusual. The French Quarter got all kinds and people usually thought I was a cabaret singer.

"Hello?" I said over the small glass deli case filled with sausages, cheeses, and several odd salads. There might've been gator in there.

A bald man stuck his head around a rack of chips. "Can I help you?"

"Can I still get a club sandwich?" I said, giving him the big eyes.

"Sorry. Deli's closed." His brow wrinkled. "Carolina?"

I grinned. "Mercy. I'm Carolina's daughter."

He threw up his hands. "Hey. Hey. Hey. You visiting your grandparents?"

"I'm just here for a few days."

"I saw you on the CNN." His brow furrowed. "You're smaller in person. Tiny."

"I'm not *that* small."

He let out a belly laugh. "You look like an Amazon goddess walking up that beach in that bikini."

"Trick photography."

"I guess so. You want a club?"

"Do you mind?" I asked, trying not to look pathetic. Matassa made the best club sandwich in the world. I wasn't sure why. It was just heaven on sandwich bread.

"Anything for Double Black Diamond's new cover girl." He grinned.

"You heard about that?"

"It was in *The Times-Picayune*. You want a cold drink with that?"

"No, thanks."

I wandered around the store, while he fried my bacon, and marveled at the sheer amount of stuff they managed to get on the narrow aisles. I got a basket and picked out some Angelo Brocato ice cream, stracciatella, not the truly weird spumoni. The deli guy found me in the cereal aisle and gave me my sandwich, then ducked his head and asked for my autograph. That happened now that DBD named me as their cover girl, but I didn't expect it in New Orleans.

"Really?" I asked.

"I collect autographs. Brad Pitt was in here last week."

"How did that happen?"

"I think he was lost."

"Doesn't he live like three blocks away?"

He shrugged. "Tourists. So whaddaya say?"

I took a pad and pen out of his apron pocket and wrote a little note.

"Thanks, cher. Trix will take care of ya."

I paid and walked back to the house. The street was nearly empty, but I could hear Bourbon St. a few blocks over. It was a whole different world over there. I put on my PJs and ate in bed. Actually, I fell asleep with half a sandwich in my mouth, waking only once during the night when I was suddenly awake and absolutely sure someone was in the room. There wasn't. I went back to sleep to be awakened in the morning by the sun streaming through the windows.

I yawned, rolled over, and discovered I wasn't alone. Sitting on my dresser was a black cat. It was tall and skinny with unblinking green eyes. Weird. My grandparents weren't pet people. They liked Swish and Swat less than I did. Pop Pop called cats "Snobs that poop in your house."

I slid out of bed and went into the kitchen. The cat followed me and sat in the kitchen doorway. I put the rest of my club in the fridge, hoping the cat hadn't licked the mayo while I was unconscious.

"Do you live here?" I asked the cat.

It stared at me, still without blinking. Even the evil Siamese blinked. I got a bowl of cereal and ate at the counter while the cat watched. It was so weird. I had to call Mom, something I usually would've avoided while out of her sphere of influence.

"Hey, Mom," I said.

"Don't make a mess. Did you make a mess?"

Groan.

"There's no mess. I've been here twelve hours."

"You take less than twelve minutes to make a mess. I have it on video."

"For crying out loud, Mom. There's no mess. Does Nana have a cat?"

She hesitated and then said, "Yes, yes they do."

"When did that happen?"

"I don't know. They just got a cat."

"What's its name?"

"Um...Blackie."

"Original."

"Not everyone wants to name their cat something as lovely as Skanky."

"Point taken." I looked around the kitchen. "Where are the cat bowls?"

"Stop harping on this," said Mom.

I made some much needed coffee. "I'm not harping. I have to feed it."

"No, you don't. I think the neighbor is supposed to be taking care of it. Just throw the cat out."

"What neighbor?"

"I don't know. Where are you heading today? We need to be updated frequently. Your dad and Morty are handling the other Berrys."

"Handling how?"

"We want to know who that Andrew is that they mentioned. He could be the connection between them and Blankenship," said Mom.

I took my first gulp of coffee. Oh my god did I need that. "Mom, I didn't get the feeling that they orchestrated the shooting at Tulio. I think they saw the chance to make some serious bucks off their family tragedy and jumped on it."

"Your father has a feeling."

Enough said. Dad was famous for his feelings. He knew when something wasn't right. If he thought there was a connection between the other Berrys, Tulio, and Blankenship, there probably was, but the idea made me sick to my stomach.

"Mercy?" asked Mom.

"Does Dad think they sent Blankenship to Tulio?" I asked.

"Not exactly. He thinks you're right about them, but there's something there. You have to find the source of the Listeriosis. We'll handle the shooting."

Mom lectured me for another ten minutes about safety. I scored some points for bringing the Mauser and plenty of pepper spray, but she was more worried than usual. If my parents were so freaked, why didn't they send Aaron with me? I kept expecting him to wander in. Aaron was normally like Velcro during my investigations, but I didn't mention him. I didn't need that little weirdo dogging my footsteps, although I did miss the food.

After the rundown on locking doors, Mom started on checking for tails as if it was a given that someone would be following me around New Orleans. I had to tell her I felt an impending bout of diarrhea in order to get off the phone. Once we hung up, I realized she never told me which neighbor was supposed to take care of the cat, but I wasn't risking another call. No way.

"Alright you," I said to Blackie, who stared at me from the door. "You're going out."

I picked him up and put him out the door. He stared at me with those intense green eyes and then sauntered across the courtyard to sit next to the fountain and proceeded to stare at me. Great.

"Shoo," I said. "The food isn't here."

Blackie didn't care and he still didn't care after I'd showered and packed Grandpa's Mauser in my purse. When I went out the door to start backtracking through Abrielle and Colton's last day in New Orleans, the cat was still sitting by the fountain, not moving or blinking. He made Skanky look normal. At least my cat blinked.

I passed Blackie and headed down the alley. When I looked back, there he was sitting at the entrance. Still watching. Creepy damn cat. I locked him in and trekked off to Mom's old elementary school. It was only three blocks, but I had a chance to soak up the French Quarter. It had its own particular smell. Moist (yes, that is a smell) and earthy with a hint of vomit and flowers thrown in. Mom wouldn't like that description. She would say the French Quarter smells like the Old World. Now I've spent considerable amount of time in the Old World, traveling with my godmothers, Myrtle and Millicent. The Quarter is completely unique. That's not to say bad. In fact, I love it. It's real and it doesn't care what you think.

That's exactly how I felt walking down the cracked sidewalk. I didn't listen to my mom, who advised a floppy hat and shapeless sweatshirt to make me less obvious. Experience has taught me that when I try to be less obvious, I attract a lot of attention. Mom wouldn't know that. Her hats are anything but dull affairs and she doesn't own a sweatshirt. I did put on sunglasses and yanked on the hem of the tank dress, but it rode up anyway. Mom would be horrified. I caught her trying to burn my dress once, but I stopped her just in time.

I came around the corner and crossed the street in front of Lafitte's Blacksmith shop, a really cool old bar which probably had nothing to do with Jean Lafitte. The elementary school covered most of the block and looked the same as when Mom went there, red brick with arched windows and white trim. I trotted up the stone stairs and got myself buzzed in by saying I was a friend of Donatella Berry.

A woman waited for me in front of the office. She was about twenty-five but had a distinct old lady vibe about her. Her hair was knotted up in a tight bun and she wore some of the dowdiest clothes I'd ever seen.

"Hello," she said in a squeaky voice.

I stuck out my hand. "Hi. I'm Mercy Watts."

"I'm Chelsea." She looked at my hand and forced herself to shake my fingertips. I could see her struggle and it made me feel bad for putting her on the spot like that.

"I'm helping out Donatella. I'd like to speak to your principal, if I may," I said.

Chelsea burst into tears and began to snuffle like a Truffle pig. I didn't see that coming.

"Are you okay?" I asked, restraining myself from touching her shaking shoulder.

"I...I...I"

Another woman came out. She was older with feathered blond hair circa 1983. She heaved a sigh and said, "Alright Chelsea. What is it now?"

"Dona...tella."

The new woman rolled her eyes and shooed Chelsea back into the office. "Go blow your nose and have some chocolate."

Chelsea stumbled back into the office in an ugly cry and I was momentarily speechless. My showing up to interview people got various reactions, but that was a new one. Donatella took it better than that.

"You are?" asked the woman.

I explained the situation and she introduced herself as Kathy Brun, the assistant principal. She led me back into her office and we sat down in well-worn, but comfy, chairs.

"So what do you want to know?" Kathy asked.

"Was Donatella having any problems with anyone? Any trouble at all?"

Kathy chuckled softly. "Not Donatella. The thought is ridiculous. Everyone loves her. She's a great administrator. No problems at all."

"You're friends?"

"I think so," she said with confidence. That meant no, not real friends, not the kind you tell your husband stories to.

"Did anything unusual happen on the day she left for St. Louis?" I asked.

"Nothing. Typical day. Donatella left early to see if they could get on an earlier flight. But you know that, right?"

"She told me. Did you tell anyone that she left early? Was anyone curious about it?"

"It wasn't a secret. She was dreading the trip, actually."

"Why was that?"

"Well, Colton's a handful. He doesn't like changes in his schedule. Donatella likes to keep things consistent for him."

"So why did she decide to leave early?"

"She thought if she could get him to the hotel and let him have a swim in the pool before the dinner, he'd be in a good mood. Don't let me give you the wrong impression. Colton is a great kid, very smart."

"But..."

"Like I said, he's a handful. She wanted to give him a little time to adjust and calm down."

"What would happen if she didn't?"

"He might refuse to eat or want to leave right after they got there. Nothing big."

"Does everyone know this about Colton? Did it surprise you that she decided to leave early?"

Kathy smiled and got a little teary eyed for the first time. "We're a close community in this school. Donatella didn't hide her struggles with Colton. No, I wasn't surprised when she asked to leave early."

I didn't like that. It sounded like Donatella was an open book. If someone wanted to predict what she was going to do, it wouldn't be too hard. I could do it, based on what Kathy just said. I asked if Donatella was close to anyone else on the staff and we went to see a third grade teacher by the name of Erika Cullen.

I knocked on the door. Erika excused herself from her class and Kathy took over while we talked in the hall. I gave her a brief rundown of the situation and Erika crossed her arms. Not a good sign.

"I'm trying to help Donatella," I said.

"So you say," said Erika.

"You can call her and ask. I have no objections, but do it soon. I've got to figure this out fast."

Erika started to text someone and I had to bite back a groan. I had things to do, beignets to eat. Time was a wasting.

After about two hundred texts, Erika pocketed her phone. "She said it was okay."

All that for okay? Fine.

"Has Donatella had any problems with anyone, for any reason? I don't care if it's about a parking space, tell me," I said.

She crossed her arms again. "She said to tell you, but—"

"Go ahead. It's just information to me."

"There's a rumor going around about her and Mr. Donnelly, the science teacher."

"An affair?" I asked.

"He wishes."

"So, no affair?"

"Donnelly likes her a lot, but she made it plain that she's very married. She adores...adored Rob. And he adored her. They had no secrets." Erika teared up and wiped her eyes on her sleeve. "She'd never cheat on him."

"Was he angry, insistent?" I asked.

She nodded. "He got a bit weird. Leaving her flowers and notes on her car, but he never threatened her or anything."

"Did Rob know?"

"Sure. She told him everything. They were very close. Rob called Donnelly and told him to knock it off."

"Did he?"

"As far as I know."

"When was all this?" I asked.

"About six months ago. You don't think that Donnelly had anything to do with Abrielle and Colton getting sick?" She gasped. "Or the shooting?"

"No, I don't." I said it as firmly as I could. "But I'm checking everyone out. The kids weren't around here on the day they left, right?"

"Nope. I haven't seen them in weeks. They go to school outside the city."

Kathy came out into the hall. "How's it going? Getting everything you need?"

Erika looked uncomfortable and I didn't mention Donnelly. "Yes, Erika is very helpful. Can we have a couple more minutes?"

"Sure," said Kathy and she went back into the classroom.

I raised an eyebrow at Erika. "Kathy doesn't know about Donnelly?"

"No," she said. "Donatella said not to tell her. You know how it is. She's the assistant principal. She'd have to do something about him. Donatella didn't want that. He's a fabulous science teacher. The kids love him and he stopped after Rob talked to him."

"Do people think that maybe something was going on between Donnelly and Donatella?" I asked.

She shrugged. "You know how people are. They love to talk."

"I know all about people talking."

"I bet you do with a face like that." Erika smiled. "I can't decide if it's a good thing or a bad thing."

"It depends on the day," I said. "What's Donnelly's first name? I need to exclude him."

"Calvin."

I asked her to point me in the direction of Calvin, the lovesick science teacher, and took off down the hall. Calvin was in his room, running an experiment. The door was open and laughter billowed out into the hall. The teacher's back was to me. He was a large guy. His body said he'd played football at some point. It was probably at the college level, if I went by the size of his thighs. Calvin stood at a stainless steel-topped table, pouring a greenish liquid into a beaker and producing a pillar of steam, oblivious to me.

"Who can tell me why that happened?" he asked.

Half the class raised their hands and the other half looked as though they wanted to. A great science teacher. A great suspect. No doubt about it. A science teacher would be able to figure out how to poison a couple of kids. He'd have the science, the planning ability, but not the access. He'd need a partner to get the bacteria into the kids.

Several kids got called on, giving various answers that were almost right. Calvin made every one of them feel like they won the lottery. There was clapping and high fives. One of the girls noticed me in the door and Calvin turned around with a broad smile on his face. "Come in! exclaimed the ghost —come in! and know me better, man!"

A third of the kids' hands shot up.

"LaDonna!" shouted Calvin.

"*A Christmas Carol* by Charles Dickens. The character is the Ghost of Christmas Present!" LaDonna had the whitest teeth I'd ever seen in her dark brown smiling face.

"We have a winner!" Calvin launched something at LaDonna.

She caught it and announced, "Bit O'Honey!"

There was more clapping and I wasn't sure what to do. Calvin grinned at me again. "Sorry about that. I head the Lit Club. Come on in."

I smiled back. Calvin Donnelly's class was infectious. Why weren't any of my science teachers like that? I had the Ferris Bueller-type teachers, droning on and on, making you want to stab yourself with a spork just to escape.

"Actually," I said, "could you maybe step out into the hall?"

"Certainly. Class, go over your notes on combustion. I'll be back in a minute."

Calvin joined me in the hall and I closed the door behind him. That peaked his curiosity. His rather grizzled eyebrows went up. Calvin Donnelly had multiple scars. One split his left eyebrow in half. I was wrong about the football. It was probably heavy-weight boxing.

"We haven't met, have we?" he asked. "I'm sure I'd remember someone like you."

"We haven't. I'm a friend of Donatella Berry."

His face fell. All the joy vanished in a blink. "Poor Donatella. How is she? How are the kids?"

"They're recovering. Donatella is pretty much how you'd expect." I told him why I was there, talking to him specifically.

"You don't think I poisoned Donatella's kids. I'd never in a million years do something like that," said Calvin.

"I'd like to cross you off my list," I said.

"Well, cross me off. There's no way."

"You were giving Donatella some trouble at the beginning of the school year."

Calvin blushed and it looked ridiculous on his weathered cheeks. "Yeah, I admit I was an idiot. I was new to the school and, well, you've met Donatella. She's beautiful. I've always had a weakness for the redheads. I lost my mind. I admit it. Her husband, Rob, called me and I stopped. I'm embarrassed to say it took his voice to bring me back to reality, but it did."

"You talked to Rob?"

"He called and told me to knock it off and I did."

"That's it?"

Calvin shrugged his huge shoulders. "That's it. Seriously, how are the kids? Colton going to be alright?"

"You know Colton?"

"Yeah. He's a great kid. Whip smart. Love that kid."

"Kathy said he was a handful."

Calvin made a face. "Don't take this the wrong way, but some female teachers have a hard time connecting with boys. They don't like the activity level or the noise. Colton is a lot, but in a good way. I'll take five Coltons over some kid who couldn't rustle up the imagination to cause trouble."

"How do you know him so well?" I asked.

"He was in my Christmas break robotics camp. He picked it up like that." Calvin snapped his fingers.

I watched Calvin's face and body language carefully. I didn't see any signs of lying. Good eye contact. No inappropriate facial expressions or looking to the left when answering questions. Unless he was a sociopath, Calvin Donnelly was telling the truth. He came off better than the other Berrys. He asked about the kids and more than once, too. Calvin couldn't think of anything out of the ordinary the day Donatella left early, but he was pretty distracted. The science kids were going nutty in the room without supervision. They'd be throwing beakers in a second.

"I have to go back," he said.

I thanked Calvin and gave him my card. "If you think of anything that might help Donatella, please give me a call."

"I will," he said, flinging open the door. "Jefferson put that down."

Calvin ran into the science room and I made a few quick notes on my phone. Not too much to say. So far, the other Berrys were the best suspects as far as motive went. But Calvin Donnelly was at least in the state when the kids were infected and spurned love was nothing to ignore. But if Calvin did it, I'd have to be medicated for depression. Great science teachers are hard to find.

I finished my notes and went back to the office. Kathy was there and said she'd walk me out, amid the echoing sobs of Chelsea. I glimpsed her curled up in a chair in the waiting room outside Kathy's office. She was shaking and bright red.

"She's very sensitive." Kathy's eyes were redder and she looked on the verge of breaking down herself. "This has hit us all very hard. The whole family. I don't even know what to say. We've sent flowers. Will you give Donatella our love when you see her?"

I said I would and I left with a new suspect, but not a good one.

CHAPTER ELEVEN

My first beignet was bliss. My second was filling and my third was completely uncalled for. Those little rectangles of fried dough were exactly what I needed, not to mention the mountain of powdered sugar. The coffee wasn't bad, either, nice and milky. The Café Du Monde was about half full and I didn't have to stalk anyone to get a table, which was a new experience for me. I ordered another coffee and decided I'd had enough sugar to brace myself for a call to Uncle Morty. I promised to check in and, to be honest, I was a little lonely. I kept expecting Aaron to plop down in a chair next to me, but the chair remained empty. I couldn't help but wonder when that little weirdo would show up. I hoped he would. Aaron wasn't much of a conversationalist, but my own thoughts weren't as scintillating as you'd think. My head was downright boring on the inside.

I dialed and held the phone a good inch from my ear as protection from the inevitable bellow.

"What?" Uncle Morty burst out.

"It's me, checking in," I said.

"I know. I got caller ID. Hurry it up. I gotta go."

"Really?"

"Yeah, really. I got a life."

That was up for debate. Uncle Morty barely left his apartment. He was a world-famous epic fantasy author and worked as a hacker, just for fun. He barely left his apartment.

"I went to Donatella's work. I've got a crappy suspect for you."

"Define crappy."

I told him Calvin's history with Donatella and not surprisingly, he liked him for it. Morty liked him for the shooting, too. Get rid of the kids and the husband and Calvin might figure he could pick up the pieces. Hideous crimes have been committed for less.

"He says they were all good," I said.

"Yeah, right."

"Colton was in his Christmas break camp. They wouldn't put their kid in Calvin's camp if it wasn't over."

"Maybe he's lying," said Uncle Morty. "Did you confirm this camp with the principal?"

"Well..."

"Idiot. I gotta do everything."

"Everything? I'm in New Orleans."

"And I'm at the airport. Gotta go. Security."

"Oh my god. Where are you going? Not here. I don't—"

He hung up on me. Groan. Double groan. If Uncle Morty was coming, he wouldn't be alone. He'd bring Aaron, Rodney, and possibly a slew of his Dungeons and Dragons cronies. They'd expect to stay with me and Nana's weird cat. That house wasn't big enough for me and that many nerds. Aaron I'd accept, but the rest of them? No way.

I tried calling him back. No answer. Nobody answered. I thought about calling Mom but she'd just ask what I was wearing. I'd end up getting lectured twice in one day. Dad would be okay. He didn't care what I wore, but his phone went to voice mail. Who else could I call? I had to know how many nerds I was dealing with, so I could book the hotel rooms and somehow get them to stay there instead. Pete. I hated to admit it, but my doctor boyfriend was a full-out nerd, gaming, lightsabers, the whole deal. He'd know when to expect my nerd crew. If I could get a hold of him, that is.

Pete answered on the first ring. Weird. "Mercy, how's the investigation going?"

"Hi. I can't believe I caught you in between patients."

"Patients? There's no patients today. Am I right, guys?" Pete said away from the phone. That was when I picked up the hubbub around him and it wasn't hospital hubbub either.

"Where are you?" I asked.

"The airport, of course."

Yes! I could cry. I really could.

"You're at the airport. Really. That's great." I could take the guys if Pete was with them. I'd fit them all in somewhere. They could game in the living room all night and smell like very old tacos. I didn't care.

"I'm surprised," said Pete. "I thought you might, ya know, think it was lame."

"Lame? Why would I ever think it was lame?"

"You know, all the costumes."

Costumes?

"Costumes? It's not Mardi Gras."

"It is in Portland." There was a bunch of whooping around Pete and my heart sank. I could hear Uncle Morty and Rodney in the background. Aaron would be there. They didn't go anywhere without Aaron.

"Portland?" I asked.

Pete's voice got softer. "You got my note, right?"

"Note?"

"I left it for you with the chocolate. I didn't get an answer, so I thought you might be mad. It's the Portland Comic-Con. We're all going for three days. I asked you to go in the note before this whole Berry thing came up."

That damn Skanky.

"I think Skanky ate the note."

"Not possible. I hid it in the cookie jar."

"He broke it," I said.

"Oh damn. I thought it was safe in there. Did he eat the chocolate?"

"I got to see it recycled all over him."

"I'm so sorry. How can that cat be so smart and so stupid at the same time? I'll buy you a new cookie jar. How about a *Game of Thrones* cookie jar?"

"What would that be? Like a severed head?"

"That would be sweet."

I gulped down my burning hot coffee and said, "Got to go. Have a good time."

"Mercy?" said Pete. "Did you think we were coming to New Orleans?"

"Kinda."

"I'll make it up to you, I swear. In the meantime, have fun investigating by yourself. You always hate it when Aaron tags along."

"Yeah, I do hate it."

We hung up and I looked around the café. I think my bottom lip poked out a little. What a loser. I could investigate on my own. I could be by myself. No problem. What was wrong with me? So the skinny doctor and the little weirdo were going to Portland. I was in the Big Easy. If I couldn't find a party, I may as well give up on life itself.

I paid my bill and took off to Jackson Square, enduring the whistles and catcalls that came with that part of the Quarter. For some reason, men think rude hand gestures are a compliment. I'm here to say, they are not. Two obnoxious businessmen, carrying bloody marys, followed me down the street. They loudly debated whether or not I was female and how I liked *it*. I considered showing them my Mauser or, at the very least, giving them a squirt of pepper spray. But I hailed a cab instead and left them in a sudden tropical shower that they so richly deserved.

The cab took me to the far side of the CBD and dropped me at Rob's office in a grey concrete building that looked like it shouldn't have been in the same state as the French Quarter, much less the same city. The Central Business District was a towering concrete maze. I avoided it at all costs, since I usually got lost.

I went into a sumptuous lobby and headed up to the fifteenth floor. The doors opened and the temperature dropped twenty degrees. I should've brought a sweater. Mom told me to. I wouldn't be mentioning the cold unless I wanted another lecture.

Schwartz Realty took up half the floor and their lobby was filled with antiques that were probably new but made to look old. I longed to look under the end tables. Posers.

"Can I help you?" asked the receptionist, a young woman wearing so much blue eyeshadow I was surprised she could open her eyes. It was thick, like it was done with crayon.

I gave her dad's card and told her I wanted to see Rob's boss.

"Mr. Schwarz is with a client right now. Do you have an appointment?"

"No. It's about Rob Berry's murder."

The receptionist gulped and the other clients in the waiting room perked up. Murder in New Orleans wasn't exactly rare, but in that office it was.

"I'll be right back," she said.

I perched on a hard leather sofa for exactly seven seconds when the receptionist rushed back in. "Mrs. Schwartz will see you now. Right this way."

She led me through a warren of wood-paneled halls covered in tasteful paintings of the city. One wall had a row of portraits of the company's top realtors with their names engraved on brass placards underneath. The largest was of the founder, Mr. Jared Schwartz, a lantern-jawed man with close-set eyes and a forced smile. The row of portraits was long and Rob Berry was near the end, smiling out at me.

"Wait a second," I said, backtracking to his picture. Since I'd avoided the media coverage of the Tulio murders, I'd never seen Rob Berry's picture. He came as a surprise. Given Donatella's looks, I expected a stunner along the lines of Chuck, but Rob was average at best with a soft doughy face and thinning hair. He did have kind eyes. The eyes got me. Donatella must've loved his eyes.

There was a sniff next to me and I turned to the receptionist. Her lower lip was scrunched up tight, like she was fighting back a sob.

"Nice picture," I said.

"Yes," she squeaked out.

"Did you know him well?"

She nodded.

"I'm sorry for your loss." I patted her shoulder and she buried her face in her hands. Wrong thing to say, I guess. Her sobs went up in

pitch and I looked around the hall for clue where to take her, but all
the doors were closed. I wasn't confident I could retrace my steps back
to reception. Heck, I got lost in St. Louis and I lived there.

A door opened at the end of the hall. A blond woman stepped out
and what a woman. She was six feet tall and built like Kim Kardashian
with curves that put mine to shame and I'm no beanpole.

"Sheila, I'm waiting," she said in a husky voice that reminded me of
my dad when he'd gone on a drinking binge after a tough case.

Sheila wiped her eyes and straightened up. "I'm sorry, Mrs.
Schwartz."

"I haven't got all day. Move it along. You can cry on your own
time."

"Yes, ma'am." Sheila touched my elbow. "This way."

She took me into Mrs. Schwartz's office and sat me in a Scandina-
vian-style chair. The whole office was done in blond wood and clean
lines, jarring after the dark-paneled hall. Mrs. Schwartz sat down
behind her glass-topped desk and steepled her fingers. "That will be
all, Sheila."

Sheila started to say something but thought better of it. She left,
closing the door behind her.

"So you work for Donatella Berry," said Mrs. Schwartz.

"I'm looking into the poisoning of her children. I'd like to ask you a
few questions."

She leaned forward and placed her chin on her perfectly manicured
hands. Actually, everything was perfect about Mrs. Schwartz in a weird
way. She wasn't beautiful, but she did a damn good impression of it.
Her makeup was flawless. She almost looked sculpted with the way the
blush worked with the bronzer to hollow out her cheeks. Her hair was
in an updo and there was no way she did that herself. It flowed back in
carefully designed waves that were fascinating. It reminded me of a
Lego figure's hair.

"What would you like to know?"

I went on to ask her all the standard questions. Problems, enemies,
blah, blah, blah. Her answers were just as standard. Everything was
"no" until I got to Donatella. When I asked about their relationship, a
flicker of dislike passed over Mrs. Schwartz's finely-tuned features.

"You don't like her," I said.

Her head jerked back. "I didn't say that."

"You didn't have to. What's the deal?"

She blew out a breath and, to stall for time, she ordered a couple of coffees over her intercom.

"Just tell me," I said. "I'll find out anyway."

"You assume there's something to find out."

"There is."

Sheila brought in two coffees on a silver tray and hurried out without a word. Mrs. Schwartz frowned at the door after she left.

"It's not Sheila's fault," I said.

"What do you mean?"

"I asked her about Rob."

Her face took on an odd cast. There was not quite an expression. "Yes, well..."

Ah, there it is.

I steepled my fingers and smiled. "She's awfully upset over a mere co-worker. What was going on between Rob and Sheila? " I asked.

She looked at me directly without a hint of deceit. "I'm unaware of any impropriety."

"Don't you mean you're not directly aware?"

Something changed in Mrs. Schwartz's eyes. They lit up, but it wasn't reflected anywhere else on her face. That's when I got it, the perfection. Mrs. Schwartz had discovered Botox and she was in love with it.

"I don't know what you mean by 'directly aware'," she said.

"You didn't see anything with your own eyeballs."

"No, I didn't."

"But something could've been going on."

"I suppose. Possibly."

That's all I got or would get. Mrs. Schwartz was a nightmare to interview. I was used to people showing me who they really were and what they thought with a wrinkle of the brow. Mrs. Schwartz's brow might as well have been made of stone, for all the good it did me. I pushed for some more information, but there was none to be had. Rob was their highest performer and he'd be sadly missed. Sadly missed was expressed with zero eye moisture. I gave her Dad's card and stood up to leave.

"I have to ask," she said.

"Ask away." I knew what she wanted to ask. I just wasn't sure if she'd have the nerve to come right out with it.

"Who's your surgeon?" I have to know. He's a genius."

"Mother Nature."

She tried to wrinkle her nose and failed. It was so weird to watch. Note to self: never do Botox unless you want people to stare at you and wonder what's wrong with your face. I had enough people staring at my face already.

"You don't believe me," I said.

"Marilyn Monroe had a chin implant. You expect me to believe you don't."

I tipped back my head to show my scarless chin.

"Your surgeon is extremely talented," she said.

I don't like you.

I left without speaking. Snotty woman. I wanted to punch her in her unnatural nose, but I doubt she could feel it. Mrs. Schwartz didn't ask me about the kids or Donatella. That might be telling or it might mean Mrs. Schwartz was as cold-hearted a she looked.

I wandered around for ten minutes before I got back out to reception. I'd planned on pumping Sheila for personal details. No Botox there and the girl was a tearful mess. I'd know in an instant if she and Rob were having an affair. But Sheila wasn't at the desk. She'd been replaced with a nearly identical substitute. Where did they get those girls? And when did blue shadow come back and where was I?

"Hello," I said. "What happened to Sheila?"

"Sheila?"

"The other receptionist."

"They sent her home," she said.

"Do you have her address by chance?" I asked.

"Address?"

"Sheila's address. Her last name."

"No. Why would I?"

"She works here."

"Uh, huh."

The eyes were open, but there was a vacant lot behind them.

"Do you know Sheila's last name?" I asked.

"No."

I had to push. I had to see how empty her vacant lot was. "What color is Sheila's hair?"

"I don't know, like brown or something."

Sheila was a blond. The lot was swept clean.

"Did I get it right?" the girl asked.

"Yes. Sheila's a brunette," I said.

"Good. I wanted to get it right. Can I help you with anything else?"

"I seriously doubt it."

"Alrighty then. Have a good day."

I left, mentally flogging myself for thinking my nursing student, Brittany, was a nitwit. She was a rocket scientist compared to that girl. I rode down the elevator with a businessman who tried to sniff me. I practically ran out of the office building into the warm sun. There was a tour group passing by and I joined them for a block before cutting out to go to Mother's. Mother's was Dad's favorite eatery and Mom's least favorite. She's not the fan of debris that Dad and I are. Debris is basically pan juices with lots of meat bits in it. I wished they sold it by the pint. It's life sustaining.

It was the lunch rush, but I squeezed into the last counter seat available and ordered a debris po'boy. Mom would've been disgusted and that made it extra good. I texted a picture to Dad and then got down to business. Morty and the nerd crew—it pained me to think of Pete as one of them—wouldn't be in Portland for another couple of hours, so background on Sheila would have to wait. I didn't want Rob to be a cheater, but an insanely jealous girlfriend would come in handy. Other than that, I didn't have much. A trip out to Donatella's house was in order. It was a reach, but I could search and see if anything turned up. I'd get some samples of the milk and cereal they ate for breakfast, just in case, but that was probably a waste of time. Threatening letters from a homicidal maniac would be nice, but I wasn't feeling lucky.

CHAPTER TWELVE

My cab screeched to a halt in front of Nana's and I slipped my shoes on. My beaded wedges looked so cute that morning when I picked them out, but when I started to walk back to the Quarter, three blisters popped out in a matter of four blocks.

"Wait here," I said. "I'm just getting new shoes and then it's out to Belle Chasse."

The cab driver smiled. "Sure thing."

I got out and rummaged around for the key. I found it about the time an older English couple came down the alley and unlocked the gate.

"I'm calling Caro. We will not stay here, if this isn't rectified," said the woman.

"Darling, don't get yourself in a tizzy. Caro has the highest standards. One call and she will fix it," said the man, who looked pained and bored at the same time.

"It's disgusting. This can't go on."

I waited for them to exit, but they ignored me and purposely let the gate close. Nice. The couple walked away, discussing how to inform Caro of the situation. Caro was Nana, so I was mildly interested, mostly because I might be expected to do something. Get a plumber. Unclog a toilet.

I unlocked the gate and checked my messages. Nothing from Nana or Pop Pop. If I got out quick, I could deal with it later. Unclogging toilets should be done later, whenever possible. I always hoped for a miracle and sometimes I got one.

But it wasn't a toilet or bugs or any of the things that could go wrong with a vacation rental. It was something that could only go wrong in my life. I was halfway down the alley when the smell got to me. Not hot dogs, which I kept expecting, but something else much less savory. Sausages, and not good ones. The sort of sausages that ought to have been thrown out, not barbecued.

There was no one in the courtyard. I headed back to the pool on the other side of the servant's quarters and found it empty, too. Maybe it was a neighbor. Nana couldn't be expected to control them. The high brick walls on the three sides of the property blocked my view, but there wasn't any smoke that I could see. Weird. And that's when I got worried. I went back to the courtyard and looked at the back of Nana's house. Smoke. A layer of it drifted around Pop Pop's room like heavy cloud cover.

"Oh shit!" I didn't cook anything. Did I cook something? I ran to Nana's door with my key, but it was unlocked. I flung it open and ran into the kitchen. There standing over the stove was a lanky man with limp black hair. I could barely see him through the greasy smoke billowing out of the pan he was holding.

I pulled my pepper spray out and aimed. "Who the hell are you?"

The man forked a rancid-looking sausage and turned to me with a goofy smile. Stevie, the loser son of Big Steve Warnock.

"Hey, Mercy. Hungry?

I sprayed him.

A humid breeze blew in through the kitchen window, but it didn't help. The smell of rancid sausage had taken hold. If I didn't figure something out, Nana would kill me. Stevie did it, but that would hardly be seen as a good excuse.

Honk.

The cab!

"Don't move!" I yelled at Stevie, who had his head under the kitchen faucet. He sputtered something through the water and I ran out.

The cab driver didn't look so much relaxed as angry. "What happened to your shoes?"

I'd forgotten all about the shoes. "Something came up. I'm sorry." I thrust the fare at him, plus a generous tip, and ran back through the gate.

Stevie did move. He never listened or learned. He was back at the stove and the burner was fired up.

"Stevie!"

He jumped and clonked his head on the hood. "What happened?"

"Turn that off."

He didn't. I did. I have never seen a grosser sausage in my life. I put a lid on the pan so I wouldn't have to look at it anymore.

"Go lay down, while I figure out what to do with this...this stuff."

"Let's eat it."

"We're not eating it. I'd throw it out the window, except I'm afraid a stray dog will get it and die."

Stevie ambled out with a dripping face. Of course he did. Why would he bother to dry off like a normal person? I checked to see if the stove hood had a higher setting than turbo. It didn't, so I put the pan on the granite countertop to cool off.

I found Stevie on Pop Pop's favorite leather sofa, dribbling all over it and rubbing his eyes.

"Don't rub," I said and went to get a towel and a wet washcloth.

I wrapped the towel around his sopping head, trying to be gentle when I so didn't want to be.

"Ow. My head hurts," he said.

"Sorry," I said, pressing the cool cloth to Stevie's red eyes.

"Why'd you spray me?"

"Instinct."

"I didn't do nothing," he said.

"You try my patience."

"Patience?"

"Never mind. What are you doing at my grandmother's house?"

"Hiding out."

"You're not even going to bother to lie?" I asked.

He lowered the cloth and gave me his sad puppy eyes. "I cooked."

"That smells like salmonella, so I'll pass. How'd you know I was here?"

"Your mom told my mom in an email. I have her password," said Stevie.

I put the cloth on my forehead. This was just great. "Is it your birthday?

"It's 'my sweetie boy.'"

Gag.

"Of course, it is. Who are you hiding from this time?"

"Your dad."

"You're hiding from my dad in my grandmother's house? How stupid are you?"

Pretty stupid. I don't know why I asked.

"Ernie told me about hiding in plain sight, I thought I'd try it out."

I sat back. This better not be going where I thought it was going. "Who's Ernie?"

"Ernie Costilla."

"Oh my god. You're hiding from one of the Costilla brothers?"

Stevie gave me the blank look that he did so well. "Yeah. He wants to kill me."

I smacked him with the cloth. "You're hiding from Ernie Costilla here? Are you crazy? He'll kill me to get to you." I wasn't exaggerating either. Ernie Costilla was the criminal that Mexican drug lords looked up to.

"No." Stevie shook his head like I was silly for having such an idea. "I'm hiding from your dad. If I go to jail, Ernie'll have me killed."

"You have an arrest warrant out then. What state?" I asked.

"Just Missouri." But he didn't look all that sure about it.

"I'm calling the cops."

"You'll get me killed," he said.

"You did that yourself. What idiot thing did you do? Tell me you didn't steal from the Costillas."

He shrugged. "I didn't think he'd notice. There were a lot of stereos in that warehouse."

"How many stereos did you take?" I asked.

"Sixty-two."

I dropped the cloth and punched him in his bony shoulder. "I'll kill you myself. Sixty-two stereos? Who wouldn't notice sixty-two stereos?"

"You want one? I got 'em in a storage unit out in Slidell."

"No, I don't want a stolen stereo. I want you out and you can take those disgusting sausages with you." I picked up my phone. "Time to go, Stevie. I'll give you a five minute start, just to be sporting."

He crossed his arms. "I'll stay here."

"You can't stay with me. I'm working and you're, you know, you. There's probably a trail behind you wider than a semi."

"No way. I was careful. All cash for travel and I used a fake name at the storage place."

I had to ask. I couldn't help myself. "What name did you use?"

"Steven Warnockski."

I slapped my forehead.

"You like that. See how I added the ski at the end? Nice, huh?"

There were no words.

"Besides, you're not working." He stretched out and put his hands behind his head.

"Yes, I am."

"You packed four pairs of stilettos."

"You went through my stuff?"

"Yeah and I am digging the thongs. They're getting a little ratty though."

I smacked him with the cloth again. "You touched my panties, you freak? What is wrong with you?'

"I'll take you shopping. I saw a Frederick's of Hollywood on Bourbon."

"That was probably a porn shop."

"Close enough."

I looked up New Orleans police department on my phone. "I hope they put you in the general population."

"No, you don't. You like me. We're the same."

"We're not the same. I'm surprised you can breathe on your own."

"Our dads are the same," he said.

Stevie had me there. Big Steve and Tommy Watts were showstoppers and cast big shadows. But that didn't make me the same as Stevie, the guy who once tried to sell drugs to the undercover cop who arrested him the week before. I'd been arrested, but never for being a complete idiot.

"If you think I feel sorry for you, you're wrong," I said.

He tilted his head. "Do you feel sorry for my mom?"

"I feel pity for your mom. It's gone way beyond sorry."

"Works for me. Mom would be crazy upset if I went to jail and got killed. She'd never forgive you."

"You need to go to jail."

Big Steve was a powerful lawyer and, so far, he'd managed to keep Stevie out of jail with a series of questionable deals. He did it for Olivia, Stevie's long-suffering mother. She believed with all her warm heart that Stevie would turn out great, if only they could just get him through his awkward phase. Keep in mind that Stevie's awkward phase started in Kindergarten where he'd eat anything on a dare, including rocks and worms.

"Jail won't help. The Costillas will kill me and Mom'll be devastated. I'm her sweetie boy."

"Why do you have to be such a dirtbag?"

"I'm a good guy." He said it with big, red eyes, and he believed it. Stevie never really hurt anyone but himself and his parents. He wasn't violent. Did he deserve to die because he stole from criminals? Darn it. I'm such a sucker.

Stevie grinned. "I knew you couldn't do it."

"Fine. I won't turn you in, but you can't stay here. When the Costillas show up and kill you, they'll get blood all over and I am not cleaning that up."

"Deal. You want a sausage now?" he asked, grinning.

"Do not eat those sausages. Throw them away and don't cook

anything else. There's a club sandwich in the fridge that I left out all night. You have a better chance of survival eating that. I have to go out. I want you gone by the time I get back."

"Sure thing."

"Where will you go?" I asked.

"There's always a place for a guy like me."

A guy like Stevie? That would be what? A failed criminal with a low IQ.

"I'm charming," he said.

I gave him a look meant to convey my doubt, but he didn't get it. He looked rather pleased with himself. As long as he left, I guess I didn't care. I had a bacteria to track down and it was bound to be way more wily than Stevie the worm eater.

CHAPTER THIRTEEN

My cab pulled up in front of Donatella's house in the upper-middle class suburban of Belle Chasse. It was a new plantation style house with lots of white pillars and wrought iron on the balcony.

"You want me to hang?" asked my driver.

"No. I could be awhile." I paid him and went up the long walk to the big front door. My code worked and I let myself into the two-story foyer. I froze. It was one of those sixth sense things. Something was wrong, but the problem wasn't immediately apparent. The foyer was gorgeous with highly-polished floors and a gleaming crystal chandelier. The flowers on the side table had died in Donatella's absence and petals littered the table and floor. That was normal, but something else wasn't.

I stepped back out and took a look at the alarm keypad. It didn't tell me if there had been any other entries. It had been armed and the door was locked, so why did I feel so exposed? I called Uncle Morty, but it went straight to voice mail. Still on the plane. Damn. There was nothing else to do, but to go in. I pulled out my Mauser and stepped back into the cool foyer. The room to the right was a formal living room and it was also perfect. I crossed the foyer and entered a home office. At first glance, it looked fine, too. But when I walked through, there were a few things that caught my eye. The desk drawers weren't pushed all the way in. The top of the desk had a few items on it, a lamp, calendar, a pen holder, and several family photos taken recently by a lake. All these things were carefully arranged, but one thing wasn't, an address book. It lay open off to the right side. Whoever looked at it wasn't seated. Odd. Donatella was obviously a neat freak. Everything that I'd seen so far had a place. That address book wasn't where it should've been.

From there I went into the family room. It was tidy, except for some family albums tossed about on the coffee table. The kitchen and the rest of the first floor were all perfect. I went up the stairs, gun still in hand, with the hairs rising on the back of my neck. I expected to find someone up there. Since there was no smell, I had to assume they'd be alive and aware of me. But there was no one in the master suite or the guest room. Abrielle and Colton's rooms were more lived in than the rest of the house, with clothes and Legos strewn about, but empty as well. Their older brother Christopher's room was where I found it, the thing that had been freaking me out since the second I walked in. Christopher's room was trashed, and I mean trashed. The mattress had been thrown on the floor and shredded. The plaid wallpaper hung in ripped strips off the wall. His desk and bookshelves were tipped over. His lamp had been thrown against a wall and was shattered to bits.

I checked the walk-in closet and found it empty, except for the clothes and shoes that were hurled to the floor in a fit of rage. If I had to guess, they didn't find what they were looking for and, boy, did it piss them off.

I stood with the Mauser hanging limp by my side. What the hell? I thought I'd get nothing but an expensive cab ride. This was crazy. What did Christopher have to do with anything? He was never supposed to go to St. Louis. If Blankenship was targeting him, someone screwed up royally. He didn't get the listeriosis either.

There was a creak from somewhere in the house and my arms snapped up into firing position, exactly the way Dad drilled into my unwilling head.

A shrill woman's voice came up the stairs. "I told you. I saw her go in."

"Stay outside, Mrs. Palladino," said a husky male voice.

"I'm not staying out here alone."

"Stay here."

I heard a gun slide out of a holster. Cop. That was a good news/bad news kind of thing. I really didn't want to have to explain my presence or be slowed down now that something had turned up. On the other hand, at least it wasn't the crazed Christopher-hater.

"Hello," I called out, sticking the Mauser back in my purse. With any luck, I wouldn't be searched.

"Come out where I can see you," ordered the male voice.

"I'm coming out." I walked slowly out onto the second floor landing with my hands up.

It was a cop in uniform with his gun trained on me. Standing next to him was a gaunt woman of about forty-five, wearing skin-tight spandex.

"That's her. I told you. Breaking and entering. That's a crime. I want her arrested," she said.

"I'm not breaking and entering. I have permission to be here from the owner."

"No, you don't."

My hands went to my hips involuntarily. "How would you know?"

"Hands up," said the cop.

I put my hands back up, but now I was irritated. That woman needed to be quiet. She didn't want to mess with me. I had a job to do and I had to do it while smelling like bad sausage and having giant blisters. I did not want a delay of her kind.

"I'm Mercy Watts, friend of Donatella Berry."

"No, she's not. I know Donatella's friends," said Mrs. Palladino.

I groaned. "I live in St. Louis. You wouldn't know me. Can I come down and show you my ID?"

The cop dropped his weapon. "Come on down and we'll get this settled."

"Put your gun up," said Mrs. Palladino. "She could be dangerous."

"I think I can handle it," he said with a sigh.

"Are you sure? Don't you want some backup?"

I walked down the stairs slowly for the cop's benefit, not Mrs. Palladino's. He looked like he'd had a long day without her freaking out more. I stopped at the foot of the stairs next to the newel post. "Can I get out my ID?"

"Go ahead," he said.

I held out my driver's license and he gave it a cursory glance.

"Good," said Mrs. Palladino. "Now arrest her. This private property."

He rolled his eyes and took his radio off his belt. "Unit 33. All clear."

Mrs. Palladino stomped her foot. "It's not all clear. Arrest her."

"I'm not arresting her. That's Mercy Watts," he said, smiling for the first time.

"So what?"

"Haven't you seen her on CNN?"

"I watch Fox News."

The cop holstered his gun. "She's been on there, too."

"As a burglar?" she asked.

"As a detective," he said. "What brings you here, Miss Watts?"

I was tempted to lie. Sometimes it was a reflex, coming from years of fatherly interrogation, but it occurred to me that Christopher's room wasn't something to be kept quiet. It would be needed as evidence. I didn't want to taint that.

"Donatella asked me to come down and look into the source of her children's listeriosis." I gave him a brief outline of my activities and then said, "You probably are going to need backup."

Officer Czuchry went stiff. "What did you find?"

"Christopher Berry's room is trashed and someone has been searching the house," I said.

"Yeah," said Mrs. Palladino, "you."

Czuchry pointed out the door. "Outside. Both of you."

I sauntered by Mrs. Palladino, noting that she wasn't forty-five. She was so thin her face looked older than it was. Up close, I'd put her at thirty. It was depressing.

Czuchry ordered us to stay there and he went upstairs. I leaned on a stately pillar while Mrs. Palladino eyed me with obvious conceit. She thought I was fat. Not just fat, morbidly obese. I'd had that reaction before. Some people saw curves as a disease that must be cured.

"Are you really a detective?" she asked with a hint of interest.

"No."

"What? Why did you say you were?"

"I didn't. I'm a nurse."

She crossed and recrossed her arms. "In a real hospital?"

"No. In porn," I said sarcastically, but she totally bought it.

Officer Czuchry came out, looking freaked. "I called it in. You found it that way?"

"Yep," I said.

"She's in porn," said Mrs. Palladino.

He looked at her for a split second like she'd been speaking Russian, and then went back to me. "Who do you think did it?"

Mrs. Palladino stepped in front of him. "Why are you asking her? She's in porn."

He took her by the arm and put her in his cruiser, calling her a vital witness. She couldn't stop smiling after that. He returned to me and said, "Did you tell her you were in porn?"

"Yes," I said, finishing a text to Uncle Morty who so far hadn't responded.

"Why?"

"I really don't know."

"Well, you can't leave. We'll need a statement and we have to verify your connection to Mrs. Berry." Then he started to fiddle with his radio. "Miss Watts, can I ask you a personal question?"

I wish you wouldn't.

"How personal?"

"What's Nina Symoan like?"

"Oh," I said, crossing my arms. "So you're a Nina fan."

He blushed under his hat brim. Nina Symoan was the wife of Mickey Stix and former cover girl for the band Double Black Diamond. Nina fans were a bit obsessive, but usually sweet.

"Go ahead," I said.

Officer Czuchry went on to pepper me with questions for the next ten minutes until a pair of detectives showed up. They looked at Mrs. Palladino in the squad car and then strolled up to the porch. They were in plain clothes, blue suits and nearly identical striped ties. They may as well have been in uniform.

The taller of the two looked me over. "Well, I never thought I'd see the day."

"What day is that?" I asked.

"Having another Watts in my jurisdiction," he said, sticking out his hand.

I shook it and his partner's hand. "I take it you've met my dad."

"John Truesdale. This is my partner, Robert Sweenie. I met your dad about five years ago on the Gator Bait case."

I nodded sagely, like I knew what case he was talking about. "Do you want me to make a statement? I really need lunch and a nap." I didn't say the truth, which was that I wanted to keep my head start before they had a chance to muck it all up.

"Sure," said Sweenie.

I told them what I told Czuchry. Then I walked them through the house, reiterating that I'd touched absolutely nothing.

"What did you hope to find?" asked Truesdale when we landed back in the foyer.

"I was going to get some samples and have them tested," I said.

"Samples of what?"

"The milk and cereal the kids ate."

"But you don't think that's how they got it."

"No, but it pays to be thorough."

Truesdale tapped his foot and tilted his head. His soft brown hair was greying at the temples and he was rather distinguished. Sweenie wasn't. He was round and sweaty with black-framed glasses that kept slipping down his shiny nose.

"What were you going to do with the samples?" asked Sweenie.

"Have them tested at RDT Analytical Laboratory. My dad arranged it," I said.

"We can't let you do that now. It's a crime scene," said Truesdale.

"No problem. You'll want to run it though, considering the connection to Tulio and the listeriosis."

The detectives glanced at each other. I wasn't going to argue and they weren't sure why.

"Can I come in later to make my statement?" I asked.

Truesdale said I could and gave me his card with the address written on the back.

"Tomorrow at the latest," he said.

"Absolutely." I gave him one of Dad's cards with my address in the Quarter and then called a cab. Surprisingly, one showed up five minutes later and Czuchry walked me to it under the watchful eye of Mrs. Palladino.

I opened the back door and he put his hand on it. "So why didn't you try to get your own samples? A private lab would probably be faster."

"There's no need now." I slid in and closed the door.

Czuchry watched me drive away with a puzzled expression. He seemed like a bright guy and Truesdale certainly was if he worked with dad. They didn't put just anyone with Dad. They'd figure out why I didn't want those samples before the prints were run. This case was about Christopher Berry. He was the target, not his siblings. Next stop, Tulane University.

CHAPTER FOURTEEN

But I didn't go to Tulane. It was four o'clock by the time we drove back into the city and I knew from experience that weaseling information out of Student Services was going to take longer than the half hour I had before the office closed. Uncle Morty still wasn't answering his phone and neither was Pete. I broke down and called Donatella from the cab, but she was in the middle of a crying jag. I didn't have the heart to tell her about her house, much less my suspicions about Christopher. The last thing she needed was another kid in peril. Then I called Truesdale and asked him to hold off on calling her. I gave him Clem's number at Children's, in case he wanted to confirm my story with the nursing staff. He didn't need to call. As soon as I said crying, he was more than happy to wait.

There was no point in wandering around Tulane without knowing where Christopher lived or what his classes were, so I went home. The Quarter was still quiet. The party would start for real in a couple of hours. Maybe I'd take a ghost tour to take my mind off the sound of Donatella's voice. I could still hear it in my head and it wouldn't go away. From what I could understand, the kids were doing okay. The rest of what she said was lost in sobs. I just told her it was going well and that I would be home soon. I don't know why I said that. It sounded soothing at the time, but I had no idea what I was going to find at Tulane, if anything. I was sure Christopher was the key, but that didn't make it simple.

Then the cab turned onto my street and I saw him. Instant recognition. If I could've told the cab to back up and go the other way, I would've. But he saw the cab and me in it. Chuck was leaning on the wall next to Nana's gate. He was unmistakable, even at a distance, with his snug t-shirt and his long legs clad in boot cut jeans. They ended in the new cowboy boots he adored, probably because they added another two inches to his already considerable height. He wore a baseball cap that emphasized his strong features and his smile when he saw me.

Groan. Stevie better be gone. Getting rid of Chuck was almost as hard as getting rid of Aunt Miriam. Which is to say, nearly impossible. I might have to sink so low as to plead women's troubles to lose him. Women's troubles worked great on Dad. He was always afraid that I'd tell him something he didn't want to know, which was anything about anything below the neck. I once said the word mammogram and he ran out of the room.

The cab stopped and I dragged out paying, so I could think of a plan in case Stevie was still in the house. Who was I kidding? He was in the house. I'd have to manually throw him out to get rid of him. And he rented that storage unit in basically his own name. The Costilla brothers would be joining the party in no time. I could just go to a hotel. The Quarter was lousy with hotels.

My cab door opened and Chuck leaned in, filling the cab with his scent of cologne and wintergreen gum. "What're you doing? Thinking up an escape?"

"No," I said with what I hoped passed as honesty. "I'm paying."

Chuck gave the cab driver some twenties and pulled me out. "You've paid. See how quick that was?"

"You're ever so much smarter than me, I guess," I said while trying to brush by him, but he held my arm tight.

"Where are you going so fast?" he asked

"I'm tired and I have to...to feed the cat."

"Your grandparents have a cat? That's weird."

At least I wasn't the only one who thought so.

"Yes, they do. Let go."

He did let go and trailed me to the gate. "Aren't you going to ask me what I'm doing here?"

"I assume it's to bother me," I said, stuffing the key into the lock.

"It is, of course, but I do have other business." He smiled and leaned over me.

"Go and do that."

"Oh, I'll *do* some things," he said.

Ew.

"There're no things here that require doing. Get lost." I yanked opened the gate and he pushed it back closed. It locked automatically. Damn it.

"Aren't you going to ask me in?" he asked, ruffling my hair with his wintergreen-scented breath. "Your nana would ask me in."

"She likes you," I said, sticking the key back in the lock.

"Everybody likes me."

"No, that's Aaron. You probably have hundreds of people who hate you. Criminals, boyfriends of the girls you've seduced."

"I've never seduced anyone's girlfriend. They don't always mention the boyfriend."

"Or the husband."

He nodded. "Or the husband. Especially the husband."

"You are a menace." I managed to open the gate an inch. "Get out of my way."

Chuck grinned. "You're nervous. We are alone in a romantic city."

"*I'm* alone in this city and *you* are alone in this city. *We* are not anything."

"Ask me why I'm here then," Chuck said.

"No."

"Okay. Then I'll show you." He opened the gate, despite my best effort to close it, and walked down the alley. "Don't worry. I know the way."

I ran after him, grabbing his hand. "No, you don't. Get out."

"You're holding my hand. About time."

"Ew." I dropped his hand, but I could still feel its heat.

He laughed and easily out-paced me. I ran into the courtyard and dashed in front of the door, blocking it with my body. "You can't go in there. Because..."

"You're hot for me. I know." Chuck smiled so wide it looked like it hurt.

"No, I'm not and that's not the reason. Pete. Pete wouldn't like it."

Chuck went over and sat on the wall in front of the fountain. He wasn't going anywhere. "I'm sure he wouldn't, but that's not why you don't want me in the house."

"Yes. Yes, it is." I fumbled with the house key and calculated the odds of me unlocking the door and getting in before he got to me. They weren't good.

"There are a couple of reasons you don't want me in the house. I'm me, for one."

I sneered.

"And, for two, Stevie Warnock's in there."

I gasped and he laughed.

"He is not. Don't be ridiculous," I said.

"You thought it was just dumb luck that Stevie ended up here at your nana's house right when you're here? Stevie's not lucky. He's an idiot. We set him up."

Oh my god. I'm the idiot.

"How?" I squeezed out.

"Stevie knows his mother's password. We planted the email from your mom, saying you'd be here, so we could swoop in and nab the moron before he gets himself killed."

"If you knew that I'd be here, why'd my dad and Big Steve send you down?" I asked. "I wouldn't protect Stevie."

"You'd never turn him in to the cops. You've got a soft spot for misfits and fools and Stevie qualifies on both," said Chuck.

"I do not. I've tased him more than once, for heaven's sake."

"And you've let him go more than once. Big Steve wants him brought home immediately."

"What's the point? It's his life."

"It's Olivia that Big Steve is protecting. Word on the street is that he stole from the Costillas. They'll kill him if we don't get him into custody and he needs to surrender in Missouri."

"They'll kill him in jail," I said.

"Come on, Mercy. Stevie's going to end up in prison or dead, one way or another. At home we have a better chance of keeping him alive. He's dead without us. He's a complete idiot."

Before I could confirm Chuck's assessment, Stevie did it himself. He leaned out the second story window and yelled my name. We looked up in amazement. Anybody else would've spotted Chuck, climbed out a front window and ran for it, but not Stevie. How had that guy come from Big Steve and Olivia? His gene pool was stellar, but it was like he forgot to dive in.

Chuck laughed. "You were saying something about not protecting Stevie?"

"Hey, Chuck," Stevie called down. "What are you doing here?"

"Guess," said Chuck.

"You and Mercy finally hooking up? I get it. A little romantic thing down here at Nana's house. It's cool with me. You guys want to go see a movie? How about dinner?"

"Dude, if I was here to get it on with Mercy, why would I want to go to a movie with you?"

"I'm a fun guy."

Chuck shook his head. "See what I mean? Prison or dead. Open the door, Mercy. It's unavoidable."

It was, so I did.

The cat watched us from the top of a bookshelf. Its green eyes glowed in the gloom. Stevie claimed he didn't let it back in and I almost believed him. Stevie could be quite sincere.

"There's something weird about that cat," said Chuck. "How did he get up there? I don't see any claw marks on the shelves."

"I really don't care," I said. "Can you get him for me?"

Chuck took Blackie off the bookshelf and gave him to me. The cat was warm and smooth in my hands and he looked completely unconcerned when I tossed him out the door. He landed gracefully, gave me a sidelong glance, and stalked across the courtyard toward the servant's quarters.

"What's up with that cat?" asked Stevie. "It never meows."

"Why would it meow?" I asked, increasingly worried. I left Stevie alone with Nana's cat. I'd never known him to be violent or cruel. But still, there was a first time for everything. "Did you do something to the cat?"

"I poked it," he said.

"Why?"

"'Cause it's weird. You know it's weird, right?"

"It's a cat."

"Nah. That's a weird cat." He plopped down on the sofa and propped his feet up on the trunk that served as Pop Pop's sofa table. "I gotta eat. Let's go eat."

"You're not eating. You're leaving with Chuck," I said.

"Where are we going?" asked Stevie.

"Back to St. Louis, so the Costillas don't kill you in my nana's house."

"Nah. I'll stay here," he said. "I could use a good po'boy. You want a po'boy?"

"No, I don't want a damn po'boy. I want you two out."

Chuck stifled a laugh and made an effort to drop the glee off his face. Then he sat down and turned on a hockey game. He didn't even like hockey. "I think we'll stay a while. See if we can help you out."

"I don't need any help from either of you. Get out." I didn't mind Aaron, tagging along, so much. He was unobtrusive and came with an endless supply of chocolate. Stevie came with endless stupidity and Chuck came with irritating hotness. Neither were helpful.

Chuck sniffed. "You need help cooking. What is that smell?"

"Stevie made rancid sausages. I made him throw them away," I said.

Stevie burped. "I ate 'em."

I slapped my forehead. "I told you they were bad."

"Nah. They were good. I wonder if I could find that guy again."

"What guy?" asked Chuck.

"The guy that was selling the sausages out of the back of his van."

Chuck crossed his arms. "Give me a description. Do you remember the license plate number?"

"It was Louisiana. Maybe started with a T." Stevie's forehead wrinkled. He might've been thinking. It was the first time I'd seen it happen.

"What are you doing?" I asked.

"Getting a solid description," said Chuck, "so we can find that van."

"So you can turn him in to the health inspector?" I asked, hopefully.

"So we can buy some sausages."

I threw up my hands, went upstairs to my bedroom, and slammed the door so hard the pictures rattled on the walls. How was I going to get rid of those two? I looked out the window and bit my lip. Climbing out might work. There was a stone ledge where I could inch along until I got to the garden wall. I could lure those two outside and then lock them out. That would definitely work with Stevie. I'd managed to lure him into my truck with a hamburger once. Then I tased him and took him to his dad. Chuck was another story. I could probably get him out, but it would take a hot woman to keep him out. While I was looking outside, the cat came sidling across the garden wall, sat on its slim butt, and stared at me.

"You *are* a weird cat," I said.

It yawned. If it hadn't, you would've thought it was stuffed.

My phone rang and made me jump. Uncle Morty. Finally.

"Stop sending me texts," he snarled.

"I wouldn't have to, if you answered," I said.

"Yeah, right. You're such a girl."

"What does that mean?"

"Girls love the hell out of texting. I'm putting it in a book," he said.

"Your books have swords and dragons. Where do cellphones fit in?" I asked.

"I can put a cellphone in, if I want. I'm the damn writer. You want that shit you been bugging me about?"

"Yes." I drew the word out nice and long, just the way he hated.

Uncle Morty growled and gave me a quick rundown. Calvin Donnelly, the science teacher, was at school the whole day of the Tulio shooting so he had no access to Abrielle and Colton. There was no connection between Donnelly, the other Berrys, or Blankenship that Uncle Morty could find, and it pissed him off.

"So we can push Donnelly to the back burner then," I said.

"Hell, no. I'm gonna keep working him," he said.

"Why? Donatella and Rob trusted him with their kid, didn't they?"

"Yeah. Colton was in that science camp, but he's still a good candidate. Scum bag."

I rolled my eyes. Calvin Donnelly was no scumbag and I knew scumbags. "What about Sheila and Rob? Anything there?"

"Big time."

"Tell me they weren't having an affair. I so don't want to tell Donatella that," I said.

"They had a thing. Flirting on email. Questionable compliments. It progressed to low-grade cybersex. Never got to actual sex."

"Gross. Was it still going on at the time of Rob's death?"

"Nope. Sheila made an ass of herself at the Christmas party by rubbing on Rob and Donatella made a scene."

That explained Mrs. Schwartz's expression when I mentioned Donatella. She wouldn't like a scene. She liked perfection no matter how thin the veneer.

"How much does Donatella know?" I asked.

"Only the Christmas party stuff. Rob convinced her that nothing was going on. Sheila was sloppy drunk and everyone blamed it on the punch."

"I'm surprised Donatella didn't check out his phone. She's pretty sharp."

"She might've, but he probably used a disposable cell."

"How do you know they were even having a thing then?"

"Hello, Mercy. Rob was smart, but that idiot girl wasn't. She used her normal phone. I got it all. Texting is freaking wonderful. That sleaze is forever."

"Ick."

"You got no idea. Anyway, Rob broke it off after the party. Said he loved his wife and apologized for being an asshole. Little Miss Sheila couldn't get the time of day out of him after that."

"How'd she take it?" I asked.

"Like a twenty-two-year-old girl. Lots of calling her mother. Shit like that. I'll tell you one thing that chick didn't give up. Sheila thought Rob didn't love Donatella. She thought he didn't want to lose the kids in a divorce."

"Any evidence of that?"

"Nope. All in her head as far as I can see," said Uncle Morty.

"But she believed it. That's the important thing."

He cackled. "Ya damn skippy. You get rid of those kids; you get rid of the wife."

That sounded so cold. Sheila didn't seem like the vicious type. The type to get it on with a married man maybe. But kill his kids? I doubted it.

My door vibrated with a loud banging. "What are you doing in there?" yelled Chuck.

I put my hand over the phone. "I was taking a nap! Thanks a lot!"

"No, you weren't." Chuck paused. "Really?"

And he's the pro detective, paid and everything.

"Yes. You've had girlfriends. They took naps, didn't they?"

"I guess. I'm sorry." Chuck pounded back down the stairs.

For the record, I'm not much of a napper. My mind's too busy. I have to be pretty tired to nap. Chuck's known me since we were kids. He ought to remember Mom forcing me into bed with threats of outing my naplessness to Santa.

"Hey," squawked Uncle Morty. "I ain't got all day."

"Sorry. Where were we?"

"Getting pissed off."

"But that's your normal state," I said.

Uncle Morty surprised me by laughing. "Yeah? Well, you bother me."

"I live to serve. Did you get my text about Donatella's house?"

"Yep and that's an interesting tidbit. Enough to keep me yakking with you instead of at John DiMaggio's table."

"Who?"

"Know your Futurama, girl!"

"I'll get right on that. What about the house?" I asked.

"Alarm was turned off at 2:23 p.m. the day after Tulio happened. And get this, it was done remotely."

"Really? That's interesting. Somebody hacked the security company?" I asked.

"Yep."

"Um...it wasn't you, was it?"

"Shut up."

I laughed. "Any idea who it was?"

"Not yet, but I'll get this dillweed."

He sounded like he took offense at the whole alarm disarming thing. I don't know why. Uncle Morty did it all the time for Dad. He'd do it for me. If I paid him, that is.

"What bothers you about this?" I asked. "You're not above it."

"That's different. Tommy's a stand-up guy. Even you're okay."

"Thanks," I said. "I'm touched."

"Quiet! This dill let in a murderer. I let in the good guys and you."

So I wasn't a good guy. Alright then. At least he didn't say I was bad. Uncle Morty gave me Sheila's address. She didn't have an alarm so I was all set with my trusty lock picks, although I wasn't certain if I'd bother to search her place. Sheila didn't strike me as a hacker or somebody who had the money to pay one.

I hung up and thought it over. Maybe a search of Sheila's place was in order or maybe just a girl-to-girl talk. I could go out to Tulane, but it'd be easier to blend in during the day.

I slipped off my shoes and opened the window. I could do it. No problem.

Don't think about the drainpipe incident. Don't think about the drainpipe incident.

As luck would have it, there was no drainpipe to climb down and eventually fall off, like I had in Honduras. Not one of my finer moments, but this was bound to go better. Chuck and Stevie were watching hockey, and the ledge was a reasonable size if I squinted.

"I'm doing it," I said to the cat.

It hissed and arched its back into a curve that would've made the Gateway Arch jealous.

"It's not that bad an idea."

Bigger hiss.

Whatever cat. I slung my purse over my shoulder and leaned out just as my door banged open. "Going somewhere?" Chuck pointed at me.

I froze.

"I knew you didn't take naps. Your mom used to threaten to duct tape you to the bed."

Ah crap!

I fixed a look of dignity on my face. "I was looking at the weird cat, if you must know."

Chuck walked over and looked out at Blackie, who'd settled down and was cleaning his sleek side. "What about him?"

"I don't know. Nothing. I was just looking."

"Uh, huh. Where were you going?"

"Nowhere." I opened my purse and dug for my favorite lipstick. It was under the Mauser, like always. I proceeded to put on a generous coat. Chuck watched me like I was the last beer on earth.

"I'll take you. I'm pretty good at this," said Chuck in all serious-ness. That was the last thing I expected. He couldn't help me. It wouldn't look good, if we got caught.

"I thought you were here to nab Stevie." I narrowed my eyes at him.

"I am."

"But?"

"But this is a big case. If Blankenship—"

I pushed past him and ran down the stairs.

"Where are you going?" Chuck yelled after me.

I spun around on the bottom stair and he nearly ran me over. "I knew it. You're here to watch me. Dad thought I couldn't handle it without Aaron. Is that it?"

Chuck took off his baseball cap and smoothed his thinning hair. "Tommy has nothing to do with it."

"He knows you're here."

He grabbed me by the shoulders and pushed me gently back against the wall. His scent washed over me and my stomach did a flip. Stupid stomach.

"He does, but you can't be here alone. Blankenship is a mass murderer," said Chuck.

"Blankenship is in Hunt."

"But you think he had a partner. Tommy told me."

"I don't know," I said, avoiding his intense blue eyes.

"Yes, you do. You've got Tommy's instincts. I'm not leaving you here alone. No freaking way."

I struggled in his grasp. "My dad didn't send you?"

"For Stevie, he did."

I didn't know what to make of it. Dad trusted me. That was new.

"So you don't have to stay here."

"I want to stay here. This is where I want to be," said Chuck, his face bending down closer to mine. Oh, no.

Stevie popped his head into the stairwell. "Hey, guys. What's you doing?"

Chuck didn't look up. "Stevie, go away or I'll smack you until you bleed."

"I used Mercy's laptop and there's a ghost tour at eight. What do you say? Let's party down at the Cat's Meow and see us some ghosts."

"Stevie," Chuck's voice took on a threatening growl.

I broke our eye contact. "Great. But no Cat's Meow. I don't do karaoke."

"Karaoke rocks." Stevie did a little uncoordinated hip shake. "Let's do it."

I hooked my arm through his stringy one. "The Costillas might spot you."

"Screw those guys!"

"You know this is how you always get caught," I said.

"You think?"

"Could be."

That puzzled Stevie, like most things. We walked off, leaving Chuck glowering in the stairs. I held back a laugh. He was going to watch me, huh? Fine. So be it. I had Stevie, the human shield. I'd get those two liquored up and slip away while they were sleeping it off. Easy-peasy.

CHAPTER FIFTEEN

The snoring was incredible. It surrounded me, coming up through the floorboards and barreling in through the bedroom door. I didn't know human beings could make such hideous noises with their faces, and I'd spent the night at Uncle Morty's. I called him Captain Cacophony when I was a kid.

The night out on Bourbon Street hadn't gone exactly as I planned. Chuck and Stevie both got ripping drunk, but at separate times. Chuck did it on the ghost tour. Our tour guide made a generous stop at the unhaunted Lafitte's Blacksmith shop and we were all encouraged to buy hurricanes and some purple drink. Chuck had both, chugging them in a dark corner, glaring at me. By the time we were in front of LaLaurie house and listening to fantastic tales of extra limbs being sewn onto people, he was bumping into walls and telling everyone that he loved them, including a lesbian couple, five frat boys, and a bridal party. He even loved Stevie for being so great at being Stevie. I was the only one he did not love. Chuck told me to go jump in the Mississippi and kiss a catfish. Okay. He was very popular. Only Chuck could become more attractive when slobbery drunk. At the end of the tour, the bride was ready to dump her fiancé and run off with that 'tall drink of sexy.'

I would've considered this a great success if Stevie wasn't completely sober. He drank three times as much as Chuck and didn't slur a word. He said he had an Irish liver. My dad boasted of the same thing on a regular basis, and I very rarely saw him drunk. Stevie and I carried Chuck back to Bourbon and propped him in a corner of a bar, where he told me I was mean and then passed out. I couldn't believe it. Chuck was a lightweight. How did I not know that? Stevie, on the other hand, was ready to party. Maybe his brain cells couldn't get saturated with booze because he had so few of them that the alcohol couldn't locate them in his empty head. We karaoked. We danced. I was felt up so many times I got used to it. Stevie was charming in his goofy way and we had people buying us drinks left and right. Mine were virgins and Stevie didn't care. He was too busy, hitting on transvestites and the odd prostitute. He didn't believe either were what they were. Seriously, women don't have calves like that. We just don't.

Stevie finally tipped the scales at two in the morning, but he was so drunk he couldn't help me with Chuck. I had to hire a bouncer named Jerry Curl to carry him home. Jerry dumped him inside the door and he was still there in a heap, laying on the floor. I couldn't manage to drag him to the sofa. Even if I had, I wouldn't have been able to lift him up onto it. So I covered him with a quilt, gave him a pillow and a mixing bowl for the inevitable vomiting, and went to bed. Stevie disappeared somewhere in the house. I might've thought he escaped if it wasn't for the dual snoring.

I gathered up my clothes and opened my creaky door, wincing at the noise. The house was so old that there were no en suite bathrooms. Actually, it started out with no bathrooms at all, just an outhouse at the back of the courtyard. Thank goodness for plumbing.

I crept into the guest bath, closed the door, and pulled back the shower curtain.

Ah crap!

Stevie was asleep in the tub. His gangly limbs hung over the side and his head was propped up against the faucet. I guess a guy like Stevie was used to sleeping in odd places. I left him there and went into Nana's bathroom. I showered and dressed quickly, leaving my hair to dry in ringlets since using the dryer was asking for the guys to wake up.

I found Chuck where I left him, but the mixing bowl was full. Gross. Since he was blocking the main door, I went to the front. That door opened onto the street, but nobody ever used it. I had to scoot a trunk out of the way to get to it, only to find it dead bolted by a key I didn't have. Fantastic. I'd have to escape through a window. Not ideal, but I'd done it before. First, I tried the windows in Pop Pop's room, but they squeaked so loud Chuck started to stir. I hoofed it upstairs and looked out my window. Full circle. I was destined to go out that window.

I got out on the ledge and shinnied across to the garden wall. It was easier than it looked. No wonder Nana made a habit of it when she was a teenager. I stepped, lost my balance and caught myself on the branch of a live oak that was drooping over from the neighbor's garden. When I looked back down at the wall, the cat was sitting directly in my path. He blinked his green eyes but didn't meow or purr or anything. He was so still, I began to wonder if he could make any noise at all. I didn't relish stepping over him, since he probably had sharp claws and might take offense. But he just sat there and watched me tiptoe across the wall toward the servants' quarters. The building butted up against it and I had to be careful. Once I got to the back courtyard, I could climb down the trellis next to the pool.

The trellis looked sturdy so I headed straight for it when I heard whispering.

So close.

"Yes, it is," said a woman in a British accent.

"No, darling. I'm afraid not," said a man, also British.

"I'm telling you that I recognize her."

"You weren't wearing your glasses."

"I was," she said.

"You weren't. That's why you nearly fell into the pool," he said.

"I tripped. It's her."

I sighed and turned to see the older couple that I'd seen the day before, sitting at a table next to the pool. It didn't occur to me that any of the guests would be up at seven, much less outside eating a full breakfast.

"Hello," I said with a limp wave.

They said hello and waved back.

"I'm not a burglar or anything. Don't worry."

"We didn't think you were," said the woman. "You do seem to make a habit of this, I must say."

I walked along to the trellis and tested its bolts. Nice and secure. "A habit of what?"

"Walking on the wall, naturally."

I looked up and frowned. The husband rolled his eyes and said, "I told her it wasn't you on the wall last night, but will she listen?"

"Wait. You saw someone on this wall last night?" I asked.

"Are you saying it wasn't you?" asked the woman.

"It wasn't me. What did they look like?"

"You."

"No, it didn't. It was a man," said her husband as he got up and helped me down the trellis. The two of them introduced themselves as Bea and Jonas, Londoners on a tour of America. They went on to quibble about whether or not it was a man. Bea had no clue. But Jonas gave a description of what could've been a smallish man in a black hoodie and jeans at eleven last night when we were on Bourbon, belting out Bette Midler hits.

I got a little dizzy when they said hoodie.

"Are you feeling unwell?" asked Jonas.

"Did you see where he went?" I asked.

"He walked along the wall in the direction you came from and then he came back about ten minutes later. We were having a nice glass of wine right here and he didn't see us." Jonas sounded completely unperturbed by the situation. I was plenty perturbed. First, the hospital parking lot and now this.

"See anything else odd?" I asked.

"Odd?" asked Bea after sipping her tea.

"Odd, like people climbing over the wall."

Jonas topped off his cup and added a lump of sugar. "Now that you mention it. We were getting ready to go out yesterday morning and I heard someone rattling the gate. It's sturdy and didn't give way."

"Did you see anyone?" I asked.

"No. Only the other guests. Nice boy named Stevie asked me if I wanted some nice sausages, but we had reservations."

"Those sausages were disgusting. They stank up the entire courtyard," said Bea.

"You're sure it wasn't Stevie on the wall?" I asked.

"No. Stevie's taller," said Bea. "It was a woman."

"It was not. That was a man, but not Stevie."

I got the key to the back gate out. "Why aren't you worried about this?"

Jonas shrugged. "We live in London. Nothing surprises us anymore."

I gave him Dad's card and asked them both to keep an eye out. They never asked me why I was using the wall instead of the perfectly good walkway and I didn't volunteer the information. I wasn't sure what I would've said anyway. I left them to their traditional English fry-up. Where they got the black pudding would remain a mystery not worth solving. Millicent insisted I try the stuff when I was six on my first trip to London. If I try hard, I can still taste it. I fear only senility can wipe that particular food memory away. That was one good thing about Aaron not being with me. He wouldn't be inspired by the pudding and make it into a hot dog. Aaron could put anything into a hot dog, and I mean anything. The Christmas morning ham and chestnut dogs will live in infamy.

I shook off that breakfast memory and headed down the street after I made sure no hooded strangers were lurking around. I'd packed my Mauser and some pepper spray, just to be on the safe side. Now it was smart, instead of just paranoia.

The Ruby Slipper Cafe was open with no waiting. I requested a table with a good view of the street and smiled at the guys sitting at the table next to me. I recognized them from Bourbon. It was a Stag weekend and they didn't look like they'd been back to their hotel yet. They each had a bloody mary and trembling hands.

"Hey," said the bridegroom, who was now wearing his shirt backwards. "Do you have any aspirin or maybe a handgun so I can blow my head off?

I have both.

"How about we skip the handgun for now." I gave him my aspirin and the groom's party divided the pills.

"Weren't you with some guys last night?" The best man belched. "How'd they get so lucky? We could barely get you to look at us."

The waitress brought me some more coffee, gave the groomsmen a disgusted look, and took my order. Tasso cream sauce. Thank you, Lord.

"I know them," I said. "Family friends."

"Are you sure about that?" asked the third groomsman. He had a big three on his shirt. At least it looked like a three through the multiple layers of stains he added over the night.

"Well, Chuck wasn't my biggest fan last night."

"The cop," said Number Two. "Yeah, he kept calling you 'that woman.'"

Number Three shook his head. "Not him. The other one."

"Stevie? I can't explain it, but he likes me," I said and it was true. Stevie did like me. Maybe all the times I'd tased him had fried his tiny brain.

"The skinny guy that sings like a chick?"

"That's him."

"No, I mean the other other one," said Number Three.

A little chill went down my arms, raising the hairs to spikes. "I was only with two guys, Chuck the cop and Stevie the Bette Midler wannabe."

The groomsmen's brows furrowed.

"Who was that other guy then?" asked the groom. "He was sticking with you like shit on a shoe."

"Yeah, he was," said Number Two. "He followed you outside when Stevie started to sing *The Rose.*"

"God. I hate that song, but he was pretty good," said Number Three.

The waitress brought my food and it smelled fantastic, better than fantastic, but my appetite was zero. "You were outside, weren't you?" I asked.

"Yeah," said Number Two. "We were talking about something. What were we talking about?"

"Girl bands. What did this guy look like?"

"Oh, yeah. Mel B was hot, like super hot."

"Focus, Number Two. What did the guy who followed me outside look like?"

He took a big drink of his bloody mary and his eyes focused. "He wasn't with you?"

"No."

"Maybe I'm wrong. He was just watching you a lot. There were a lot of people, coming in and out. And let's face it, people watch you. Old guys, young guys, chicks, even."

"But you all thought he was with me?" I asked.

They nodded.

"Who remembers what he looked like?"

Various expressions of puzzlement crossed their faces.

Okay. Don't suggest anything. Let them find the answer.

"What color was he?" I asked.

White was the instant answer. Younger, not like an old married dude came next. Black hoodie and jeans after that. As for his face, they had nothing. I guess it didn't stand out and they were still soused enough that if I suggested a big nose or a scar, they would've thought he had it.

"Do you remember what time you first saw him?" I asked.

Stupid question. They didn't know what time it was, period. And no, they wouldn't recognize him again. Only the obviousness of my face made them remember me. I was, as always, hard to forget. Whoever that guy was wouldn't have had a hard time finding me on Bourbon Street. Ask enough people if they've seen Marilyn Monroe, and you'd have me.

CHAPTER SIXTEEN

The St. Charles streetcar was packed with natives going about their lives and tourists swiveling their heads to catch sight of every stately home. You couldn't look fast enough. There were so many on both sides and interspersed with restaurants and shops that popped up unexpectedly amid the grandeur.

The wooden seat rattled away under my rump and I stopped worrying about the hoodie guy. He wasn't on the streetcar. I'd checked and rechecked. So I allowed myself to relax and remember. Pop Pop loved the streetcars. When we came down to visit, he'd buy me a pass and we'd ride and ride with no particular destination in mind. We might step off on the Loyola campus and walk around. There'd be lunch at a place we spotted through the open windows. It would invariably be down market and frequented by locals and cost about eight bucks. It was always good in its way. I think Pop Pop wanted to make sure I knew life wasn't only lived on the refined Hawthorne Avenue. He didn't resent the Bled family. He liked them very well, but their life wasn't ours. He made that very clear and I didn't mind. I always knew who I was.

The car screeched to a halt in a way that sounded like it was broken. I got off, behind a lady who looked like she'd just finished a twenty-four hour shift in drudgery and cut to the right to walk in front of the stone Tulane sign. No one followed me, but I kept an eye out, the way Dad had taught me, always scanning behind my sunglasses. I'd have to be sharp. The campus was alive with students running to class, campus employees heading to work, and various people who appeared to be out for a leisurely stroll. Security was in evidence. I passed two guards as I went deep into the campus and searched for PJ's, the campus coffee shop that Pop Pop always took me to. It was the way I remembered it, crowded with students studying or avoiding studying. I ordered a latte and went out to sit on the green bench that we always sat on to people watch, except I wasn't people watching in the traditional sense, more like people fearing. I scanned every few minutes and input Christopher's frat address that Uncle Morty sent me, along with his schedule.

The building was close, off on the left side of campus. There wasn't exactly a fraternity row, but most of the houses were on one street, according to Google. I drank my latte and formulated a plot. Christopher was in St. Louis, so I'd say I was there to check that no one had gotten ill. I might not have to say anything at all. In my experience, fraternities weren't as closed off as sororities. After all, the girls were lovely targets for Richard Speck types and the guys were only good for playing beer pong.

I mapped out my route to the frat and then strolled through campus past the science buildings and then the dorms. There were plenty of Christmas lights still up in the windows and various signs like, "Call your mother" taped to the glass. My nursing school experience had been much more sedate. My school was attached to the hospital and security was high. No parties. No Christmas lights. Dad loved it. He considered student nurses to be a high value target so we must be locked down.

The area by the dorms was mostly empty, broad expanses of green lawns. I was alone. Somehow that made me feel awfully exposed and nervous, more nervous than when I'd been in the crowds by PJ's. Then a man came around the corner and I jerked back at his sudden appearance. He wasn't wearing black at all and I relaxed. He was a brother in a long white cassock with the traditional beaded belt and large wooden cross. That's where tradition ended. He was also wearing neon green Nike tennis shoes and a John Deere baseball cap. He smiled at me when we crossed paths and I felt safe again in a world where brothers like John Deere caps.

I exited the campus and joined the hubbub on the street. Cars were honking as students darted in front of them and ran for the campus. Delivery trucks pulled up onto the sidewalk and the drivers hauled open their big metal doors with grinding clangs. Much better than the quiet of the dorm area. Down the street I saw Christopher's frat without trying. It was hideous and funny at the same time. The house was a two story, craftsman style, probably built in the thirties. There were wide concrete stairs down to the cracked sidewalk and they were painted in thirds, green, red, and orange. The house's pillars were painted like barber poles and there were fake palm trees on the front porch and part of the lawn. The roof was missing some shingles. Half the windows were cracked and most of them were covered in what looked like beach towels instead of shades. Next door was a well-mannered sorority house. If it had a nose, it would've been wrinkled in distaste at its garish neighbor.

I stopped in front and lowered my glasses. "Wow."

Two girls passed me, overburdened with enormous backpacks. They'd come out of the sorority and glanced up at Christopher's house with sneers.

"Don't go in there," one hissed at me.

"Why not?" I asked.

"They're being investigated."

"Really? For what?"

The other girl drew back and said before hurrying away, "What do you think?"

Overwhelming roach infestation? Underage drinking? Hazing? I had no idea what they'd be investigated for if it wasn't the normal stuff. Girls could be so difficult sometimes.

I walked up the stairs, dodging beer cans and a couple of bongs, and wondered if Donatella had actually seen where Christopher was living. The front door was locked so I knocked, even though it didn't look like a knocking kind of joint. To my surprise, the door opened and I was face-to-face with one of the most straight-laced guys I'd ever come across and that's saying something, since I was dating Pete. The guy wore pressed khakis, a snow-white polo, and heavy-rimmed black glasses. His skin was flawless and he showed zero surprise at my appearance.

"Can I help you?" he asked in a soft New Orleans accent.

I smiled broadly. "I hope so. I'm here about Christopher Berry and the illness in his family."

His smooth brow furrowed under his sleek brown hair. "Christopher's in St. Louis."

"I know. That's why I'm here." I held out my hand. "Mercy Watts and you are?"

"Toby Granger. I can't tell you anything. We believe in privacy here."

Please.

"Sure you do. I assume you know what happened at Tulio."

"Tulio?"

"The restaurant in St. Louis where his father was murdered," I said.

Toby swallowed hard. "Yeah. I know about that. Have you seen Chris?"

Best not to lie in such moments. I didn't even know what Christopher looked like. "No. I'm friends with his mom, Donatella. They're spending their days in the PICU with Abrielle and Colton."

"Are they okay? I heard they were really sick."

"They are. How well do you know Christopher?" I asked.

He shrugged and, I swear, his polo crackled. "A little. I'm a junior. Look, I've got to go." He didn't move or invite me in. I'd been counting on the frat guys not really caring what happened. Toby cared. Damn him.

"Okay. Look. Are you perhaps pre-med?" I asked.

"How'd you know that?"

"Educated guess. I'm a nurse. What do you know about listeriosis?"

He stared at me, so nothing. I gave him a quick rundown and then asked, "Can I come in? It's getting hot out here."

Toby sighed and opened the door wide. "Sure, but I have class in fifteen."

I walked in and was surprised at how clean it was. The wood floors were shiny if a little scarred from use. No beer can pyramids or trashed furniture in the hall or in the TV room where Toby brought me. It was cheap particle board furniture, but nice. I guess they kept their crazy outside. Toby offered me a seat on a well-worn sofa but didn't sit down himself. Message received.

"So, did you see Christopher on the day his father was murdered?" I asked.

"Probably. I don't remember," said Toby.

"Do you perhaps remember seeing his brother and sister on that day? I believe their mother brought them here before they flew to St. Louis. She's rather striking."

"Oh, yeah. I guess I did. It was in the afternoon. I was going out to my Calc three study group."

"Did you notice anything odd when they were here? Strangers hanging around the house? Stuff like that."

"No, but I wasn't really paying attention. Everything was fine," said Toby, shuffling his feet and looking at his watch.

"How was Christopher doing? Any problems?"

Toby's eyes shifted to the left before he answered and I perked up. "No, no, he's fine."

"So no problems whatsoever?" I asked, making sure I focused hard on him.

Another shift to the left. "No. Nothing."

"Do you have any problems with Christopher?"

He looked me right in the eyes. "No. He's a good kid." He said that a little strongly, like someone might disagree.

There was movement in the hall, a brief flash of an arm. I hesitated, but they didn't come in. I had the strong impression they were standing there, listening.

"I really have to go," said Toby.

"Just a couple more questions," I said. "What's going on with the house? Some girls came by and told me that you're being investigated."

Toby flushed, his cheeks turning tomato red in an instant. "People say lots of things. Nothing's going on. Nothing big."

I watched him silently without blinking.

"We had a party. We're a frat. We have parties. It's not our fault if underage assholes come in and get wasted."

"And that's it?"

"What else could there be?"

"Something with Christopher perhaps," I said with a winning smile, the one that had been known to disarm men much more experienced then young Toby. But I'd left it too late, an error on my part. I should've batted my eyelashes at the beginning. Dad would be so disappointed in my lousy timing. Toby was already too agitated to fall for my face and he just wanted to escape.

"I have to go." He went for the door and I wasn't going to talk him out of it.

"That's fine, but I need to take a look at Christopher's room."

He stopped in his tracks. "What for?"

"Just a look-see. His siblings were poisoned with listeriosis. I'm supposed to find out where it came from."

"It didn't come from here," he said.

"How do you know?" I asked.

"Nobody else is sick. I told you already."

"So what will it hurt to let me take a look? Maybe the guy in the hall could take me up."

"What guy?"

"The one hovering by the door, listening to our conversation," I said, still smiling.

Toby flushed harder and walked into the hall. "Derek, what are you doing?"

A bulky kid with a good set of pimples stepped into the doorway. "Sorry. I was curious." He glanced at me and I realized his red face was about me not about being caught eavesdropping.

"I was just going." I stood up slowly and tossed back my hair. I really had no shame. I needed to get into Christopher's room and that kid could get me there.

I walked over to Toby, while keeping my purse back out of his line of sight, and pulled one of Dad's cards out. I held it low by my hip and slipped it to Derek as I passed. Then I thanked Toby for his help and sallied out the door with a good hip swing for Derek's benefit. With any luck, I'd be back with a quickness.

Toby lied. He did not have class in fifteen or even in thirty. It took a painful forty-five minutes for my straight-laced obstructionist to leave the house. Minutes I spent standing on the corner next to a bar covered in band flyers and questionable substances. I hadn't been to a college bar since the Byers case and I hadn't missed it. There were five separate vomit spots along the front wall that someone had made a cursory attempt at washing away. The strong wee smell wasn't helping my mood either. To be fair, the smell wasn't much different than Bourbon Street and the surrounding blocks, but I found Bourbon much more diverting. At least there was music and interesting, if odd, people to watch. Toby made me stand in the muggy New Orleans sun, smelling vomit and getting hit on by delivery guys who thought their tongues were somehow enticing. Not so much. I could've kicked that over-starched liar in the shin. Get out.

And then he did. Toby walked out of the front door with a back-pack, that was either brand new or ironed, and walked off toward the Science Buildings on campus. I waited until he vanished around the corner before I crossed the street to try my luck with Derek, who answered the door after one knock. He'd been waiting, a very good sign for me.

I stuck out my hand. "Mercy Watts, daughter of Tommy Watts."

"I know," he said breathlessly.

"Because of the card?"

"Because of you. I'm a criminal justice major."

Sweet.

"I see, and you overheard me talking about Christopher?"

"Sorry, but I had to know why you were here." Derek led me back into the TV room and closed the door behind us. "I saw you out the window, talking to those girls. I couldn't believe Mercy Watts was at my frat. I about freaked the fuck out. Sorry. I shouldn't have said that."

"It's fine. Toby was pretty evasive. I could call Christopher's mom and ask her what's going on, but I'd rather not, if I don't have to."

"I don't think she knows."

I gave him the full Marilyn wide-eyed smile and this time it wasn't too late. Derek blushed like crazy and started stammering. Okay. Maybe I laid it on a tad too thick.

"Knows what?" I asked.

"We're not supposed to talk about it, but since it's you, I think it'll be all right."

"It's more than alright. I need to know and so do the police."

"Christopher was charged with rape," whispered Derek.

I almost fell over. My knees actually went weak, and they never do that. I have rock-solid knees. I groped for a chair and dropped into it just the way my godmothers taught me never to do. "By who?"

"Faith Farrell. But he didn't do it. She's crazy."

How many times had I heard that? Too many to count.

"What makes you say that?" I asked in what I hoped was an even tone.

"She's a psycho. She was stalking him."

"Did Miss Farrell report this to the police?"

Derek frowned. "I don't think so. No regular cops ever came. Chris had to go talk to the campus police about it, though."

"What happened?"

He shrugged. "Nothing. He didn't do it."

Campus police. Great. Why they were ever allowed to decide anything on a rape case was beyond me. Some schools even allowed student courts to decide whether or not an assault had taken place. And people wondered why girls didn't want to report rapes.

"When did this happen?" I asked.

"I don't know when she said it happened," said Derek.

"Okay. When did she accuse him?"

"Christopher got called to campus security in December. I think it was before finals. Could've been the second week. I heard you talking about the Listeriosis thing with Chris's brother and sister. What's this got to do with that?"

"I'm not sure. Maybe nothing. Did Christopher have any problems with anyone?"

"Besides Faith? No."

"Nobody threatened him? Was there anyone hanging around the house that shouldn't have been?" I asked.

"No. Everything was regular. We all thought the rape thing was bullshit."

"But some people didn't agree?"

"Just some of the girls around." Derek rolled his eyes. "They love drama and pumpkin spice lattes."

I grinned at him. "You've got us pegged. How about Faith? Drama girl?"

"I don't really know her. She was around at the beginning of first semester and then she wasn't. No big deal," he said.

"Do you remember when you stopped seeing her? It could be important."

Derek got out his phone and looked through some things. "October."

"Really?" I didn't expect him to know.

"Yeah. She was at our Halloween party, but she wasn't at sexy savages."

"Huh?"

He came over and kneeled next to my chair, holding his phone in front of me. "Here she is. The French maid in the back."

The group shot had twelve people in it. Faith stood far off to the left, not really part of the group. She was tall and curvy with dark brown hair cut in a pageboy style. Her smile was plastered on and she looked uncomfortable in her sexy getup, while everyone else hammed it up.

"Is Christopher in this picture?" I asked.

"That's him." Derek pointed to a gangly redhead that reminded me of Prince Harry, but not as good-looking. He was definitely Donatella's son, curls and all. Two identical blonds, wearing Cleopatra costumes, were hanging all over him and he was loving it.

"Who are the Cleos?" I asked.

"Rory and Rachel. They're twins and they love redheads."

"So they were with Christopher that night?"

"Oh, yeah. Big time."

I got out my phone and typed in the names and dates that Derek repeated for me.

"What was this sexy savages thing?"

"Thanksgiving party. You know sexy savages and pimping pilgrims. It's kinda stupid."

"And Faith wasn't there?"

Derek showed me all the pictures he had of that night and it was pretty stupid. Any excuse to drink, right? Faith wasn't in any of his pictures. Of course that didn't mean she wasn't there. Derek might not have seen her. There were plenty of shots of Christopher though with the twins again. They were half-dressed as pilgrims. Christopher was a savage in a loincloth.

"Any parties after that?" I asked.

We went through all the pictures Derek had taken since then and Faith wasn't there. Maybe she'd run into Christopher somewhere else, but Derek didn't think so. The pledges stuck pretty close together. They did cleaning details and cooking, plus they had to study group, but he admitted that they weren't joined at the hip.

"Were you here when Christopher's mother came the day his father died?" I asked.

"No. I have three back-to-back classes on Friday afternoons. My schedule sucks."

"And nobody in the house has been sick?"

"Nope."

I stood up. "I need to see Christopher's room."

Derek's eyebrows shot up. "What are you looking for?"

"No idea. Probably nothing, but Abrielle and Colton were here. I have to look."

Derek pumped his fist. "Let's do it."

We used the back stairs, so no one would see us and went into Christopher's room. Derek said I was there at the right time. Most everyone was in class or out getting lunch. The house would get busy in a couple of hours.

Christopher's room was tiny, more like a walk-in closet with clothes strewn everywhere. He had a single bed and posters of cars and various movies pinned to the walls and ceiling. There was something about that room. It was messy and all guy, but I had the sense that there was a clue buried in the mess. This was the last stop for Abrielle and Colton before the airport. Something happened in that room. I could feel it. I just had to find it.

Christopher had a little dorm fridge stocked with only some cheap beer and Red Bull. No open containers. I rifled through his drawers and the papers on his desk. I found a half-empty box of ribbed condoms and some pictures of the twins, naked. Nice. But no sign of Faith, pictures, cards, or a mention of her in his papers. Derek said Christopher had a laptop, but it wasn't there. I assumed he took it and his phone with him to St. Louis. If there was any evidence of a connection to Faith, it would be there. Moreover there was no food, certainly no food that could've been contaminated with bacteria and eaten by the kids. Damn. Now I had a new possible crime and no evidence in the old one. Fantastic. Job well done.

"Are you finished?" asked Derek, looking vaguely disappointed.

I was missing something. I should've found some sort of clue. It was there. It had to be.

"Sadly, yes. I'm not seeing anything."

We left the room and headed back down the stairs. Now I'd have to look into the rape. No avoiding it. Someone hated Christopher Berry and who was a better candidate than a possible rape victim? Nobody. That's who. Crap on a cracker. I'd rather dive headfirst into a dumpster than find evidence that Donatella's son was a rapist.

"Wait," I said. "We have to go back."

"Why?" asked Derek.

"Dumpster."

"Huh?"

"Where's the trash? Did you see a basket in Christopher's room?" I asked.

"Oh shit!" Derek ran up the stairs past me.

I chased him yelling, "Don't touch it!"

Derek stopped in the middle of Christopher's room with his hands up. He listened to me. That was so rare, I was speechless for a minute.

"I didn't touch anything," he said.

"Wow. Good." I looked around, not seeing any trash basket or any trash. "He had a basket or can, right?"

"I think so. Should we look?"

"Yes, but I have a feeling. There's—"

"A Tommy Watts kinda feeling," said Derek, buzzing with excitement.

"You've heard about my dad's intuition then?"

"It's legendary. You have it, too?"

"Sometimes. If we find the trash, don't touch it."

Derek and I went through the room systematically, starting at the window and working our way to the door. I found it at the foot of the bed. The covers had been thrown off and draped over the footboard. In the corner was a small wire trash basket, full but not overflowing.

I got out my phone and snapped several pictures. So did Derek, to my amusement. There wasn't much to see: four crushed beer cans, a couple of Red Bulls, and lots of crumpled paper.

"Anything?" asked Derek.

"Not so far." I used my pen to shift the contents. Under the cans, I saw a bit of pleated paper. A little more shifting revealed crumbs.

"Do you see something?" Derek loomed over me, blocking the dim light from the overhead lamp.

"Cupcake wrapper."

If that cupcake was our culprit, the kids must've split it. That thing must've been loaded with bacteria to have the effect that it did.

I took a close shot of the wrapper and encouraged Derek to do the same. He was so happy and I started to get why Dad loved mentoring. Derek was so damn excited.

I dug out Truesdale's card and texted him a picture of the cupcake wrapper. He called me in two seconds flat. You gotta love cellphones.

"Don't touch it," he said as an opener.

"I'm not going to touch it. Do you think I'm an idiot?"

Truesdale ignored that question and pelted me with others about how I found it, how I got in, etcetera.

"Look, I didn't do anything illegal. One of Christopher's frat brothers let me in. We found the wrapper together. I was in his company the entire time. Remember, I'm not an agent of the police. I'm doing a favor for a friend. This is clean."

Derek beamed at the word "we."

Truesdale grumbled a bit and then said a unit was on the way. Tulane wasn't in his jurisdiction. The New Orleans cops would handle it.

"Do you have good cooperation with them?" I asked.

"Sure. I sent Vicky Cortier over. She was part of the Gator Bait case, too. Sit tight."

"We're not going anywhere." I hung up and gave Derek a recap.

"So what do we do now?" he asked.

"Nothing. Cortier will collect the evidence and we'll tell her what happened."

His face fell. "What about us?"

"What about us?" I asked.

"What do we do next?"

We? Oh, right. I said "we." Great.

"You are going to figure out what to say to Toby. He's going to be pissed that you let me in."

I expected him to get all worried, but instead he said, "I don't care. Someone tried to murder Chris's family and we just found a clue. Toby can suck it."

"Alright then. No fear. I like that." And I did, too. Unfortunately, it meant I had another guy to deal with. Chuck and Stevie were bad enough. But Derek was a good kid and intimidating if you paid attention to his size, not his pimples. There was the hoodie guy to worry about and it might not be a bad idea to have someone in tow as long as it wasn't the two I'd left behind. Neither of them took orders. "Okay. I'm going to call Donatella to ask Christopher about this cupcake. You're going to see if you can find out where Faith Farrell lives."

"No problem. I'll call my friend Olivia. She'll know." He went into the hall to track down Olivia and I girded my loins to call up Donatella.

Please don't let her be crying. And please don't let me make her cry.

Donatella answered with a surprisingly strong voice. I went ahead and told her about Christopher's trashed room, because I had to tell her at some point, and she took it well. I guess, compared with every-thing else she had to deal with, a vandal in her house was a minor annoyance. I asked to talk to Christopher and she handed the phone over to her oldest child.

"Hello," he said in deep husky voice.

"Hi. Are you in a room with your mother?" I asked.

"Yeah."

"Step outside where she can't hear you."

"Why?"

"Just do it. We're going to talk about Faith Farrell."

Silence and then he whispered, "Okay."

"Did you do it?" I asked in an angry voice that surprised me. Was I angry? I didn't know.

"No. Hell no."

It was a good instant answer. No hesitation whatsoever and I felt a little weight come off my chest. Not all the weight, just a little.

"Okay. We'll leave that for now. Tell me about the cupcake wrapper in your trash."

"Who said you could search my room?"

"Someone poisoned your siblings. Do you really want to quibble about privacy?"

"I guess not," he said, all resentful teenager.

"So I found a cupcake wrapper in your trash. Where'd it come from?"

"How the hell should I know?"

"It's in your trash."

"I didn't put it there," he said, indignant.

Derek popped his head back in and gave me a thumbs up. I returned it and told him to ask anyone in the house if they knew anything about a cupcake in Christopher's room. Another thumbs up. Excellent.

"You're sure you didn't eat a cupcake recently?" I asked Christopher.

"I'd remember if I ate a cupcake. I'm not stupid."

"I know you're not stupid, but the trauma of the last few days could make you forget. You've had bigger things to worry about."

He was silent and I sensed that he was holding back tears. The moment was uncomfortable for the both of us. I hated making him answer questions in the hospital feet away from sick siblings with his father in the morgue, but it had to be done. I just wished it'd fallen to someone else.

"I'm sorry for what's happened, Christopher. But your mother has asked me to do this for her, and I'm going to chase it to the end. I have to ask you about all of it."

"Okay," he squeaked out, his voice an octave higher.

"So you didn't eat a cupcake. Was there one in your room? Maybe somebody gave you one?"

"I don't think so. I don't really like cupcakes that much. What kind was it?" he asked.

"Looks like chocolate."

"I don't like chocolate."

"Tell me you're not serious," I said.

He chuckled a bit. "I'm serious. No chocolate. Everybody knows I don't like it. My girlfriend in high school made me a shirt that said it."

Not everybody knew. Someone very important didn't.

"Give me the sequence of events the day your mom came by to pick up the picture you drew for your grandparents. Start with waking up."

Christopher went through his day step-by-step and it was undeniably boring. Typical day in college. It got interesting when it came to Donatella's visit but only because I'd found the wrapper. Christopher said he ran into his mom and siblings as they arrived at the house. He was coming back from class. They went into the TV room and he sent his brother and sister up to his room to get the drawing, which was lying on his bed. They brought the picture down, everybody hugged, and Donatella and the kids left. Christopher said he hadn't been in his room since that morning. He didn't lock his door. Anybody could've gotten in there and left the cupcake.

"You think it was poisoned?" he asked in a voice that dripped with doubt.

"I think the bacteria came from somewhere and this cupcake is awfully suspicious."

"Then..."

"Then you were the target. Yes. That's what I think. Let's talk about Faith."

"Do we have to?" He sounded much younger than eighteen, a little boy caught out.

"I'm afraid so."

"You're not going to tell my mom, are you? She can't handle it. She'll freak out."

I walked over to the window and saw a woman dressed in a slouchy suit get out of a blue sedan that had motor pool written all over it. Cortier had arrived. I didn't have much time left.

"Your mom's going to find out, but I'll put it off as long as I can. Tell me the story. The cops are here."

Christopher's tale was awash in clichés. He met Faith Farrell at a party. They hooked up. She was the clingy girl, average girl. He was the hot guy with other girls to do. She wouldn't leave him alone. He ignored her until she did. There was no breakup or even a date, just sex and drinking. It was nothing to Christopher, but I suspected it was everything to Faith. Christopher claimed he was shocked when he was called into the campus police on a rape charge. He told his side and it went away. He made it sound simple. Nothing is that simple.

He'd had no other problems. No fights. No enemies. No enemies that he knew of that is. Christopher didn't consider Faith an enemy and he wasn't particularly angry about the charge. He called her crazy and that was it.

I told him that I'd be texting my dad and to expect him soon. I gave him a warning about Dad and bullshit. He wasn't a fan, and Christopher wouldn't like the reaction if he tried to hold out on Tommy Watts. The boy was glum when we hung up and I didn't blame him. If he had any secrets, my dad would find them.

I texted Dad the basics and he replied with, "On it."

Cortier stepped into the room as I finished and stood there, looking at me with a puzzled expression. She was an older lady with auburn hair, no makeup, and smile lines that made her appear jolly despite the serious look on her face. "Well, I'll be damned. It really is you."

"It is," I said.

"Alright. Run it down for me."

I told the detective everything, except the things I didn't want to tell her. I sort of forgot about Faith. She just slipped my mind. Derek stood there, watching our interview and wisely said nothing. I was beginning to really like that guy. He backed me up on everything and we watched as Cortier bagged the cupcake wrapper and the rest of the trash.

"You don't know if the Berry kids ate it?" she asked.

"I will in about a half hour."

"Why a half hour?"

"I told my dad."

She smiled. "Ah. I give it fifteen." Then she raised an eyebrow. "Anything else you want to tell me?"

Want is a no. Should is a yes.

"What are you looking for?" I asked, giving her the big eyes.

Cortier chuckled. "You are your father's daughter."

Derek lifted his lip in scorn and she chuckled again. "In attitude, not looks. You two may as well tell me what you're hiding. I'll find out anyway."

I'll keep my head start. Thank you.

"I don't know what you mean," I said.

"Your father isn't the only one who has feelings."

"No one is as accurate."

"I can't argue with that, but this investigation just kicked into high gear. Withholding information isn't going to look good."

I smiled. "You want me to do all the work for you?"

"You *want* to do all the work, unless I miss my guess. Your father's the same way. Control freak."

That wasn't the first time I'd heard Dad described that way, but it was a first for me and it stung a little. I was the good one when it came to control. Years of being ordered around will do that, but this was my job first. Mine. Mine. Mine.

"There's nothing I can do that you can't," I said.

"Have you seen you?"

"You've got the badge."

She switched her gaze to Derek. "What about you?"

"I wasn't here that day. One of the other guys might know who brought in the cupcake." Derek neatly moved the conversation away from us to the investigation. Nice. Cortier didn't miss that, but she decided we were hopeless. I've been thought of that way many times.

"Who would've been here that Friday afternoon?"

Derek listed the most likely candidates as I edged closer the door.

"Where do you think you're going?" asked Cortier.

"Lunch. I'm starving," I stuck with the truth, at least a partial one.

"You expect me to believe that you eat?"

She thought I was skinny. I didn't get that very often. She should talk to Mrs. Palladino. That woman didn't eat.

"I eat plenty. And it's time to head out. You need anything else from me?"

"I do, but I'm not going to get it."

Correct.

"I'll do anything I can to help," I said.

"No, you won't," she said with a hint of bitterness.

I crossed my arms. "I gave you the murder weapon and the intended victim. You had nothing until I showed up."

She glowered at me. "Get out."

And I did with a big fat grin on my face.

CHAPTER SEVENTEEN

Derek knocked on Faith Farrell's dorm room door and we waited. Getting into the dorm was easy. Everyone knew Derek, and a girl let us in with no questions asked. Probably not the best idea for security reasons, but great for me.

"Are you sure this is her room?" I asked when no one answered.

"That's what Olivia said," said Derek. "You could leave a note."

A note about rape. Not going to happen. A couple of girls came down the hall, carrying heavy loads of books and weary expressions.

"Excuse me," I said. "Is this Faith Farrell's room?"

Both girls wrinkled their noses slightly and the one on the right said, "Not anymore."

"She moved?"

"I guess."

"Any idea where she moved to?"

The girl on the left rolled her eyes and unlocked her room, disappearing inside without saying anything. The other girl shrugged. "She was just gone after Christmas."

"And you didn't care to find out where she went." I couldn't keep the edge out of my voice. Maybe nursing school was different, but I knew everyone on my floor right down to their shoe size and preferred alcohol.

"Why would I?" she asked, genuinely puzzled.

"She lived three doors down."

"That didn't make us friends."

"Does her roommate still live here?" I asked.

"Sure." She edged into her room. Interest over. "Nice makeup, by the way. Are you like a pro or something?"

"I'm not wearing any makeup."

She frowned and stepped back out to get a closer look. "Holy shit. You're not. So how did you," she made a sweeping gesture, "do all that?"

"It's the family face," I said. "Who was Faith's roommate?"

"Anne Marie Murphy."

She was still peering at my face. Looking for what, I had no idea, but it was odd and uncomfortable. I snapped my fingers and she refocused on my eyes, instead of my lip line. "When will Anne Marie be back?"

She called into the room and the other girl said Anne Marie had back-to-back labs, and then she would be working at the school paper. She'd be back late. Interesting how they knew everything about Anne Marie and nothing about Faith.

"What's her shoe size?" I asked.

The girl popped out an eight without hesitation. Faith's shoe size? She had no clue. Weird. She did know the name and room number of their resident advisor. Peaches Skelton on the third floor. I didn't know girls got called Peaches anymore.

The girl went in her room hastily before I could ask any more questions. I stood there for a second, mulling the encounter over. It wasn't what I would've expected at all. Girls are gossips in my experience. Why didn't she want to spill it all about Faith, a girl who accused a popular frat boy of rape? If that wasn't ripe for the rumor mill, I didn't know what was.

"That was kinda weird," said Derek, picking a pimple on his chin.

"You don't know either of them?"

"They haven't been to any of our parties."

"Well, let's go visit the RA and see what Peaches has to say."

We headed down the hall and I heard the door to the stairs slam. I whipped it open and sprinted down the stairs with Derek close on my heels. I caught a glimpse of brown hair on the stairs below us. I leapt down the rest of the flight, cornering with the help of the metal handrail, and caught the guy at the entrance where he got tangled up with some other students trying to come in. He attempted to squeeze between two girls carrying multiple pizzas, and I snagged him by the grey hoodie.

He shot out one arm and hit a stack of pizzas, which tumbled to the floor.

"Hey, asshole," the girl yelled, diving down after them.

"You are such a freak, Grayson," said the other girl.

Grayson made a break for the door, but I'd wrapped his hoodie around my hand and he was going nowhere fast.

"Let go," he yelled.

"Forget it, Grayson," I said, pleasantly. "We're going to have a little chat."

"Tell him to stop being a freak," said the girl who'd dropped the pizzas.

The girls stomped up the stairs after giving Grayson venomous looks and Derek got in front of him. He towered over our captive, but Derek wasn't all that large. Grayson was pretty small for a guy. He was barely taller than me, maybe five foot five, and delicate with slender wrists and narrow shoulders. I felt hefty next to him, not something that happens with guys very often. He could be the one Jonas and Bea saw on Nana's garden wall. Size was hard to gauge from a distance and personal feelings about size do factor into a witness's impressions.

I gave Derek a don't-let-him-get-away look and let go of Grayson's hoodie. "Why are you following me?"

Grayson's brown eyes lost their fear and went blank. "I wasn't following you."

"Oh, really. Why'd you run?"

He looked at the well-worn Vans on his feet and said softly, "I'm not supposed to be up there."

"Up where?" asked Derek.

His voice got even softer. "On Faith's floor."

Derek raised his eyebrows and flushed with excitement. "Why not?"

Grayson tried to dart away, but Derek caught him by the arm easily. He squirmed and said, "Peaches told me not to. Okay?"

He wasn't my guy. I guess that would've been too easy. "What did you do to Faith?"

"Nothing. I just liked her. Okay?"

"Apparently, it wasn't okay. What did you do?" I asked.

"I just talked to her. It was no big deal."

It was a big deal if the RA had to intervene, but that wasn't my concern at the moment. "So you were listening to us talk. What's up with that?"

"I heard you mention Faith before you went inside. I thought you might know where she is. That's all," said Grayson, a bit defiantly.

"Why didn't you ask around?"

"I did. Nobody will say anything about Faith and I'm not exactly popular, in case you didn't pick that up."

"I picked it up just fine. Why is everyone protecting Faith?" I asked.

Grayson snorted. "Protect Faith. Nobody protected Faith. If they did, she'd still be here."

"Then why don't they tell you where she went?"

"Because they like me even less than they like her."

"What were they supposed to protect her from?"

We stopped talking as a group of guys came down the steps. They casted curious glances at us and left.

"You already know," said Grayson when the door closed.

"I do," I said. "Did you want to protect Faith?"

"Of course I did. Faith was the only one around here that under-stood me or anything worth understanding and that fucking frat boy..." He turned away, his eyes reddening.

"Would you like to kill him?" I asked.

"Yeah, I would. He's the son of a bitch who—" Then he stopped. "Did something happen to Chris Berry?"

"Do you know him?"

"I've seen him. Did something happen? Is that why you're here? Who are you?"

"You don't know?" asked Derek, clearly astonished. "She's Mercy Watts. She's a famous detective."

Grayson jerked backwards, knocking against the wall. "He's dead. I'm fucked for sure."

"He's not dead."

He stuck his finger in my face. "Then he should watch his back. I'm going to beat the shit out of him the next—"

Derek started laughing. "Come on, man. You couldn't beat up a twelve-year-old girl."

Grayson shoved me into Derek and darted past us, slamming open the door. I lunged for the door but stopped. Grayson was small, but quick, and already out of sight.

"I'm sorry," said Derek, hanging his head. "I shouldn't have laughed. It was just so stupid."

"Don't worry about it."

"He really is a freak, isn't he?"

"I suspect so. Let's go see Peaches." I went up the stairs, and I could practically hear the wheels turning in Derek's head. Grayson was a very nice suspect. He knew about the rape and something was off about him, but he hadn't been hanging around the frat house. He'd been at Faith's dorm.

"Derek, do you know his last name?"

"That guy? No."

I stopped on the stairs and faced him. "I need you to go find out. Try the girls we talked to before."

"What makes you think they'll talk to me?" he asked.

I smiled at him in my most winning way. "Nothing, but you have to start interviewing sometime if you're going into law enforcement."

Derek grinned up at me, full of confidence, just like a guy who's never been spit on, drugged, or chased by dogs. That would be me. He'd be safe with girls who carried *A Handbook to Literature* and French dictionaries.

"What else should I find out?" he asked, not doubting that he could.

"Where he lives? The problem with Faith? Anything and every-thing. Call me when you have it?" I said and trotted up the stairs to the third floor. Derek would probably get the basics, but mostly I needed to get rid of him. As helpful as he was, I didn't think an RA was going to say squat to me about a rape with a guy from his frat there. She'd have to be the world's worst RA and stuck with a name like Peaches, she couldn't be.

I was right about Peaches, sort of. She was a good RA and a careful one. It took me ten minutes to talk my way in. I'm sorry to say it was a video of Dad on Dateline that did the trick. Peaches loved that Lester Holt, and she was about as big as the anchorman at a good six two. I assumed when she opened the door, and completely filled it, that the name Peaches was one of those cruel joke things that stuck. It turned out Peaches was her real name and she was thrilled to be wide, a real advantage in the crease, whatever that was.

Peaches talked to me about lacrosse for a solid fifteen minutes before I got her back to Faith Farrell. I had the feeling Faith wasn't someone she wanted to think about.

"I can't really talk about it," said Peaches, squeezing her muscular body in her desk chair.

"Why not?" I asked, directly with a pleasant, conversational tone. That disarmed her as I knew it would. Some things are assumed to be right and people are always surprised when you don't assume it.

"Because...because it's private," she said.

"Are you saying you have some sort of RA/dorm confidentiality?" I hated to push, but I needed to know what happened.

"No, but this is Faith's private business."

"And Christopher's."

Peaches wrapped her arms around her waist and said, "He doesn't get any privacy."

"Why not?" I asked.

"Because...he..." she trailed off.

I raised an eyebrow. "Because you're sure he did it?"

"Yes," she said loudly.

"Why?"

"She reported it to campus police."

That's when I got a feeling, not a pleasant one. A report makes you guilty? I sure hoped not. There were plenty of *reports* about me. From the set of Peaches' jaw, I knew this wasn't the path to go down, but there was a little self-righteousness in me that took away my common sense.

"Anyone can make a report," I said.

"People think it can't happen or that it's...it's the girl's fault. It wasn't Faith's fault." Peaches shrunk down in her chair, diminished from the kickass goalie she obviously was, and I instantly regretted every word.

"No," I said softly. "It wasn't her fault. I didn't mean to imply that it was. I just want to know what happened. I'm not here to prove Christopher's innocence. It's about his brother and sister. That's all. Nothing else."

"But you'd protect him, if you could. Guys like that always get protected."

It was a question I hadn't thought about. Christopher. Would I protect him? No. No, I wouldn't. I'd seen too many rape victims in the ER to seriously consider it. The pain would hang in the air, always just a breath away. If Christopher caused that, he deserved what he got. Donatella was a different story. I very much wanted to protect her and to a lesser extent Ameche. He was a good guy and a good cop. Having a rapist in the family wasn't great for the career. The truth, all the truths, would have to come out. The truth about the listeriosis was first on my list.

"I won't protect him. You have my word on that." Then I told her about the listeriosis and the Tulio murders.

Peaches went pale and clinched her strong hands. "I can see why you'd want to help his mom, but I don't know how I can help."

"Tell me about Faith."

If anything, she went paler. "You think she tried to poison Christopher?"

"If he did what she claimed, revenge isn't unheard of," I said.

"She wouldn't. She's not that kind of person." Peaches shook her head. "No, no way."

"Okay. What kind of person is she? How well did you know her?"

"Not well at all. She was a typical freshman, busy with classes."

"And boys?"

She flushed. "That's not abnormal."

"No, it's not. I'm trying to get a fix on her. Was there drinking involved?"

"She wasn't a drinker that I'm aware of."

"Was she that night?" I sounded like a defense attorney and I hated myself for it.

"I don't know," she said.

"What did Faith tell you about it?"

Peaches fidgeted and flexed her fingers. I sat up straight. "She didn't tell you anything."

"No. She cried and wouldn't say a single thing about it."

"Did you take her to campus security?"

"She'd already been when her roommate came up and asked me to talk to her."

"Anne Marie? What did she say?" I asked.

"That Faith wouldn't stop crying long enough to pack, and she needed help with her."

"She was packing to go home for Christmas?"

Peaches leaned forward and lowered her voice. "No. She withdrew from school. That's how I know it's true. Faith was a straight A student. Gifted. She was working on dual degrees in physics and engineering."

Whoa. What was a girl like that doing at Christopher's frat, dressed up like a French maid? Physics and engineering. If she was as smart as Peaches thought, Faith would be able to figure out how to spike that cupcake with the bacteria.

"Maybe she transferred," I said.

"No. She didn't. I asked."

So Faith lost a lot, including her school. I assumed her parents knew. That wouldn't be fun to deal with, even if they handled it well. Faith was a good candidate for revenge. I would be, if I were her.

"What do you think she was doing with Christopher Berry?"

"I heard he's good-looking." Peaches looked off into the distance past my head. "Girls do stupid things when it comes to a good-looking guy."

I wanted to say something comforting. But there was no way I wouldn't come off as self-serving or flippant. That would be terribly insensitive. Peaches had endured an assault. I was sure of it. I would've reached out to her, if I could've thought of a way to do it.

"You're right. We've all done stupid things for guys that weren't worth it."

The line of her mouth changed from grim to bemused. "I doubt you can say that personally."

"Nobody's immune," I said.

"You're Tommy Watts's daughter."

"That doesn't stop me from being an idiot. Ask him. He'd be happy to tell you all the stupid stuff I've done."

She brightened up at the thought of my famous father not being my biggest fan. It didn't cheer me up, but I'm not the one who needed it. We chatted for a few more minutes until my phone started buzzing in my purse. I thanked her and asked her to call me, if she thought of anything else. She wouldn't. She believed Faith because of her own experience, but she didn't have any real knowledge of Faith's situation. She did describe her as distraught about leaving school. There was something there. I just had to find out why Faith withdrew and didn't transfer instead. First, I had to find Faith.

CHAPTER EIGHTEEN

I shielded my eyes from the bright sunlight coming down through the branches of the live oak above me and squinted at my phone. "Damn." Dad had texted the bad news. The kids' memories of the day they got sick were spotty at best. They couldn't even remember being in Christopher's room, much less eating a cupcake. Dad said I'd have to do better. Thanks for the tip, Dad.

After that, I decided snarkiness from my father wasn't enough to round out my day so I called Uncle Morty.

"I don't have time for this shit," he bellowed after picking up on the first ring.

"Are you serious?" I asked.

"I'm doing my thing."

"Apparently not."

"Hey," said Uncle Morty. "I got obligations to my fans."

"You don't go to Comic-Cons as you, the author. You go as Morty the super nerd."

Click. He hung up on me. It couldn't be the super nerd comment. In his world, that was a compliment or maybe it was super geek that was a compliment.

Ah crap. Now I have to apologize to the super whatever.

Morty's phone went to voicemail. This was serious. I was running up a big bill and Morty did love my payments. I wasn't going to pay him if he didn't actually help. I tried three more times before I broke down and called Pete. He answered all breathless. I didn't like the sound of that. I'd seen the pictures of the girls in costume at Comic-Cons. They made my bikini shots look tame. Plus, those girls carried swords. I couldn't compete with swords and skin.

"What are you doing?" I asked.

"I just got my bicep signed."

Seriously?

"Oh...um...by who."

Be calm. It's Pete. He wouldn't do anything.

"Lt. Uhura. She rocks hard. I can't believe it. You know what? I'm an idiot. I'll have to wash it off. Damnit. I should've had her sign my shirt."

"Lt. Uhura?"

"From Star Trek. You know, the communications officer."

"But she's like seventy," I said. Visions of Pete hooking up with Halle Berry as Catwoman spun into dust.

"Eighty-two, but she still has it."

"I don't know what to say to that. Congrats, I guess."

"Thanks. I'm going to see if she'll sign my shirt. It's the one you bought me. You don't care, do you?" he asked in a rush.

"Go for it."

"There she is. I gotta go. Oh my god. Zena, Warrior Princess!"

"Wait!" I yelled, but he hung up, off to chase down Lt. Uhura or Zena. I wasn't sure what to do with that. Should I be relieved that he wasn't cozying up to hot girls painted green and wearing costumes made of thongs, or should I be worried that he was more interested in an octogenarian? I googled Zena and came up with a hot woman in her forties. Not feeling better.

I tried Uncle Morty again. Voicemail. So I broke down and called Aaron. I had to be desperate to call Aaron. He wasn't a talker and not particularly useful, except by accident. But there was a first time for everything.

"Hey, Aaron," I said.

"Yeah."

"I called Uncle Morty a super nerd and now he won't answer his phone. Can you tell him I'm going to contact Spidermonkey if he doesn't speak to me?"

Aaron didn't really answer. There was more of a mumble and then the clamor of the convention center. Lots of happiness. I only hoped my boyfriend wasn't getting too happy. Hopefully, Aaron was looking for Uncle Morty. If the threat of hiring his archenemy didn't get him on the stick, I didn't know what would. I would hire Spidermonkey, if necessary, but I really didn't want to distract him from the Klinefeld mission he was on. Plus, he was more expensive than Uncle Morty.

"Double," Uncle Morty bellowed into the phone.

I sighed. Of course, this would cost me. "Fine. What've you got?"

He did a bunch of grumbling about calling him a nerd when clearly, he was a geek. Someone had outed him and he was being besieged by fans. I made all the right sympathetic noises, although it was very hard to imagine fans fawning over a man so crabby and difficult that he'd been blacklisted by every pizza joint in delivery distance.

"What've you got for that?" he asked.

"Huh?" I must've faded out after the tenth description of a fan costumed as one of his sword-wielding dragon killers.

"Triple!"

"Double is as high as I go. Chuck gave me Spidermonkey's number."

"He wouldn't."

"He did."

"Alright, you pain in the ass. You at Sheila's?" he asked.

I stretched out on the grass. "Tulane, looking into Christopher." I told him the whole sordid business, Faith and all.

"What do you think you're doing? We don't need more suspects. You're supposed to be narrowing it down."

"I had to check out Christopher. It was his room that got destroyed."

"That's just swell. So now you've got this Faith, Grayson, Sheila, and Mrs. Schwartz."

"Mrs. Schwartz? What the heck does she have to do with it?" I asked.

"Not my job to find out. But she called Donatella's school on the day of the Tulio murders." Uncle Morty chuckled and then said, "Have fun with that."

"Are you serious?"

"Yep. You're screwed. There are too many clues in this room." He said the last sentence in a strange singsong voice.

"Thanks. Wait a minute. I know that line."

He laughed and I remembered why I liked my father's odd best friend. He watched movies with me that didn't include gore.

"*Murder on the Orient Express*. Did I get it?"

"Yes and you don't even like mysteries."

"I like that one and you're right. There are too many suspects and too many clues."

"What do you think Miss Poirot?"

"First of all, I'm not nearly so fussy."

Uncle Morty snorted.

"And if I were Poirot, I'd have already figured it out." I heard footsteps and my eyes popped open to find Derek walking toward me.

"Poirot?"

I told Uncle Morty I'd follow up on Faith and go from there. He'd rather have had me interrogate the lovelorn Sheila, but since I was on Tulane already, I decided to stick to my plan. Uncle Morty didn't believe that college freshman, despite her rumored IQ, orchestrated a complicated poisoning. I had my doubts, too, but you never know.

Derek helped me up. "If you're Poirot, then that makes me Hastings."

"If he wasn't in *Murder on the Orient Express,* I have no idea what you're talking about." I brushed off my backside. "Where's the campus police?"

He pointed the way and I trotted along beside him, trying to keep up with his longer strides. "Slow down and tell me about Grayson."

"Sorry. On TV, you're not so..."

"The word you're looking for is short. It's not a character flaw, shortness," I said with a grin.

He laughed and told me about Grayson Harris. He was well-known and disliked most everywhere for general oddness. Some thought he was bi-polar. Others favored ADD or Asperger's. Grayson was known to have a huge crush on Faith Farrell and he followed her around. They were lab partners in three different classes. He was the only one who could keep up with her, but she wasn't interested in Grayson for anything more than science and he knew it.

Derek had talked to dorm people, two professors, and a teaching assistant. Faith and Grayson weren't very popular. I could see it in Grayson's case. He was odd on the face of it, but Faith? What did she do?

"I don't know," said Derek. "Nobody knew her well and they didn't want to. She kinda sounded like a know-it-all, but they weren't specific."

"Did they know about the rape charge?" I asked.

"I think so, but I couldn't get them to say anything about it."

"Alright. Let's go find someone who definitely knows what happened to Faith."

"Who?"

"Whoever she made her report to." I smiled and headed off in the direction of the campus police.

Sgt. Wellow wasn't impressed. He knew exactly who I was and didn't care for me.

"You should've reported it to us," he said, puffing up in his cushy desk chair.

"It didn't occur to me." I didn't try the big eyes. I didn't dare.

"And now you're here, thinking you're a big shot, coming down to solve our crimes for us. No, thank you."

"I don't care who solves it as long as it gets solved." I wiggled on the hard plastic seat Wellow had offered me, not the soft fabric one three feet away in his small, badly lit office.

"Are you implying that we won't solve it?" he asked.

Derek blanched, looking like he was ready to run out of the room. I patted his knee and said, "Not at all. I apologize. I should've called you. I already knew Truesdale and that's why I thought of him."

"How do you know Truesdale?"

I told him about Donatella's house and Christopher's room. He leaned back in his creaking chair and whistled. "You're not here to make trouble for that boy?"

The cop likes Christopher. Interesting.

"Christopher? No. I'm supposed to find out who poisoned his brother and sister. I ran across the rape. Faith Farrell is as good a suspect as any."

"That girl wouldn't poison anybody. I doubt she's had an original idea in her whole life."

"She's supposed to be very smart."

He made a face at me. "Just because you're in the physics program doesn't mean you're smart."

Yeah. It kinda does.

"How do you think she got in the program?" I asked.

"Oh, don't get me wrong. Miss Farrell is book smart, but she's not creative smart, if you get my drift."

"She can learn anything, but she can't make anything up."

His hand made a pistol and he fired it at me. "Bingo."

"If Miss Farrell can't make anything up, how come you think she's making up the rape? I asked and heard a quick intake of breath from Derek beside me.

A slow, almost sensual smile crossed Wellow's craggy face. "I don't think *she's* making it up."

I bit my lip, mulling it over for a second, before I said, "When Miss Farrell reported the rape, was she alone?"

"This is a police investigation. All information is confidential."

What investigation?

"Since when is the identity of the person you arrived with confidential? I'm not asking what you or they said. I'm here for the Berry family. I want to help Christopher."

Well...sort of.

"Her father came with her," said Wellow. "That's all I'm saying."

"Did you like him?" I asked.

"Miss Watts, you are persistent. I'll give you that."

You've given me way more than that.

"Your personal impression isn't private. Did you like the man or not?"

Wellow let out sigh of exasperation. I get that a lot. "No, I didn't like the lord on high coming down to tell me my business. Happy?"

"Thrilled," I said. "Has the name Grayson Harris come across your desk?"

Wellow blinked in surprise. "That's a change of topic, no transition."

"I ran into him and he was rather odd about Miss Farrell."

"The kid's got issues," he said.

"I got the impression he's some sort of genius."

Wellow rocked forward in his chair. "We've got plenty of geniuses around here. Most of them don't have a lick of sense."

"Like Grayson Harris."

"He's a good example, but if you're thinking he had something to do with Miss Farrell's supposed rape, think again. He thinks he's in love with her as much as he knows about love, that is. He wouldn't hurt her."

"Would he hurt someone he thought hurt her?" I asked.

"A nose wipe like that? Forget it. All he'd do is follow her around. He was always places he shouldn't have been."

"If Grayson was always following her, did you question him about the night it happened?

"I didn't need to ask him, because it didn't happen. Case closed."

Derek whispered under his breath, "Oh, shit."

Wellow focused on Derek for the first time. "What have you got to do with this?"

"Um," muttered Derek.

"He's my assistant," I said.

"So the world-famous Mercy Watts needs a pimply college kid to help her investigate," said Wellow.

Derek flushed to the roots of his spiky blond hair and so did I. What an ass.

"He gets the job done," I said.

"Desperate, huh?"

Oh, it is on, old man.

"Care to put your money where your mouth is?" I asked sweetly to cover up my desire to smack the crap out of him.

"What do you have in mind, Miss Watts?" he asked with plenty of smug on his face.

"I solve the rape and poisoning before you and it's dinner at Irene's."

"You know about Irene's?" Surprise replaced the smug.

"My mother's a native. What about it? Up for the challenge?"

"What do I get?" asked Wellow.

"What do you want?"

Don't say anything gross.

He steepled his fingers. "I'll take Irene's. My wife's heard the soft shell crab is to die for."

"I wouldn't know."

"You've never been there then."

"I hate crab," I said with a shudder.

Wellow grinned over his bitten-to-the-quick fingernails. "Me, too. Let's make it interesting. The loser pays for dinner at Irene's and has to eat a crab."

I leaned forward and spat out, "Make it two."

What the...

Wellow stuck out his hand. "Done."

We shook on it and I tried to look extremely confident, which I wasn't. What the hell was I thinking? I'd rather chop off a useless pinky toe than eat two crabs. Two! I took it from one to two, like a kamikaze moron.

"Anything else I can't do for you?" asked Wellow.

"We're good," I said. "I hope you have a lot of space on your credit card, because I love wine pairing."

A flash of fear went through Wellow's eyes. Ah! The bastard.

I laughed and couldn't resist taking it further. "Can't you tell? I'm a luxury few can afford."

"Um…well."

"I look forward to meeting your wife. I bet she likes pairing, too. Irene's has an extensive wine list and their wait staff has excellent, if expensive, taste."

"She…um…"

"We better be going now. People to see, crimes to solve, you know. Bye now." I stood up and flounced out.

We left the campus police station and blinked hard at the glaring light outside. The temperature had gone up ten degrees and I fanned myself with my hand.

"What's next?' asked Derek.

"We need to find Faith and get her story. That'll be my job," I said.

"Do I have a job?" he asked.

"I want you to go back—"

"Hey, Mercy," called out an all too familiar voice.

No. Seriously. No.

"Whatcha doing in the cop shop?"

There was Stevie, out in broad daylight, leaning on a fire hydrant and holding a drippy mess of an ice cream cone.

I went over with Derek in tow. "What are you doing here?"

"I'm gonna help you."

"You're going to help me? Did Chuck put you up to this?"

"Nah. He's still asleep on the floor."

I stared at Stevie in all his goofy, clueless splendor. "How did you find me?"

"Pretty impressive, huh?" He grinned at me and took a huge slurp of his ice cream.

"You used to take finals in classes you didn't have because you wandered into the wrong room. There is no way you found me on your own."

"Yeah, I did. Chuck installed an app on your phone." He held up Chuck's phone. "And I tracked you with it."

My mouth fell open. I never pegged Chuck as the stalker type and I knew stalkers. "I can't believe it. What a jerk. And you're no better. Where's my privacy?"

"You don't need privacy. We're family," he said.

"No, we're not."

"Well, you're Chuck's family."

"His mother is my ex-aunt."

He nodded sagely. "Family. He's looking out for you. Like always."

"He doesn't look out for me. He bothers me, the big sleazebag."

"You like it."

"I will punch you in the face."

Stevie laughed as if I was joking and looked at Derek. "Hey, man. How you doing?"

"Hi," said Derek, looking thoroughly confused. Who could blame him?

"Stevie," I said, "you can't be out in public. You know that."

"I went out with you last night," he said after more slurping.

I lowered my voice. "Chuck was there. The Costillas wouldn't take you out with a cop right there. Come on."

"Who's the Costillas?" asked Derek.

"Just some brothers that wanna kill me," said Stevie, casual, like people say that all the time.

"People want to kill you? For real?"

"You see I stole some—"

"Stevie!" I hissed.

"Huh?"

"You can't be telling people that." I dragged him over to a tree and shoved him into the shade as if that would protect him from prying eyes. "You have to stay at the house or just disappear before Chuck takes you back to St. Louis."

"Nah. I'm having a good time. New Orleans rocks. There's a haunted pub crawl tonight. I say we do that," said Stevie.

"You're going to get killed on my watch," I said, slapping my forehead.

"I'm good."

"No, you're not. You've never ever been good."

Derek held up his hand. "So you two are friends and you're a detective and he's a..." The knowledge took root in Derek's eyes, "a criminal."

I often forgot that normal people didn't know criminals as a general rule. Just another clue that I wasn't normal. I knew lots of criminals, ranging from Blankenship, the mass murderer, to the criminally stupid, Stevie.

"We're not exactly friends. Our parents are friends," I said.

Stevie flashed a wide grin. "We're totally friends. I tell people about her all the time."

"Please don't."

"Too late."

Groan.

"Fine. We're going back to the house." I pointed at Derek. "Forget you ever saw this numbskull. It's better for your health."

"I thought I had a job."

I rubbed my eyes, suddenly very tired. I told him to go back to his frat and ask if anyone had seen Grayson Harris, lurking around on the day Christopher's father was murdered.

"You think he did it?" asked Derek.

"Not yet, but Wellow said he was always where he shouldn't be. He couldn't stalk Faith anymore, so why not stalk her rapist?"

Derek took off, after promising to update me if he found anything, and I called a cab. Stevie finished his cone and wiped his hands on his pants before plaguing me with tour suggestions. He was even willing to tour The Gallier House. 1830's elegance didn't sound like Stevie at all. He was full of surprises.

The cab drove into the Quarter with Stevie giving me his take on the best karaoke spots that we absolutely had to try out.

"Stevie, the best you're getting out of me tonight is a game of Yahtzee and that's if you're lucky," I said, turning away from him.

I really meant to stick to that. My feet hurt. I was starving. I had suspects cropping up every which way and now there were three crimes. I was staying in and sleeping like I meant it.

But it was not to be. We walked in the door to find the floor empty. Chuck waited for us in the kitchen, showered, shaved, and burning for revenge.

"You!" he said with a long finger pointing at my chest.

"What's your problem, stalker," I said, kicking off my shoes and going for the ice cream. Dessert before dinner. Yes. Yes. Yes.

"You got me drunk, so you could skip out on me."

"And they said you weren't very bright."

"Payback's a bitch."

"I'll show you bitch."

"You and me. Mano a mano."

I took a bite of stracciatella and said through the creamy coldness, "You want to fight me? Did you hit your head when you passed out?"

"I mean, you and me, we're going out drinking. I'm serving the drinks and you're drinking them."

I laughed. "I'd rather lick Bourbon's gutter."

"That can be arranged."

Stevie pumped his fist. "Party!"

"No party," I said. "Sleep."

"No sleep," said Chuck. "You owe me."

"For what? You're not even supposed to be here. You've got Stevie. Hit the road."

"I've got the spare keys." Chuck held up Nana's spare set and shook them.

I shrugged. "So what?"

"I will go out on Bourbon, find a party, and bring it home."

I gasped. "You wouldn't. This is my nana's house."

"Try me." Chuck leaned over and sneered in my face. Oddly, he was never so handsome as he was in that moment. His blue eyes glittered and there was a flush in his cheeks. I was momentarily stupefied.

"What?" he asked.

"Nothing. You're on. Give me the keys," I said.

"You can have them at midnight."

"Fine, but I'm not getting wasted." I tossed the ice cream back in the freezer and glared. Why did he have to be so handsome and down-right annoying at the same time? But all I had to do was get the keys back and I was home free. I'd curl up in bed and watch something mindless. I could use a little mindless.

"Fine." He somehow squeezed Nana's keys in the pocket of his very snug jeans and grinned at me like he knew what I was thinking. I was sure I could still get the keys with the help of a distracting female or two. It could be done.

I was wrong. I was very, very wrong.

CHAPTER NINETEEN

Waking up was like swimming through Jell-O and lime Jell-O at that. I was half right about our night on Bourbon. I didn't get wasted, but I didn't get the keys either. Chuck couldn't be distracted. He drank virgin margaritas and teased me with his sobriety. Luckily, he couldn't help watching hot women walk by and I was able to dump half my drinks, and fake being wasted. Unfortunately, the half I didn't dump I had to drink. I hadn't been that drunk since Mom and Dad's anniversary party when Uncle Morty made the punch and it was eighty percent vodka.

I groaned and tried to roll over, but something heavy was pinning me down. I suffered a minor panic attack until I realized it was an arm, then I had a major attack. I screeched and shoved the arm.

"What? What?" yelled a bleary-eyed Chuck as he sat up bare chested.

I screeched again.

"What's wrong?"

"We're in bed. Together." I jumped out of bed and patted my fully-clothed body.

"You wanted to," he said.

"No, I did not."

Chuck smiled and smoothed the sheets. "You begged for it, baby."

"Don't call me baby."

"That's what you called me last night."

"Oh my god. That is not true." My eyes migrated down his taut torso. Was he naked? Did I sleep with a naked Chuck?

His smiled widened. "Are you sure?"

"Yes!"

"Really?"

No!

I pointed a shaky finger at him. "You took advantage of me?"

He stretched and the muscles on his torso rippled. My friend Philippa was right. He did have an eight-pack. I slept with an eight-pack. I probably touched him. I probably touched him a lot. Hell, I wanted to touch him right then.

Blackie jumped up on the bed and nudged Chuck's hand for a pet. He stroked the animal as it watched us with expressionless eyes, and then Chuck raised an eyebrow at me. "Advantage? You're still dressed."

"You're not."

"I sleep nude."

"Ew."

"Hey, you kissed me first."

I gasped and ran out of the room.

"Mercy!" yelled Chuck. "I was kidding."

Too late. I was already on the move. I grabbed my purse and shoes, which I found next to a snoring Stevie on the couch, and ran out of the house. The courtyard was empty and wet. It must've rained heavily. One of the Birds of Paradise plants was so saturated that it drooped over the edge of the planter. It brushed my bare leg as I paced. I didn't remember the rain, but things were coming back. The warmth of Chuck's body, dancing, touching. We might've kissed. He said he was joking, but...

"Mercy!" called Chuck from inside the house.

I took off past the door, ran down the alleyway, and banged my way out the gate. Coffee. What was open? Wink's was always open. I headed off in the direction of the riverfront, making sure my phone was off. Chuck could try to follow, but he wouldn't know about Wink's. He'd probably try the Café du Monde.

The streets were empty. It was very early. I only saw a couple of delivery trucks, rumbling through the narrow sodden streets. Wink's was open, but only just. I opened the door and the best smells rushed out. Fried dough and fresh coffee. The place was empty. A counter girl with gold gauges in her ears gave me a wave and went back to her phone while I perused the pastries.

"Have you decided?" she asked after a few minutes.

"Half a dozen buttermilk drops and a large coffee, please."

She poured my coffee and eyed me over the edge of the pot. "Rough night?"

"It shows, huh?"

"You look like you slept in your clothes."

I patted the fabric of the halter dress I'd wore out last night, but it was hopeless. The nice lines now looked like a blue garbage bag. "I did."

"Bummer. I thought you'd be out of that dress pretty quick." She filled a bag with drops and handed it to me.

I squinted at her. "Do I know you?"

"My second job is at the Cat's Meow. I served you last night."

I groaned. A witness.

She smiled and gave me my total. I paid and hesitantly asked, "How bad was it?"

"Depends on what you consider bad," she said.

"Did I happen to kiss anyone?"

"Not that I saw, but," she whistled, "that guy you were with was fine. I thought you went home together."

"We did."

"And you slept in your clothes? I would've been naked before we got through the door. Goddamn, he was fine."

I took my change and gave her a weak smile. "He's also obnoxious."

"Who cares with a body like that?"

I must've still had a buzz on, because I wasn't sure why I cared. Nobody else did. I found a seat, took a sip of coffee, and pulled out my phone. Turning it on probably activated the tracking thingy Chuck installed, so I couldn't check messages or call Derek for an update. Faith Farrell was next on my list or Mrs. Schwartz, but she wouldn't be in the office yet. The drops were fabulous and the combo of caffeine and sugar cleared my head. I needed my phone. I needed help. The counter girl had an edgy confident look to her. Someone who didn't exactly follow rules very well with her neck tattoos and gauges.

"Excuse me," I said. "Are you good with phones?"

"I guess," she said with interest.

"That guy you think is hot—"

"He's crazy hot," she interrupted.

"Well, he's crazy. I know that. He put a tracking app on my phone, so he knows where I am. Any idea how to get rid of it?" I asked.

"That sucks."

"Still think he's hot?"

"I'd do him." Then she smiled wickedly. "But I'd never let him near my phone."

"Good tip. Any ideas?"

"I've got a friend. I'll call him."

The counter girl's name was Phoebe and her friend, Burt, said to call my provider on Phoebe's phone. They would fix it. Sure enough. Chuck was now on my account and he'd added the tracking. I smelled Uncle Morty, maybe Spidermonkey, but I didn't think he'd agree to someone spying on me. Uncle Morty had no problems spying on anyone for a buck. My company apologized and, after much haggling, gave me a month free and took Chuck off my account. I tipped Phoebe heavily and turned on my now safe-from-tracking-phone.

Uncle Morty had been busy and he was pissed that I wasn't answering his texts. There were twenty-three all together and contained everything I needed to start the day and avoid Chuck altogether.

He gave me Faith Farrell's address. She lived in the Garden District. I'd have thought she was out-of-state. Tulane was mere blocks from her house. She could've gone home during the Christopher situation, but I had the impression that she stayed on campus until she left at Christmas. Odd. I would've gone home. No doubt about it. Then Dad would've killed my rapist and made it look like an accident. But

Faith didn't go home. Morty confirmed her major. She finished the semester with straight As in some pretty heavy-duty classes. She'd withdrawn for personal reasons and her transcript had not been forwarded. It got weirder. Uncle Morty found out Faith's phone had been canceled the day she left the university and he couldn't find another one in her name. There was no hospital visit charged to her insurance and she wasn't seen at the campus clinic. Maybe it wasn't that odd. Some girls don't want anyone to know. She reported the rape at her father's insistence, if Wellow was to be believed. He could've found out too late for there to be any point in an exam. Still, something felt a little weird about her being so close to home. Where was her mother? Wellow didn't mention her.

Seven forty-five. Uncle Morty might be awake. His sleeping habits were the subject of some speculation. He rarely slept and when he did it was during the day. Some of my friends were still convinced he was a vampire, despite his distinct non-sexiness. I decided to brave his wrath and called him on my way out of Wink's

"What?"

"You owe me," I said.

"For what? Puttin' up with you?"

"For my phone and tracking me. Thanks a bunch."

Silence.

"Morty?"

"I didn't do it. Get out of your nana's house. I'm calling Tommy. Go to a hotel with good security." He was panicked. So bizarre I couldn't speak for a second.

"It's okay. Chuck did it," I managed to get out between his multitude of safety orders.

Then there was a string of cuss words so creative I think he made them up on the spot. They involved donkeys and icebergs. I passed by a woman opening a shop and got a strange look. He was that loud.

He took a breath so I said, "Are you done?"

"Hell, no."

"To be continued then. Did you get anything on Christopher?"

Uncle Morty grumbled, but finally gave me the scoop. Christopher was squeaky clean. No problems anywhere at any time. He had a slew of recommendations from both male and female teachers. That wasn't terribly unusual for a date rapist, if that's what he was. If Wellow had done a report, it wasn't in the system. Morty thought he round filed it.

"Anything on Faith's mother?" I asked.

"Dead when she was two. Carbon monoxide poisoning. Ruled accidental."

"What about her father? What's his deal?"

"I'm working on that guy. Not much on him. Works for a tech company specializing in interactive media. Travels a lot. Russia is a frequent spot, but he goes to Hong Kong and Malaysia, too."

"I hear you can get anything in Russia, if you know the right people," I said.

"That's the same everywhere. He doesn't text or use the phone much. His email is all work-related and would bore you to tears."

"No private email?"

"None that I can find. No mortgage. Leases his Mercedes. Credit cards are paid off every month and they're only used occasionally, mostly for travel. He likes cash, unfortunately. No arrests. No tickets. He likes Breaking Bad and writes book reviews on Amazon, mostly Sci-fi."

I laughed. "You hate him."

"Ya damn skippy. Nothing there and everybody's got secrets. I'll break him."

"Maybe he's just a regular guy."

"Screw that. I'm a regular guy and I cheat on my taxes. Everybody has something."

Uncle Morty wasn't a fan of goodness in general. He might not believe in it at all. If Mr. Farrell had a secret, Uncle Morty would kill himself to find it. If nothing else, he wanted to prove himself right.

"Anything new on Mrs. Schwartz and the call to the school?"

"You can handle that."

"How am I supposed to do that?" I asked.

"Go to the school, ya moron. I got shit to do."

"Like what? Are you hitting on Star Trek actresses?"

He growled. "Mind your business and get 'er done."

He hung up and I got on the streetcar out to the Garden District.

A light rain started and I closed my window, shivering in the chill. The driver was the chatty sort and we talked about Wink's and po'boys until I got off at a row of shops before the Latter Library and bought a jacket and umbrella, before heading off into the wilds of Uptown.

That was Nana's territory. She loved houses, architecture, and history in general. She and I would walk the Garden District streets, comparing Italianates and French Second Empires. I googled the Farrell address and found it was right in the center of all the best addresses. Mr. Farrell must have some bucks to have paid that off.

It took me a half hour to find the address, despite Google helping. Somehow, I made two wrong turns and ended up back on St. Charles. But I found it, eventually, and I wasn't disappointed. Mr. Farrell had serious bucks as in Bled family money. The mansion took up half a block and was a Greek Revival with two story white columns and black shutters. I'd seen that house a million times, but never paid much attention to it. Nana didn't like it. She said it had more money than style and preferred the smaller Italianates with their black ironwork and lush greenery. I hadn't thought much about it at the time, but now I decided I agreed. That house was the equivalent of a trophy wife. She was an eye-catcher, meant to impress, but with little else to recommend her, except the price tag.

I took a picture and sent it to Uncle Morty. He texted me, "On it."

That house had to cost around seven million. What the hell did Mr. Farrell do for that tech company?

I turned off my phone and slowly walked across the street, taking in the broad expanse of the mansion's front. It was pristine icy white and the landscaping was minimal, lots of green lawn and a few plantings up by the front gallery. Very clean. Little imagination. So this was Faith Farrell's house. I sort of felt sorry for her in a strange way. I grew up in what a lot of people considered a mansion and The Bled mansion was my second home, but both houses had a warmth that the Farrell house lacked.

The front gate opened without a creak and I walked up the brick walkway, feeling more and more nervous with every step. The floor of the front gallery didn't creak. My flats padded over the shiny slick surface with only a whisper of noise and that made me more uncomfortable. Old houses were supposed to make noises, plenty of groans and grumbles. The Farrell house was plenty old. 1850's was my guess, but it felt new and...unhappy.

No doorbell, of course, so I lifted the weighty brass knocker shaped like the god Pan. He was fierce and held the actual knocker in his grimacing mouth with bared teeth and a hint of tongue. Pan was older than the house he was attached to. He didn't quite fit. The knocker thunked down and I imagined the echo through the mansion. There would be servants and who knew how long it'd take them to get there. I dropped the knocker a second time and went to the right of the wide black-lacquered door to peer in through the sheer curtain that hung over the glass side panels. The fabric was excessively gathered so I could only make out the forms of the interior but none of the details. There was a wide open stair rising out of the center of a receiving room. No furniture at all. Only a huge chandelier graced the room. Then I saw movement on the staircase. Someone was coming down from the left, but they stopped only a third of the way down. My instinct said it was a woman.

I dropped the knocker twice in quick succession and went back to the window. The figure was still there. Not moving. I tried again and then finally someone went past my window and I heard the methodical sound of locks being thrown open with force. I closed my umbrella and fluffed my damp hair as the door opened six inches. I expected an elderly housekeeper wearing the usual getup of a grey sweater and gum-soled practical shoes. What I got was a young Hispanic girl about twenty, wearing a stiff black uniform. Her hair was pulled back so tight into a bun that it held up her thin brows and gave her a mildly surprised look.

"Yes," she said.

"Hello. I'm Mercy Watts and I'm here to see Faith Farrell." I said it louder than necessary for the benefit of the person on the stairs. I couldn't see if they were still there.

"Miss Farrell isn't taking visitors," said the maid.

"Is she ill?"

"No." She tried to close the door and I stuck my foot in the crevice. Ouch.

"I think she'll see me. It's about Mr. Berry," I said, not withdrawing my foot, even though she was pushing the door against it.

The maid frowned, but in a way that said she had no idea who Mr. Berry might be.

"Miss Farrell," door shove, "is not taking visitors at this time." Another shove and I felt the bones of my poor foot sort of stack up on each other. I threw my shoulder against the door and knocked her back a little. That door was seriously heavy.

"Look. You might as well let me in. I'm not leaving until I see Miss Farrell. This is important." I shoved again and I caught her off balance. The door opened and I saw her, Faith Farrell, standing on the stairs. She couldn't have been more different than the girl in Derek's pictures. She wore a navy blue A-line skirt, a white oxford, black Mary Janes, and thick tan pantyhose. If Faith wasn't so young and fresh-faced, she could've passed for a middle-aged secretary.

"Faith, I need to speak with you!" I called out, my voice echoing through the empty room.

She didn't move and stared at me with a mixture of curiosity and fear.

"Callie!" yelled the maid.

There was the sound of running footsteps and another person hit the door, forcing me back. It slammed shut. My last image was of Faith, leaning over to get a last look at me. I darted over to the window and saw two black-clad figures dragging a third up the stairs. Faith. What was going on?

"Who are you?" asked a deep voice behind me.

I spun around and found a man standing on the gallery behind me. He wore a light grey suit of the two thousand dollar variety and a tasteful tie. Above the tie was a face I wouldn't like to see ever again. It was that unfriendly. People didn't usually look at me that way unless they were trying to kill me. He glared at me with brown eyes under heavy black brows. His skin was thick, full of folds and lines from extensive sun damage, making him seem older than he probably was. His full lips were pulled back in distain, showing teeth that were so white they had to be veneers. I would've darted past him, but the rain had started in earnest again. It came down in sheets, giving the feeling of a solid wall.

"I said who are you?"

His voice made my heart go tight in my chest, but I said with a smile, "Mercy Watts. I'm here to see Faith Farrell."

"My daughter isn't taking visitors." If anything, his eyes got harder. "She isn't feeling well."

"So I hear, but this is about her case."

He said nothing and I almost mentioned the poisoning, but something held me back.

"It'll only take a minute," I said.

"She's been through enough. I'm not going to have you upsetting her."

"I understand, but—"

"But nothing. Leave."

With anyone else, I would've argued, but Mr. Farrell wasn't one you could win an argument with. He didn't move so I went around him, forcing myself not to be a coward and pass by closely when I wanted to keep at least five feet between us. I walked into the downpour and opened my umbrella. When I got to the gate, I glanced over my shoulder. He was watching me. And I thought my dad was a looming presence. Tommy Watts was nothing compared to that.

I walked down the street, measuring my footsteps so I didn't look like I was hurrying away. I wanted to, badly. When I turned the corner toward Tulane, my phone rang. Think of the devil. It was my dad and a feeling of relief washed over me.

"Where are you?" he asked.

"I just left the Farrell house," I said, tripping over a heave in the brick walk beside a much more pleasant Greek Revival.

"Get anything?"

"Oh, I got something alright."

"Spill it."

Dad liked facts. I had no facts, just feelings. I knew nothing more than I did before.

"Sorry. I've got nothing, really. I couldn't get in. The guards were in place."

"What *did* you get?" Dad asked in a tone that was sharp and wary.

"I told you. Nothing."

"Who did you see?"

"Faith at a distance, a maid, and Faith's father."

"Tell me what you felt, Mercy. Just say it. It's okay. Whatever it is."

"He killed his wife." I slapped my free hand over my mouth. Where did that come from? I got to St. Charles Ave. and waited for an opening in the traffic to cross. "I don't know why I said that."

"Don't you?"

"No. I wasn't thinking that at all."

"The evidence says you were."

A tour bus stopped to let me by and I dashed across to make my way to campus.

"You can't listen to me. Uncle Morty says the mother's death was ruled accidental."

"It was, but that doesn't mean it's right."

I headed past a rather ramshackle Tudor style house, down the street toward Derek's frat. I didn't plan on getting him to go with me, but Faith's father and the rain changed that. I felt vulnerable after his hostility. With the decreased visibility, the black hoodie guy could walk right up to me, and I wouldn't know it until it was too late.

"What are you going to do?" I asked.

"I've got a few markers I can call in."

"To do what?"

"To take a second look at Pamela Farrell's death, of course. Morty just texted me. Her insurance settlement was huge."

"Do we really have to borrow trouble?" I asked as I turned to walk up the garish steps of Derek's house.

Dad's voice grew hard. "We didn't borrow shit. Donald Farrell tasked us. He could've been polite to a young woman who showed up on his doorstep, but he wasn't. He scared the shit out of you, didn't he?"

I rang the doorbell. "Maybe a little."

"Well, I'm going to scare the shit out of him. I'm damn good at it, too. Ask anybody."

I didn't need to ask. I knew firsthand. Dad chased one of my dates down the street with a bat after he showed up for our date with a bottle of Colt 45 in hand and smelling like weed. I never saw Shane Ridley again, but I heard through the grapevine that he had to throw his underwear away. Dad was plenty scary when he chose to be.

"Don't we have enough victims to deal with?' I asked.

"We don't make the victims, Mercy, my girl. We just deal with their deaths."

"Well, if you're sure."

"Oh, I'm sure."

That had an ominous tone to it, and I felt a bit sorry for Mr. Farrell. Dad would make his life miserable until he was satisfied, which he rarely was when it came to crime. If he got a whiff of something not adding up, he'd be on Farrell forever.

"I only wish Chuck was still there. You could use some backup on this," he said.

I rang the doorbell again. "He is, unfortunately."

"What the...Chuck is still there?"

"I left him at Nana's this morning."

"Are you kidding me? Stevie didn't show? I thought we had that skinny idiot."

"Oh, yeah. I've got him, too," I said.

"Then why is Chuck still there? He's supposed to get him and get out before the Costilla brothers get wind of Stevie's whereabouts. I don't want one of those freaks anywhere near you."

"I don't know what to tell you. They're still here."

"What did you do?" asked Dad. Darn it. I was so enjoying him being pissed at someone else for a change.

"I didn't do anything. I don't want either of them."

"I knew I shouldn't send a boy to do a man's job."

I laughed. "Chuck will be thrilled that you consider him a boy."

"He's a boy when it comes to you. You need to stop it now."

"Stop what?"

"You know."

"I don't." The door opened and an unknown frat guy looked out at me curiously. "Gotta go, Dad."

"Mercy!"

I hung up with pleasure and smiled past the dripping curl that hung in my face. "Hi. Is Derek here?"

"Dude. You really know him?"

"I'm here, aren't I?"

"I thought he was bullshitting me," he said.

"Is he here?" I asked.

His shoulders slumped. "Nah. He's at Intro to Criminology, I think." Then he perked up. "I can help you."

"Thanks, but I was looking for an update." I put my umbrella back up. "Tell him I stopped by."

Darn that Derek. Any normal student would've taken one look at the downpour and said screw it, but not my guy. He had to be good and go out in this deluge. I'd have to find the one person who might know exactly what happened to Faith Farrell on my own. I wasn't leaving Tulane until I found Anne Marie Murphy.

CHAPTER TWENTY

Anne Marie was a girl after my own heart. I found her in her dorm room, wearing pajamas, not going anywhere. She knew who I was and, after a moment's consideration, she asked me in and offered me a mug of Swiss Miss that she made in her mini dorm microwave.

I accepted and sat on her new roommate's bed, blowing on my steaming mug and watching her fuss around to avoid talking.

"This isn't going to hurt," I said after she rearranged her books for the third time.

Anne Marie pulled her shoulder-length curly hair back into a big barrette and plopped onto her bed, resigned to talking at last. "I know." Her heart-shaped face tried to look glum but couldn't manage the expression. She was just too adorable with pale Irish skin and a sprinkling of freckles below her green eyes. Her face was made to be happy.

"You know why I'm here?" I asked.

"About Faith."

"About the rape specifically, yes."

"Why do you care?"

I sipped my cocoa, allowing her to stew for a moment. "I shouldn't care if a rape was brushed under the rug?"

Anne Marie tucked her legs under her bottom. "Of course, you should." She was not convincing at all.

"I really came here about Christopher Berry."

She'd been about to reach for the books again, but her hand stopped in mid-gesture. "What about Christopher?"

"You heard about his father's murder?"

"Everybody has. I haven't seen him, though. I heard he was still in St. Louis," she said, now very attentive.

"He is." I ran down what happened to his brother and sister.

She shook her head. "I didn't know about that."

"It's not common knowledge. In any case, the trail brought me to you," I said.

"Me? I didn't have anything to do with any bacteria."

"Not you exactly. You because you knew Faith and it doesn't look like anybody else did or wanted to."

Anne Marie grimaced. "Yeah...well...Faith wasn't real popular, but I liked her." She paused. "Sort of. You don't think Faith did something to Chris's brother and sister."

"It's a lead. I have to follow it." I took a drink of the watery mixture. Too bad Aaron wasn't there. He would run out and come back with amazing hot chocolate in order to educate her in the ways of awesome. On second thought, maybe it was better that I was alone. First of all, I didn't want to talk about rape or sex of any kind in front of Aaron. Second, if Anne Marie was happy with Swiss Miss she was really better off that way. I craved the good stuff all the time to the point where I dreamt about it and woke up drooling. It wasn't pretty.

"What do you want to know?" asked Anne Marie.

"Tell me about Faith. Could she have come up with the plan to poison those kids?"

"Sure. She's smart as in straight As without study grouping."

"Do you think she would to do?"

"No. Faith was sweet. She wouldn't hurt kids."

"Even after what happened with Christopher?" I asked.

She sighed. "I don't really know what happened."

Anne Marie was hesitant to say anything about Faith. She did like her or, rather, she wanted to like her. "She was just very young, you know. I thought we were going to get along great. We did on paper."

"But?"

"But she had no clue about real life. She acted more like she was in middle school than college. It made everybody think she was weird and I guess she was. I don't know how to explain it. She was just really, really young."

"Not much experience with guys."

Anne Marie shook her head. "Zero. I don't think she'd ever been on a real date. She had dates for Homecoming and Prom, but I think they were arranged by her dad. Their parents worked in the same company or something. She never had a second date with anybody. She was real close with her dad, though. They talked every day. I mean, seriously, I like my dad, but not that much. He was always checking up on her and he knew where she was, like he was tracking her. If she didn't answer her phone, he'd call me. Like I was supposed to watch her or something. Totally weird."

"Did you know that she lives over in the Garden District?"

"She told me. She said she wanted to go away to college, but her dad said she wasn't ready."

"Sounds like he was right," I said.

"Yeah, I guess. But how is she supposed to grow up with him calling her all the time?"

"Good question. He probably thought he was doing the right thing. My dad always does."

Anne Marie laughed. "Mine, too, but he has no clue."

"Faith's dad had a clue. He went with her to report the rape," I said.

"He's the reason she went at all." She crossed her arms.

I finished my cocoa and rolled the cup between my palms. "Tell me what happened. I suspect you're the only one who knows. Christopher's mom hasn't found out about this yet. I'd like to clear him before she does if that's possible."

"He didn't do it." Anne Marie told me in a straightforward manner that spoke of the absolute truth. Faith was crazy about Christopher. They hooked up a few times, but she couldn't play it cool. She called and texted him constantly, found reasons to be waiting outside his classes, and told everyone that they were going out. They weren't, not in any traditional sense anyway. Christopher liked Faith well enough, but he got sick of her and stopped answering his phone sometime in early October.

The revelations embarrassed me for Faith. I went through a phase like that. But I was thirteen at the time, not a college freshman.

"How long did she keep it up?" I asked.

"Oh my god. Forever. Like November. It was so embarrassing. She would go into people's rooms and talk about him and ask them what she should do. I told her it was over, but she didn't understand. She thought if she could talk to him, he would understand how much she liked him."

"Probably not helpful."

"I felt sorry for her, but get a clue."

"When was the rape supposed to have happened?" I asked.

"Her dad said it happened in early September."

September? Her dad said?

I watched her closely. "Her dad told you, not Faith?"

"Yep. It was her dad. I never got to talk to Faith about it. He was always there after they went to the campus cops."

"So it happened in September, but she was still into Christopher through October?" I asked.

"Yeah. Who texts their rapists?"

No victim I've encountered.

"Did Faith tell her dad that she was raped in September?"

"No, I don't think so. Everything was fine until right before Christmas break. She woke up and her bed was full of blood. I think she had a miscarriage. I wanted to call an ambulance, but she made me call her dad instead. He came and took her away. She was gone for three days. When she came back, they'd already been to the cops. She was hysterical. I had to call our RA to calm her down. We packed up her stuff and I never saw her again. I tried calling, but her phone's disconnected. Then I got called into campus security and I told them what I just told you."

"You told them about the miscarriage?"

Anne Marie fiddled with her blanket. "No. I should've."

"Why didn't you?"

"The cop was sure Chris didn't do anything, so I thought it would be okay," she said, her pretty eyes growing moist.

"If you were so worried about Christopher, why didn't you tell Wellow everything you knew?" I tried not to get irritated and failed. Tell the truth. How about that? Everyone tell the truth and save me some time.

"Well, Faith was freaking out."

"Understandable from what you said about the blood."

"I mean, really freaking out. I asked her if she was pregnant and she acted like I was nuts, but I know she did it with Chris. She told me her spleen must've ruptured. Spleens don't do that." Anne Marie paused. "Do they?"

"No. That's not a spleen," I said. "I'm still waiting for why you didn't tell Wellow."

"Faith's dad kind of threatened me," she said, her voice trembling.

Now we're getting down to it.

"Threatened you how?"

"That morning, when he was taking her away, I said she had to go to the hospital. That I thought she was pregnant. There was a lot of blood. I mean, a lot. It soaked through the mattress and got on the floor."

"You were right," I said. "She should've gone straight to the ER. What did her dad say?"

"He said she wasn't pregnant and I'd regret it, if I told anyone. He's an alumnus. He said he'd get my scholarship pulled. I have to have my scholarship. My parents can't pay for this school."

"So, you didn't tell anyone?"

"I couldn't chance it. Besides, it was Faith's business, not anybody else's. You won't tell her dad, will you? He's crazy."

"Oh, he's crazy alright."

I left Anne Marie curled up on her bad with the assurance that her scholarship was safe. I wouldn't tell Mr. Farrell a damn thing. I would tell the cops, but I left that part out. No use in freaking her out. I couldn't conceal a vital fact. Christopher didn't rape Faith. He probably never knew she was pregnant. Heck, she didn't even know it or didn't want to know it. All of this was fascinating, but I wasn't sure where it got me. So Faith's dad was crazy. That didn't necessarily make him my poisoner though. There was still Mrs. Schwartz's call to Donatella's school. Why would she call? She had to know about the party in St. Louis. Rob had taken off work for it. The only thing I could think, was that she was checking to make sure the whole family would be there. A chilling thought.

I needed a latte. Double espresso. I could've used Aaron, too. Something about that little weirdo and his copious amounts of food helped me to think and I needed to think. Instead of thinking, my brain just felt full up with knowledge that I didn't know what to do with. Aaron could've helped me sort it all out. With lots of chocolate, of course.

I walked down the stairs with my full brain in my chocolate-less state. I wasn't paying attention to anything, save that. If I had been aware of my surroundings, I would've seen him before he grabbed me, avoiding the whole mess. But I wasn't, and he did.

The hand shot out from around the stairs the second my foot hit the bottom landing. He rammed me into the concrete block wall. I got my bell rung pretty good and my eyes wouldn't focus for a second.

"Where is she? Tell me where she is."

A face got up in mine, but everything was fuzzy. He shook me hard, cracking my head again. Somehow Dad's never-ending training kicked in without me thinking about it. I grabbed him by the ears and drove my knee up into his crotch. Twice. Because I could. He screamed and dropped to the floor, but not easily. My fingernails were dug in deep and he took me down with him. I landed painfully on my hip and let go, scrambling back and lunging for the metal handrail to support me. It was Grayson Harris writhing on the floor. I resisted the urge to kick him, because you're not supposed to do that. Instead, I pepper sprayed him. From the screaming, I suspect he'd have preferred a kick.

I shoved the canister in his face and screamed, "Did you try to kill Christopher Berry?"

More screaming. I would've threatened to spray him again, but he'd clamped his hands over his streaming eyes.

"Did you try to kill Chris?"

Screaming.

Idiot! I shouldn't have sprayed him. Now he's useless.

People ran into the stairwell and leaned over to get a look at the commotion.

"Holy shit. What happened to him?" yelled one guy.

"That's Grayson Harris," said a girl.

Two guys in hockey jerseys came down the stairs. "Grayson? That shithead." They looked at me. "Did he do something to you?"

"It's fine. Call the campus—" I didn't get the rest out, because they leapt over the railing and went at Grayson with fists flying. I guess they didn't get the memo on not kicking/pummeling people when they're down. "No! Stop it!" I grabbed one by the collar and kicked the other one. Grayson's screaming went up a notch. Somehow, I was protecting the guy that attacked me and doing a terrible job at it.

Quite a crowd was forming, but nobody moved to help. I yelled at a girl. "Call the cops!"

"What for?" she asked.

"They're gonna kill him, moron!"

"Oh. Ya think?"

"Yes, I think. Call the damn cops!"

The jersey ripped and I stood there holding a collar. Both guys were still punching Grayson. I don't know what he could possibly have done to deserve that. I couldn't pull them off, so I decided to go the other way. Push them over. I shoved ripped-jersey guy. He landed on his face and his nose exploded. Served him right. Before the other one straightened up, I kicked him in the butt, thankful the toe of my shoe was so pointy. He yelped, leapt forward, and rammed himself into the wall. He went silent, but his partner started yelling, "My nose! My nose!"

"Shut up or you're going to lose a few teeth," I said, kneeling beside Grayson. He was moaning in the way that told me he wasn't fully conscious. I couldn't check his eyes because of my pepper spray and he was bleeding from the nose, mouth, and ears. I managed to check his torso. Broken ribs. Several. Extensive bruising and abdominal pain that might indicate internal bleeding. First, the eyes. Grayson was having a strong reaction. I hadn't been all that close to him when I let loose.

"I need some saline! Who has contacts?" I yelled.

One of the girls yelled, "I do." She ran off and came back with a little bottle of saline solution.

"Grayson, I'm going to decontaminate your eyes. This is saline. It won't hurt."

I crawled to the top of his head and clamped it between my knees. He moaned, but there was little resistance. I pried one eye open a tiny bit and gently spray the saline into the opening. I did the same with the other eye. After two repeats his eye relaxed and the lids fluttered.

"Does anyone have any milk?" I asked.

Another girl ran for it and gave me a carton of skim. Not ideal, but what are you gonna do? I poured the milk over Grayson's red, swollen face in hopes that it would staunch the reaction.

"I'm going to pour some milk in your mouth," I said. "Just swallow."

He did swallow, but I think it was more reflex than anything I said. Grayson looked like he'd been interrogated by the CIA. At least his eyes were somewhat open. That was the best I could do. Once the cops got there, I'd be trapped. The next five hours would be spent making a complaint and getting checked out at the hospital for nothing. Grayson was in no shape to talk. Wellow would just love that. He'd keep me wrapped up for hours. Wrapped up and then forced to eat crab. Nope. Not going to happen.

"Did anybody call the cops?" I asked the stunned crowd.

Nobody moved.

"Oh, for crying out loud. How did you people get into college? Is there affirmative action for the intellectually challenged?" I went for my purse, currently being stepped on by three guys in bare feet. Yuck. I slapped their legs until they got off. But Anne Marie came through the crowd. "I got it, Mercy." She held her phone up. "They're on their way."

"Cops and EMTs?" I asked.

"That's what 911 said."

"Good. I'm outta here." I made for the door, but she ran after me.

"Where are you going? You have to tell them what happened," she said.

"You tell them. Grayson grabbed me, cracked me on the wall a couple times, I kneed him and pepper sprayed him. Those two happy heroes jumped in and pummeled him for no good reason. That's it."

"But you're bleeding."

"Where?"

She pointed to my hands and I'll be damned, I was bloody. Only it wasn't my blood. I got Grayson's ears pretty good.

"I'm fine. If Wellow catches me here, he'll keep me for hours."

"What for?"

"He thinks I have no business being down here looking into the listeriosis. The last thing he wants is for me to figure this out before him."

Anne Marie's pretty face got all wicked. I wouldn't have thought it possible. Her eyes glittered and she said, "Because you're a girl."

"I don't know about that. My dad's a famous detective. That doesn't help."

"It's because you're a girl. He didn't believe Faith. He had a thing about her."

"You didn't believe her either," I said.

"I had a good reason. He's the police. Isn't he supposed to get the facts before he decides?"

"Ideally, yes."

"Well, he didn't. Wellow decided she was full of it before I told him what I knew. I could tell."

Interesting. This could help me win. No crab. No crab.

The sound of sirens filled the stairwell. Not much time.

"Well, then do me a favor," I said. "When Wellow shows up, don't tell him where I went."

She glared out the door. "Don't worry. I'm not telling him anything."

I ran out and darted around the building, away from the multiple sirens, and ran smack dab into Derek in the middle of the quad. He wore a soaked windbreaker with the hood up and I screamed when he grabbed me.

"Mercy! What happened?" he said, taking my umbrella and opening it. I hadn't noticed the rain until he did that and now my mascara was down to my chin. Nice.

"Grayson and I had an issue. It's fine. Come on." I dragged him off between two of the dorms. "Where's a bathroom? I need a bathroom."

"Are you sick?"

I held up my hands. "I'm bloody."

Derek recoiled. "What the…"

"Not mine. I need to wash and get out of here."

We struggled through the rising tide of students and faculty heading for the dorm and the sirens. I put my hands in my pockets, so no one would notice them, and Derek brought me to the nearest bathroom in the bookstore. I washed up and splashed some water on my face, fixing the mascara issue. It didn't help the screaming headache Grayson gave me, but I was thinking a more clearly. I texted Dad about Grayson and then called a cab to meet me at the corner of Loyola and Calhoun then went out into the shop. Derek was looking out the window in the direction of the sirens. We'd go the other way.

"Anything interesting?" I asked.

"I count five sirens. That's interesting," he said.

"Why?"

"How many cops do you need for one guy?"

"Well…it was really three guys." I led him outside and explained what happened in detail as we walked to the corner. The cab pulled up and we got in quickly.

"Where to, pretty lady?" asked the driver.

I raised an eyebrow at Derek. "Do you have anywhere you're supposed to be?"

"Are you kidding? I'm not leaving you alone again."

I gave the driver Sheila's address and then asked what he'd found out from his brothers at the house. He flushed and looked down at his stubby fingernails. "Nothing. They know I let you in and I'm on the shit list."

"I should've anticipated that. Toby was less than helpful. I'll deal with them."

"If they won't talk to me, they're not going to talk to you," he said.

I shifted in the seat, leaned over, and batted my eyes with a slightly open mouth a la Marilyn. "Did you ask nicely?"

Derek scooted back and stammered, "I...I...I."

"Boy," said the driver, "I'd tell that little lady anything she wanted to know."

"Thank you for your vote of confidence." I grinned at him in the rearview mirror.

"Always happy to help. What information you looking for?"

"Who might've been prowling around a certain frat house at the time a cupcake was dropped off," I said.

"Are we talking cupcake or *cupcake?*"

I grinned wider. "The edible kind."

"Some would say you're good enough to eat."

"It has been said."

"Many times."

"A few. It's true."

"I will say it again. You are good enough to eat."

"I'll take that as a compliment," I said.

"That's what it was."

Derek looked back and forth between me and the driver with a confused, slightly embarrassed expression.

"How'd you end up in the back of a cab with this lady, boy?" the driver asked Derek.

"I really don't know. Luck, I guess."

"That I believe."

"He's helping with some research."

The driver grinned in the mirror. "I shoulda gone to college."

My phone rang and I didn't recognize the number. Normally, I didn't answer for people I didn't know. I had a history of obscene callers and had to change my number on a regular basis. It was a hassle, but you get used to it. This time I answered out of desperation. Uncle Morty hadn't called and I was hoping it was him. It wasn't.

"Hello."

"Mercy Watts?" asked a low male voice.

"Yes."

"I'm calling on behalf of Tulane University. We're sending you a cease and desist letter."

I licked my lips. "Oh, really. Whatever for?"

"You must stop harassing our students and faculty immediately," he said.

"How are you going to send it?"

"Huh? I mean, I will be mailing out the letter immediately. If you do not comply, we will sue you."

"Are you using a courier, USPS, FedEx? Is the letter registered? What am I looking at here?"

Derek and the driver looked at me curiously and I rolled my eyes.

"Courier," said the guy. He even sounded sure.

"What address?"

"For what?"

"What address are you sending the courier to?" I asked.

"Oh, well, your address."

"Which is?"

"I have it right here."

I leaned back and sighed. "Look. I don't know who you are, but here's a tip, so far in my life I've been drugged, beat up, and nearly drowned. If you're going to try and intimidate me, you're going to have to do better than that. Bye now."

I hung up and Derek stared at me. "Who was that?"

"No idea, but he sucked. I've dealt with thirteen-year-old girls that are tougher than that."

"Really?"

"Yes, and smarter." I texted Uncle Morty about the so-called Tulane threat and asked him to look into it.

The driver came to a halt at a stop sign and shifted in his seat. "I'm going to have to go around. There's some kinda nonsense goin' on up there."

I looked down the street and my stomach twisted. There was police tape and a crowd of bystanders under wide umbrellas, craning their necks to get a look.

"Where's that address I gave you?" I asked, feeling sicker by the moment.

"Up there somewhere. Don't know for sure."

"Pull over."

"Yes, ma'am." He turned left and parked on the cross street. We were in a down market area, but it was clean with little shotgun houses painted in cheerful pastels. I bit my lip and then told Derek to stay in the cab.

"Why? I better go."

"No. You stay here." I grinned at the driver. "Make sure he doesn't leave me here. I'll be back in a minute."

"But Mercy, I think I better—"

I got out and closed the door on more protests. My umbrella popped open and I crossed the street, hopping over the gushing gutter to a cracked sidewalk. The crowd was oddly silent. That's how you know something horrible has happened. Even in the taxi I knew. Disaster has a look about it, a way of being draped over those who are on the outside watching. I knew what had happened, and I knew who it had happened to.

I reached the edge of the crowd and, sure enough, the address was Sheila's, a pink shotgun house with green shutters. There were two patrolmen holding back the onlookers, not that they seemed inclined to rush the scene. They stood together, holding hands and sometimes murmuring with the rain beating on their umbrellas, drowning out what might've been said.

"Excuse me," I said to a little old lady with skin the color of well-roasted coffee beans. "What happened?"

"Oh lord. It's a terrible thing. Terrible thing."

"What is?"

"Young girl living in that house. She's dead. I've known her for months. Sweet girl. Not too bright, mind you, but a sweet, sweet girl." She wiped away a tear and I felt tears rise in my own eyes.

"Sheila," I whispered.

"You know her, too. Wasn't she a sweet girl?"

"I think, she was. What happened? She was awfully young."

The lady edged closer to me and said in a low whisper, "Man come in, tear up the house, and strangle Sheila. Sweet girl. Why he want to do a thing like that? Those girls didn't have a pot to pee in."

I swallowed hard. *Why indeed?*

"When did it happen? I asked, all choked up. I couldn't help it and it disgusted me. I was supposed to be a professional. Sort of, anyway.

"I saw her come home the day before yesterday. She was all crying about some man at her work who got himself killed. She was torn up about it. Didn't want to talk, though. She went inside and never come out again."

"Who found her?" I asked.

"Her roommate last night. The house was torn clean apart and there Sheila was dead in the kitchen. Poor little Leslie. What a thing to find. They had to take her away in an ambulance. She was wailing something fierce," said the lady.

"Where does Leslie work?"

"She's one of those airline stewardesses. I don't know which airline, but that girl's always gone." She looked at me closer with hazy cataract-filled eyes. "Do I know you?"

"No, ma'am. I'm from out of town, but I met Sheila a couple days ago."

"Were you coming to see her?"

"Yes, I was."

She patted my arm. "What a shock for you."

Yes. Quite a shock.

I thanked her and went back to the taxi, feeling heavier and heavier with every step. Sheila gets strangled right after I show up at Rob Berry's office, asking questions. That couldn't be a coincidence.

I got in and slammed the door, dropping my sodden umbrella at my feet.

"What happened?" asked Derek.

"Someone got murdered."

"Jesus. What is this world coming to?" The driver shook his grey head. "Are we going now, little lady?"

"Yes." It was hard to get that little word out, but I did it.

"To the address you give me?"

"No. Tulane."

He looked at me in the mirror and nodded. "Yes, ma'am. Right away."

I sunk into the door, ignoring questions from Derek and wishing I'd never come. Dad should've been the one. I couldn't handle this. It was too much. Sheila was dead. Dead. That was so damn permanent I wanted to scream.

But I didn't scream. Dad always said feel however you want, just keep it on the inside. So that's what I did. I had the driver drop a protesting Derek off at the frat and then told him to take me to St. Louis cemetery No. 1. Feeling the way I did, I needed family. It wasn't required that they be alive. In fact, they listened a lot better if they weren't.

CHAPTER TWENTY-ONE

The heavy bunch of sunflowers and yarrow on my lap cheered me up considerably. The driver took me by his favorite florist, so I could pick up flowers for the family vaults. His wife required flowers on a regular basis and he knew just where to go for a good deal. I combined three bunches and the pile covered my lap with cheerful goodness. I've always thought that sunflowers are the happiest plant. If I ever have a garden, it will have sunflowers.

"You sure about this, little lady? You had a shock with that murder and all. The dead might not be good for you," said the driver kindly.

"I always come to see them. Now might be my only chance while I'm here," I said.

"Not a good day for it."

I looked out at the passing buildings, grey and lifeless in the continuing drizzle. "It's okay. They don't mind."

He pulled up at the gate, a black wrought iron affair between two white blocky pillars. The gate was open, which surprised me. I had terrible luck with that gate. Half the time when I showed up, the gate had a chain wrapped around the metal bars and was sealed with a big padlock for no apparent reason other than I was there.

"Do you want me to wait?" asked the driver.

"No, thanks. I'll walk."

He made a grumbling noise in his chest.

"It's okay. I've done it bunches of times." I pulled out the fare with a generous tip.

He gave me his card and told me to call if I changed my mind. He'd be in the neighborhood. I got the feeling that he would be just for me. I gave him his money and he didn't bother to count it. I guess he liked me, a nice feeling considering the day I was having.

I stepped out onto the sidewalk right into a puddle, of course, popped open my umbrella, and waved to the driver before he drove away down the misty street toward Canal. My sopping shoes crunched the gravel as I walked past the pillars into 'the domain of the dead' as Pop Pop called it. He avoided it at all costs. It was all those generations stacked up in their ovens or worse jumbled up together under the floor when their vaults had been taken over by new occupants. He hated the idea that all those generations had come down to just one. Me. I was the only egg left in the family basket. Pop Pop thought it was a lot of pressure. I didn't agree. It wasn't my fault we weren't good breeders. Nana was always asking about Pete and hinting about marriage and babies. She thought six was a nice number. I thought she was insane. Six of me? My parents could only handle one.

I took a left past Nick Cage's future resting place, a white pyramid big enough for three, and meandered through the warren of tombs. Most were no longer cared for. Their families had died out or forgotten their responsibilities. But some, like ours, were very much loved. Nana kept up the maintenance. She did the cleaning on both tombs, actually, Pop Pop's family and hers. They were in different parts of the cemetery. The old dividing lines of religion and race were still in place. Nana's family was Catholic and Pop Pop's were Protestant. She made a point of telling me that someday those tombs would be my responsibility. Now that was a daunting thought. All those generations counting on me not to be a loser and keep their bricks from showing.

Pop Pop's family tomb appeared in front of me first. It was very tall and ochre yellow with a double row of vaults, each with a plaque inscribed with names and dates. I divided the sunflowers and put them in the vase at the base. I'd forgotten about water, but, with all the rain, it was taken care of.

"Hi, everyone. It's Mercy, the last egg, come to see you," I said, feeling silly, but Nana said you had to talk to them out loud or it didn't count. She was probably crazy, but what the hell. The cemetery was empty, not a tour group in sight, so I told them, my people, all that had happened. I ended with Sheila and found myself overcome with regret and tears.

"I think I got that girl killed." I put my hand on the plaque that contained my great grandmother Amelia's name. "I wish you could tell me I didn't. Maybe you could give me a sign. Anything would do."

I waited like an idiot and nothing happened. I dropped my umbrella and let my tears get washed away. The rain kept coming and all was silent in the domain of the dead. I wasn't surprised, but you never know.

I leaned over and kissed the plaque as I'd been taught to do. "Look out for Sheila, if you can. I'd appreciate it."

My phone started ringing, but I wasn't inclined to answer. This was my time to feel rotten and I didn't want any intrusion. But it wasn't family. It was Spidermonkey. I'd completely forgotten about him and the Klinefeld Group. New Orleans made me forget that there was another world entirely.

"Where are you?" Spidermonkey asked.

"New Orleans."

"Still?"

"Connecting the dots takes time."

"They're not connected yet?"

"I'm on to something. I'm just not sure if it has anything to do with Donatella. I think it does. I have a feeling that it does."

"So it does."

"Let's hope. What've you got?"

"I, too, have been finding some dots. I found the first connection between your family and the Bleds prior to Myrtle and Millicent giving your mom the house. It took me two days in the St. Louis University archives to do it, but I got it."

"Seriously? What has SLU got to do with it?"

"The Bleds helped your mother get in. Josiah Bled wrote a letter to the Dean of Admissions."

"How in the world did you find that?"

"I got desperate. Nothing was coming up. The Bleds donate big bucks to the university yearly. Your mother went there. I was going through the records to see if their paths ever crossed. Josiah was a guest lecturer. I thought they met that way."

"They didn't."

"Not that I know of, but did you know that your mother received a 50 percent scholarship to the prelaw program?"

"No way. I didn't know that."

"Well, she did and all the freshmen that received scholarships got together to take a picture. Your mother was in that year's picture, naturally. And surprise, surprise, so was Josiah Bled."

"Why would he be there?"

"He's named as a university benefactor, but he never appears in any other photo with the scholarship winners. Then I took a look at your mother's application and, no offense, she shouldn't have gotten that scholarship. She'd done well in high school, just not that well."

"That's weird."

"I thought so, too. So I looked into admissions. Turns out Josiah Bled and the Dean of Admissions were old friends. Knew each other during the war. I went through the dean's papers and that's where I found the connection."

"Which is? Don't keep me in suspense."

"Josiah Bled wrote a recommendation letter to Dean Frank for your mother. He suggested that she be admitted and given a 50 percent scholarship as a favor to the Bled family that he would personally fund," said Spidermonkey.

"Did he say why?"

"Unfortunately no, but Frank knew Josiah very well because all Josiah said was that Frank would know the reason and left it at that. Your mother was admitted and given the scholarship. Carolina wasn't to know anything about it, and I can't find any evidence that she did. She still might not know, even now."

"Why do I feel like we're getting both closer and farther away at the same time?”

“We’re getting closer, much closer. It just isn’t coming together yet.”

“What’s next?” I asked.

“I’m looking into the job that brought your grandparents to St. Louis and you are looking into your grandparents.”

“Me? What can I do?”

“You’re staying in your grandparent’s house. Search it.”

“I can’t do that. They’re my grandparents.”

“Exactly. Something in that house connects your family with the Bleds. Go find it.”

“I’m not going through their stuff. It’s creepy and weird.”

Spidermonkey heaved a sigh. “Look. Public records will only take us so far. This is personal. Very personal. The Bleds trusted your parents. We have to find out why.”

“Would you want your granddaughter searching your house if she suspected you were Spidermonkey?”

“I see your point. So start with the easy stuff. Check out their books. There might be inscriptions by the Bleds. Photo albums. Expensive artwork. Your grandparents were known to the Bleds before your mother applied to college. Look around. The answer might be right on the wall.”

I hung up and rubbed my eyes. Great. Just great. I didn’t want to look through anything in my grandparent’s house. And how was I going to do that with Chuck and Stevie right there? Impossible.

I touched the cold stone. The marble was real and sent a chill up my arm. “One of you knows, don’t you?”

A couple walked by and gave me a funny look. Talking to graves. That wasn’t so odd, was it? What was the point of visiting if I couldn’t talk to them? They were my people, after all.

I waited for the couple to turn the corner and then rested my forehead on the stone. “Please help me figure it out. Millicent and Myrtle need this. I need this. The Klinefeld Group isn’t joking.”

My phone rang again. I expected Spidermonkey this time, but it was Oz.

“Andrew Marlin,” he said.

"Who? What?"

"The other Berrys' Andrew is Andrew Marlin."

"Great. Who is he?" I asked.

"I don't really know. All I have is the name," said Oz.

"Well, how'd you get that?"

"Ken Berry bankrolled a small-time meth operation and this Andrew is involved."

And these were the people trying to take Donatella's kids. Scumbags.

"That's it?" I asked.

"I'm sure your Uncle Morty can take it from there."

I thanked him and hung up as the rain increased, deepening the puddles. I had to hop over one to avoid getting thoroughly soaked. Even so, my toes were freezing. I sped up to find Nana's family tomb. It was very different from Pop Pop's. His was conservative, simple. Nana's wasn't. That side of my family made a show of death. Don't tell anyone, but it was my favorite. It was so big that I could see it several rows over. The gothic stone cross on top towered over the neighbors and proclaimed exactly who they were being compared to.

I rounded the corner, smiling, only to stop short at the sight of a figure inside the wrought iron fence. The gate was hanging open and I squinted through the increasing sheets of rain. I couldn't make out the intruder at such a distance, only that they had a huge black golfing umbrella and were on my family's property. I pulled out my pepper spray. If this was the guy in the black hoodie, he was going to get a face full. I stomped over in my squishy shoes and hollered, "What are you doing in there?"

The umbrella tilted to the side and it was Chuck, leaning on my family tomb and reading a book. "About time."

"What are you doing here?" I asked, coming through the gate. I reached back to close it and my umbrella tipped and let the rain hit my face. Chuck put his umbrella over me and closed the gate.

"I'm waiting for you. I had a feeling you'd make your way here."

There was no vase for Nana's tomb, so I placed my flowers on the altar in front and wished fervently that Chuck would go away so I could talk to them and ask them for their guidance. But he wasn't going anywhere, the big clod. On second thought, this could be useful to me.

"Can you do me a favor?" I asked.

He moved in closer. "Anything."

"I want you to give Morty a name for me, but you can't say where it came from."

"And where'd you get it?"

"Doesn't matter. Promise?" I asked, wanting to put my damp hand on his dry chest.

"Promise." Chuck crossed his heart and grinned.

"Andrew Marlin."

"As in the Andrew the other Berrys mentioned?"

"Maybe. I hope so." I could tell he was curious about how I got my information if it didn't come from Morty or Spidermonkey. Clearly, Aunt Miriam hadn't told anyone about my meeting Oz at the convent. Maybe senility was kicking in. She never missed a chance to nail me. Chuck started to say something, probably designed to get the info out of me, so a distraction was necessary.

"Why are you really here?" I asked, giving him a knowing glance.

"Tommy called," he said.

"Tell you off, did he?"

"You could say that. He's afraid Stevie will lure the Costillas to the grandparents."

"He probably will."

"If they show up, I'll be there," he said, the brilliant blue of his eyes had darkened to a grayish hue, making him seem more serious than usual.

"Going to take on the Costillas single-handedly?"

"If necessary, I'm not leaving you here alone."

My hands went to my hips. "And why is that? You think I can't handle it by myself?"

"It's a lot."

I thought about Sheila. I hadn't told anyone about her yet. I don't know if it was the steady rain, sealing us in under Chuck's umbrella, or my ancestors theoretically looking on, but I blurted out, "Sheila's dead."

He stiffened. "Who?'

I explained who she was, my interview with Mrs. Schwartz, and the mysterious call to Donatella's school.

"What has this got to do with the listeriosis?"

"Maybe nothing. The Berry's might just have hideous luck."

"Or great luck, depending on how you look at it. The kids are alive because of that little bacteria."

"Eye of the beholder, I guess." I turned away and pressed my palm against one of the plaques.

Please help me. Nana believes you can. I believe it, too. Or maybe I'm just desperate. Desperate and standing next to Chuck. Not a good combo. He smells good. And he hasn't done anything sleazy. That's good. No. Stop it. It's Chuck, woman. Get a grip.

I opened my eyes and my hand was on the oldest vault. Robard Boulard died Nov.1831.

Of course it's you. Here I am, standing next to Chuck and asking you for help.

Robard was the one who purchased the tomb and, according to family legend, was quite something. He made and lost several fortunes. If the rumors were correct, Robard was a serious ladies man. There was another tomb a few pathways away that belonged to the Plasketts, a gens de couleur libres family. Robard was supposed to have had a mistress, Josephine Plaskett, that he signed a binding marriage-like contract with and then fathered a second family with her. Mom said it wasn't true. Our ancestor wasn't a dirtbag. In my experience, whenever you have to say someone isn't a dirtbag, they most certainly are. I'd seen Robard and his wife's portraits in The Cabildo museum. She was a small blond with a tight look around the mouth and he was a handsome devil, sure of himself to the core. Actually, he reminded me a lot of the man standing over me with his knowing attitude and rakish grin. Trouble, pure and simple.

"I can't stand it," said Chuck, edging closer and filling my mind with his presence. "What are you doing?"

"Thinking." I removed my hand from the cold stone and tucked it in my pocket, away from troublesome, yet alluring men.

"About me?"

"In a way."

His eyelids lowered to half-mast. "Really? I consider that progress."

"You shouldn't. I was thinking how like Robard you are."

"I hope he was irresistible."

I rolled my eyes. "Probably more like incorrigible."

"I'll take it." He lifted the damp curls off my forehead and brushed them back with practiced ease. "You are the only woman I've ever known that is beautiful with wet hair."

He's trying to suck me in. Fight it.

"And no makeup," I said with a sneer.

"Especially with no makeup. You're all clean and red cheeked."

Oh, no.

"And fabulous."

Pete who?

"And you make me..."

What do I make you? What? What?

Chuck's head tilted down; his blue eyes warm with genuine affection. "So horny."

I shoved him back and he hit the fence. "I can't believe you. Idiot! Why do you always have to ruin it?" I spun around and stalked out through the gate.

"Wait!" he yelled.

I slammed the gate right into his knees and he grunted. Served him right. Bastard. No. Horny bastard. I hurried off, jumping over puddles and struggling with my umbrella that had chosen that precise moment to collapse.

"Wait, Mercy! What did I ruin? Was there something *to* ruin?" Chuck yelled after me.

"No! Stay away from me!" I ran out through the front entrance and into the street, dodging traffic and ignoring Chuck's pleas. I lost him easily in the streets of the Quarter. I knew them. He didn't.

I beat Chuck to the house and walked into the smell of sausages so thick Pop Pop's room was hazy. The cat was back on the mantel, staring at me with unblinking eyes.

Why me? Seriously. Why?

"Stevie!" I hollered as I peeled off my soaked jacket and kicked off shoes that would never be the same again.

Stevie came out of the kitchen wearing Pop Pop's Kiss the Cook apron and carrying a meat fork with a sizzling sausage. "Yo, Mercy. You're just in time."

"What did I tell you about sausage?"

He thought about it. Thinking for Stevie included staring at the ceiling a lot. "That you like them?"

"That you're not supposed to cook."

"Oh, yeah. You want one? Extra juicy. I found a new sausage guy."

"And where did he have those sausages? His trunk?" I asked.

"Where else you gonna keep 'em?"

I threw up my hands. "Fine. I give up. Get salmonella. Just open a window. This place is going to have to be professionally cleaned to get rid of the stink."

Stevie chuckled. "Yeah. It does kinda smell."

"After the Costillas kill you, I'll remember this and my mourning will be cut short," I said.

A huge smile came over Stevie's goofy face. "You're gonna mourn me. See? We are friends."

"Whatever. I'm taking a bath. If Chuck ever comes back, tell him not to bother me. I'm armed and female." I tromped up the stairs, fast at first and then slower. Nana had lots of art on the walls. What had Spidermonkey said? Look for expensive artwork. No. All their stuff was local artists or inherited pieces with a few portraits and framed photos. Robard had been the heyday for my family's finances. Between cotton market crashes and the Civil War we had become firmly middle class. There sure weren't any Monets on Nana's walls. Scratch that. There was a framed Monet poster in the guest bath, but that was probably worth fifty bucks.

I went into my room and found the sausage stink had made its way up there. I opened the window and then dumped my purse in search of a peppermint. That stink was getting to me. One sad, lint-covered mint dropped out onto my Mauser. Five second rule! Sort of. I picked off the lint and popped it into my mouth. Soothing, in spite of the added purse favor. I put the Mauser and its clip in the side table drawer where Dad kept trying to get me to keep it normally. He thought purses and Christmas sweaters weren't good enough to store the precious Mauser. Whatever.

Now for the bath. I filled the tub with steaming hot water and bubbles, and then peeled off my clothes, sinking down into the suds. It was so hot it was almost painful. I'd washed and conditioned my hair and exfoliated every inch of my skin before I heard a telltale thumping, coming up the stairs.

The bathroom door rattled with a hard pounding. "Mercy, we need to talk."

"No, thanks. Taking a bath."

"Let me in," said Chuck.

"Gross. No."

He went away. It was a miracle. Maybe this was the sign from the family. Nice one. But then there was a different rattling, a little clinking metal on metal.

"What are you doing?" I asked.

"Picking the lock."

"I have a gun!"

"In the tub? I don't think so."

There was a loud click.

"I'm coming in," said Chuck.

"Do not come in here," I said, looking around for an escape. All I had was a tiny window that wouldn't begin to fit my generous rump.

The door creaked open an inch. "I brought you something."

Intriguing.

"What is it? You better not say your penis."

Chuck laughed. "It's not my penis." Then he got quiet. "You weren't hoping that I'd—"

"No, I wasn't!"

I kind of was. What the hell was wrong with me? Was it the romance of the New Orleans' old and storied streets, the case, the fear…No. I had Pete. He was safe, predictable…far away.

"Here I come," said Chuck. "Don't shoot me."

He crept in, carrying a large wicker basket. It took him a second to find me in the tub, since I was up to my nose in bubbles. "Oh." Then he blushed and I mean blushed, about half his blood rushed to his cheeks.

"I told you I was in the bath," I said, snottily as possible.

"I thought...I thought you were just messing with me."

"Well, I wasn't. What have you got?"

He held out the basket. "I'm sorry."

"I'm not taking that," I said. "You might see something."

The blush faded and a wicked, familiar grin came over his face. "Would that be so bad?"

I snorted. "There you go again, ruining it."

"Alright then. I won't say anything." He sat down on the toilet with the basket in his lap.

"What are you doing?"

Silence.

"Fine. Go ahead and talk but be warned I have soap on a rope and I'm not afraid to beat you with it," I said.

Chuck opened the basket and pulled out a bottle of good Bordeaux, a pair of hand-blown wine glasses, chocolate croissants, and a set of flannel PJs. "You want some wine?"

"You bought all that after the cemetery?'

"I can shop. You want it or not?"

"Yes."

He poured two glasses and we sipped in silence. I didn't quite know what to do, and he was blushing again.

"I am sorry, you know," he said after finishing his glass, rather hurriedly.

"I know, but you can't say that stuff."

"Why not?" He wasn't looking at me, but at the tile on the wall.

"Because I have Pete, and you have half the tri-state area."

His eyes dropped down to mine. "I've given you the wrong impression."

I smiled. "I seriously doubt it."

"I'm not that guy."

"Please. You are so that guy. Look at you."

He sat up straight, and I swear I could see the abs through his tee. "Look at you. Are you that girl? I've heard what people say to you. Are you her?"

It was my turn to look away. "You think I am."

He gasped. He actually gasped. I didn't think men did that. "Never."

I glared at him. "What you said back there was the kind of thing heavy breathers say to me in the middle of the night on the phone."

"I never thought of it that way. I'm not a prank caller. It's you and it's me."

"My point exactly. You can't say that stuff."

He poured me a second glass. "I'll be more careful. Let me make it up to you."

I smiled in spite of myself. "You already bought me PJs."

"I'll help you with the Klinefeld Group. I know you're working with Spidermonkey."

"How'd you know?"

"I'm a detective. Hello, Mercy. Think," he said with a grin and a voice just like my dad.

I grinned back. "So how do I know you won't tell anyone what I'm up to?"

"I haven't told anyone yet and I won't. You can trust me."

His eyes said it was true. My secrets would be kept.

"Alright." I told him everything that Spidermonkey and I had found out, including the connection to SLU. By the time, I got done my water was cold and I was half drunk from the very good Bordeaux.

Chuck nodded and packed up the basket, except for the PJs.

"Where are you going?" I asked. My bubbles were getting scant and I was starting not to care.

"There's a lot of books in this house. We better get started and, by the way, I'm helping you with Donatella's case tomorrow."

"I didn't agree to that."

"Too bad, beautiful," Chuck said as he walked out the door. "It's you and me getting it done."

Ah crap!

CHAPTER TWENTY-TWO

The rest of the night passed quickly enough. We drank more wine, ate questionable sausages, and went through every book in the house. We peeked behind paintings and prints. We looked through photo albums until our eyes ached but found exactly nothing. If my grandparents were connected to the Bleds, they'd hidden the evidence very well.

I woke up on the sofa tangled in blankets, wearing Chuck's flannel PJs. Something smelled fantastic, all apple-y and sweet. And there was something else. Singing. A Christmas song. Christmas was over a month ago. I yawned and untangled myself before going to the kitchen. I don't know what I expected to find. It certainly wasn't what I found, that was for sure. I made it to the kitchen door and didn't go any farther. It wasn't a radio or CD or iPod. It was Chuck, standing at the stove wearing only a pair of flannel PJ bottoms, singing The Eagles' "Please Come Home for Christmas." And he was singing it really well, like better than Don Henley. He'd take a deep breath before each verse and the muscles in his back would ripple. I couldn't stop watching. I was addicted to watching.

Then he stood back and flipped a pancake. It landed right in the pan, just the way mine never did. Stevie came up beside me. "Hey, Mercy."

Chuck turned around with his frying pan and saw me, standing there like weirdo stalker.

"What are you doing?" he asked.

Watching you.

"I was hungry."

He smiled and I did my best not to look down from his face. Those PJ bottoms were hanging low on his hips. Very low.

"Great. I made pancakes and cinnamon apples."

"Um...good. Great. I'm just going to go back to the living room and do some stuff that I have to do."

Smooth, Mercy.

"We can eat in there," said Stevie.

"Yeah, great." I practically ran out. What a loser.

We ended up sitting around Pop Pop's sofa table, eating, and watching *The Hobbit*. The pancakes were fabulous. Aaron had competition, except there wasn't any chocolate. The cinnamon apples were very tasty, though.

Chuck kept looking at me the whole time and it was unnerving. I think he expected me to Fike him at any minute. My dad had a partner named Michael Fike, who used to lose him on purpose. Getting ditched came to be called getting Fiked. I knew I should Fike Chuck at the first opportunity, but my mind was dulled by copious amounts of sugar. I wasn't sure where to start. We now had listeriosis, mass murder, a rape, and a strangling. Why couldn't we have a nice white collar crime? A little tax evasion or fraud? Something that didn't cause the victim physical pain.

"I'm sorry we didn't find anything on the Bleds," said Chuck after scraping the last of his syrup off his plate and licking the fork clean. I think I was supposed to watch the licking. I didn't. Well, maybe out of the corner of my eye.

"It was a long shot," I said. "At least we can say we left no stone unturned."

The cat walked in from the kitchen and jumped up onto Pop Pop's chair. The same place I'd found him three times that morning before tossing him out.

"How does that thing keep getting in?" I asked.

"While you were gone yesterday, I did a little investigating," said Chuck.

"And?"

"I have no idea. There are no open windows and no cat flap."

Stevie belched, loud and juicy. "No, we didn't."

Chuck and I looked at him, but the goofball didn't elaborate. He started licking his plate. His mother would have had a heart attack. Olivia didn't approve of any kind of licking. How that prim woman gave birth to Stevie was a mystery and made me wonder if I should remain the last egg in the family basket. If I did breed and came up with someone like Stevie, it wouldn't be worth it.

"Okay," said Chuck. "I can't stand it. We didn't what?"

"Huh?" asked Stevie, peeking over the rim of his plate.

"You said we didn't do something. What didn't we do?"

"Oh, yeah. We didn't look in there." He pointed to the sofa table. Of course. The sofa table wasn't a table at all. It was a tool chest, made by Pop Pop's grandfather. Pop Pop didn't have much use for tools, so he made it into a sofa table. We cleared off all the rubbish. Pop Pop did like his sports magazines. He had everything from *Sports Illustrated* to *Golf Digest*. We made stacks next to the chest and then examined its padlock.

"I can pick it," said Chuck.

"And relock it?" The padlock was an old brass job with a large keyhole. If we needed the key to relock it, covering up our snooping would be a lot harder.

Chuck examined the lock. "Maybe not. Let's look for the key."

We searched the house for a half hour and came up empty. It was pick the lock or give up.

"I say you pick it," said Stevie.

"You would," I said.

"You want to know what's in there, you gotta be bad." He grinned. "They'll get over it. They always do."

"That's your parents."

"You're their only grandbaby. What're they gonna do? Take away your birthday?"

"Fine. Go for it, Chuck," I said.

"Music to my ears." He waggled his eyebrows at me.

"Will you never learn?"

More waggling. "Probably not, but I'm hoping you will."

I rolled my eyes.

"Learn what?" asked Stevie.

"Never mind."

Chuck got his picks and had the lock off in two minutes flat. The chest opened with a loud creak. It was filled with photo albums, old ones with crumbling paper pages and black and white photos held on with little black triangles on the corners. We carefully lifted out each one and went through the pages. The oldest album was from the 1920s and it was filled with family pictures of a car trip out to the Grand Canyon.

"One more," said Stevie.

I leaned over and looked, gripping the side of the trunk. "That's it."

Stevie and Chuck scooted over on either side of me and all three of us gazed down at the last album in the bottom of the trunk. It was large and square with an embossed cover that said, 'Our Friends.'

"How do you know?" asked Stevie.

"It's identical to the scrapbook Florence Bled kept on Stella Bled Lawrence during the war," I said.

"There's a scrapbook on Stella?" asked Chuck as he lifted the album out and put it into my lap.

"There's probably lots of books like that," said Stevie.

"No way. It's exactly the same. Look at this clasp and the border. The Bleds don't buy things at Walmart. Stella's book was specially made. This is hand stitching."

"What does Stella's book say on the front?' asked Chuck.

"Tarragon," I said.

"Like the spice?"

"I guess."

"Open it. Let's see what we've got," said Chuck.

I opened the cover and found a large portrait of a couple under a sign that said 'Happy 40th Anniversary.' The man was thin and studious-looking with thick glasses and thinning grey hair. His wife was a buxom blond.

"Hey. She looks like you, Mercy. Not so Marilyn though. Who is it?" asked Stevie.

"Amelie and Paul. They're my great-great-great-grandparents."

I turned the page and found pictures of the party. There were tons of people. Amelie and Paul must've been pretty popular.

"What year is it? The hair is weird," said Stevie.

"Has to be the thirties." I carefully pulled a photo out of its triangles and read the back. It was dated September 24, 1938 and had a bunch of names identifying the people in the photo. I didn't recognize any of them.

"Are there any Bleds?" asked Chuck. "I only know a few."

I thought back to all the portraits in the Bled mansion and in Prie Dieu, the family seat. I did know Bleds, but there were a lot of them. I'd only recognize the ones closest to Myrtle and Millicent, their father, uncles, and close cousins like Stella. There was a certain look to the Bleds, a self-assurance that great wealth brought. I didn't see that in the photos.

I leafed through the pages and the photos changed from the party to what I assumed was Amelie and Paul's anniversary trip. They took a huge ocean liner called *The Destiny* and went to Europe. No Bleds in any of the shipboard photos or on their Grand Tour around Europe. They landed in Liverpool and toured England, then Italy, Greece, Austria, and Germany (a questionable idea in 1938). I was about to give up when I got to the last country, France. Gorgeous pictures of a happy couple still in love after thirty years decorated the pages as they traveled through Burgundy and the Loire Valley. There were lots of laughing shots and a few where Paul was grinning in a bad boy sort of way and Amelie's eyes were narrowed, shades of my parents. Chuck leaned in and slid his arm around my waist. He was smiling down at my ancestors and I didn't stop him. I didn't want him to stop.

"Maybe it's not there. The album could be a coincidence," he said.

"It could be, but it's not. I know it's not. I have a feeling."

"Then by all means, flip the page," he said, his breath warm on my ear.

And I did. Amelie and Paul were in Paris in1938. They went to all the usual spots. Notre Dame. The Eiffel Tower. Then I was on the third to last page, scanning the faded photos and there they were, sitting at a table in a little café overlooking the Seine. Stella Bled Lawrence and Nicky Lawrence. They were squashed together to fit in the frame with Amelie and Paul. I couldn't breathe. We'd found it. The connection in black and white.

"Is that..." Chuck squeezed me.

"It is."

"Check the back."

I gingerly slid the picture out. The back was blank. I put it back and stared at the faces. Amelie and Paul were much as they'd been throughout the entire album. Happy. Perhaps a bit tired. Stella and Nicky were smiling, but happy wasn't in their eyes. I remembered that they'd gotten married in 1938 and went on their wedding trip through Europe, a trip the entire family tried to talk them out of. There was a photo of Stella and Nicky in Venice, sitting in a place of honor in the Bled mansion. It was my favorite of the family pictures. They stood in front of a gondola being amazingly gorgeous, set for a big adventure which they had in World War Two. That picture was taken...what did Millicent tell me?

"What are you trying to remember?" asked Chuck.

"When the photo of Nicky and Stella was taken, the one at Myrtle and Millicent's, it was their honeymoon, but I think they'd already been to France. There was some story about Stella buying a whole new wardrobe in Paris at the beginning of the trip. Her mother was furious. Her original honeymoon clothes are in the attic at Prie Dieu. She had them sent back. I don't think they would've gone to Paris twice on the same trip. Look at their faces. They were blooming in Venice, but in this picture, they look like they've lost twenty pounds at least."

We flipped through the rest of the photos. Stella and Nicky didn't appear again. The next shots were of Marseille and then of another ship, not the one they'd taken over.

"Stevie, can you run up and get Nana's magnifying glass? It's on a pole next to her bed for stitching."

He got the magnifying glass and I went back to the picture with Stella and Nicky. I held it over the photo. It was easy to see with magnification. Stella was wearing heavy makeup in an attempt to conceal a split lip and some faded bruises. Nicky's hands had something wrong with them. He held them in his lap like he was in pain. The clothes were brand new and off the rack, nice, but the fit wasn't quite right. Stella's clothes were always custom as were Nicky's suits. He was a very tall man with broad shoulders and the suit he had on pinched and bunched.

"You see the bruises, right?" asked Chuck.

"Oh, yeah," I said.

"What do you think happened?"

"No clue, but it was something serious. The clothes aren't right. There's the weight loss and bruising. Look at the rings under their eyes. They wouldn't have gone to Paris twice. That's not how the grand tours worked."

"It looks like Paul and Amelie were only with them a short time."

"Long enough to bind my family to the Bleds for life."

"For generations."

"Well, we know when Paul and Amelie left for Liverpool," said Chuck. "So we can figure out the date or at least get damn close."

"From the way they're all dressed, I'd say November."

"That's one long anniversary trip," said Stevie. "Are we done?"

"Not quite," I said.

I got out my phone and took multiple shots of the Stella and Nicky photo, and then documented the ship names and the countries Paul and Amelie visited to pin down a date. Then I sent it all to Spidermonkey.

He texted back, "Paydirt."

"You know," said Chuck, "when I said I'd help, it was just for you."

"Yeah," I said.

"But now I have to know. Amelie and Paul spent an afternoon with Stella and Nicky in Paris and fifty years later Millicent and Myrtle give your parents a house. Why? It's going to drive me crazy. What could possibly have happened on that one day that would make you a Bled godchild and your parents so important?"

I smiled. "We'll just have to find out."

"I like that we."

Me, too.

"First, there's a little matter of rape, murder, poisoning."

Chuck snorted and smiled. "Are you still on that? We're talking history here. Major stuff."

"I think Donatella considers the poisoning of her children pretty major. Get dressed. We've a school to visit and crimes to solve."

Chuck didn't move. "Are you going to Fike me?"

Stevie laughed. "She is so gonna Fike you."

"Actually, I'm not. You two are clearly not leaving and the longer you're here, the better chance I have of waking up to a Costilla banging on the door. Let's finish this and get Stevie home."

Chuck stuck out his hand. "Agreed."

We shook on it and I meant to keep my word. Mostly.

CHAPTER TWENTY-THREE

By the time we got out of the house, the sun had turned the previous day's rain into a weighty humidity that made my hair curl into corkscrews by the time we walked by Lafitte's Blacksmith shop. Chuck and I went straight on St. Phillip and Stevie juked to the right.

"Not so fast." Chuck shot out a long arm and snagged Stevie by the collar as he tried to make a break for it.

"Come on, man. I'm no detective. I've got business to attend to," said Stevie.

Chuck let go and patted his sidearm. He'd decided to go professional in the clothes department and wore a blue blazer over his shirt and tie in order to look more cop-like and conceal his shoulder holster. I thought the jeans and snakeskin boots made him look like a TV cop instead of a real one, but he said that's what people want cops to look like and he never got any complaints. The way he said it, made me think it was the ladies who weren't complaining.

"What business?" asked Chuck.

"I gotta see a guy about a thing."

"What guy? What thing?"

Stevie smiled his goofy, oddly winning smile and I was about to say, "Let him go."

"Knock it off, dipshit," said Chuck. "I'm not a chick."

Stevie continued to smile. The idiot couldn't help it. He was genuinely happy most of the time. "You know, I got to see about my next move. Can't stand still. I gotta—"

"I'm going to stop you right there. If you think you're selling those stereos, you're out of your damn mind. Those are evidence of a crime. After we wrap this Donatella thing up, I'm bringing you to Big Steve and we're reporting those stereos to the locals."

"Man, I got to get some cash."

"You want to die?"

"The Costillas haven't found me yet."

"You've been lucky. I would've left you at the house, if I could trust you, but you've got that look in your eye," said Chuck.

Stevie squashed up his face. "What look?"

I didn't know what the look was either. Stevie only had two expressions, goofy and dumb.

Chuck patted his side arm again. "The look like you're going to take off and get killed. Come on. You're with us for the duration. I promised your dad I'd keep you alive."

Stevie shrugged, resigned to the situation. I took his arm and we stayed on St. Phillip until we arrived at the school. It was quiet but humming with life the way schools do.

"You two stay out here," I said. "I'll get the scoop on Mrs. Schwartz's phone call to the school."

Chuck's left eyebrow shot up. "You wouldn't be trying to Fike me, would you?"

"No. I've already been here. They like me."

"Are they women?"

I clenched my jaw. "Yes."

"Then they'll like me better."

"Hoy-day, what a sweep of vanity comes this way," I said with a sneer.

"You don't think I know where that's from," he said.

He didn't. Not because he was stupid or uneducated, but because he didn't have Mr. Sheridan for AP Lit. Mr. Sheridan loved Shakespeare and was a nightmare grader. Only my ability to memorize quotes kept me from getting the dreaded C in his class. That and I agreed to wear hose and those weird puffy shorts for the Bard's birthday.

"What's it from then?" I asked.

The door of the school opened and Kathy Brun, the principal, came out with a student. "Miss Watts, you're back. Good news, I hope," she called down the stairs.

"Not exactly." I turned to Chuck. "Saved by the teacher."

"Shakespeare. Timon of Athens." He grinned at me.

"What the?"

"I helped you study for that final. As I recall you still owe me a kiss." He started up the stairs and turned his smile on Kathy, who was momentarily stunned.

"I didn't get an A," I whispered and then said, "Hi, Kathy. Do you have a minute?"

She shooed her student off to a waiting car. "Yes, of course. Is it about Donatella? We've had no news."

"Abrielle and Colton are better, but they won't be released any time soon."

I introduced Chuck, and Kathy blushed. The woman actually blushed. I had to bite my tongue to keep from telling her that behind that body and face was a true pain in the ass. But I needed her to like Chuck and, honestly, I doubt it would've made any difference from the way she looked at him. He wasn't *that* good-looking. Get a grip, woman.

Then I introduced Stevie, not as easy. I said he was my assistant and Kathy didn't buy that for a second. She looked like she wanted to register him for special ed.

After the introductions, we settled into her office and I told her about the phone call. She shook her head. "I don't remember any call about Donatella. Do you think it's important?"

"Possibly," said Chuck and he went on to dazzle her with why. It was boring and I stopped listening after the second sentence. Stevie was biting his nails and I itched to get a move on. I had a weird feeling that moving was important and that dazzling a principal wasn't.

"Wait a minute," I interrupted the love fest. "The call came in late, like at three-thirty. Were you still here?"

"Absolutely. We have after-school activities and I always stay."

Chuck sat back in his chair and watched me. I'd never had anyone watch me interview before. Well, nobody like Chuck anyway. He was a pro and suddenly I was self-conscious.

"Go on," he said.

"Um...so are you sure you were in the office at that time?" I asked.

Kathy thought about it. "I did have to go down and handle a fight in the courtyard. Boys. You know how they are."

"How long were you gone?"

"Twenty minutes at most."

"Someone answered the phone. Who else was in the building?"

She named six teachers and a custodian. "There may have been some parents, but I don't think they'd answer the phone."

"Can you ask if anyone took that call?" I asked.

Kathy called each teacher in their classroom and got six negative answers. The custodian, Mr. Hobbs, came into the office and said he never answered phones. Too busy for that nonsense. The man turned to leave and I called after him. "Wait. Did you see any other teachers here that day?"

"Other than those six?" asked Mr. Hobbs.

"Yes."

"I think Mr. Donnelly came in for a bit. He said he forgot some papers."

Mr. Donnelly. Perfect.

"I'll go see him." I waved everyone back into their seats. "I know the way. Mr. Donnelly and I have a great rapport."

I left with the weight of Chuck's frown on my back and trotted down the hall to the science classroom. The door was open and kids were shouting answers. It sounded like some sort of chemistry bingo game was going on. I popped my head in and waved. Mr. Donnelly turned and his jovial face got serious in an instant. "Miss Watts, you're back."

"I have a quick question, if you don't mind."

"Not at all. Joey, you're in charge."

Joey, a gangly boy of about twelve, ran up to the front of the room, knocking into three girls in the process and eliciting screams of protest. Mr. Donnelly suppressed a smile as he came out into the hall.

"Boys. No sense at all," he said. "What can I do for you?"

"Did you answer the office phone on the day Donatella flew to St. Louis?" I asked.

His brow wrinkled. "I never answer the phone. Why?"

"Are you sure? Someone answered the phone. The call came in after school was out. Mr. Hobbs remembers seeing you in the building."

"That was a Friday, right? No. I don't have after-school activities on Fridays. I leave immediately."

My shoulders sagged. Fantastic. I thanked him and he headed back to his now raucous classroom. But he stopped in the doorway and spun around. "Wait, Miss Watts." He pulled out his phone and checked something. "I did come back in. My fifth graders' chemistry essays were due on that day and I forgot them."

"So you answered the phone."

"I completely forgot. When I came in, the phone was ringing, I ignored it because, like I said, I don't answer the phone. But on the way out, it was still ringing and I thought it might be an emergency. They just asked if Donatella had left for St. Louis and I said that she had. That was it."

"What did she say exactly?" I asked, crossing my fingers for something, anything significant.

"She? No, it was a man."

Holy crap! The fingers worked.

"A man? Are you sure?"

He smiled and I saw the charm in him. If Donatella hadn't been married...

"I know a man's voice when I hear it." There was a crash and a squawk in his room. "I have to go. Sounds like giving Joey a shot wasn't my best idea."

I grabbed his arm. "All he asked was if Donatella had left?"

"Yes."

"Did you tell him that she left earlier than she planned?" I asked.

"No, he didn't ask."

"It wasn't Rob by any chance?"

"No. Definitely not. I know his voice. This voice was much deeper." Mr. Donnelly patted my hand on his arm. "I'm sorry I forgot. It was a ten second conversation."

"It's fine. Don't worry about it."

"Will this help Donatella?"

"It will. I have a feeling."

"And that's important?" he asked.

"Very in my world."

Another crash erupted in the science room followed by a burst of laughter.

"Gotta go," said Mr. Donnelly and he dashed through the door yelling, "Joey!"

I walked back down to the office and heard more laughter. Kathy loved being left with Chuck. There they were kicking back, eating cookies and drinking coffee. I leaned on the doorway and crossed my arms. He was supposed to be investigating, not flirting.

"Oh, Miss Watts," said Kathy. "You're back."

"Yes, I'm back."

"What's wrong?" asked Stevie.

"Nothing. Absolutely nothing," I said.

Chuck gave me a twisted smile. "Nothing wrong, eh?"

"Nothing. Not a thing. Donnelly answered the phone and get this, it wasn't Mrs. Schwartz. It was a man."

"A man? That's interesting."

"That's right. I'm going to the frat. You can go interview Mrs. Schwartz and find out who made that call. You'll like her. She's right up your alley." I thanked an astonished Kathy and flounced out, quickly trucking out of the building. I was mad. Not mad. That wasn't right. I was steamed. It was coming out of my ears, hot angry steam. That Chuck. Making me crazy. How could anyone be that irritating and rude and obnoxious and so completely, unfailingly Chuck.

I was halfway down the street before they caught up with me. Chuck snagged my arm and spun me around. "What is your problem?"

"I don't know what you're talking about," I said, wrenching my arm out of his grasp.

Stevie's hand shot up and waved around like he was answering a teacher's question. "Oh oh. I know."

"No, you don't," I said.

"You're jealous."

I protested and they laughed. I lifted my foot to stomp on a shiny boot, but my phone rang. Uncle Morty. Finally.

"Where you been?" he bellowed.

"You haven't answered the phone in forever. Where you been?" I snapped.

Silence for a moment and then in a soft voice, the kind you'd use on a skittish horse, he said, "It's alright. Everything's fine."

"Damn right it is."

"Now, I have some information. Would you like to hear it?" he asked.

"Yeah, I guess." I turned my back, but I think Chuck and Stevie were still stifling laughter. Bastards. Jealous. Puh-lease.

"First of all, Tulane doesn't know who the hell you are. They aren't sending you a thing. Second, the hospital released that Grayson kid, and nobody told the cops who was involved. Grayson and your two helpers have refused to press any charges. Wellow is pissed. He thought he had you. What the hell were you thinking? You never bet a cop on crime."

"I wasn't thinking. I was pissed."

"Yeah, well, the guy's an idiot. He's telling everybody and his mother's brother that he's going to kick your ass."

"What do you think?" I asked.

"I think you better move fast. Wellow shows some signs of intellect. Not much, but some."

"What else have you got?"

"Nothing on Schwartz. No connections between her and Blankenship or the Farrell family or the other Berrys."

"Great. Did you find anything new on Donald Farrell? I'm not crazy about that guy."

"I didn't, but one of my guys did."

"You have guys?"

"I subcontract. You'll like this, Farrell's been calling Wellow repeatedly over the last week," said Uncle Morty.

"Why? Faith's case was dropped. The evidence didn't back her up," I said.

"Maybe her dad decided it ain't over. I'd be pretty damn mad if I thought my kid got raped and the cops didn't give a shit about it. Now Farrell's pissed off Tommy something good. He's seeing about the wife. Farrell pulled some strings. No autopsy. First cop on the scene didn't feel good about the suicide finding. Tommy's working it hard. That woman will be out of the ground in a week. They informed Farrell this morning. He ain't happy."

"Imagine that," I said with a smile.

Chuck came around me, no longer amused. "What'd he say?"

I shooed him away, but, of course, he didn't leave. He never does.

"What about the other Berrys? Did Dad get anything on them?" I asked Uncle Morty.

"Nothing. They're greedy and not burdened by grief or guilt over the whole family annihilation thing."

"They're special. Get anything on that name they dropped? Anything on Andrew Marlin?"

"Tommy got him. Took two days of surveillance, but Ken Berry finally met with Marlin at a Denny's."

Nothing about a convenient tip from Chuck aka me. So typical. Dad just found Andrew. Right.

"Denny's? That doesn't say lawyer to me."

"That's 'cause he ain't a lawyer. Not anymore. Marlin got disbarred in Mississippi three years ago for bribing witnesses. He moved to Illinois and does some paralegal work for a couple low-class sharks."

"How do the Berrys know him?" I asked.

"Ken sued another driver last year after a minor fender bender in a Walmart parking lot. Andrew was working for the lawyer he used. Bogus claim. The insurance company had Ken followed and caught him moving furniture and skeet shooting. Idiot. If you're gonna commit insurance fraud, you gotta lay low."

"What about Andrew and Blankenship? Do they know each other?"

"Nothing so far, but there's something there. Tommy has a feeling," said Uncle Morty.

"That's a good sign...in a bad way. Do you have any pictures of this Andrew character?"

"Yeah. I'll send 'em."

"Excellent."

Chuck poked me in the shoulder. "What'd he say?"

"Nothing. Go away," I said.

"Huh?" asked Uncle Morty.

"Not you. Chuck. He's bothering me."

"That moron's still there? What the hell? Give him the phone!" he yelled.

I grinned. "Gladly." I handed my phone to Chuck, who held it six inches from his ear.

There was a lot of yelling, mostly cursing and name-calling. Chuck hung up after a good three minutes of misery. It was hilarious because it wasn't me.

Chuck gave me my phone back, looking a bit shaken.

"It's fun being me, huh?" I asked. "What's the deal with the Costillas?"

"Last seen in Florida."

"Heading this way?" Stevie almost looked worried, but it might've been hunger.

"They don't know," said Chuck. "What did Morty have on Donatella's case?"

"Aren't you supposed to be leaving?" I asked.

"I'll leave when I'm ready. What'd he say?"

I told him with reluctance since my phone starting ringing again. The photos of Andrew Marlin had come in. I opened them and frowned. Andrew Marlin was new to me. No, not exactly new. I didn't recognize him, but he was familiar.

Stevie looked over my shoulder. "What? Are they coming for me? Who's that guy?"

"Andrew Marlin," I said with a discreet look at Chuck. He acknowledged with a nod. "But I've seen him before. Sort of."

"Sort of?" asked Chuck.

I covered my eyes. "He's really familiar."

"Here or at home?"

"Here. Give me a second." I ran through the events of my investigation. It wasn't anyone I'd talked to. That was a rather limited list. "I've got it. He was on the wall at Rob's realty company."

Chuck grabbed my arm, his fingers wrapping completely around my bicep. "Are you sure?"

"Yes. At least it was someone very like him."

Chuck pulled up the company webpage to the staff page and there he was. Not Andrew, but Jared Schwartz. An older version, but very similar.

We held the phones together and Stevie said, "They're like brothers or something."

"I feel a little sick." I leaned on a signpost.

"How come? Isn't this good?"

Chuck shook his head. "Not exactly."

My eyes got watery. "The other Berrys lured their own family to their deaths."

"How'd you get that?" asked Stevie.

"Andrew Marlin is the connection. He looks exactly like Jared Schwartz, who worked with Rob, *and* he knows the other Berrys. The other Berrys recommended Tulio, a restaurant they'd never been to. Their family and, more importantly, Rob gets killed there. They aren't exactly broken up about the murders and neither was Mrs. Schwartz. The other Berrys had everything to gain. If Donatella and the rest of the Berrys died at Tulio, they'd inherit millions."

Chuck scratched his chin. "We need to connect Marlin to Blankenship. If we don't, this is all just coincidence."

"Do you really believe this could be a coincidence?" I asked, flushing with anger.

"Don't get me wrong. I like it, except for one thing."

"What's that?" I asked.

"Why would the Schwartzes want Rob Berry dead? He was a

freaking realtor." asked Chuck. "Did you get a hint of financial troubles at the office?"

"No, but they have a shiny veneer. This has to be about Rob though. He was having a thing with Sheila. Mrs. Schwartz didn't know that until I told her, and now Sheila's dead. If Rob knew something, who would he tell? His wife, brothers, his online mistress? If Donatella had been at that dinner, the possibilities would've been wiped out."

"That's sick, man," said Stevie. "They killed kids. Like, on purpose."

"Yeah, they did." Chuck turned me around and pointed me back the way we came. "I want you to go home now. Stevie, you're with Mercy."

"No way. I'm going to the frat," I said.

"You're going home. This is huge. I'll call Tommy and fill him in. He'll get our guys on Andrew, but I don't want you out until we nail this down."

I shook him off. "You're forgetting the listeriosis. I'm going to the frat."

"I don't give a shit about that."

"I do. I promised Donatella, and it has nothing to do with the Schwartz thing."

"Just because the left hand doesn't know what the right is doing, doesn't mean you're safe."

I groaned. "I'm going. Unless you want to spend the rest of the day trying to control me and failing, I suggest you go interview the Schwartzes and let me get on with it."

Chuck stood there, weighing his options. He didn't seem to like them all that much. A myriad of emotions crossed his face before he finally said, "Alright. Go to the frat, but you're taking Stevie with you."

Stevie pumped his fist. "Score. Hot college chicks looking for a bad boy to sow some oats with."

"You're not dangerous. You're a petty criminal," I said.

"Same thing."

"It's really not."

"I got plenty of looks the other day."

"I'm sure you did, but you're not going," I said.

"You'd take Aaron," said Stevie.

"You're no Aaron. I don't know what you are."

Chuck looked up from texting. "I told Morty. He agrees. Stevie is with you or forget it. I'll be on you like white on rice until you get on a plane."

"I won't be any safer with Stevie tagging along. The Costillas don't use bacteria to do their bidding. We could be shot on the street easily. No elaborate plan required. Stevie should go home."

"The Costillas aren't interested in you. If they figure out where Stevie is, they'll just snag him and leave you. You're Tommy Watts's daughter. They won't pick a fight with him and you need backup."

"Are you listening to this?" I asked Stevie, who was looking up at the cloud cover rolling in. I poked him in the side.

"Huh? Oh, yeah. Snag me off the street. Uh, huh," he said.

"This doesn't worry you?'

He shrugged. "They don't know where I am."

"Do you ever worry about anything?" I asked.

"I'm worried I won't meet some hot college girls. Can we go to a sorority instead?"

I rolled my eyes and dashed past him to a cab that had stopped at the stop sign. I jumped in with impressive speed, but it wasn't fast enough. Chuck grabbed the door before I could close it and I wasn't strong enough to slam it on his fingers. I tried and my attempt was pathetic. He waved Stevie in the other door and leaned in. "Good luck, beautiful. I'll be collecting that kiss when this is all over."

"I told you—"

He slammed the door and thumped the cab's roof. We pulled away from the stop sign and I looked back. Chuck was standing in the street, watching me go. He didn't look happy about it, despite his small victory.

CHAPTER TWENTY-FOUR

A spattering of raindrops hit the multi-colored steps of Christopher's frat and I looked up. Gloomy clouds rolled in over the peaked roof, darkening the sky and making it seem like dusk rather than midday.

"There's a sorority right there," said Stevie, running up the steps behind me.

"Later," I said.

"Really?"

"No." I rang the doorbell and, when there was no answer, I pounded on the door. Toby answered and his face looked like he wanted to punch me.

"What are you doing here?" he asked.

"I have some more questions."

He tried to close the door and I stuck my sandaled foot in the opening. Ouch.

"Please. This isn't a joke," I said.

"No kidding. Thanks to you. The Counsel is looking at us again over the Farrell thing."

"It didn't happen."

"I know that, but now the cops are crawling all over us. They're asking questions and it's not like the campus cops. Cortier is serious," said Toby.

"She is, but there's nothing to find. Christopher didn't do it, but Faith's father believes he did. Have any of you seen him around the house?"

"No, we haven't." He shoved the door against my foot and I winced in pain. "Go the fuck away."

"I will not. Someone tried to kill those kids."

"Nobody here."

A guy I didn't recognize jogged down the stairs behind Toby. He wore a stained Metallica tee and boxer shorts over his extremely hairy legs. He chugged a Coke and yelled, "Hey man, you gotta see Alex."

I took the distraction as an opportunity to throw my shoulder against the door, but I didn't manage to budge it. Then Stevie slapped his hand against the door with a force that wasn't typical of him. Toby wasn't expecting it. He jumped back and I tumbled into the entry hall, nearly landing on my face. Stevie ran in behind me and lifted me to my feet. "Bastard. You always let a Watts in."

"Says who?" asked Toby.

Stevie put his finger in Toby's face. "Everybody."

I pushed his arm down. "It's fine. I'm not exactly fragile."

"Dude," said the guy on the stairs, "It's Marilyn in the flesh. Come to see the hottest dudes on campus?"

I straightened up with what I hoped passed for dignity. "It's Mercy Watts. Is Derek here?"

"What do you want with that fresh?"

"Don't worry about it." I leaned over the bannister. "Derek!"

My helper ran down the stairs, completely decked out in Tulane gear. He looked like a walking advertisement. "I'm here."

Toby pointed at him. "I told you to drop it."

"Alex is sick."

"Mercy's a nurse," said Stevie.

Boxer short guy laughed. "He's not sick. He's drunk. Freaking lightweight."

"It's barely noon," I said.

"So?"

Good point. It is a frat.

Derek pushed past him. "He barfed all over himself."

Toby grabbed my arm. "Get out. We don't need your help."

"Did Alex eat anything odd today?" I asked.

"He lives on kimchi and pork sausage, so yeah," said boxer short guy.

A groaning moan came from upstairs. Not like a drunk coming to. There was real pain in it.

"Mercy," said Derek. "I don't think it's booze."

"It's booze," said Toby.

"Did he eat anything else?" I asked. "Cupcakes?"

Toby dragged me toward the door. "No."

Boxer short guy scratched his hairy belly and said, "There're cupcakes in the common room."

"Shut up, Dillon."

I broke away from Toby and ran into the TV room. On the sofa table were two plastic containers filled with store-bought cupcakes in Mardi Gras colors. Five cupcakes were missing. Shit.

Stevie went for the cupcakes. "Alright. I'm starving."

I smacked his hand. "Those are bacteria bombs."

"Are we sure about that?"

"Pretty sure."

"Toby, where'd those come from?" I asked.

Toby shrugged. "I don't know and I don't care."

"Some girl brought them this morning," said Dillon, still scratching.

My stomach twisted. "Faith Farrell?"

"Who?"

"The one who accused Chris of rape, moron," said Derek.

"Oh. Nah, it was a blond chick. Never seen her before. Sweet body, though." He gave me a horn-dog look. "Not as sweet as yours though."

"Gross," I said. "Derek, find out who ate those cupcakes. Dillon take me to Alex."

Toby stepped in front of me. I expected another protest, but his face was in a deep frown. "You really think—"

"Yes, I do. Get out of the way."

Stevie shoved him to the side and we ran up the stairs. Alex was lying on his bed, clutching his head and moaning. His fingers were pressing so hard into his dark hair that they were white up to the second knuckle. I ran over dirty clothes and pizza boxes to his bed. There were two cupcake wrappers on his bedside table, and he'd vomited so much that it coated the side of the mattress and dripped onto a pair of sweatpants on the floor.

"Alex?" I pushed him onto his back, but he stayed in the fetal position with his knees drawn up to his chest. I didn't try to check his pupils. His eyes were screwed shut and the sound of my voice made him flinch. I turned to Dillon. "Call 911."

"Really?" he asked.

"Now!"

He picked up Alex's phone and called, telling them it was the flu.

"It's not the flu," I said. "He's been poisoned with listeriosis."

"Listerios...what?" asked Dillon.

"Bacterial meningitis. Tell them now!"

Alex groaned and another guy walked in carrying a half-eaten cupcake. "What's going on?"

I leapt at him and smacked the cupcake out of his hand.

"What the fuck?" he yelled.

"How many have you eaten?" I asked.

"You are one crazy bitch."

Stevie gave him a light smack on the cheek. "Mercy asked you a question. How many?"

His mouth fell open at the minor assault on his person and then he said to me in a respectful tone, "Just one. I mean, half of that one."

"They're sending an ambulance," said Dillon, holding out the phone.

"Tell them there are multiple patients." I turned back to Alex and squeezed his shoulder. "An ambulance is coming. When did you eat the cupcakes?"

"My head," he groaned.

"I know, Alex, I know, but try to remember. How long ago?" I asked. "An hour?"

"No." Tears dripped down his face and his body jerked as he dry-heaved.

Less than an hour. Very fast. Double dose.

Toby and several other guys had squeezed into the room.

"Toby, every cupcake is contaminated with the bacteria. I want you to bag all the remaining cupcakes for the cops and call Cortier. Tell her I'm here and what's happened."

"Dillon said it's bacterial meningitis," said Toby.

"It is. A form of it, anyway. Everybody who's had one, even a tiny bite, has to go to the hospital," I said.

"I have to go?" asked the guy who'd eaten a half.

"Yeah, dipshit. What'd she just say?" asked Stevie

"Call your parents," I said. "Call all the parents."

"What for?" Dipshit asked. "They'll get pissed. They're always pissed at me."

That kid was making Stevie look like a rocket scientist.

"You've been poisoned, dipshit," said one of the new arrivals, a guy with shaggy red hair and a good-sized beard. "What can I do?"

"Name?" I asked.

"Avery."

"Take Dipshit into the bathroom and make him throw up."

"Gross," said Dipshit.

"Like you don't throw up every weekend," I said.

Everyone, but Alex laughed.

"You do, dude," said Dillon.

"I do not," protested Dipshit.

I got up in his face. "Do you see Alex? You're next. Stick your finger down your throat or they'll be shoving a tube down it."

"Alright. Alright. Jeez. Keep your panties on."

Avery went to go with Dipshit, but he waved him off. "I'll do it. I don't need an audience."

Derek ran in and grabbed Dipshit. "Did you eat a cupcake?"

"Yeah, yeah. I gotta go barf." He left, grumbling about pushy girls, and Derek came to me at the bed.

"I've got them all. There are six. Sean ate three. He just started vomiting. Oh, man. It, like, went all the way across the room and hit the wall."

"Six? How can there be six? Five cupcakes were missing. Alex ate two and that guy ate one. There's only two left."

Derek's mouth formed an "O" and he ran back out. Alex started to rock with the pain, moaning, and his teeth were grinding so hard I could hear it. He was the worst. The first infected.

"Alex, who brought the cupcakes?" I asked. "It's important."

He wouldn't answer. He couldn't. I doubt he could hear me through his agony. Sirens sounded in the distance. Thank god.

"Did anyone see the girl who brought those cupcakes?" I said to the solemn group in Alex's room.

Avery raised his hand. He looked like he was about to get paddled. "I did."

"Who was it?"

"Probably that crazy Faith Farrell," said another guy.

"No," said Avery. "I wouldn't take a toothpick from that chick. It was Vanessa from my American Lit class."

"Do you know where she is right now?" I asked.

"No. I'm not some freaking stalker."

Toby squeezed back in the room. "I do. She's on my girlfriend's floor."

"Good. Go get her."

Toby rushed out and the room went silent. Alex's body had gone limp. He was unconscious. I grabbed the phone from Dillon and dialed 911 again. I told them we needed another ambulance and that Alex was now unresponsive. He was burning up. I guessed his temperature at 104. The operator said two more ambulances were on their way.

The siren was outside. I ran downstairs with Stevie on my heels and met them at the door. Derek had all the infected guys in the TV room. Sean was bent over a trash can, shaking violently, but he was conscious, so I sent the EMTs up to Alex. They had him assessed and out the door in less than five minutes. The second ambulance showed up and they took Sean, who'd begun screaming and clutching his head. The rest of the guys stood in the entryway, white-faced and talking to their parents on their cellphones.

"Okay. Who are the rest of my cupcake eaters?" I asked.

Dipshit and three others raised their hands tentatively

"Did you all vomit?"

They nodded and told me their names.

"Good. How are you feeling?"

They were all nauseous and had light headaches, except for Dipshit aka Leo, who'd only gotten a small dose and had cleared it pretty quickly.

Two more sirens were in the distance. I didn't have much time. This had to be about Faith. It had to be. Derek came in, holding an empty plastic container. "I found it in the dumpster out back. I think that's it."

"Excellent. Avery, was that all the boxes?"

He nodded. "Yeah. There were three."

"How come you didn't eat any?" I asked.

"Look at those artificial colors. That shit'll give you cancer."

Leo snorted. "You are such a loser."

"I didn't have to make myself barf, did I?" Avery crossed his skinny arms. "My mom was right. Don't eat stuff if you don't know where it came from."

"Tree-hugger."

"Barfer."

I put my hands over my ears. "Quiet! I have to think."

"About what?" asked Leo.

"Who tried to kill you, for one."

Toby flung open the front door as the third ambulance rolled up with a squad car right behind it. He held a thin blond girl, wearing a push-up bra and a skintight tee, by the arm.

"I didn't *do* anything," she protested.

I peeled Toby's fingers off her arm. They left pale marks in her thin skin. "I know you didn't, but you know who did."

"No, I don't. I just deliver for Gardenway," she said.

"What's Gardenway?" I asked.

"Grocery store," said Toby.

"Yeah," she said. "They give me stuff to deliver and I deliver it. That's it. I don't know anything about any poison."

The EMTs raced up the stairs with a gurney and I pointed at Davis. He'd eaten one and a half cupcakes and had been the last to vomit. They were assessing him when the cops came through the door, looking bored and sweaty, each with a good thirty extra pounds to carry up those long steps.

"What's going on here?" asked the first one, so red faced he looked worse than Davis.

I told him and he acted like I was nuts, complete with sputtering.

"You're telling me that somebody spiked their cookies?"

"Cupcakes."

"So they got some bad pastry," he said.

"Call Cortier," I said. "This is her case."

He snorted. "Cortier. That woman."

"Yes." I gritted my teeth. "That woman. The detective. The one that outranks you."

His partner, less corpulent but a wheezer, put up his hand. "Yeah, Jones. You know her. She's a good one."

Jones snorted again and I wondered what that meant. Either she wasn't a good cop, or she couldn't be, because she was a woman. I got the feeling it was the latter.

"Just call her," I said. "Tell her Mercy Watts is here. It's about the Farrell case."

"Oh, yeah. I'll call her," said Jones. "I'll tell her some tranny wants her to investigate some poisoned cookies."

"Cupcakes."

His partner put up his hand again. "Did you say Watts?"

Derek walked over and stood behind me. "Yeah, as in Tommy Watts."

"Who the hell is Tommy Watts?" asked Jones. "It's time for lunch, Moe. Do we have a crime here or what?"

"Yes," I said. "Poisoning is a crime."

The EMTs laid Davis on their gurney and the woman said, "Six cases of bacterial meningitis in the same household and they all ate the same cupcakes? Something's rotten in the state of Denmark."

"What does that mean?' asked Jones.

"It means, do your job, Jones. Donuts can wait. We've got six kids that need spinal taps here. You better find out why," she said, opening the door.

Davis's head popped up. "Spinal tap. Nobody said anything about a spinal tap."

She gently pushed his head back down. "It'll be fine, baby. Just a little poke."

"With a needle?"

"It ain't with a garden hose. You'll live." She rolled her eyes and looked around at the rest of the guys. "Who's next?"

Nobody moved.

"Come on," she said. "You may as well admit you ate one of them cupcakes. A screaming headache is on the way."

Leo's shoulders slumped and he raised his hand. While I was being surprised by Leo, the delivery girl made a break for it by running into the TV room. I chased her through the first floor and caught her by the back door, trying to unlock the deadbolt.

"Where do you think you're going?' I asked, grabbing her by the arm.

"Back to work."

"Cops need to talk to you."

"I don't know anything."

"Sure you do," I said.

She shook her head as Jones's partner came in the room. "Who's this?"

I filled him in and then said, "She's lying."

"I am not. I do deliver for Gardenway," she said.

"That I believe. But this delivery wasn't for Gardenway."

Moe crossed his arms and smiled. "Who was it for?"

"Somebody who wanted to punish this fraternity and she knows who," I said.

She shook her head so hard; I'm surprised she didn't give herself a concussion. "No, I really don't."

"Who gave you the cupcakes?"

"Nobody."

I crossed the room to Moe and leaned on his arm, giving our reluctant witness the stink eye that I'd learned from Aunt Miriam. I must've learned it quite well, because she backed up and bumped into the door. "Isn't it a crime to withhold evidence, Moe?"

He nodded. "Obstruction. This could be a murder investigation, so the penalties could be severe."

She paled. "I...I..."

"You what?" I asked.

She let out a ragged breath. "There was a guy waiting outside the store. He had these cupcakes and he paid me to deliver them. I didn't know he'd done anything to them."

I took her by her shaking shoulders. "What exactly did he say?"

"Nothing. He paid me twenty bucks. I needed the money."

"That's fine. Did he say anything about the frat?" I asked.

"Not really."

"Not really, or he didn't say anything?"

She frowned. "Just something about a reward."

I gripped her tighter. "A reward for what? It's important."

"Ouch. You're hurting me."

"Think. What did he say?" I asked, not loosening my grip.

"Um...a reward for good behavior." She nodded. "Yes, that's it."

Good behavior? Who rewards goodness with meningitis and a side order of death?

"Are you sure he said *good* behavior?" I asked.

"Um...yeah. You don't give cupcakes for bad stuff."

"What did he say? Close your eyes and picture the conversation. Picture his face. What did he look like?" I asked.

"I didn't really see his face. He had on this fedora and a raincoat, but he was older with dark hair."

"Now think about what he said."

Her eyes opened. "It wasn't good. He just said behavior. That's weird."

I looked at Moe. He nodded and took his radio off his belt. "This 781. We need Cortier over at Tulane ASAP."

I hugged Vanessa. "Thank you."

"You're welcome. Is it that big a deal?"

"It's a huge deal." I urged her to the front of the house to wait for Cortier with the rest of the guys. I had to think. It was Faith Farrell's father at Gardenway with his poisoned cupcakes. But this wasn't the first time. I ran after Vanessa and caught her in the TV room.

"Have you delivered here before?" I asked.

"Huh?'

"Cupcakes. Have you ever delivered cupcakes here before?"

"Yeah, but it was just one."

Yes! Eat crab, Wellow!

"Who did you give it to, and who gave it to you?" I asked.

"You know what? I think it was the same guy, but he had on different stuff. I didn't think about it before. He gave me a twenty then, too."

"Who got the cupcake?"

She shrugged. "I don't know. I was supposed to leave it in a room as a surprise for his son."

"Which room?" asked Moe.

"Second floor. I don't remember exactly which room," said Vanessa. "Is that bad?"

"It's okay. Go on to the entryway. I'm sure the detective will be here any second to take your statement."

Moe and I stood there, quietly looking at the cupcakes of death in the Ziploc bags marked, "Do not eat. Poisoned."

"Do you know who did it?" asked Moe.

"Donald Farrell. He thinks one of the guys raped his daughter and got her pregnant," I said, my mind spinning.

"Did the kid do it?"

"No on the rape. She was pregnant, I think. He may have been the father. I didn't get that far."

"That's pretty far. So, if you don't mind me asking, what's your dad like? He's kind of a legend around these parts. The Gator Bait case, but I guess you know all about that."

"Not really. He never mentioned it," I said. "What was it about?"

"Guy murdered his wife's lover. He brought the body down here and fed it to the gators. Then the psycho started killing the lover's family one-by-one. They knew about the affair. Gator bait. He was fishing with their parts."

"A nasty case of revenge."

"Yep. We had people going missing all over the city. Can't believe your father never told you about it. That was a huge case," he said.

One-by-one.

"Miss Watts? You alright? You didn't eat one of those cupcakes, did you?"

"He was getting revenge on the people who wronged him? The Gator Bait guy, I mean," I said.

"Yeah. Crazy. He blamed the lover's sister for introducing his wife to the guy. Crazy connections like that."

"Anybody who he thought caused the affair?"

"Yeah. What are you thinking?"

"Something's rotten in the state of Denmark."

"Huh?"

"Hamlet's about revenge and how revenge is inadequate sometimes."

"You lost me."

"Farrell tried to kill Christopher, failed, and now he's out of reach. That's inadequate. More punishment is needed."

"Who's Christopher?" Moe asked.

"The supposed rapist. Today Farrell tried to take his revenge on Christopher's frat. This is where Farrell thinks his daughter was harmed, so it's their fault."

"Oh, I get it. This Farrell needed more revenge, so he poisoned these kids. I'll call it in. We'll pick up Farrell."

"He's not done," I said.

"What do you mean, not done?"

"These guys wronged his daughter, but they're not the only ones." I dug around in my purse and came up with the scrap of paper with Anne Marie's cellphone number on it. She didn't answer. Oh, no.

"He'll go after his daughter's roommate." I gave Moe her room number and I kept calling.

Anne Marie, answer the damn phone.

Moe grabbed my shoulder. "I'm going over there. The school is getting her schedule. We'll find her."

I nodded and he left the room, yelling for Jones.

Revenge. Is a little ever enough?

"Derek!"

He ran in, out of breath. "What's wrong?"

"We've got a problem." I dialed Wellow's number. No answer.

"What should I do?" he asked.

"Keep calling this number and tell Wellow that Farrell is going to try to kill him." I shoved my phone at him.

"What about me?" asked Stevie.

"You're with me."

"Where're we going?"

"To save a man so he can eat some crab."

"Is it me?"

"No!"

CHAPTER TWENTY-FIVE

The door wouldn't open. I yanked on the metal handle a second time, but the campus police station was locked. Locked. What the hell?

Stevie gave it a try as if I hadn't done it right. "I've been to a lot of police stations."

"Don't I know it," I said.

"I never saw a locked one."

I pounded on the glass, rattling it on the hinges. "Me, neither."

We both started pounding, so hard I half expected the glass to break.

"Wellow! Wellow!" I yelled.

Students walking by stopped and stared. We must've looked like total nuts. Who the hell is desperate to get into a police station? I called Wellow's number again and then the general number. No answer for either.

"Maybe there's a window open," said Stevie.

"In New Orleans. Please. It's 80 degrees today and 100 percent humidity." I gave him my phone. "Call 911. I'm going to circle the building."

"Probably shouldn't."

"How come?"

Stevie pointed through the glass at something on the floor. I pressed my nose against the door. It was a shoe. A shiny black oxford. A cop shoe up on its heel and barely visible behind a desk. There was a foot in that shoe and a body on the floor.

I frantically rattled the door again. "I have to get in there."

"How about this?" Stevie stood next to me, cradling a small decorative boulder.

"Where'd you get that?"

"Flower bed."

I tried to pull it out of his grasp, but he held on tight. "Let go."

"I'll do it. Your sheet is clean." Stevie stepped back and heaved the rock. The door exploded and I glanced back. About fifteen people had their phones out, documenting our breaking and entering of a police station. If that didn't make it on YouTube it would be a miracle. At least I wasn't wearing a bikini.

Stevie kicked the remaining glass out to make a hole big enough for me and I stepped through, slipping on the shards of glass on the tile floor. I nearly went down and Stevie caught my arm as my feet went out from under me.

"You okay?" he asked.

I dove for the desk and cleared the glass. The cop on the floor wasn't familiar to me. He was ten years older than Wellow, balding and well-muscled. I knelt by his side and checked his pulse. Strong and steady. No blood. No obvious wounds. I felt around his head and neck. There was a large hematoma on the back of his head. I checked his pupils. Both dilated. They did react to my penlight slightly. Not great, but it was something.

"What's wrong with him?" asked Stevie.

"Closed head injury." I pointed at my phone in his hand. "Tell them."

"Tell them what?"

"Give me that." I started the rundown when a series of gunshots went off over our heads. Four shots in quick succession. I shoved the phone at Stevie and jumped to my feet. "Stay with him."

"Hell, no!"

A crowd of students were gathered around the broken door, all looking up in bewilderment at the second floor.

"Hey! Any med students?" I yelled.

An African-American guy the size of a twelve-year-old shot up his hand.

"Get in here!"

He ran in, slipping on the glass.

"Talk to 911 and find the defibrillator. Monitor his heart rate and breathing," I ordered, shoving the phone at him.

"Yes, ma'am."

I sprinted for the stairs while fumbling through my purse.

Where is it? Where is it?

The Mauser wasn't there, but my hand found my pepper spray as I leapt up the last two stairs.

"Mercy! Don't go up there!" yelled Stevie.

I ran onto the second floor and found the two desks empty. Wellow's office was on the other side of the floor with the door open. A second volley of gunshots went off. A full clip from the sound of it. The large glass window next to Wellow's door shattered and the drawn shade billowed into the open area. I ran across the room as Stevie called my name behind me. I hit the wall next to Wellow's door and that's when I heard the screaming and the sound of something hard hitting something wet.

Stevie reached the wall beside me and grabbed my arm. "You're not going in there."

"Wanna bet?" I bit his hand. He screeched and let go.

I kicked the door open, crouched, and looked in. I was eye level with Donald Farrell. He sat on Wellow's chest, a brick in his left hand poised to strike. Wellow's hands were up, bloody as his face, which looked like meatloaf.

"Stop!" I screamed.

Farrell's arm continued a swing back—lucky for me—and he exposed his face fully to my can of pepper spray. I doused him right in the kisser. He flipped backward, dropping the brick and clutching his face. I leapt at him and did what my mom taught me. I kicked him in the junk. Dad would not be proud. Junk-kicking was not to be included when the guy was going down. Mom would've kicked him a couple more times to be on the safe side. I only kicked him once and that was plenty, if I went by the screaming.

I dropped to Wellow's side and grabbed his Smith & Wesson revolver, lying on the floor next to a writhing Farrell. I handed it back to Stevie and he snapped open the cylinder. "He got off four shots."

"There's another weapon. Find it."

I checked Wellow's vitals. Heartbeat, yes. Breathing, no. I grabbed a pair of latex gloves and my CPR mask out of my purse. Nurses have these things next to their lip gloss. I'd never had the occasion to use the mask before, but Mom got it for me after I graduated. I was so glad I didn't have to put my mouth on Wellow's blood-filled one. I gave him two quick breaths and reassessed. It was enough to jump-start him and he took some shallow breaths on his own. He moaned and I checked his pupils. Equal and reactive.

"Wellow, it's Mercy Watts. You're okay. EMT's are coming."

His mouth moved and he gasped in pain. I checked the line of his jaw. Multiple fractures, and he was missing several teeth.

Stevie walked around the desk. "Oh, shit!"

"What?"

He pointed into the corner behind me. Chuck was lurching to his feet. Blood dripped down his jaw and soaked into his shirt. He held his Glock loosely in one hand and groped vaguely behind his hips with the other. "I can't find my cuffs."

"You don't have them," I said. "Stevie. Belt."

Stevie trussed up Farrell with an efficiency that only comes from being cuffed many times.

Chuck staggered toward me and grabbed the desk for support. I jumped up and caught him before he went down. "Are you okay?" he asked me as his knees buckled.

I'd like to say I eased him to the floor, but he took me down with him. Stevie had to roll his limp body off me. I checked his vitals. No breathing. I positioned his head, not bothering to retrieve my bloody mask. I never imagined I'd need two of them. I pinched Chuck's nose and saw, a second before his lips touched mine, a small flutter of his lashes. I sat bolt upright and punched him in the sternum.

"Ow!" he yelled.

"You deserve it, you big faker," I said.

"I told you I was going to get that kiss you owe me."

"I was going to give you CPR."

"Close enough," he said.

"You are an idiot." I shifted his head to the left. He had an open laceration about the size of brick on the side of his head. He'd need stitches.

Chuck smiled. "It works in the movies."

"What movies?"

"I don't remember. Probably bad ones. I've been injured in the line of duty. Don't you want to kiss it and make it better?"

"I've got pepper spray and I'm not afraid to use it," I said. "See if you can track my finger."

"I'm tracking your lips."

"Shut up."

"How can I tell you what I'm tracking if I'm shutting up?"

I groaned. "You're impossible."

Wellow's moans took on a desperate quality so I crawled back over to him, taking his hand. He had several compound fractures with one bone splinter poking through the skin. Nasty. It was his gun hand and it looked like Farrell had bricked it pretty good.

"Get up, Chuck, and tell me what happened. Why are you even here?" I asked.

Chuck crawled dramatically into a chair. "When I got to Schwartz's office, guess who was already there?"

"Just tell me."

"The FBI."

"Seriously? What for?" I asked as I tilted Wellow's head to the side and cleared the accumulating blood from his mouth. "Stevie, where the hell is that ambulance?"

"I think I hear the sirens," he said.

There were sirens. I could barely make them out over Wellow's distress. "Good. Go down and get a crew up here. What did you say, Chuck?"

"I said, it was bid rigging and mortgage fraud. The Schwartzes had quite a ring going," said Chuck.

An EMT ran in, carrying his trauma bag. He knelt by Wellow and gloved up in purple. I got out of the way and took Chuck's Glock out of his hand, ejecting the clip.

"You emptied the clip and didn't hit him once? Seriously? That's embarrassing," I said.

"I'd been clobbered with a brick," said Chuck, a blush creeping across his cheeks.

A cop ran in with his gun drawn and pointed it at me. I held up my hands and Chuck flashed his badge. The cop bagged Chuck's Glock and Wellow's revolver and then took a quick statement from us. Chuck would probably never live down that series of events, but it wasn't his fault. He was seated with his back to the door when Farrell came in and cracked him with the brick. Chuck went down and Farrell dove for Wellow, who had his gun in a drawer. He was able to get it and fire the first four rounds, none of which connected. Farrell got Wellow down and started clubbing him as Chuck came to. He was disoriented and seeing double. He emptied his clip in the general direction of Farrell. We didn't find out until later that he did hit Farrell twice. Once in the thigh and a graze to the head. I couldn't tell, because of all the blood spatter from Wellow. Farrell didn't seem bothered by either wound. He was screaming about injustice when they dragged him from the room, half-blind from my pepper spray and holding his crotch. They wouldn't discover the thigh wound for another fifteen minutes. Frankly, I don't think anyone was trying all that hard.

After the EMTs carted Wellow and his partner off, another ambulance arrived for Chuck. It was a standoff of epic proportions. Chuck didn't want an ambulance and the EMTs didn't care what he wanted. Chuck was about to win when he got nauseous and barfed in Wellow's trash can. I pinched him until he agreed to get into the damn ambulance. He sat on the gurney, looking wobbly and pathetic. It made my heart twist a little. I am such a sucker for a wounded cop. Stevie and I climbed in and sat with him.

"I think I might throw up again," he said.

The EMT gave me a basin and I held it under his chin. "Go ahead. Nobody cares."

"This isn't how I thought this trip would go."

"No kidding. Usually I'm the one who goes to the hospital," I said. "It's a nice change for me."

Chuck did throw up again, and we laid him down for the ride to the hospital. A short ride thankfully, since the nausea increased with every bump.

"So, how did the FBI find out about the Schwartzes?" I asked to distract him.

"Rob tipped them off before he got on the plane to St. Louis," Chuck whispered.

"So the agents just told you all this in the midst of arresting Mrs. Schwartz?"

"She was already gone when I got there. They were executing a search warrant."

"Still. That's awfully nice of them."

Chuck smiled. "I have my ways."

"Of course, you do."

"Jealous?"

"Terribly."

"I thought so."

We arrived at the ER, cutting off anymore insinuations. Chuck was diagnosed with a serious concussion and admitted for observation. I stayed with him on the sleeper chair in his room. Stevie charmed his way into the nurse's lounge and got a date with a nurse that was way too good for him. Lana was charmed by his tale of peril at the campus police station and the blood on his shirt didn't hurt. I gave him a hundred bucks to take her to dinner, but it was really to keep him from talking to anyone who would listen. The hospital was crawling with cops and nobody, as of yet, had thought to ask him who he was beyond his cursory statement that he'd been with me. Pretty soon somebody was going to ask and he'd be arrested for whatever he'd done in Missouri.

It took forever to get Chuck settled into his room. He had a screaming migraine and squeezed my hand so hard I expected bruising. Once the Vicodin was onboard, he relaxed and I retreated to my chair to watch his monitor and the nurse coming in for repeated unnecessary blood pressure checks. She asked me several times about our relationship. I suppose she was hoping we were blood related, which we weren't, despite the same last name. My uncle adopted Chuck during his brief marriage to Chuck's mom and it stuck.

The nurse left reluctantly after the third check and Chuck gazed at me, all drugged and bleary. "You can come over here."

"I'm not getting in your bed if that's what you're thinking," I said, crossing my arms.

"You could. There's room."

"Go to sleep."

He held out an arm that looked completely out of place in a hospital gown. "I can't sleep, if you're so far away." His eyelids drooped and my resolve softened. There were still traces of blood on his face, a good section of his hair was shaved for the twelve stitches he required, and he hadn't been able to keep down Jell-O so far. In short, he was pathetic and it hurt me to see it.

"Alright, but don't be trying to feel me up or anything." I dragged my chair over to his bedside and lowered his side rail. "Better?"

He reached for my hand and I gave it to him. "Much. Now get in bed."

"What does it take to get you to sleep?" I asked.

"You. Naked."

"If I was naked, you'd go to sleep?"

"Oh, yeah. I wou..."

And he was out. I leaned on his bed and put my head on the mattress.

"Mercy," said a woman's voice.

I looked up and found Cortier peeking around the curtain. She was wearing skintight workout clothes and her hair was in a ratty ponytail.

"Can I come in?" she asked.

I rubbed my eyes. "Sure. What's up?"

She laughed softly. "Plenty, with you in the center."

Chuck stirred and reached for me. I took his hand again. "Right place and all that."

"Definitely the right place for Wellow," she said.

"How is he?"

"Looks like someone put his face in a meat grinder."

"They let you see him?"

"No. That's what the wife said." Cortier pulled up a chair on the other side of the bed. "How's he doing?"

"He'll be fine. They'll keep him overnight, but it's nothing dramatic."

She eyed the stitches. "That's not what I'd think if it were me."

"Could've been worse," I said.

"It was worse. Johnson had a stroke. He's in a coma."

I nodded, thinking of nothing useful to say. Stroke after a head injury could happen. I shouldn't have been surprised, but I was. Surprised and saddened. I had a pit in my middle. Not a new pit. An old one, freshly opened. Rory Dushane, from my adventure in Copper Mountain, was still in the hospital, trying to learn how to hold a fork. I couldn't think about that at the best of times and now wasn't the best of times. Change of subject required.

"The lab confirmed listeriosis in both the frat boys and the remaining cupcakes," I said.

"I know," said Cortier. "Have you seen the boys?"

"Briefly. Alex's having a rough time, but it looks like they'll all recover fully. Did Vanessa pick Farrell out of the lineup?"

"We did a photo array, but no. The best she could do was a probably. We did get one print off of a cupcake box. It looks like he tried to wipe it clean and missed a spot."

"What did Farrell say?" I asked.

"Not a damn thing. Bastard clammed up tight. He has four lawyers hovering outside his room." Cortier rubbed her hands together. "God, I'd love to get him in interrogation."

"Do you think it would do any good?"

She sighed. "It'd make me happy to harass the hell out of him. But no, he wouldn't give anything up. That's what I wanted to talk to you about."

"Harassing Farrell?"

"His connection to the Tulio case in St. Louis."

"If there's a connection, it's news to me," I said.

She leaned back and rubbed her jaw like my dad did when he was thinking. "I heard this big lug was over at Schwartz Realty when the Feds raided it."

"He was going to interview Mrs. Schwartz."

"What for?"

"Rob Berry worked for her and—" My phone rang. Dad. 911. "I have to get this."

She shook her head. "This is important. Why was he talking to Schwartz?"

"Sorry. It's my dad."

She sucked in a breath and a muscle twitched in her jaw.

"Hi, Dad," I said, turning away.

"Don't tell her anything!" he burst out.

"Who? What?"

"Cortier. She's on her way to find you. Don't tell that woman diddly-squat."

"Oh, well..."

"She's there, isn't she?" he asked.

I looked back at Cortier. She was trying to look nonchalant and failing miserably. "Yeah, she's here."

"What'd you tell her?"

"Nothing."

"Good girl. Now tell her to piss off," said Dad with glee in his voice.

"I don't think so."

"Alright fine, ya goody two shoes. Now I want you to get yourself over to the lockup and interview that Schwartz woman pronto. I can't find any connection between her husband and Andrew Marlin, neither can Spidermonkey."

My chest went tight. "Spidermonkey?" I squeaked out.

"You've heard of him?"

"Um...Chuck uses him sometimes, I think."

"Yeah, he does. Morty's partying at that Comic-Con and I needed this ASAP. For god's sake, don't tell Morty."

"No problem. So you don't have anything?"

Cortier flashed a smile and then quickly concealed it.

"We've got Andrew Marlin. Cortier doesn't have anything. I need you to get the connection from Schwartz. Her husband ran for it, so all we've got is the wife."

"Dad, I'm not the one for this. Think about it," I said.

Cortier perked up.

Dad mumbled something. "Yeah, yeah. This is up Chuck's alley. He could charm the skin off a snake."

He didn't know. I hated giving bad news and this news felt like a huge screwup on my part. If I'd figured it out sooner…

"Mercy?" said Dad.

"There's been a complication," I said.

"Ah, shit. I knew I should've sent Aaron with you. All that chocolate makes you think. What'd you screw up?"

"I solved the poisoning." I glanced at Cortier and she nodded with a smile.

"Really? That Farrell kid?"

"Her father."

"What's the bad news?" Dad asked.

"He tried to kill Chuck and two other cops."

Dad let out a string of curses that would've made Uncle Morty take note. Very creative. When he calmed down, he asked, "How'd you solve it if people almost died?"

I told him what happened and he grudgingly gave me a few props.

"So there's really no point in me going down there," I said. Schwartz wasn't going to tell me anything. If Chuck was on his feet, maybe.

"Figure something out!" Dad yelled. "I'm not eating catfish!"

I glanced at Cortier. "Catfish?"

"I hate freaking catfish!"

"Okay. Nobody is going to make you eat catfish, Dad."

Cortier raised her hand. "I am."

"What the…"

"That woman's trying to bogart this case."

"Let her. I need a vacation. A real one. No blood."

"To hell with that. We have a bet. Loser eats catfish."

So that's where I got it from. All my stupidity was Dad's fault.

Mom would be thrilled. The argument about where my brain came from was long-running.

"How can she take the Tulio case? It happened in St. Louis," I said.

Cortier smiled.

"It's complicated, but there's some small basis, if the crime was planned in her jurisdiction and the Berrys were lured to St. Louis. The Schwarz employees are going to be locked up tight and most of them are women. You're no use there."

"Thanks, Dad."

"Why'd you let Chuck get clobbered?"

"Not my fault."

"I'd like to know whose fault it is?" he asked.

"I'm going with the guy that did it. Farrell."

Dad started typing in the background. It helped him to think. "Yeah, yeah. Who else would know about the Schwartzes and doesn't owe them anything? Who else have we got to ask?"

"I'll think of something," I said.

"You better. If I eat catfish, you eat crab."

Crab again. It always comes back to crab.

I hung up and looked at Cortier.

"So the big man has told you to shut up," she said.

"Yep."

"He's a huge pain in the ass."

"Nobody knows it better than me."

Cortier tried to pump me for information, but it didn't last long. She paced and then walked through the curtain only to pop her head back in. "Where's your partner? I need to interview him."

"Comic-Con," I said.

"What?"

"My partner, Aaron, is at Comic-Con in Portland."

"Not that partner. The other one. Gangly, but charming."

"Oh, him."

Think fast. Nope. I've got nothing.

"He's on a date."

That flummoxed her. I guess people don't generally get romantic after going through a bloody crime scene. She didn't know Stevie and, if I had my way, she never would. When he got back to Nana's, I was shipping him off. Anywhere was preferable to New Orleans and Chuck was in no shape to take him home. Dad could snag him at some later date, assuming he could avoid the Costillas.

I fussed with Chuck's blankets and he grabbed my hand. "What's wrong?" he slurred.

"Nothing."

"Don't believe…"

"Go back to sleep."

He was already out so I put up his side rail. A connection between Marlin and the Schwartzes. Who would know that? Rob Berry, possibly. Donatella? I hated to bother her, but, at least, I had good news. It took a half hour of trying before she answered. She was shaky and so sad, she sounded like she was talking to me from under the ocean. I suppose I was hoping for happiness when I told her she was off the hook in the listeriosis case, but she only accepted what I said and waited. Grief can be like that, even the things that matter terribly cease to matter for a time.

"Donatella?"

"Yes."

"Have you ever heard the name Andrew Marlin?" I asked.

"No."

"You're certain?"

"Yes."

She didn't ask why I wanted to know. She couldn't have cared less so I let her go. If Rob knew the connection, he took the knowledge with him to the morgue. Sheila was the other possibility and she was dead. Cortier hadn't mentioned her. Maybe she hadn't put it together. I doubted anyone knew about Rob's relationship with Sheila. No, no. That couldn't be right. Sheila was young and none too bright. She'd have told someone. She couldn't resist. Of course she did, and that person would know everything she knew.

I jumped out of my chair and Chuck raised a hand. "Where are you going?"

"Nowhere. I'm getting hungry. Be right back."

He tried to sit up. "Liar. You've got an idea. I'm going to." His mouth twisted and he grabbed his head.

I pushed him back and gave him a basin. "You're not going anywhere. I'll be right back."

He protested, but I was out the door, calling Spidermonkey and avoiding the cops.

CHAPTER TWENTY-SIX

I met Tiny at airport security and he was exactly what you'd expect in a Tiny. He was six foot six and morbidly obese. I was mildly afraid that he would fall on me. He looked that bad. Sweating and out of breath after walking the five feet to greet me at the front desk.

"You must be Mercy," he wheezed.

This guy is going to die, like right now. I don't have time for that.

"That's me. Did Detective Cortier call you?"

"She did, but there's nothing I can do. Got to have a ticket."

Damn.

"Any ideas?"

"There's a flight to Naples, Florida in thirty. 350 bucks."

I groaned. "Tiny, you're killing me."

"You're lucky I'm here. Joe would strip search you and still wouldn't let you on the concourse."

"Joe's a stand-up guy."

"He's a dirtbag, but he's my boss," said Tiny and his cheeks changed from their dark brown to crimson. It's not easy to get skin that dark to go red.

I took a step back, just in case of eminent collapse. "Are you okay?"

"Oh, yeah. I'm good. Just ate lunch."

There was a choice to be made. I could sit Tiny down, loosen his tie, and assess his condition which was obviously bad. Or I could buy that over-priced ticket and get out on the concourse, saving myself from a crab dinner and Dad's wrath. I didn't know which would be worse.

Damnit, Tiny!

I took him by the arm and attempted to steer him back to the extra-large office chair behind the desk. I failed. Tiny stood there and watched me tug on his elbow which was, incidentally, right in my eye line. I'd never felt so short.

"What're you doing?" he asked.

"Trying to sit you down." Now I was out of breath from tugging on that enormous arm.

"Don't you have to get on the concourse?"

I let go. "I'm going to give it to you straight. I'm afraid if I leave you here, you're going to collapse and die. I can't have that on my conscience. There's too much on there already."

Tiny chuckled. "I'm not going to die. Why you think I'm going to die?"

"I'm a nurse and I've seen people in the ICU that look better than you," I said. "Please sit."

"You're a nurse? How'd that happen?"

"It's a mystery."

"Cortier said you was a detective," he said.

"Are you going to sit or what?" I asked.

Tiny laid a twenty-pound hand on my shoulder. "I've got a job to do. You want that ticket? Her plane takes off in twenty minutes. You don't have a lot of time."

"I'd rather lose her than you."

He laughed again. "You dramatic, girl. I'm all good. Let's get you that ticket."

Tiny steered me out the door into the hubbub of the airport. He lumbered along beside me at a pretty good clip, considering his size and the odd turn to his right knee. We took the elevator up to the United desk and I plunked down my credit card. 350 bucks for a flight

I wasn't going to take. It pained me. It really did. Physical pain. That money would've been better spent on a flight to Germany with Spidermonkey to research the Klinefeld Group. Spending it on anything would be better than spending it on nothing.

Tiny used his radio to call for a zippy little airport cart. When he got on, the thing lurched so hard to the right I wasn't sure the tire would rotate. But it did and we made it out to A33 quickly.

Spidermonkey had sent me a picture of Sheila's roommate. She was a pretty girl of twenty-two. Leslie Hutton was at the gate, waiting with the other flight attendants and not happy to see me. I get that a lot. I jumped off the cart and sprinted to catch her before she made it through the door.

"Leslie!" I yelled as I ran.

Leslie stopped at the door and turned, frowning. She had big bags under her eyes and a papery look to her skin. Not a lot of sleep since she found Sheila strangled in her kitchen.

I stopped in front of her, gasping. "Leslie."

"We've boarded. I have to go."

"No, no. Just one second. It's about Sheila."

She flinched and turned right into the attendant at the boarding pass scanner, bursting into tears.

"Sheila!" The woman grabbed her by the shoulders. "What's wrong?"

"Nothing," she sobbed.

The woman, her tag said Mary, glared at me and folded Leslie into her narrow chest.

I put myself between them and the door. "I wouldn't be here, if it weren't important."

"Doubtful," said Mary.

Tiny lumbered over. "Stand down, Mary. Miss Watts is legit."

Mary wasn't convinced, but she didn't try to move Leslie around me either. Tiny grabbed the scanner kiosk to support himself. He'd sweated through his uniform and was puffing at an alarming rate. The kiosk tilted and I lunged to keep Tiny upright. Once steady, he shook his head as if clearing a fog. "I'm okay."

"No, you're not," said Mary.

Leslie lifted her head, wiping her tears. "I'm sorry for all this."

"Nothing to be sorry for." Mary's expression turned from caring to vicious when she looked at me. "You go away. Running around upsetting people."

"That is my M.O. I can't help it," I said.

"Yes, you can. You're making a show of yourself. It's disgusting."

Not the first time I'd heard that, but it was the first time with that nasty tone. It stung me for an instant until I remembered that I was a book with a showy cover. I would be judged by it. That's how it is. Deal with it, Mercy.

"Leslie found her roommate strangled two days ago. My job is to find out who did it," I said with dignity, I hoped.

Mary clutched Leslie tighter. "Oh my god. That was you, honey."

Another flight attendant came out and tapped Leslie on the shoulder. "You need to board. Now, Leslie."

Tiny held up a finger. "Hold it. We're solving a murder here."

"Are we?" she asked.

"We are," I said. "I hope we are. Leslie, you were close to Sheila, right?"

She nodded and her face squinched up, prepared for the ugly cry. "I knew her forever. And now... and now, she's..."

I took her away from Mary and looked into her weepy eyes. "Did she talk to you about Rob Berry?"

Her eyes widened and cleared.

"It's okay. I already know. Did she talk to you?" I asked.

"We told each other everything."

"And Rob told her things."

She nodded.

"About the company. What they were up to? Illegal things?"

Another nod.

"Did she ever mention a man called Andrew Marlin?"

Leslie frowned. "No. That's a funny name. I'd remember that."

"Are you certain?"

"I'm sorry."

I gave her arms a brisk rub. "It's okay. I thought I had something there for a second. You better get on your plane. It's best you're out of town for a bit."

"Won't the police want to talk to me?" asked Leslie.

"It can wait. Get on the plane and get some distance between you and the Schwartzes."

Mary and the other attendant dried Leslie's eyes and straightened her uniform.

"Rupert, can you take Miss Watts away?" asked Mary. "People are staring. They'll be getting nervous about," she whispered, "terrorism."

"They're not staring because of that," said Tiny.

Mary gave him a look that said she didn't agree. I was a dime a dozen. Harlot. Tramp. I ignored her and took Rupert/Tiny's wrist. His pulse was racing and the sweating wasn't letting up.

"So you're a Rupert?" I asked to distract him while I looked in his eyes.

"I prefer Tiny."

"It's a good nickname."

Nickname. Tiny was his nickname. Of course!

I spun around and grabbed the door just as it was about to close. "Leslie!"

Mary grabbed me. "Stop that! Rupert will arrest you."

"No, I won't," he said. "But you better stop anyway."

"Leslie!" I yelled again and she came back around the corner.

"What?"

"What about Andy or Drew? Either ring a bell?"

She shook her head. "No."

"Wait, wait. What about Fish? That's a nickname for Marlin. Anything?" I asked.

Leslie brought up her finger and tapped her chin.

Yes? Yes?

"I've heard that one. I thought it was a weird name, but it has nothing to do with Rob Berry," she said.

"I'll take it. Where did you hear it?"

"From Sheila. She said some guy called Fish showed up at the office a couple of weeks ago.

Right before the Tulio murders.

"He hit on Sheila in front of Rob. The guy was really obnoxious."

"Who was he, Leslie?"

"Well, Sheila said Mr. Schwartz called Fish a distant cousin but he seemed more like a brother. He was sleazy enough."

Another flight attendant came around the bend, tapping his watch. "Leslie, get a move on. Do we have to replace you?"

"No, no. I'm sorry," said Leslie, but she didn't turn to go. She reached inside her carry-on and pulled out a pink flowered book with a little brass lock.

"Diary?" I asked.

"Whoever...hurt Sheila searched for it, but they didn't find it."

I took the diary and pressed it to my chest. "Thank you. We'll get him. I swear."

She wiped a stray tear as the other flight attendant tugged on her sleeve.

"Just out of curiosity, where was it?" I asked.

"Brown sugar canister. We never bake." Leslie turned away and disappeared around the bend. Mary tugged me backwards and slammed the door.

"You," she pointed, "go."

"Alright then," said Tiny. "Let's get you back."

We got on the cart and zinged through the crowds back to the elevator. I got off, but Tiny didn't.

"That girl's friend was murdered?"

"Yes," I said.

"And that book's gonna solve it?"

I laughed. "It's never that simple. It's evidence, much needed evidence."

"Evidence, like what you see when you look at me," said Tiny and the sparkle went out of his eye.

"I suppose so."

"You think I'm going to die."

"Yes, I do and pretty soon if you don't do something. I'd hate for that to happen."

He stuck out his big hand. "Pleasure to meet you, Mercy. I hope you got what you needed."

"I did and thank you for not arresting me."

"Ah, shoot. I can't arrest you. I'd have your old man down here, doing a dance on my head." He slapped the hood of the cart and they drove away. I'd probably never see Tiny again. But I'd read too many studies, looked at too many fatty livers, not to know. It broke my heart. Tiny was one of the good guys.

I went down the escalator to find a convenient cab, waiting at the curb. I gave the driver Nana's address and was once again told it didn't exist. After a five minute argument, we were on our way into the city. I relaxed on the cold vinyl seat in the back and read Sheila's last words with a lump in my throat. I was in those flower-patterned pages and she'd been kind. Lucky for me, Sheila had an eye for detail. She noted that I had green eyes, instead of Marilyn's blue. It was an important distinction that few noticed. She also noticed that Fish looked a whole lot like Mr. Schwartz and that Fish glanced at Mr. Schwartz with a frown when he called him a distant cousin. Sheila wrote her opinion in purple ink. She thought Fish and Mr. Schwartz were brothers.

I snapped the diary shut and pulled out my phone. "Dad, I got it."

CHAPTER TWENTY-SEVEN

Dad found Andrew Marlin, aka Fish, in a Motel 6 with a teenaged prostitute before Chuck got his eleven o'clock pressure check. My father was a lot of things. He was not slow. Or restrained, for that matter. There was some talk of a police brutality charge, but since Dad wasn't a cop anymore, it came to nothing. Dad figured if a forty-year-old man takes a sixteen-year-old girl into a hotel room, he deserves to get punched in the ear six times. It turned out that plenty of people agreed, me included.

After Andrew was arrested in Missouri, I handed over the diary to Cortier. She wasn't happy. First, that I hadn't told her about Andrew and his resemblance to Mr. Schwartz and second, because Dad was flying down to watch her eat catfish. The other Berrys had readily admitted to suggesting Tulio to their relations at Andrew's suggestion. They hadn't been charged, but it wasn't out of the question. Dad thought they were clueless pawns in the scheme to kill Rob and Donatella. No one was certain how Blankenship fit in, but nobody thought the shooting was a coincidence. Dad said it would take some time, but they'd find the connection.

I curled up on my sleeper chair next to Chuck's inert body and let Dad lecture me on the death penalty in Missouri vs Louisiana. It was better to have Andrew in Missouri, for some reason. I couldn't have cared less either way. It was over. Dad graciously said he'd let me tell Donatella the whole story and I pretended to be grateful. I wasn't, not a bit. The whole story included Sheila and who wanted to tell the wife about her? At least Abrielle and Colton were safe from living with the other Berrys. I'd done my job as Dad kept telling me over and over. But I didn't exactly feel like I'd done it. Blankenship's smile crept back into my mind and the thought of him was like having an intestinal parasite, gross and bad for the digestion.

I went to sleep with his face in the forefront of my mind and when I woke up, he was still there. I began to feel like Andrew and the Schwartzes were getting away with it. Dad was confident that the connection between Blankenship and Andrew would be found. The more I thought about it, the more I doubted it. If the cops didn't lock down the part they played in the Tulio murders with solid evidence, Andrew and the Schwartzes would go to some federal prison to play tennis. The other Berrys would walk away untouched. The thought made me sick. I sat in Chuck's room, watching his monitor, waiting for an idea to come to me. None did.

Chuck woke up migraine-free and starving. He ate the hospital breakfast and everything I brought up from the cafeteria. I got one apple chip and a latte, only because the doc didn't want Chuck to have coffee. One apple chip? I was starving and trucking down the hall in search of a vending machine when I happened upon Derek, who was studying a room's placard.

"What are you doing here?" I asked and the kid jumped a foot. "Sorry."

"It's okay," he said. "I was looking for you."

"I'll pay you twenty bucks to get me a chocolate croissant from the pastry cart next to the information desk downstairs," I said.

He frowned. "How come you can't go?"

"Doc's coming up to examine Chuck and I want to be there."

"Okay. Sure."

I gave Derek twenty-five dollars that he tried to refuse and I ended up stuffing the money in his back pocket. He took off for the elevators and I went back to Chuck's room to find him flirting shamelessly with Cortier. She wasn't happy to see me. That bothered me even less than usual, since her questioning was solely to get one over on my dad.

"It's well known that Tommy uses you for grunt work and doesn't pay you," Cortier said to me. "This is your chance to pull one over on him."

"Pass. He's my father, remember? I'm stuck with that weirdo for life."

Cartier had no hope. Nobody beat my dad, except my mother. That was only because he loved her so much. She brought out the stupid in him and, believe me, it wasn't much. If I had any secret ammo to use against Dad, I'd use it for myself. Cortier could eat her catfish. Bummer for her.

Chuck laughed and crossed his arms. The muscles bulged under the short sleeves of his hospital gown. I tried not to notice and failed. Miserably.

"Come on. Can't you give me something on him? I'd rather eat a homeless man's underwear than eat one bite of catfish." She looked desperate. I knew the feeling. I could've lost to Wellow. My victory was hollow, considering that he would be eating through a straw for the foreseeable future. As much as I liked to win, I wouldn't be serving liquid crab.

"I can't because I don't have anything," I said.

"You're his kid. You've got the genes."

"Do I look like I have the genes?"

"You've got the brain. I'm not eating that catfish." She pointed at me like that was going to do something for her. Puh-lease.

Derek walked in with a beautiful little white pastry bag. "Here you go."

Chuck reached out. "You are the man. Gimme."

I smacked his hands. "Back off, buzzard. That's mine."

"But I'm starving."

"You've had 1200 calories so far today. You're good." I took the bag from Derek and gave him a hug just to irritate Chuck. It worked. He crossed his arms and glared at Derek, who retreated to the far side of the room.

"Don't scare off my assistant," I said. "If it weren't for him, you'd probably be in the morgue with a brick-shaped hole in your head."

Chuck snorted, but Cortier got interested. "Oh, yeah. Derek, the frat boy assistant."

Oh, no. Did Derek do anything illegal? No. Maybe. No. Not sure. Oh, no.

Cortier took off her jacket and exposed her badge clipped at her waist. Derek looked at it and then me. Fantastic. The poor kid didn't know anything that would help her, but she'd grill him until he peed. Literally.

Chuck tapped my thigh with his foot and when Cortier advanced on Derek, he mouthed, "Remember Stevie. Get her out."

I'd completely forgotten about Stevie. Now he was something Cortier could use against Dad. She'd arrest Stevie, instead of letting him surrender, and ruin Big Steve's scheme to protect his goofy offspring. Dad couldn't have that and she'd win.

"So," I said, "let's go for a coffee and talk about it."

Cortier turned, her eyes glittering. "That's right. I know Tommy Watts."

Huh?

"This kid is your assistant, your protégé."

Where is she going with this?

"Yeah, sure. He's been a huge help," I said.

"In other words, you owe him," said Cortier.

Derek brightened up like my cat, Skanky, when I brought home smoky cheddar. A cat's gotta have his smoky cheddar.

"Yes," I said, slowly.

"I can help you out with that," said Cortier.

Chuck mouthed, "Oh shit."

"That's right, handsome," she said. "Everybody knows that a Watts takes care of their people. Hell, that's why Miss Mercy's down here in the first place, taking care of Officer Ameche. He's Donatella Berry's brother, isn't he?"

"Yes," I said.

"He helped you out, and now you're helping him."

"Yes."

"So Derek helped you and he wants to be in criminal justice." She looked hard at Derek and he nodded. "I can help him. I can be his mentor here in New Orleans, on the scene. That is..."

Groan.

"If I help you get out of catfish," I said.

She fired a finger pistol at me and I contained a grimace. Derek was looking so damn shiny and eager, what could I do? "How much mentoring?"

"Plenty. That kid'll skip the police department and go straight to the FBI," she said.

Derek was doing the wee-wee dance, he was so excited.

"And all I have to do is get you out of catfish?" I asked quickly, so he wouldn't pee himself.

"That's the deal."

I stuck out my hand. "Deal, but it might take a few days."

Cortier nodded and I hustled her and her new protégé out of Chuck's room. Derek couldn't stop gushing about how he'd work so hard and blah, blah, blah. I had to get them out of there. It was near eleven. Stevie was a late sleeper, but he could show up at any second. If Cortier got interested and decided to run his name, I'd be screwed and so would Derek. She wouldn't owe me a thing.

I grabbed Derek by the shoulders. "It was great having you on my team. You are going to be an asset to Cortier." I hugged him and whispered in his ear, "Get her out of here."

"Sure," he said.

"Sure what?" asked Cortier.

"Sure would like to...buy you a cup of coffee, so I can pick your brain," said Derek, masterfully covering.

"Sounds great. Always in need of coffee."

They said goodbye and walked away. Derek gave me a thumbs up as they turned the corner and I returned it. He was a good kid. I hoped Cortier would really help him, and then I smiled. If she didn't, Cortier would answer to Dad. He was serious about taking care of people.

Back in Chuck's room, I found him trying to take out his IV.

"What do you think you're doing?" I asked.

"I'm checking myself out."

"This isn't a hotel."

"It is now. I'm not sick," he said with his best smile. "All I need is some Motrin and I'm all good."

"No NSAIDS post-concussion."

He gave me a lecherous grin. "I hope that's not no sex."

"It's no Motrin, dumbass."

"We're all set then."

"Hardly." I pushed him back onto the bed. "You have a head injury, which is made all the more apparent by this craziness."

Chuck snorted and picked at the tape on his wrist. "I've been hurt worse, playing tennis."

"What kind of tennis are you playing?"

"Combat tennis."

"That's not a thing."

"It is in my world."

I didn't know what to say to that. It was off the wall, even for someone in my life.

"Did I hear someone say combat tennis?" asked Dr. Purdy, walking in with an open chart.

"You play?" asked Chuck.

"It's the best rush you can get on a flat surface."

Chuck waggled his eyebrows at me. "I don't know about that."

Dr. Purdy laughed. "I take it back. You play double points?"

"Is there any other way to play?"

I plopped down on my chair. "This cannot be a thing. What's double points?"

"You play doubles and you can score points against the other team and your own partner."

"What do you do, tackle them?"

Chuck showed me his pearly whites. "I bite."

He and Dr. Purdy shared a hearty laugh and got down to business. We reviewed Chuck's stats, checked his stitches, and went over his aftercare instructions. Then they moved onto the intricacies of combat tennis and I went to my happy place; me on my sofa, under an afghan, drinking Aaron's hot chocolate and watching Pride and Prejudice, the good version.

"Mercy?" Chuck's voice broke into my luscious thoughts.

"Huh?"

"Doc says I'm outta here."

Dr. Purdy nodded. "Pronto."

I smiled at pronto. In hospitals, pronto means eventually, when we get your paperwork done.

In Chuck's case, pronto meant four hours. His latest labs went missing for a time and there were two codes on the floor. If I hadn't taken out his IV, we might've been there for the rest of the day. But I did take it out and we got home at two. Despite Chuck's protests, I made him take a nap. He was asleep before I tucked him in.

I decided I'd better locate Stevie before taking a shower. The Costillas hadn't shown up yet, and I figured they were past due. A part of me was afraid Stevie'd been nabbed on his date, possibly along with his date, and the thought was bothersome. I called him and heard a faint ringing on the second floor. I checked all the bedrooms and ended up in my bathroom. Stevie was asleep in the tub with his phone ringing away on his chest.

"Stevie," I said.

One unfocused eye crept open.

"Why are you in here?"

"Feels good on my back."

"You're twenty. Everything feels good on your back. Go to bed."

"I did." He turned off his phone without answering it and rolled over. I sighed before covering him with a couple of towels. No shower for me in there so I went into my bedroom to get my robe and found Blackie perched on the headboard, watching me as if I were late.

"How do you keep getting in here?" I asked as I plucked him up and tucked him under my arm for the trip to the back door.

No meow. No nothing. I had the vague notion that the cat didn't much care what I did. I certainly didn't have any effect on him.

I tossed him out the back door and he plopped down on his skinny rump and watched me in the doorway. I made a shooing motion. "Go away. The neighbor's supposed to have food for you."

Nothing. If I didn't know better, I would've questioned whether or not he was breathing.

"Blink," I ordered.

The cat didn't blink, not a whisker moved. So disturbing.

"Fine, you freak. One of these days I'm going to figure out how you're getting in and then I'll fix your wagon." Pop Pop always said the wagon thing and it never made sense to me. How was fixing someone's wagon a bad thing? Now I was saying it. Pretty soon, I'd be telling patients to finish their dinners because it would put hair on their chests.

I closed the door and, since Stevie was in my shower and I had nothing better to do for once, I went to bed to dream of green-eyed cats and menacing shadows that I would later realize were the Costilla brothers.

CHAPTER TWENTY-EIGHT

Chuck woke up before me. I found him in the kitchen, freshly showered and reading a *Sports Illustrated*. He glanced up and frowned at my rumpled appearance. I'd slept in my clothes. Not sure how that happened. I meant to put on a big tee and somehow missed the mark.

"Wow. You look worse than me, and I got hit with a brick," he said.

"Coffee." I stumbled toward Nana's beloved espresso machine.

Chuck headed me off. "I'll make you a latte. You go get ready."

"For what?"

"You won the bet, didn't you?"

I blinked slowly. My eyeballs felt like parchment paper. "I'm not making Wellow eat crab. He's been punished enough."

"Nobody's eating crab, especially not Wellow. They wired his jaw shut, remember?"

"Oh, yeah."

"I'm taking you to Irene's to celebrate," said Chuck, assuming a triumphant stance. I don't know who he thought he'd triumphed over, but I had a suspicion that it was me.

"What for?"

"You solved the listeriosis case."

"Farrell confessed?" I asked.

Chuck snorted and looked like he pitied me. "No. There was a truckload of evidence in his attic, including pie charts and case studies. Why do you always ask that? They never confess. This isn't Perry Mason."

"Perry Mason?"

"You know, that old detective show. Lawyer in a wheelchair. They always confessed on the stand."

"How old are you?" I asked.

"My mom says I'm eighty-five," said Chuck, smiling.

"That's because your mother is perpetually fifteen."

"I'd give her sixteen, but you're close. So it's Irene's at seven." He turned me around and pushed me by my rear toward the door. "Hurry up."

I tried to go back to the espresso machine. "You got reservations at Irene's in prime time. I don't think so."

He turned me again. "I have my ways."

I eyed him over my shoulder. "Do you perhaps have a date later with a buxom maître d'?

"Yes, to the buxom. No, to the maître d'. Go."

"Waitress?"

"You. I have a date with you."

I was out the door, but my heels were digging into the thick oriental carpet runner. "It's not a date."

"It's not a business meeting," said Chuck.

"I have a boyfriend and you're you."

"We'll see about that."

"Yeah, we will. It's not a date."

Chuck stopped and squeezed my shoulders. "You sure are protesting a lot."

"Not a date," I said.

He pushed me into Nana's bathroom and said, "A celebratory dinner then."

"Good." I closed the door. That was alright. Just a celebratory dinner and we were family. Pete wouldn't think anything was wrong with that. Except that we weren't really family. Not blood, anyway. No.

Pete wouldn't mind. It was fine. Why wouldn't it be fine? Of course, it was fine. Not a date. I wouldn't *date* Chuck. Nobody would date Chuck. He was so...

I turned on the water and stripped. Boiling hot water. Good for sterilizing dirty objects as well as minds. In other words, good for me.

Irene's at seven was crowded, dimly-lit, and smelled the way I hoped heaven would. Everything was good at Irene's. The patrons were happy and used to goodness. The wait staff are pros, not people waiting for their big break. Of course, I could barely see my hand in front of my face, but that was good. I looked as tired as I felt. Chuck's latte, while excellent, hadn't perked me up. I needed to good sleep, three days at least.

They sat us in a prime corner spot and Chuck ordered a hundred dollar wine. I started to protest the expense, but decided a serious celebration was in order. The prosecutor in the Farrell case called. Farrell was screwed. There was so much evidence, he'd have to agree to a plea bargain or risk a life sentence. The guy was so anal and controlling, evidence collection had never been so easy. His lawyer was already saying that Farrell saved Abrielle and Colton, because the listeriosis kept them and Donatella out of Tulio, where they would probably have been shot and killed. But since he tried to brick two cops to death, the prosecutor wasn't worried. Plus, Farrell had, in his piles of paperwork, the name and number of a Russian who worked at a Moscow medical research company. It looked like he was the one who supplied Farrell with the bacteria, since Farrell had returned from Moscow the day before the poisoning. The prosecutor was surprised when I asked about Faith, but I had compassion for the girl. Her mother's sister had taken her home and was staying with her. Faith was mute with shock at her father's arrest and she had suffered a miscarriage. That fact was on one of her father's spreadsheets, labeled "Evidence of Guilt." There was no other real evidence against Christopher Berry on the rape charge. The fact that he was a boy, and had slept with Faith, was enough for Farrell to condemn him to death. Faith wouldn't say anything about anything. They'd gotten the exhumation order on Faith's mother and expected to find that she'd been murdered. The medical examiner on the case had been put on administrative leave, pending the outcome of the new autopsy. He'd received an influx of cash around the time of her death that they hadn't been able to trace yet. The prosecutor said my dad was a genius. He said I was lucky. Thanks, loser.

"Fill 'er up," I said when Chuck offered.

He poured a big glug and I watched the ruby red liquid fill my glass. I felt better just looking at it.

"You're not still pissed about that prosecutor, are you?" asked Chuck.

"Lucky," I hissed before taking a sip.

"You were lucky. Tommy, too. Me, most of all. We're celebrating here, not obsessing." He poured me more wine and I drank it while going through the menu, squinting.

Our very mannish waitress, who was inexplicably named Jessica, came back and Chuck tried to order crabmeat gratin for the appetizer. I kicked him in the shin and he laughed. Jessica probably thought we were nuts, but she hid it well by recommending the escargot. I'm not usually a snail girl outside of France, but Chuck looked so horrified I ordered it. They weren't nearly as bad as he expected, since they didn't come in shells but were instead tucked into mushroom caps. Chuck ate most of them and declared snails to be a do-again. We ordered and got a second bottle of wine. The edges of the room were getting fuzzy in the best possible way. Chuck was smiling across from me and managed not to say a single sleazy thing. Was this the Chuck that Philippa got to see?

It was very warm in the dining room and the buzz of quiet conversations wrapped us in cotton wool, safe from everything. I forgot there was a world outside of Irene's, away from delicious food and fabulousness. I completely forgot everything but him.

Our plates came and, before I could pick up my fork, Chuck's hand slid across the white linen. "Mercy?"

"Yes?"

"I think—"

"There you guys are." Stevie grabbed an empty chair from the table next to us and plunked himself down with a bright-eyed grin.

I whipped my hand away and Chuck growled. He actually growled, like he did when the phlebotomist came in his hospital room with her tray full of bloodletting equipment. That woman ran away and was replaced with a former Army medic. He laughed and jabbed Chuck hard and fast. If Stevie had any sense, he would've been afraid of Chuck but he was Stevie and no Army guy, so he wasn't.

"Is she still pissed about the lucky thing?" asked Stevie.

"I'm not," I lied. But it stung. People were always saying I was lucky. Nobody ever said I was smart.

"She was, but I *was* getting her over it before *you* came," snapped Chuck.

"Then I'm just in time to help."

"You're not helping."

"I am," said Stevie, taking a big drink of my wine. "That's good. Tastes like one of my dad's favorites."

Chuck and I stared at him.

"You shouldn't be pissed, Mercy. Your dad gets things wrong all the time. It's just that nobody notices. Take me, for instance. He got me all wrong."

I took back my glass. "What are you going on about?"

"Tommy sent Chuck to get me and bring me home. He was expecting me back days ago, but you're here. Chuck's not going to hurry back to St. Louis with *you* here. He was a right idiot, when you think about it. Feel better?"

I looked at Chuck, but he was studying the wine glass in his hand.

"It does. Thanks," I said.

Jessica came over, her face placid but I could feel the tension in her. Irene's didn't like disturbances. "Is this gentleman with you?"

"Yes," I said before Chuck could utter the "no" that was dancing on his lips. He growled instead.

"Would you like a menu, sir?" asked Jessica, holding out a menu.

Chuck swiped the menu before Stevie had a chance to take it. "I'll give you five hundred bucks to throw him in the freezer."

Jessica barely managed to keep her professional composure. "I would, sir, but the police frown on that kind of thing."

"What's in the freezer?" asked Stevie.

"Not much," said Jessica. "Our food is fresh."

"Stevie, you're ruining my life," said Chuck.

"I'm saving your life. It's not a party without Stevie."

"I could kill you and hide the body."

Stevie laughed and took the menu from him. "Yeah, you could. Now, what are you having? What's good?"

"Everything," I said.

"Nothing," said Chuck. "Go away."

Jessica bit her lower lip.

"Have the cap of ribeye," I said. "It's fabulous."

"I'll take it," said Stevie and gave Jessica the menu. "So what were you guys talking about? The case?"

"No," said Chuck.

"Yes," I said. "The Farrell case to be specific."

"That guy is a douchebag," said Stevie, taking a wineglass from Jessica. "Let's order another bottle. I'm thirsty. My date drained me dry."

"Ew," I said. "I didn't need to know that."

Stevie didn't much care what I needed or wanted to know. He was going to tell us every gory detail. The nurse was even dumber than I thought. Stevie claimed he used a condom, three to be exact, and I only hoped he was being truthful. I once had to hunt down the girls he gave VD to. Stevie wasn't the cleanest character, but girls rarely figured that out.

Stevie's food came quickly and he ate even quicker. Chuck ordered a third bottle. Halfway through it, he lightened up and was cheerful by dessert. We laughed our way out onto the street after Chuck paid the enormous bill. I was tipsy enough not to feel too guilty as we walked down the center of the deserted street, still smelling the wonderful aromas drifting out of the door of Irene's.

Stevie hooked his arm through mine. "What should we do now?"

"We should pack and clean up the house," I said.

"That is so sensible." He gazed up at the dark sky filled with billowing purple clouds. "Let's not."

"Stevie, you are going home to face the...the—"

"Music," said Chuck.

"That's right. Face the music for your wastrel life of petty crime. Is that right? Wastrel sounds wrong," I said, tipping over in my stilettos to be caught by Stevie, who'd drunk three times as much as me but appeared sober.

"It's wrong," he said. "There's nothing petty about my crime."

"How about ill-conceived?"

"That's what Dad calls me." Stevie grinned.

"Really? That's not good. The worst I get is useless. But I'm very useful. I'm here, doing stuff that people do."

Stevie straightened me up. "We are useful. Very useful. We're unappreciated in..."

"Our time. That's right," I said. "Totally unappreciated."

Chuck shook his head. "I'll give Mercy useful. But Stevie, you keep stealing your mother's car."

Stevie wheeled around and pointed a boney finger in Chuck's broad chest. "She said the tires needed to be broken in."

"All four times?"

"I think it was five." Stevie began to count cars. "The jag. Twice. Lexus was once. BMW when I was nine."

I broke in, "I don't remember that."

"Dad hid it. I convinced him that I didn't know any better." Stevie whispered in my ear, "I did."

Chuck separated Stevie from the side of my face. "Do you hear that?"

"Yes," I said. "It was four stolen cars."

"Not that. The music."

We stopped and tilted our heads in the direction of the cathedral. Definitely music and a distinctive type, too. I groaned, "It's a second line. Tourists are such suckers."

"A what?" asked Chuck.

"You know like a funeral, but for a wedding. There's a jazz band and dancing down the streets," I said with an exaggerated eye roll.

Chuck grabbed my hand. "That sounds freaking awesome. Let's do it."

"Do what?" I asked very slowly.

"Join that line thing. We can, can't we?"

"Well, yeah, but it's not a thing. My family's been here forever and we don't do wedding lines. It's for tourists."

Chuck pulled me close and I couldn't hear anything, no music, no Stevie. "I don't care if it's for chipmunks. Let's do it."

"Okay."

He dragged me down the street with Stevie trailing behind, asking if there would be bridesmaids. I would've told him he didn't stand a chance, but he did. It made no sense, but there was bound to be a woman in the line for Stevie.

We went around the corner and found the line going past. It was a huge one, too. Two bands, twin brides and a couple of grooms, who had enough sense to look vaguely embarrassed. They were all drunk, which helped. Chuck used his long arm to push us right into the middle, where we danced like fools and felt pretty good about it. I was twirled by at least twelve well-dressed men from Jersey and a couple of Germans, too. My red dress was made for twirling. We went by Lafitte's and Chuck dashed in for some well-timed hurricanes.

We danced and watched Stevie make out with two bridesmaids and, I fear, one of the groom's mothers. It was okay, she said, because her husband had gone back to the hotel to watch *Nature*. I agreed that kissing strangers was absolutely okay, if your husband is boring, and then I was twirled away by Chuck.

The music got louder and my drink got lower.

"Check it out!" shouted Stevie. "It's gonna be a dogpile."

We were coming to an intersection and another line was, too. Our first band tried to stop but was overwhelmed by the first bridal party and then the second band. Chuck danced me past the unsmiling police escort to the center of the intersection.

"We should get out of the way," I said, looking around at the drunken mayhem.

Chuck took my chin and tilted it so that I looked up at him. "I never get out of the way. Don't you know that yet?"

"It depends on what you mean by getti—"

He cupped my cheeks, bent low, and kissed me. His lips were hot and urgent. I sunk into him and then reached up, my arms going over his shoulders and then around his neck, like they'd been doing it forever. There was no awkwardness or hesitation. Nothing, but natural rightness that I'd never once felt before. I was supposed to be kissing Chuck. I couldn't imagine why I hadn't done it before.

Once we started kissing, we didn't stop. We kissed through the rest of the second line, through a karaoke bar that Stevie brought us to. We kissed through beignets at midnight and red beans and rice at two. We kissed our way through Nana's back door and landed on the sofa in a heap. I think I took a total of six breaths in five hours. I didn't miss oxygen. Oxygen was for sissies. I only needed lips. Chuck's lips. Were there any other lips? I didn't think so.

His hands were all over me and I fully expected his fingers to pull down my panties, but they didn't. I slid his hand up my skirt, but somehow, regretfully, it would slide back down my thigh. We fell asleep like that, tangled in each other's arms, faces pressed together until the morning sunlight slanted in through the big glass windows in the back of the house. My face was itchy and stinging. I wiggled back from Chuck's sleeping face and felt my chin. Beard burn. A world-class case. I could be used in medical textbooks under beard burn, see Mercy Watts.

I slid out from under Chuck's arm and fell with a thump onto the floor.

"Where're you going?" he asked.

"To make coffee."

"Okay." He rolled over and I crept to the kitchen, closed the door and pressed myself against it.

This is not good. Well, it is good. No, it's bad. What about Pete? Pete!

I turned on Nana's espresso machine and put my head on the counter. I'd have to tell him. He would be furious. Did I care? Yes, of course, I cared. I was supposed to care. I had to tell him. It was the right thing to do. Well...was it really? Did he need to know? What purpose would it serve? It would only hurt him.

Steaming hot espresso filled my cup. No milk. I deserved no such luxury. I took a sip. It was painfully strong, but, when the caffeine hit my system, my eyes focused and I saw the kitchen for the first time. We hadn't just hit the sofa. We'd hit Pop Pop's wine cellar as well. Two more bottles sat empty on the counter. How did we not pass out?

I threw away the bottles, found my phone, and stared at it while I ate a dried-out croissant. To call or not to call. They say confession is good for the soul. What I really wanted to do was go back to the sofa, fold myself into those arms, and forget about it. Not that I'd be allowed to forget. Fate doesn't work that way. It did for some people, but not for me. And just to prove it, fate, or possibly karma, made my phone vibrate. It startled me so much that I nearly dropped it. Uncle Morty's name appeared on the screen and my stomach unclenched. It didn't last long.

"What the hell did you think you were doing?" he yelled.

I looked at the phone, afraid to put it back to my ear.

"Answer me!"

"Um, what?" I asked.

"You know what," yelled Uncle Morty. "I had a good thing going. You have any idea how hard it is to find a wizard that's up to my rogue? A rogue of my ability?"

I instantly pictured a romance novel cover, *The Scottish Rogue* or something like that. Uncle Morty, bare-chested in a kilt. Ick and improbable.

"You're a rogue?"

"You know I'm a rogue."

I think I'm still drunk. Very drunk.

"Mercy!"

"Um...I don't know what's happening," I said. "You're a rogue?"

"God damn it. Are you listening?"

I must be dreaming. This dream sucks.

"We all knew it would happen. It's been happening for ten years, but did you have to do it like that? I thought you had class."

"You're the only one." Something brushed against my leg. The cat. The cat was in again. He leapt up on the counter and stared his usual stare. That felt like my usual life, not a dream. Actually, Uncle Morty yelling at me was as real as life got. "I thought I was dreaming."

"You're not dreaming. You're an idiot."

I looked at the wine bottles in the trash can. "I can't argue with that."

"What are you going to say to him?" asked Uncle Morty.

I thought of Chuck in the other room. I had no idea what I was going to say.

"He walked out of here looking like he might jump off a bridge, Mercy. You gotta fix this or I'm gonna lose a kickass wizard."

"Wait. Who...what are we talking about?" I asked.

"Pete. Who do you think?"

Oh my god.

"Why are we talking about Pete?"

"Why do you think? He saw the video. Half the western world saw the video. Hell, it's on the DBD site. The fan boards are going batshit crazy."

I was slack-jawed. Fan boards? Video? Stevie walked in, scratching his junk and looking at his phone. "Dude, you know how to kiss. This is like that famous war kiss."

"What the hell are you talking about?" I asked him. Uncle Morty heard and began a curse-laden rant.

Stevie held up his phone and there we were, me and Chuck kissing in the street. I saw what Stevie meant. We looked like that photo from the end of World War Two, the sailor kissing the nurse, except our kiss was no polite celebration. Ours was full on I-want-to-consume-you-passion.

I snatched the phone out of his hand. "Where'd you get that?"

"Chick I know sent it. She knows we're good friends."

"This is on the internet?"

"Duh. It's everywhere. You're trending on Twitter," said Stevie.

I braced myself on the counter and started to have what I'd diagnosed in others, a panic attack. I couldn't breathe. My heart pounded.

Stevie took back his phone. "What's up with you?"

"Pete," I whispered. "I have a boyfriend."

He snorted. "Not anymore."

"I'm going to be sick."

"It's the wine."

"It's not the wine," I said.

"What about me?" bellowed Uncle Morty out of my phone. I'd forgotten he was there, the bearer of bad news and inventive cursing.

I put my shaking hand over my eyes and asked, "What about you? I've just ruined my life, not yours."

"I beg to differ. You broke up the perfect Dungeons and Dragons team. Pete's going to dump us."

"Why?" I asked, not caring one bit.

"Because we belong to you, idiot. You could've dumped him like a decent chick, but, oh no, you had to do it on the freaking internet."

"I'm not breaking up with him."

"Well, what the hell was that? A proposal of marriage?"

"I don't know what it was. Alcohol. Stupidity."

"It was lust, you common hussy."

"Did you just call me a hussy?" I asked.

"Would you prefer slut?"

"I would not, and nothing happened."

Uncle Morty snorted and cleared his throat, very phlegmy. "You can't sell that. Least of all to Pete."

"How is he?" I asked, wincing.

"Fuck if I know. The poor kid took off after three guys in Iron Man costumes showed him the video. Aaron followed him."

"Good. Aaron'll make it better."

"Hell, no, he won't. You can't make this better. The bastard's humiliated, Humiliated! And after all the time I put into breaking him in, molding him. Why I oughta—"

I hung up on him. There was only so much I could take. Not that I didn't deserve it. I was a terrible person. The worst person. Certainly the worst girlfriend. I put my head down on the counter and counted to ten. It didn't help. Why did I tell people to do that when they were panicking? It didn't help. I checked my messages on the off-chance Pete had called. He hadn't, of course. Mickey Stix of DBD called three times to tell me how he loved the video, their message boards were on fire, and he was putting the video in the headliner position on the website. Mickey thought this was good news. His news made me heave into the sink. The smell was atrocious, just like my behavior.

I drank water out of the tap and Stevie handed me a paper towel. I swallowed a considerable amount of bile and dialed Pete. I got his voicemail and, after a shuddering breath, left him a message.

"I am so sorry, Pete. I didn't mean for that to happen. I really didn't. There were all these glasses of wine and drinks and that's no excuse, but it didn't mean anything. Nothing happened. Chuck was just there and it happened. I'm so sorry. I hope you'll forgive me, although I know I don't deserve it." I wiped my face with the paper towel and turned to Stevie, but it wasn't Stevie. It was Chuck, looking at me like he'd never seen my face before in his life.

"It didn't mean anything," he said, flatly.

"I didn't know you were standing there," I said.

"Clearly."

"I had to apologize. What I did was horrible. Everyone knows or will shortly."

"Was it horrible?" he asked, stepping close and leaning over me and not in a good way.

"No. I mean, yes. It was horrible. I have a boyfriend. I did stuff I'm not supposed to do."

"With me."

"It's got nothing to do with you. This is about Pete, what I did to Pete," I said.

"With me."

"Why do you keep saying that? Yes, with you. You of all people. You. My sleazy, horny, has dated half the female population of Missouri and Illinois, cousin. You!" I yelled.

"We're not actually related!" he yelled back. "I thought you finally figured it out!"

"What? That I'm an idiot? I've known that since I set fire to the Bleds' garage. You don't need to remind me"

He slapped his hand down on the counter so hard the dishes in the rack rattled. "I've been waiting for you to see me the way you're supposed to see me."

I slapped the counter. Nothing rattled and it hurt my hand. "Who are you to tell me how I'm supposed to see you?"

"Because I love you!"

I sucked in a breath and stared up into his glaring eyes. That was not the look of love. That was more like the look of, I could kill you and make it look like an accident.

"No, you don't. I'm just the one you can't have," I said.

"If that's what you think, I'm done," he said between clenched teeth and went for the door.

"Done with what?"

"You." He banged through the kitchen door and I heard him go up the stairs, taking three at a time.

Stevie handed me my coffee cup. "Well, you screwed that up royally."

"Oh, yeah? What did I screw up? There's nothing between us. We're like cousins. It's practically creepy," I said.

"Except it's not."

I banged my cup down on the counter, sloshing burning hot liquid over my fingers. "Yes, it is. Everybody's going to think I humped my cousin. Oh my god. Mom is going to kill me. And don't forget about Aunt Miriam. She thought my modeling shamed the family. This looks like we're incest people. Welcome to *Deliverance*, it's the Watts clan."

"Except it's not."

"Argh! I'm going out," I said in a rush.

"Where?" Stevie asked.

"I don't know. I'm going to where people don't have the internet."

"1965?"

"Shut up!" I grabbed my purse and bolted out the back door.

CHAPTER TWENTY-NINE

I didn't go to 1965. No one would sell me a ticket. I ended up at Wink's again, and Phoebe was there with new jazzy purple gauges in her ears. I walked up to the counter, trying to look like a girl who didn't make out with her cousin by marriage or sleep in her clothes or forget to brush her nasty teeth before storming out of the house. Phoebe wasn't buying it. She smiled so wide her blue lipstick cracked.

"You look familiar," she said. "Latte?"

"Yes and a bunch of stuff with fat in it, like triple fat. Got any of that?" I asked.

"Cinnamon roll?"

"Sure."

Phoebe went into the back and emerged a few minutes later with a celery-filled tall glass. "You need this more than a latte."

"Bloody marys are on the menu?"

"Only for special customers."

"Oh, I'm special alright. Specially screwed."

She grinned. "I hope so."

"That's the kicker. The clothes stayed on."

"It can be done that way."

"Not well."

Phoebe filled a bag with buttermilk drops and a cinnamon roll. "I'll give you that."

I paid her and then looked around at the half-filled little café, wishing there was a place to hide.

"Come this way." She pointed to a door to the back.

I picked up my bag and my hangover cure and obeyed. Phoebe led me out to a little courtyard filled with rustic lawn furniture. "You can hide out for a while until things calm down."

"That'll take a couple of months, but thanks." I sat on a rickety lounge chair and sipped the fiery bloody mary. Wow. That was hot.

"You know what? You look just like my bulldog after he ate an entire box of pralines and barfed in my closet," said Phoebe.

"That's how I feel."

"Tall, dark, and built, not the one for you?"

"Well..."

"Oh, you have a boyfriend," she said.

"Had a boyfriend would probably be more accurate," I said.

She nodded and crossed her tattooed arms. "He sure looked like the one. That boyfriend must be uber hot."

I screwed up my mouth and had to admit, "Not really. He's more nerdy but a great guy. I really screwed up."

"So, he's boring," she said.

"Not boring. He's normal, calm, trouble free," I said.

"Give me trouble any day."

"You don't understand. Chuck bothers me."

Phoebe nodded and stepped back into the building. "Stay as long as you want." She went inside and then popped back out. "My parents have been married for thirty years. My dad bothers my mom every day. He says it's his job."

She closed the door and I stared after her. My dad bothered my mom senseless, too. Maybe it was a thing, but it wasn't my thing. Pete was nice. He was...well...he was something. I couldn't put my finger on it. No, it wasn't boring. He had lightsabers, for crying out loud.

I choked down my drink and ate my cinnamon roll to ease the burning and then lay back to study the clouds. I'd lost Pete, that was certain, but a strange feeling settled in my chest, a familiar feeling and an uncomfortable one. I didn't care. No. I cared that he was hurt and that I was the one who hurt him. But Pete wasn't forever. He never was supposed to be forever. What did Uncle Morty say? That everybody knew this would happen. I sure didn't. How did they? When I thought of Pete, I felt so sad, but not the right sad. Not like I'd lost the love of my life. Did I love him? If I did, shouldn't it hurt more?

Chuck kept infiltrating my mind, the way he infiltrated my life, bothersome, sleazy, and forever there in the background. Could he possibly love me for real? It didn't seem likely, but the thought kept coming back. I sat there for a couple of hours, snoozing and thinking. I hadn't picked up my phone when I left, so I was blissfully unconnected. No one could get to me and it felt great. Eventually, a nagging thought settled into my mind. Chuck was upset and I'd upset him. I touched my lips, all bruised and raw from his beard, and my face got hot. My stomach twisted.

I went inside, gave Phoebe back her glass, and she smiled knowingly. "So you've decided it's not so bad."

"Oh, it's plenty bad. Just not in the way I thought." I headed out the glass door and down the street. It was a leisurely walk home. I stopped to pick up a good Irish whiskey for Chuck, a little peace offering. He'd be surprised after all the yelling, but I was the one who was surprised. I opened the back door and was met by silence.

"Chuck! Stevie!" I called out, going from room to room, but they were gone. Cleared out. All their clothes, everything. I checked the bathtub. Stevie wasn't in it. My phone was on the counter where I'd left it. I called Chuck over and over. He didn't answer. I left messages. Good ones, I think, but he didn't call back. It was all silence. I usually wanted to be alone when I was off on one of Dad's cases, but now that was the last thing I wanted.

I called Stevie and then I called Chuck. I repeated the process until I thought I'd go crazy. Then I set down the phone and turned on the TV. I don't even know what was on. My mind couldn't settle. Mostly, I stared out the windows or at my phone sitting on the sofa table and I remembered the picture we'd found of my great grandparents and Stella and Nicky Bled. That was something I'd done right. But then I remembered that Chuck was the only one besides Spidermonkey that knew what I was up to with the Klinefeld Group and I felt lonelier than I ever had. We were supposed to be in it together and I screwed it up. Royally, as Stevie rightfully pointed out.

Then my phone rang. I dove for it, but it was a number I didn't recognize and had no name attached. Usually that meant some sort of sleazy prank caller. I got those all the time and, with the new video, it was to be expected. But I was desperate and hoping I was wrong, so I answered.

"Hello?" I said, trying to sound as un-sexy as possible.

"Miss Watts?" said a deep voice with a Southern accent.

"Yes."

"It's me, Tiny."

Huh?

"From the airport," he said with a hint of worry.

"Oh, right. I'm sorry."

"You wrote your number on your dad's card. Is this okay?"

"Of course. What can I do for you?" I asked.

"I googled you and it said your people are from N'awlins."

"My mother's people are. I'm at my nana's house right now."

Tiny's voice went up an octave. "You ever hear the name Robard Boulard?"

Where's this going?

I turned from the window and looked at the framed family tree. "Yes. He's an ancestor of mine."

"You ever hear of Josephine Plaskett?" he asked.

"Yes," I said, softly. "There's a tomb with her name on it near my family's tomb."

"I'm looking at it," said Tiny.

"Why?"

"Cause my name is Tiny Plaskett. You're my people, Miss Watts."

I stared at the family tree and instantly pictured another beside it. "You're a Plaskett? For real?"

"Yes, ma'am." He laughed, a great warm jolly laugh. "Can you believe it?"

"It's true then. Robard and Josephine?" I asked.

"You didn't know for sure?"

My heart was beating hard. Nana would freak out. She loved family history stuff. "It was a family legend. You're not...angry with me, are you?"

"About what?"

"Well, my ancestor sort of purchased yours. It's not exactly the decent thing to do," I said.

"Plaçage was okay then. Josephine was free and it was a contract, not a purchase."

"But still..."

"We've got the deed," he said.

"The deed to what?"

"Robard gave Josephine a house in the contract. My Aunt Willasteen lives there."

I could hear a woman's voice tittering away in the background. "That is so crazy. I'm in Robard's house right now. You have to come over." I gave him the address and Tiny said he was going to bring his aunt with him. He started naming Josephine's children as they walked out of the cemetery in case I recognized the names. I walked around the sofa table to get a better look at the family tree and Blackie stalked out of the kitchen and hissed. A great big hiss, showing all his very pointy white teeth. This from the cat who never blinked. He went up in a stiff arch, but he wasn't looking at me. I turned and froze. Outside Pop Pop's bank of windows was man wearing a dark grey hoodie. A thrill of recognition went down my arms. He'd been in the parking garage at St. John's. The confidence was the same. It was him. The man stared at me from the depths of the hood with malicious dark eyes and raised a brick.

I screamed and the window shattered.

"Mercy!" yelled Tiny.

I dropped the phone and scrambled backwards, hitting the sofa as he walked in through the still falling shards of glass. "Where is he?"

I went over the back of the sofa and fell painfully on my rump. He was on the sofa, looking down at me. "Where is he?"

"Who?" I asked, my mind a blank.

"Stevie."

"Gone. I don't know where. He left." I scuttled back, hit the wall, and the family tree came off its nail and cracked me in the head. Dazed, I stared at him.

"Where is he?" He held up a knife, a small one with a four-inch blade.

"I don't know!" I screamed.

He started over the sofa. I grabbed the heavy picture frame to shield myself, but Blackie launched himself at the man's face. His claws were full out and struck him high on the cheeks. The man flipped back out of sight behind the sofa and I scrambled to my feet, looking for a weapon. There was nothing but sports magazines and furniture. I couldn't paper cut him to death. Real weapon needed.

I dashed past the sofa. It was either the stairs or the kitchen. *Knife or gun. Knife or gun. Gun.*

I juked to the left and ran up the stairs, two at a time. Three million of my dad's lessons went through my head. Don't get yourself cornered was in there and repeated. No, I wasn't cornered. I had a plan. My Mauser was still in my side table drawer. I hammered in the clip, racked the slide, and flipped off the safety in a half second, the way Dad forced me to practice it. Thank god I had the Mauser. It was so easy to arm. I ran back onto the landing, grabbed the bannister with my left hand and swung myself around to the stairs. I was down two before he appeared at the base.

"Stop!" I yelled, assuming the proper position, so well practiced.

Blood was streaming down his face in long gashes, but he smiled, reached down, and pulled a blue and silver hilt out of his pocket. A long stiletto ratcheted out with a mechanical snap and his smile widened.

"Stop now!" I screamed.

"You're going to tell me where he is."

"I don't know!"

"You're his best friend. You know."

Best friend? Damnit, Stevie!

"But I'm not his best friend. I'm nothing to him."

"Stevie came to you and now you're going to tell me where he is."

He ran up the stairs, his blade extended, and I shot him in the face.

Very Scarlett O'Hara, except the movie got it all wrong, as usual. He kept coming for another three steps and I fired a second shot, missing him completely. Then his body stopped, frozen in the moment before he arched his spine and flipped backwards. He went ass over tea kettle, striking his head on the wooden stairs twice before landing at the foot of the stairs in a heap on Nana's silk rug. It happened very fast and very slowly all at the same time. I remember it in great detail, the explosion of his facial features as my bullet struck, the blood spatter as it hit the wall, and smell of powder harsh and acidic in my nose as I watched him fall. My gun hand stayed out and I braced myself against the wooden bannister. My gun hand began to shake, but I didn't feel it. I could only see the vibration, like the hand was attached to someone else entirely. If I dropped it, my weapon would roll down the stairs to my assailant. He looked quite dead, but you never know. I pressed the hot Mauser to my chest and stepped back up the stairs to grab onto the newel post. I clung to it, trying to think of what to do. I'd just killed someone. Dad never covered that at the gun range.

"Mercy!" yelled a deep voice and I looked reluctantly down the stairs. Outside of the broken windows was Tiny and an elderly woman with a cane.

"I'm up here!"

They saw me and stepped in, crunching the glass and sending shivers up my spine. "Are you okay?" he asked.

"She's fine. Can't you see that?" The old lady walked over to the body and poked it with her cane. "He's not. Shot to the face. You don't shoot them in the face. Look at this mess. This carpet's past saving and it was expensive to my eye." She shook her head. "Gut shot is cleaner. Young people never think about the cleanup."

Tiny slapped his forehead. "Auntie, she was attacked."

"That's no excuse. You've got to think about these things. What's her mother going to say?"

I had no idea. I'd never killed anyone before. The territory was newly discovered.

"I'm sorry?" I asked, not sure what to do.

"Good enough," said Auntie. "You stay there until the cops get here." She checked the small gold watch on her wrist and frowned. "Taking their sweet time about it."

It wasn't so long. I found out later that the cops were on the scene six minutes after Tiny called 911. Not bad at all, but it felt like forever. Once the cops were there, I was allowed to walk down the other stairs, the servant stairs, on the other side of the house. I'd forgotten they existed. It was Aunt Willasteen who pointed out that a house of this age would have a second set for those who were not to be seen as they served. The cops pushed aside the bookcase in Pop Pop's office to reveal the door and I was brought down to the living room and put in his favorite chair as Cortier showed up. She walked in through the window, wearing paper overalls the color of toilet water and booties to protect the scene.

She shook her head. "You again. I should've known."

"You took your sweet time," said Aunt Willasteen over her compact as she powdered her nose and then smoothed her salt and pepper hair back into its tiny bun at the base of her small skull.

"And you are?" asked Cortier.

"Willasteen Plaskett. I see your memory is as good as your speed."

"Do we—"

"We do. Three years ago. The Flavortime shooting. Your number one witness."

Cortier's head jerked back, I suspected, in horror. Then I realized who Willasteen reminded me of, Aunt Miriam. I would say it must run in the family, but Aunt Miriam was a Watts and no relation to the Plasketts.

"Yes, ma'am. Of course I remember you." Her eyes switched to me. "Who is he, Mercy?"

"I have no idea."

She frowned.

"But I know who sent him and it wasn't for me." I gave her Stevie's details and then ran through the events. It took about three minutes. There wasn't much to say and I found it very dissatisfying. An incident of that magnitude should take longer to explain, but, as Cortier pointed out, death doesn't take that long to accomplish.

"And how did you two come to be here?" Cortier asked Tiny.

"We were coming over to visit. We're family," interjected Aunt Willasteen.

Cortier stopped writing in her little pad.

"You don't believe me?"

"Ma'am, I believe everything you say," Cortier replied smoothly as she looked for a family resemblance and found it. Willasteen and I had identical widow's peaks.

After she finished taking our statements, I refused an ambulance for a second time. I wasn't hurt, not where any doctor could find the injury anyway and I didn't want to be poked and prodded. I sat in a lawn chair, swathed in quilts, and looked through the family albums with Tiny and Aunt Willasteen. The body was directly in front of me, lying in its pool of coagulated blood. After a couple of hours, it ceased to feel like it had anything to do with me. Mom would later tag that disconnected feeling as denial. Whatever. It worked for me, because that body was there for over four hours as they processed the scene. Evidence gathering is a long, drawn out process and when they finally carted the body away, the stretcher passed my mother and Aunt Miriam. Cortier had called Dad and he got Big Steve to borrow a private plane for them to fly down in.

Aunt Miriam walked in the courtyard first, glanced at the body, and said, "That carpet is ruined."

Mom rolled her eyes and came over to crush me to her chest. "Are you alright, honey?"

"I think so," I said, my eyes welling.

"Where's Chuck? Your father said he was here."

"I don't know. Tiny called him, but he won't answer," I said.

"Tiny?" Mom asked.

I introduced them before going into the ugly cry. I wailed for two hours while Mom and Willasteen picked out a cleaning company that would wash blood off ceilings, argued with the crime scene analyst about whether or not I could have my phone back (I couldn't), and compared family lore on Robard. The Plaskett's had a higher opinion of him than we did, oddly enough. I called Chuck on Mom's phone a dozen more times, but he never answered. I considered calling Pete, but I didn't want to look like I was saying he should forgive me because I'd been attacked. I didn't call. Not that desperate yet.

Cortier reiterated that the crime scene, aka Nana's house, wouldn't be released to us for a good long time, sparking yet another argument with Willasteen and Miriam. Together the aunts were formidable, and Cortier had to pretend to take a call so she could make her escape.

One of Nana's condos in the servants' quarters was empty and Mom insisted in moving us over there. It was a two bedroom and I would share with Aunt Miriam so she could keep an eye on me. Then she hired a massage therapist for my benefit or so she claimed. It took Tiny to pry me out of my chair. I didn't want to leave. I didn't want to move or shower or eat or do anything but sit and stare at the bloody carpet. Mom, as usual, wouldn't take no for an answer and I was hauled off. Changing my location didn't remove the stain from my brain. Incessant talking did. We weren't the only ones who went to the condo. The Plasketts came, too. *All* the Plasketts. It turned out the other side of the family weren't great breeders either. Tiny was the last egg in their basket and, if anything, he was suffering more pressure to marry than I was.

Mom put me in the bedroom with the massage therapist. Lynn was a childhood friend of Mom's, which accounted for the not listening to me. Lynn said I needed a deep tissue massage and proceeded to give me one, while making me smell the stank incense she lit and put a mere foot from my face. I would rather have had Aunt Miriam and Willasteen beat me with their canes.

When I came out, reeling from the pain and stink, I found the living room filled to the brim and smelling delicious. Willasteen had made her special gumbo, shrimp and sausage with a deep dark roux. She and Aunt Miriam were in the small kitchen, arguing about the amount of sugar to put in the corn bread.

"That's cake," said Aunt Miriam.

"That's corn bread."

"Two-thirds cup makes it cake."

"It makes it good."

I squeezed through the crowd to an empty spot next to Tiny on the sofa. He wasn't watching the hockey game on the TV. Instead, he watched Aunt Miriam and Willasteen go toe-to-toe.

"Who's your money on?" I asked.

"Willasteen. She hits."

"I have news for you, so does Miriam."

"It's like they were separated at birth."

I laughed as Tiny's cousin Melody yelled, "Somebody get the door," before she darted into the kitchen. The canes were going up. I heaved myself off the squashy sofa and opened the door. It was Cortier. The bags under her eyes had grown pouchier. "Can I come in?"

"You can try," I said.

She peered past me at the crowd. "What the hell? Are you having a party? You just killed someone."

"It's not a party. It's a reunion. And if you think I'm in charge of anything, you're wrong."

She leaned farther to the side. "Um...the old ladies are fighting."

"Are you surprised?" I asked.

"Not really, but they have canes."

"Mom and Melody will deal with it. What's up? Did you find out who that guy is?"

"He had no ID and his prints aren't in the system," she said.

I frowned and my stomach got queasy. A mystery guy wasn't good. He could be anybody. Anybody could be important. "You have no idea who he might be?"

"Maybe someone new to the Costilla organization and he just hadn't been arrested yet. Stevie was important to them, but not that important. A new guy fits."

"They still don't have Stevie so they're going to keep looking. What's next?"

"Nothing. Stevie's secure. About the time you were shooting that guy in the face, he was surrendering."

"In St. Louis?" I asked.

"Yep. He was with his father, and they're working on an advantageous deal as we speak," said Cortier.

"Was Chuck there, too?"

A smile passed over her lips. "No. I asked."

My heart sunk. Where was he? I'd stopped calling. It'd gotten to the point of pathetic. "Okay."

"No one will speak about him. We're going to need him back."

You're not the only one.

"What do you mean?" I asked.

"I mean, I asked to speak to him and got nothing. Zilch. Nobody will confirm his presence in St. Louis, but they won't deny it either."

"That's weird."

"I'd say so. We need to talk about your situation," said Cortier.

Mom poked her head around my shoulder. "That's easy. Mercy will be leaving first thing tomorrow morning."

"She needs to be available to us."

Mom smiled, the way only she can, and gave Cortier a business card. "She will be. Call us when you need her."

Cortier eyed the card. "There is the issue of security."

"Tommy will look after her."

"Where is Mr. Interview?"

Mom gave out a delicate little snort. I didn't know snorts could be delicate. I made big honking ones. "I like that. Mr. Interview," she said. "Tommy will hate it."

"It's better than Howdy Doody," said Cortier.

"Or swizzle stick."

"Or carrot cranium."

I held up my hand. "Wait a minute. Who calls Dad carrot cranium?"

"Me, for one," said Cortier. "My captain, for another."

"Count me in," said Mom. "Your father is ripe for nicknames."

"But he's...Dad."

"He's goofy-looking."

My tongue felt dry and I realized my mouth was open. Mom hugged me and laughed. "Your father is fabulous, but do you really think that I could live with him and not think he's funny? He's a six foot four red head that weighs 150 pounds. He puts jalapeños on everything and thinks he might get cancer from antiperspirant."

Cortier burst out laughing. "He's still on that?"

"He is. Don't get me started."

"Mom, is this why I got that weird all-natural deodorant in my stocking this year?" I asked.

"It is. I gave you the chocolate," said Mom.

"You're my favorite parent."

"Was there ever any doubt?"

Well...

"Alright," said Cortier. "Back to Howdy. Why isn't he here?"

"Tommy's chasing down a lead. As you know, Mercy wasn't the target."

"She could be now."

"Tommy's on it."

"Good enough." Cortier shook Mom's hand and mine before she returned to the crime scene.

I started back inside, but Mom grabbed my arm. "Did I hear her mention Chuck?"

"Yes." I avoided her penetrating gaze.

She squeezed my arm. "What did you do?"

"What do you mean?" My voice was high and hamster-like. What says guilt more than that?

"He left you here alone. Chuck would never do that, if he were thinking straight. You finally let him in."

"You saw the video," I said.

"Of course, I did. Half my graduating class emailed it to me. Thanks for that, by the way. Now what did you do?"

I told her and she looked up at the ceiling, sighing. "Leave it to you to ruin it. I don't know how you're going to fix this. I really don't. Chuck is like a son to your father. How could you?"

My bare feet became very interesting, much better than looking at my mother's angry face. "Is this why Dad's not here?"

Mom tipped my chin up. "He is chasing a lead. I came. I'm your mother. You need me, not an interrogation." She gave me a fierce hug and Cortier ran back up the steps.

"Yes?" asked Mom.

"Your cat's in my crime scene again."

"I'll get him," I said.

"I thought you locked him up," said Cortier.

Mom gave her a devilish grin. "We did."

"There's something weird about that cat. He keeps looking at me like he knows the color of my underwear."

I crossed my arms and leaned on the doorframe. "You know, I spent half my time here throwing that cat out, but he always gets back in. What is the deal? Did Nana put in secret cat doors or something?"

"Do you want the truth or a lie?" asked Mom.

Lies are always more interesting and, as Dad says, lies show you something about the liar, a truth they'd think they're concealing. "Lie."

"He's my mother's cat and smarter than you apparently," Mom said with a twinkle in her eye.

"Now I want the truth," said Cortier. "That's the most boring lie I ever heard."

One of Mom's perfectly waxed brows shot up. "Alright then. He came with the house."

I made a swirling motion with my finger. "This house? Nana's house. The house that Robard bought in 1830?"

"It's the only house we've got."

Cortier nodded sagely. "I'll tell my people to be careful."

"That would be prudent, advisable even."

What's happening?

"We didn't get the house in 1830?" I asked and both women looked at me like I was dumber than a box of rocks.

"Of course, we did. Robard bought it from the original owners after one of the many cotton market crashes. You know that."

"But..."

"He came with the house, Mercy," said Mom.

Cortier patted my shoulder. "This is New Orleans. Life and death aren't so far apart."

The cat slinked up the stairs, sat on his skinny rump and stared, not blinking as usual.

"You were well looked after," said Mom.

"So that cat has been in this house for nearly two hundred years?" I asked. "How come I never saw him before?"

Mom shrugged. "I've only seen him three times before now."

"Seriously?"

"The first time was when I was staying with my grandparents. I had this terrible flu and was hospitalized for a week. The second was right before Tenne had her terrible car accident, and the third was when my grandparents died in that plane crash. We came back for the funeral and he was here."

"So this cat is a what? A ghost?"

"I don't know what he is. I'm just glad he was here for you today," said Mom. She thanked Cortier and went inside.

Cortier eyed me. "You better pick him up."

"You pick him up," I said.

"He's not my cat."

"He's not a cat."

Meow.

I froze. It was the first meow and it sounded like an affirmation of his not-a-catness. I could not have been more creeped out.

"Good luck," said Cortier and she booked it down the stairs.

"I'm not picking you up," I said to the cat.

Aunt Miriam flung open the door, her cane at the ready. "Are you alright? What are you doing?"

"Nothing. Just thinking, I guess."

She glared at the cat, who ignored her and stalked into the condo with his tail in a question mark. "Sometimes it doesn't pay to think too much. This is one of those times. What has happened has happened. Thinking won't change it. Have you called him yet?"

Him? Chuck?

The cane rapped the floor. "Don't play with me, Mercy. Call him and tell him you've finished this case."

"Chuck isn't answering," I said in a small voice and her brittle expression softened.

"Not Chuck. The Fibonacci."

I froze.

"I assume a man like that doesn't stand in a freezing convent parking lot to pass the time of day. Have you finished it with him?"

"Um...not yet."

"Then do it and collect whatever it is that you will collect."

"I'm not getting anything," I said. "How come you didn't tell Dad about him?"

"You'd just started this hunt, and I decided that you might need backup of a most lethal kind. The Fibonaccis do provide for their friends. You are a friend, are you not?"

"I'm not an enemy."

She snorted. "I should hope not." Then she brightened up. "After you've finished, we'll watch a movie."

I paled. Then remembered we were in New Orleans, far from Aunt Miriam's movie collection. "Sure. Great."

"Willasteen has the entire *Omen* collection."

No!

Aunt Miriam gave me her phone and went inside, whistling the theme song to *The Exorcist*. Nice. Just what I needed to not think about killing. Death and blood spatter. I groaned and then called Oz Urbani.

Oz's voice was harsh and angry. "Yes?"

I hesitated, but said, "It's Mercy. I wanted to give you an update, if you're in the mood."

"Sorry. I just found out that Donatella's son was the target in New Orleans. You should've told me."

"Why do you care so much?"

"I care about all of it. If anything else turns up, I want you to tell me who's involved first."

"I'm so not doing that and I don't know why you'd ask me. You wanted Donatella cleared and I did that."

His voice deepened. "I want them punished. All of them."

I felt a little chill. "They will be, but not by you."

"And if they aren't convicted?"

Ah, there's that slippery slope I've heard tell about.

"It's a done deal," I said. "Don't worry."

I could practically hear the smile on his lips. "I've given you incentive."

"I didn't need any. I always do my best."

"Yes, you do."

"Gotta go."

"Mercy, I'll owe you and no favor will be too big to ask."

"Noted."

I wasn't sure if I felt good or bad about that. Keeping a favor from Oz in my hip pocket might be useful someday or it might be dangerous. As Aunt Miriam said, some things weren't worth thinking about. I'd do whatever was necessary for the conviction. Besides, the Fibonaccis wouldn't be deterred by something as trivial as what I wanted anyway.

CHAPTER THIRTY

I looked for the cat the next morning, but he was nowhere to be found. Mom didn't want to talk about it and seemed to think his disappearance was to be expected. I didn't expect it, but, then again, very few things happened that I expected. The plane I rode home in was one of those unexpected things. It was a cushy Cessna with leather seats and I was the only passenger. I sat curled up with my forehead propped up against the little oval window. St. Louis was having a snowstorm, but we were cleared for landing. Normally, I would've been all tense and barfy in such weather, but I was oddly calm. Going home, never felt so bad. Crashing was the least of my worries. Everyone was mad at me. But, at least, *my* cat could be counted on to like me and to stay where he was supposed to. That was a comfort. Nothing else was. I wouldn't find Pete snoozing on my sofa or special chocolates hidden in my apartment. Chuck had disappeared. Mom said Dad was talking to me, but he was just so darn busy at the moment that he couldn't find the time. Yeah, right. Uncle Morty wasn't answering his phone and neither were Aaron or Rodney. Usually, I could count on them for general cluelessness, but it looked like the alienation of their wizard was enough to put them off me. I'd been trying to get rid of Aaron for a long time. Now that he was gone, I felt empty and like I didn't fit right in my own skin. Who was I without my people?

The captain came over the sound system and informed me that we'd land in ten and then taxi into the hanger. I slipped on my sweater and wondered how hard it would be to get a cab. Nobody would be picking me up. That was for sure. Normally, I'd head straight for my godmothers. Millicent and Myrtle were my comfort people. They were usually on my side, but I doubted this time would be like that. My godmothers loved Chuck. Hurting him wasn't going to be looked on with a kind eye. So I would take a cab home, call my service and see how many hours I could work for the foreseeable future.

The wheels gently touched down and we taxied into the hanger so fast that I was shocked. The co-pilot, Matt, came out and opened the door. The ground crew extended the stairs and I gathered my stuff. The whole thing was embarrassing. All that effort for one person.

"All set, Miss Watts," said Matt with a smile. "And he's already here."

"He?"

"Your father. I met him when he dropped off your mother and aunt." He cocked his head to the side. "Are you okay?"

"Um...you've seen him? He's out there?"

"Yes. He's walking over right now."

Oh my god. He's going to yell about so many things. Killing that guy. Chuck. Wrecking Nana's rug. Chuck.

There was a creak from the stairs and then Dad stuck his head in. "There you are. Let's get a move on. We have to take off."

I stared at him, looking for signs of the tongue lashing that I was due. "Who's taking off?"

"Me."

"Are you going somewhere?"

"Think, Mercy. I'm going to New Orleans." He rubbed his hands together fiercely. "I've got some catfish to serve up."

Already? Crap.

Dad backed down the stairs and I followed, holding my carry-on like a shield. At the foot of the stairs, Dad held the little carry-on that he used for business trips and his laptop bag. He was traveling light, even for him.

"Not staying long?" I asked.

"Long enough. We need to talk."

Do we have to?

I picked at the lint on my sweater. "How pissed are you?"

"Pretty freaking pissed. I can't believe he left you like that," said Dad, his blue eyes icy.

"Huh? What?"

"Chuck. He left you there when he knew the Costillas were hunting Stevie." He ran his fingers through his hair the way he did when he was trying to contain his emotions. It was really the only way I knew he had them, his voice was so clipped and business like.

"You're mad at Chuck?"

"I'm not mad. I'm fucking furious." Dad grabbed me and hugged me hard to his bony chest.

I'm in the clear. It's a miracle!

"So you're not mad at me?" I asked, all warm and filled with love.

Dad jerked me back and gave me a little shake. "Hell, yeah, I'm mad at you. You made him leave you there like a damn idiot. And now he's gone off and potentially screwed himself. Thanks to you and your... kissing and whatnot."

"There was no whatnot, Dad."

He held up his hand. "I don't want to know. Of course, I didn't want to see that video either, but I thought you'd finally gotten a clue. I can see I was optimistic to the extreme."

I rubbed my eyes. "I don't get it. Who are you mad at?"

"Everybody!"

"I did solve the case. Donatella's in the clear. Ameche, my people as you call him, is taken care of."

"Well, that's a redeeming factor," he said grudgingly.

"And I cleared Christopher of the rape allegation."

"I suppose that's a good thing, although it was only an allegation."

I smiled and hit Dad where it counted. "And you're probably going to get credit for opening up the murder case against Farrell in his wife's death."

Dad stroked his chin. "Good publicity. Good for business. Alright. I suppose I won't be disinheriting you this time."

"That's a relief," I said with a sneer.

"It should be. This thing with Chuck is beyond the pale. Don't you know how much I count on him?"

Matt brought me my suitcase and told Dad they'd be ready to take off after refueling. A bitter wind was whipping in through the open doors and we headed for the small passenger lounge. Once inside, I poured a cup of surprisingly good coffee before asking the question I was dreading. "So is Chuck not speaking to you either?"

"He's not speaking to anyone." Dad took my cup and glared at me.

"What do you mean? He has to speak to someone. What about his guys, Nazir and the other detectives?"

Dad shook his head. "So Mom didn't tell you."

I poured a second cup, so I could put off whatever was coming.

"Chuck's gone UC."

I overflowed the cup and burned my hand. Dad grabbed it, tossing it into the trashcan. Then he ran my hands under cool water in the sink and patted them dry with napkins. Dad can delay with the best of them.

"So," I said, "he's undercover. Where? Why? You never did it."

Dad tossed the napkins. "I had your mother and then you."

"And Chuck has nothing. Is that what you're saying?"

"It's done. He's gone."

"*You* don't know where he is? You of all people," I said.

"I don't know. Narcotics operation is my best guess. He's well versed."

"How long?" I asked.

"As long as it takes."

"Like a year."

Dad shrugged. "Could be or longer."

Oh my god. I'm going to be sick. Really sick. Like Exorcist sick.

Dad gently sat me in a chair and put the trash can between my knees. Matt came in, saw me, and did an about face.

"It's my fault," I said.

Dad gave me a tissue. "No point in speculating. They've been wanting him for a long time and he finally made the jump. We've got other fish to fry."

I blew my nose and swallowed hard. "Like what? It's all done."

"I can't do it, Mercy. I tried, but I can't. There's no solid connection between Blankenship and Andrew Marlin."

"They can't charge Andrew? He obviously orchestrated the Tulio shooting."

"Oh, they'll charge him and it'll go to trial, but it's all circumstantial. Why do you think I'm going to New Orleans? It's over," said Dad, sitting next to me.

Oz is going to freak.

"It can't be. You'll find something."

"I've been doing this for longer than you've been alive. The cops aren't going to find any hard core evidence and neither will the FBI. It just isn't going to happen. You get a feel for this after a while."

The Fibonacci don't care about evidence.

I pushed away the trash can and crossed my arms and legs. "Why do I get the feeling that isn't the end of it for me?"

He clapped me on the back. "That's my girl. You have it. Damned if you don't."

"I'm not going to see Blankenship again. Forget it," I said. "Never again."

"Fine." Dad pulled a rectangular gold box out of his pocket. "You can deliver this for me."

"Bissinger's lollypops? For who?"

Please say Shelley the guard, not a psycho inmate.

"Greta. I arrested her for murder when you were about ten. Anyway, I bring her treats from time to time, but since I'm going to—"

"Nope. Not going to do it. You're just trying to suck me in."

Dad put the box in my hands. "She lives for these treats. You have the time."

"Do we really care if a murderer is happy?" I asked.

Dad's face hardened and his eyes went all glittery. "I do. It wasn't her fault."

"You arrested the woman."

"It was my job, not my choice. You owe me, Mercy. You owe Chuck."

I groaned. "Dad, come on. I just killed someone that was attacking me. Can't I get a pass for that?"

"Greta likes me. You don't know how much that counts for."

"You mean Blankenship likes me. It's not about Greta. It's about him."

"It's about twenty-six people at Tulio. I never lost sight of that. You shouldn't either."

"I'd like to lose sight of it in a huge way."

"Later," he said, handing me his car keys. "Do what you think is right, not what you think is easy."

Groan.

He stood up, gathered his stuff, and walked out the door in his easy relaxed way, like he hadn't just ordered his daughter to visit a mass murderer. Two of them most likely. I dashed after him and called out, "He's not going to tell me anything."

"We'll see." Dad boarded the plane, leaving me to decide what was right. I had no idea, except that it was never what I wanted to do, so I found Dad's car in the parking lot and input the name of Hunt in the GPS. It would be a long drive in wicked weather for nothing. I was too tired and sad to be clever and Blankenship had nothing to do but rest and plot. Not a fair contest at all.

Shelley, the guard, was waiting for me at the visitor entrance. Apparently, there was no doubt I'd do as Dad asked and it irritated me.

"I thought I told you never to come back," said Shelley.

"My father had other ideas," I said through gritted teeth. "I'm here for Greta, whoever she is."

A faded wispy brow went up. "Greta?"

I showed her my box of lollies. "I've got these."

Shelley nodded like she doubted my story and brought me into the waiting area. I expected to see Blankenship's parents there, shattered and desperate. There was plenty of shattered and desperate in that small room, but it was coming from the other Berrys. Ken and Stacy were sitting in the Blankenships' spot as far from each other as possible. They wore their Rams paraphernalia, but it now was wrinkled and stained, and their faces were seriously pinched. It took a second before they looked up. Their eyes held no recognition. What a relief. I didn't want to talk to them. Being in the same room was bad enough after what they put Donatella through.

"Harve," said Shelley. "She's ready."

Harve wasn't behind the glass this time. He sat in a chair next to the door, keeping a wary eye on the other Berrys. I guess he expected trouble between them and me.

Harve nodded at me, stood up, and clipped his key ring off his belt.

"Hey. Hey. Hey. Why's this chick going in?" Ken grabbed me by the arm and I turned to look at him full in the face. Then he knew me and sweat beaded up on the bridge of his big nose. "Watts."

"You remember me. How gratifying. Now let go."

Ken dropped my arm. "They said nobody could go in."

"I guess I'm nobody." I turned back to Harve. "Ready when you are."

"I'm always ready." He laughed and started to unlock the door. But Stacy jumped in front of me and Harve put his hand on his baton.

"Please," she said. "We didn't do anything. We didn't. You know that."

"I know you're scumbags. You set your own family up to be murdered and then tried to take Donatella's kids right after her husband died. I know exactly who you are."

"No, we didn't. We thought *she* did it," said Ken. "They're talking about charging us with murder. Are you going to see him, that guy, that Blankenship?"

I sidestepped Stacy. "Harve, it's been a long day. Can you maybe whack these nutbags?"

"My pleasure." Harve slid his baton out of its holster.

Stacy clung to my sleeve, sobbing. "Please. He won't see us. Get him to say he doesn't know us. We didn't do anything."

"You're out of your head, if you think I'll help you," I said, peeling her sticky hands off my sleeve.

"Please, Miss Watts," said Ken, now crying himself. "He has to deny it. Our lawyer said so. Tell him we could go to the death chamber."

"Yes, but he'd like that, wouldn't he?" I looked at their stunned faces as they understood the truth of my words. Harve unlocked the door and I walked into the last place I wanted to be.

After another search, I followed Shelley through an unfamiliar part of Hunt. It was more relaxed somehow with few nurses about and guards sporting smiles.

"Where are we going?" I asked.

"To see Greta," said Shelley.

"Not in the fishbowl?"

She laughed. "No fishbowl for Greta. You can see her in her room." Just then she stopped in front of a thick metal door with a single bar securing it. I wasn't comforted.

"Um...you don't have to do anything first?"

"Greta's not violent." Shelley knocked on the door. "Greta, you have a visitor."

No answer.

"Do me a favor. Talk to her a little. Tommy would normally have been here a few days ago, and she's having a bad time."

"Define bad time," I said.

"You'll see. Your dad is her only visitor and he talks to her."

I swallowed. "What do I say? What does she like to hear?"

"Honestly, I have no idea, but just talk. Tell her what you've been up to," she said.

"I killed a guy yesterday," I said.

"Maybe skip that."

"Do you talk to her?"

"When I have the time. She's a good listener and it perks her up."

"I don't know about this. I'm just supposed to give her this box," I said.

Shelley patted my shoulder. "Don't be nervous. She won't hurt you. She only hurts herself." She lifted the heavy bar and started to heave the door open, but I put my hand on her forearm. "What did she do?"

"She killed her children. Cough syrup."

A child killer. My day sucks.

"Why does my dad visit her?" I asked.

"Because she's crazy. It was postpartum psychosis. Very severe, but they convicted her anyway." Shelley's voice went hard. "Your father blamed the husband."

"And you?"

She nodded stiffly. "He's walking free. I heard he has more kids now. Don't mention that to her."

"Don't worry."

Shelley pulled open the door and I stepped into a narrow room with white walls and no decoration. Greta was curled up in the corner on the metal framed bed that was bolted to the floor. She had faded blond hair streaked with grey. I couldn't see her face because her arm was up over it like a shield. There was an IV line in her wrist and, from the look of it, she'd pulled it out many times. There were odd scars and nail marks all over her skin. She was terribly thin to the point of emaciation. I looked back at Shelley and she sighed before shutting me in Greta's hell.

"Hi, Greta. I'm Mercy, Tommy's daughter. I brought you your lollies."

No reply, so I talked. At first, it was awkward, but then it smoothed out and became easy. I told her about Dad's catfish bet with Cortier and how he was heading to New Orleans. Then I took a chance and told her why I'd been there. I told her about Abrielle and Colton. She peeked at me over her arm and I saw keen interest in her brown eyes, so I told her the whole tale, except the shooting a guy in the face part. I told her about Chuck and Pete and me. I told Greta, a woman who was certifiably insane, what I would never tell anyone else. The words just tumbled out of me until I had nothing left, leaving me feeling loose and light.

"I'm sorry," I said, putting the little gold box next to her on the sheets. "I shouldn't have told you all that." I knocked on the door and I heard the bar being lifted.

"Tommy's daughter," said a hoarse voice and I turned back.

"Yes?"

"Forgiveness is divine, if you can get it. You can."

I bit my lip and scanned her scars. "And you can't?"

"I asked. God said no." Her arm went over her eyes again and she was gone. Why did I feel so comforted in such an awful place? Her crime, the most terrible crime, was there in the room the whole time. I felt it like a living creature between us. But remorse was there, too. She should ask again. God was known to change his mind.

The door creaked open and I walked out.

"How was it?" asked Shelley.

"I don't know."

She nodded. "It's weird in there like stepping into another existence. Will you come again? She talked to you, didn't she?"

"She did. Can I see Blankenship?" I asked, suddenly very sure of what I had to do.

"He's all ready for you."

I got a little chill, fear coming in to roost. "In the fishbowl? Already? How did you know?"

"Tommy said that Greta would do the trick." She smiled.

"How does he always know?" I asked. "It really pisses me off."

"He knows you."

I found Blankenship in the fishbowl exactly the way I found him before, trussed up, bolted to the floor and completely devoid of interest in me.

"Surprised to see me?" I asked.

Nothing. I got a blank stare. He was so bland with every hair in place and not a hint of stubble, a creepy type of perfection.

I sat in the chair provided for me and fluffed my hair. It helps me to think sometimes. "Well, I'm surprised. I solved the poisoning; in case you're interested. Donatella Berry's out of trouble and the other Berrys are firmly in."

Nothing glimmered in his eyes, but he said, "*You* solved it?"

"I did. What? You thought I was too girly?"

"I thought you were too stupid." He waited to see if I was hurt. I wasn't. People thought I was stupid all the time. It came with the face.

"Nope, not stupid. Clever actually." I leaned over the table and flicked my tongue out over my heavily-glossed lips.

He sat up a little straighter, as straight as he could with his heavy shackles, and stared at my lips and then my chest. "Still think I had a partner?"

"I know you did. I found him," I said.

"Really? Then what do you need me for?" he asked, his voice silky with a hint of venom.

"I thought I'd give you your last chance."

"I've already gotten all my last chances. I'm here for the duration."

"I was referring to another last chance."

His eyes darted up to mine and stayed there, interested at last.

I smiled and made sure every bit of me showed the pleasure I didn't feel. "They've got you pretty well finished. The only death to look forward to is your own. Death by the State takes a long time though."

Blankenship frowned and his right eyelid twitched. "Yes." Then he brightened up. "Shelley might die. She could have an accident or get cancer. I'd enjoy that."

"But it wouldn't be your fault. What's the fun in that?"

He grumped and ducked his head. "None at all." Then he tilted his head up and gave me the same sly look as before. "What do you want?"

"The truth. It can kill, too, you know," I said with my best honeyed voice.

"And you'll kill for me?"

"The State will. Andrew Marlin sent you to kill Rob Berry and his family, and the Schwartzes sent him. The other Berrys made sure they were at Tulio all ready for you. That's conspiracy to commit mass murder. Sounds like the needle to me."

He looked like he wanted to drum his fingers together like some comic book super villain. "Hum. Perhaps it would be enough."

"Enough to ruin their lives at the very least." My heart was pounding and my pits were damp, despite the chill of the fishbowl.

"And what about your life? What will this case do to your life?" His voice became warm and ingratiating. Gross.

I must've instantly frowned, because he smiled broadly. "Not a good effect then?"

He wants me unhappy, unhappy for a long time. Okay. Fine, you piece of...

"It won't affect me. I'm not a criminal," I said.

"You're involved. There will be the trial. I bet you're beautiful on the stand."

I forced myself to go to David's killer's trial. David was my boyfriend when I was sixteen. He disappeared on the way to a football game with a couple of friends and was presumed dead. I hated remembering the feeling of sitting in the gallery, the photos of David and my friends up on easels, the sobs of their parents surrounding me. The pain was right there. Always there. And it worked. Blankenship was aroused by my misery. His hips thrusted compulsively and I hid my revulsion.

"You've been involved in trials before?" he asked, his voice thick with desire.

"Yes," I whispered.

"Was it...fun?"

"No," I said, sharply. "Are you going to tell me or not?"

"What if it takes them twenty-five years to execute?"

I shrugged. "You have the time."

"But twenty-five years is a long, long time," said Blankenship.

I said nothing. I didn't have to. He could taste it, my being called as a witness, going to retrials, and hearings. A never-ending life of misery that he caused.

I shot to my feet and went for the door. Shelley opened it and looked at Blankenship, a look of deep disgust on her face.

"Mercy, will you visit me?" shouted Blankenship and I put my hand against the wall.

"What for?" I asked without looking back.

"I'll need updates over the coming years."

"In exchange for what?"

"I'm a man of many actions and interests."

"You have other confessions to make?" asked Shelley.

"Not to you, bitch," said Blankenship. "To her, if she comes."

I couldn't say no, however I might like to. If there were other victims, if he'd done other things as terrible as the Tulio murders, we had to know even if it took twenty-five years.

"I'll come," I said, turning to face him so he could see that I meant it.

He smiled and it was both icky and genuine. "Promise. Cross your heart and hope to die."

"Stick a needle in my eye."

"I like the sound of that."

"You would." I went for the door and he yelled after me, "The Missouri Bank."

I stopped. "Location?"

"Warrenton."

"Box?"

"432."

"Yours?"

"Oh, yes. Excited? Don't be. I have lots of interests.

And lots of boxes.

I walked through the door, followed by Shelley. A second before the door closed, he shouted, "See you soon."

I stood in the hall, holding my stomach and biting my lip.

Harve was in the corridor and he patted my shoulder. "Good job. Your dad will be very happy, not to mention the DA."

"My mom won't. She'll be pissed. It's the proverbial deal with the devil."

"Will you do it?" asked Shelley. "Come back and see that creature, I mean."

"I have to, don't I?"

Harve and Shelley looked at each other and I could tell they wanted to say that I didn't have to, but they couldn't. They wore badges and knew about sacrifice better than most.

"I think so," said Shelley.

"Then you'll be seeing a lot of me." I walked away down the cold corridor, barely able to keep myself from running. I never needed a shower so bad in my life.

I hauled my carry-on and suitcase up the stairs to my apartment. My stomach was in a red hot knot. Nobody would be there. Not even Skanky. He was living the good life with Mr. Cervantes.

I tossed my suitcase onto the landing and trudged up the last two steps. There was a scrambling noise and a sound like unpopped popcorn hitting the floor. I cringed. This was me, after all. It could be anyone, a trained assassin, a so-called journalist, or one of my usual stalkers. But it wasn't an anyone. It was a dog, an enormous black poodle, tied to my doorknob.

My lower lip quivered. Pickpocket. Chuck's poodle, the nut case he stuck me with whenever he went away. I ran down the hall and sank to my knees, throwing my arms around his fluffy neck and breathing deep the smell of Chuck and flea shampoo. Pick slurped my ear and panted.

I scratched his ears and said, "He left you here with me because he's coming back. Eventually. To me. Right?"

Pick panted and I took that for a yes.

"He can't talk," said a voice behind me. "He's a dog."

I turned and there was Aaron, holding two grocery bags and looking like he'd stepped out of a plane crash, he was so disheveled. "You hungry?"

"What are you doing here?" I asked, quite breathless.

"Making dinner. I have chocolate."

"You're speaking to me?"

His forehead wrinkled behind his thick over-sized glasses. "Huh?"

I decided not to mention that I'd lost him his wizard and thus the perfect gaming group and that nobody else was talking to me. It didn't pay to give Aaron ideas. He usually turned them into hot dogs.

"I shot someone," I said instead.

"I heard."

"It was gross."

"You hungry?"

Enough about that, I guess.

"Starved." I got to my feet, untied Pick and got out my keys. But instead of unlocking the door, I hugged Aaron, quite out of the blue. I don't know what happened. I was standing there and then I was hugging that little weirdo. I was crying. I hate that. Crying for no reason like a silly girl.

Aaron put down the bags and patted my back. "I should always go with you."

"You should."

"No one made you hot chocolate."

"Not even once." I started laughing and Pick howled at the ceiling. Aaron looked confused. Home was home again or at least it would be soon enough.

The End

Death changes you. It's changed me. I didn't think it would, but I killed a man and I'm different. At first, I thought I was fine. After all, People have tried to kill me before. I was sort of used to it or, at least, it didn't bother me much. But I'd never killed any of my previous attackers. The worst I'd done was kick them in the junk or pepper spray them. I'd say I handled the death well until I went on a diet. Diets happen and then unhappen for me, except this one didn't end. I couldn't go off my diet. I couldn't. I ate lettuce, lots of it. Then I ate tofu. I hate tofu. But I kept eating it. Death makes you eat tofu. Who knew?

"Doesn't that hurt?" asked a low voice in front of me.

I focused on Felix behind his vegetable stand under the slim red girders of Soulard Market. He held a bunch of radishes and had a bit of straw in his scraggly blond beard. "Huh?"

"Your dog is biting your leg," he said.

And he was. I had a big black fuzzy poodle gnawing on my calf. He chewed on my legs so often I didn't even feel it anymore.

"He's not my dog," I said. "He belongs to my...my... He's somebody else's dog."

"He's still gnawing on you."

"He's got separation anxiety."

Felix raised his unibrow. "You're right there."

"It's not me that he misses," I said.

Pickpocket tightened his grip while gazing up at me with shiny dark eyes. He belonged to my cousin by marriage, Chuck, who I'd kissed and then managed to alienate while working on a poisoning case in New Orleans. My father was a famous detective and sometimes I was called on to run down a suspect. In the case of New Orleans, I was paying back a favor for a friend. I solved the case but was nearly knifed. A hooded stranger with ties to the Costilla gang wanted information about Stevie Warnock, a guy who ate rocks for money and told everyone I was his best friend. As it happened, I didn't know where my best friend Stevie was, but the Costillas' emissary was willing to slice and dice me anyway so I shot him in the face. That was two months ago. Chuck had taken off on an undercover assignment and left me his dog, the slobbering Pick. It was a promise that he'd come back to me, but the promise had ruined three pairs of jeans, six pairs of tights, all my leggings, and my going-to-court pantyhose. I paid twenty-five bucks for that panty hose and he ruined them five minutes before I had to testify at a competency hearing for a serial killer. It was a bad day.

"You want these radishes or not?" asked Felix.

"I'll take two bunches," I said, trying to shake Pick off and failing yet again.

Felix bagged my radishes and I put them in my marketing cart, a gift from my godmothers, Myrtle and Millicent Bled. They supported my diet by buying me my cart and not saying a word about it, which is more than I can say for anyone else in my life.

My shiny new cart was an upright chrome affair that folded flat and could fit thirty pounds of vegetables. I tested it. So now I fit right in with the old ladies and mothers of five weaving their way through the vendors of the old outdoor market. Soulard was a comfort. It'd been the same for over eighty years, a produce paradise in the heart of St. Louis. Myrtle and Millicent had started bringing me when I was still in diapers. My mom never had the time and my godmothers had all the time in the world so I knew the vendors well even before the unfortunate events in New Orleans.

I paid Felix and attempted to walk down to my favorite lettuce vendor. That I had a favorite should've concerned me but it didn't. I was mostly worried that April wouldn't have enough to feed my habit. There was a mother with a passel of little ones eyeing the red leaf and arugula.

Back off, woman.

Pick dug in his heels and his warm slobber soaked through the leg of my only remaining pair of skinny jeans.

"Let go. What is your deal? We need lettuce," I said while trying to pry his jaws apart. No luck.

I pulled out my cell and texted Chuck. "Your dog is biting me again. Come home and do something about it."

My fingers stayed poised over my phone's keyboard. I'd sunk to a new level. Next I'd be claiming a deadly illness, the black plague or Lyme disease. Not that it would work. My phone remained depressingly silent. No vibration. No Train belting out "Drive By." Chuck didn't answer. He hadn't answered for two solid months, despite my daily texts. I kept expecting him to. Every single time I expected him to answer. I'm crazy that way.

Pick sat down while I texted Chuck, but he didn't let go of my leg. You'd think his mouth would get dry, but drool was always in good supply.

"He didn't answer," I said. "I know you're shocked. Try to contain the disappointment."

Pick shifted his jaw to get a better grip and I gave in. I always did. Pick expected it. He was smarter than me in many ways.

"I'll buy you donuts after the lettuce."

That nutty poodle let go and licked his chops.

"You're despicable and getting fat. What's Chuck going to say? You know how he loves fitness."

Pick yipped and began tugging on his leash. The mini donut shop sat at the end of a long row of healthy stuff and the smell of fresh frying donuts made both of us drool.

"Alright, alright." I let him pull me to April's ornate lettuce stand.

She liked to arrange her lettuce into pictures. Today it reminded me of the ocean, waves of green going on forever.

"Back so soon," said April. She acted like she was surprised. She wasn't.

"I ran out," I said.

She nodded and wisely said nothing. Going through twenty heads of lettuce in four days wasn't normal even if my apartment was infested with giant rabbits.

I picked out an assortment of normal stuff, reds, greens, arugula, and chicory. Then I got some frisée and mizuna to shake it up. Twenty-two bunches to be on the safe side. Running out was not fun.

April wrapped it all up and I filled my cart, placing the lettuce on top of my other staples, cucumbers, tomatoes, and whatnot. I paid April and calculated how many apples and turmeric I needed for juicing. Pick tugged harder, dragging me to the right.

"Hold on," I said, trying to picture how many wormy-looking turmeric roots I had left in the fridge.

Pick began prancing and making his I-see-someone-I-know whine. I looked up and spotted my dad standing at a stand with specialty greens like watercress and baby beet. He had his gun holster on and his hand poised like he was ready for something to happen at any second. Soulard market was pretty dangerous, all those vitamins and such. Dad was against vegetables as a general rule. He used to pay me to eat his when I was a kid so my mom would think he was eating them. A dollar per serving unless it was beets. I charged five bucks for beets. Dad called it extortion. I didn't know what that was but even at six I knew beets cost extra.

Dad saw me, but he didn't move. He scanned the area looking for something that he didn't find, then he gave me a little head cock to tell me to come over. Pick dragged me to him and wagged like he hadn't seen Dad in a month instead of a week.

"What are you doing here? Not buying veg, I assume."

"You assume right. Let's go," said Dad, not looking at me but still scanning.

"I'm not done," I said.

"You're done."

"No, I'm not."

Dad grabbed my arm and looked me in the eye for the first time. "Have you seen anyone following you? Anyone unusual?"

"All my stalkers are unusual." I smiled. Dad didn't.

"I'm not talking about the Marilyn Monroe fanatics. Anyone who doesn't want you to see them?" Dad was back to scanning.

"I had a couple of DBD fans yesterday. They just wanted an autograph." Through another series of unfortunate events I ended up being the band Double Black Diamond's new cover girl. Their fans outnumbered Marilyn Monroe's and were happily less odd.

Dad wheeled my cart around and began taking long strides toward the exit, dragging me along with him. I yanked my arm out of his grasp. "I told you I'm not done."

"We identified the guy," he said under his breath.

My heart seized up. "What guy?"

"Who do you think? The guy you shot."

"And?"

"It was Richard Costilla. The youngest of the brothers."

I felt like vomiting but I said, "So?"

"So you have to be locked down until I fix this."

"Define locked down."

"You're coming home with me. No going out." Dad glanced around. "Sure as hell no wide open spaces. The Costillas' want you dead."

"Are we sure about that?"

Dad yanked me close. I hadn't seen such fear in his eyes since I was little and ran off in Disney World. "We're sure. You need to come home."

"You mean your home," I said.

"My home is your home. It always will be. The Costillas don't play. You killed their baby brother. You think they're just going to forget that? The kid was seventeen."

"He was trying to kill me."

"They don't give a crap." Dad spun me to face him. "You're coming home right now if I have to wrestle you to the floor and hogtie you with zip ties."

"No, thanks."

"You're coming," he said between gritted teeth.

Richard Costilla's face flashed in my mind. I needed a salad so bad. "I get it."

The edge left Dad's eyes. "I'll buy you donuts."

"I don't want any donuts, but Pick wants some."

He touched the lacy greens of my carrots that draped over the edge of my cart. "I can see that, but do me a favor and tell your mother that I bought you donuts."

I shrugged. "Okay."

"And that you ate them."

"Obviously."

"Good." He took Pick's leash from me and we walked to the donut guy. The smell of sizzling dough filled the air as he dropped a fresh batch in the fryer.

Dad bought a bag and leaned over to me, his broad forehead wrinkled under his red hair. "Are you sure about the donuts?"

"I'm sure."

"How long are you going to punish yourself?"

"I'm not!" I gave my cart a hard shove and I dashed ahead of Dad and Pick. Pick yipped and his nails scraped the concrete floor of the market as he tried to follow me. My heart twisted a little. Somehow in the long weeks since Chuck left Pick with me, he'd become my dog and I hated to leave him behind but I couldn't talk and I couldn't think about talking. So the Costillas had marked me. I should've been frightened. Terrified would've been an appropriate response. Instead, I felt empty. I needed a salad. A salad and maybe some tofu.

Read the rest in
In the Worst Way (Mercy Watts Mysteries Book Five)

USA Today bestselling author A.W. Hartoin grew up in rural Missouri, but her grandmother lived in the Central West End area of St. Louis. The CWE fascinated her with it's enormous houses, every one unique. She was sure there was a story behind each ornate door. Going to Grandma's house was a treat and an adventure. As the only grandchild around for many years, A.W. spent her visits exploring the many rooms with their many secrets. That's how Mercy Watts and the fairies of Whipplethorn came to be.

As an adult, A.W. Hartoin decided she needed a whole lot more life experience if she was going to write good characters so she joined the Air Force. It was the best education she could've hoped for. She met her husband and traveled the world, living in Alaska, Italy, and Germany before settling in Colorado for nearly eleven years. Now A.W. has returned to Germany and lives in picturesque Waldenbuch with her family and two spoiled cats, who absolutely believe they should be allowed to escape and roam the village freely.